PEACE CRIES THE SOUL

Peace Cries the Soul

Leah Dawkins

Dedication

In honor of my mother and in memory of my father.

Acknowledgements

No work is ever done in a silo, and thus it is true with my second book as with my first. A special thanks to my husband, Tim, who has held my hand, stood by my side, and is the best salesman of my work a woman could ask for. I love you, now and forever.

To Kim, my editor. She is direct without being cruel and she is spot on in her recommendations to enhance scenes and notify me when I have used the same body movements too many times. And I quote, "He has shaken his head six times in the last page, I think he is dizzy." Thank you, Kim.

To Gina, my hiking buddy and one of the best people I know. she could not have been more accurate when, on our trek through El Camino, she looked at me and said, "It's about to get *real*." I am so grateful for her support and her help with all things military. Her knowledge and accuracy make my war scenes ring true.

To my very first Beta Reader, Diane, thank you. I appreciate your thoroughness and your encouragement. The BRAVO! Was all the impetus I needed to move forward on publication.

To my readers of Home Cries the Soul, thank you for taking a chance on me. I cannot thank you enough for all your kindness, honesty, encouragement, and graciousness as I have navigated these new territories of self-publication.

To my BookTok friends, Stevo and ReadbyFaith, thank you for all you have done, said, and written to spread the word on my writing. You have been the very best thing about my social media platform and I am forever indebted to you.

A special shout-out to my hometown of Sumter, SC. You showed up and supported me from day one. You made me feel like one of you, embracing me and my dream. Southern Bliss Yoga, Simpson's Ace Hardware, N Salon, Grady Ervin, and Naomi and Warner all stocked my books and supported me. And the community completely showed up. You will never know how much that meant to me. I am so thankful.

And finally, to Colligo Coffee and Brubakers, who have kept me caffeinated with Earl Grey Tea and space to write and work, you have my gratitude.

*On a side note, I was made aware that Gabriel would have been around 5 years old during the Korean War. He would have been in the war in Vietnam considering his age. I will be making that correction moving forward.

Prologue

It's the summer; the night is sultry and hot. The circadian are humming, and sweat is pouring off the two people dragging the body across the cotton field. The boy runs to the shed procuring a wheelbarrow. He grabs the torso, the girl his feet. With a great deal of effort, they lift the dead body into wheelbarrow. Both take a handle and start to push. Digging into the ground with the toes of their tennis shoes and pushing with all their young strength.

"What are we doing? What are we gonna do?" Whispered the girl. Tears streaming down her face.

"It's gonna be okay. Let's just dump the body next to the slave cabin. It won't be found for a while. Should give us enough time to figure something out. If we have to run, we do. I got some money stashed away. But we go back to our lives until or unless we have to run."

"I don't know? What if we get caught?"

"Not gonna happen. Come on! We are almost there." It takes both of them to lift the handles and steer the cart across the dirt path. The man is heavy.

They stow the body next to the slave cabin. They then take his watch, ring, wallet, shoes, belt, anything that might identify him. They even have the presence of mind to cover him with some shrubbery and corn stalks. They walk to the river. The tide is up. She puts all the dead man's belongings in a bag she steals from the Beauregard's boat. She puts a rock in the bag to weigh it down and tosses it in the water. The bag floats for a moment before sinking. The teenagers watch as the bag sinks to the bottom, praying the tide and the pluff mud will cover up the crime.

"That is as good as we can do. We have to go," says the boy.

They look at each other and look around the plantation. He takes her hand and squeezes it before running across the field and back to their respective lives. Fear and panic, and a certain amount of relief nipping at their heels.

1

Chapter One

Present Day

"Momma, who is that comin' up the drive?" Savannah asks her mother, Laura Lynne. They had just finished the special memorial service for Aunt Eileen, Melanie and Gabe's youngest sister.

"Who?"

"Yeah, I see him too. By the third Magnolia tree. He's wearing fatigues and is carrying an army duffle?" Beau, Laura Lynne's son, points toward the right side of the drive.

Laura Lynne walks toward the road. She hasn't spotted him yet. Savannah and Beau follow her. Savannah is a bit slower as she is currently six-months pregnant. All of a sudden, Laura Lynne stops in her tracks and exclaims, "Tripp!" and takes off running down the road. The man drops his duffle bag and runs up to Laura Lynne, sweeping her off her feet and doing a twirl.

"Laura Lynne, is that you?"

"God, Tripp, it is so good to see you!" Laura Lynne takes a step back, wiping her eyes. "But good Lord, you look terrible and smell worse! Have you been ill?"

"Good to see you too, baby girl." He wraps his arm around her shoulders. He is still a tall man but a ghost of the boy Laura Lynne remembers so fondly. Laura Lynne snuggles up under his arm and wraps her arms around his waist, tugging him toward the house.

"Come on. I want you to meet my children." Laura Lynne smiles up at him. "I'm going to be a grandma!"

"What? No way are we old enough to be grandparents!" She hits him in the stomach as they approach Savannah and Beau. Laura Lynne untangles herself and stands between her children.

"Savannah, Beau, this is your Uncle Tripp, well, Sawyer now, I guess, since Daddy died." Beau holds out his hand, and Sawyer shakes it, whacking Beau on the shoulder. He smiles at Savannah.

"Good Lord, Beau. It's like staring in a mirror 30 years ago," says Sawyer.

Beau laughs. "That's what everyone keeps telling me! It's nice to meet you, Uncle Sawyer."

"And Savannah. Aren't you just beautiful?" Sawyer walks over to her and opens his arms. She gives him a big hug. "I hear you are making me a great uncle."

"I am," Savannah says as she rubs her belly. "It's a boy. We finally decided on a name for him. I was going to save it, but it seems fitting to share it with you here: Nathaniel Christopher." She starts to tear up. "Wanted him to feel like part of the family straight from the get-go."

Sawyer hugs her tight against him and replies, "I think it's a fine name. Grandma Birdie would be thrilled you are using Poppy's name." Beau pulls a handkerchief out of his pocket and hands it to Savannah. Sawyer looks over at his sister, "Laura Lynne?"

Laura Lynne smiles through her tears. "I love it! It's perfect."

Under his breath, Sawyer says to Beau, "Got any more handkerchiefs? These women are a couple of waterworks. Has it been this way since y'all got here?"

Beau whispers conspiratorially, "Well, it's been emotional, that's for sure. Between the dead body, Uncle Gabe's arrest, Momma bringing down several prominent citizens of Venice, Savannah's baby, Aunt Eileen's memorial, and now you showing up, we are on a regular

Mardi Gras parade route." He snaps his fingers. "Oh, and I shot my first turkey this morning."

Sawyer releases Savannah and looks at Laura Lynne. "You want to tell me what your son is talking about? What the hell is going on?"

Laura Lynne takes the handkerchief from Savannah, wipes her eyes, and blows her nose. "Come on, let's head up to the house." She looks at Beau. "Can you grab the duffle? Take it to Pearl. Tell her to put it in Momma and Daddy's old room."

Sawyer starts to shake his head.

Laura Lynne continues, "Sawyer, it's your rightful place. May as well start getting used to it."

Beau grabs the duffle and slings it over his shoulder. As a group, they walk to the front of the house.

"Before we get to the house, you need to know Momma is there. We just had a service for Aunt Eileen." Laura Lynne wipes her eyes again. "Remember she asked to have her ashes spread in the gardens at Tea Olive when I was ready to come back." Laura Lynne gazes at the gardens. "It took six more years, but I made it."

Aunt Eileen, twice divorced and a tree-hugging hippie, she was the black sheep of the Cooper siblings. She owned River Oaks, a horse farm in Brunswick, Georgia. Laura Lynne had stayed with her following her banishment from Tea Olive. Eileen became her second mother and a grandmother to Beau and Savannah. When she passed, the land went to the Cooper Family Trust. But the executor of the ranch is Laura Lynne.

Sawyer squeezes Laura Lynne's hand. "I'm glad you did. It was never the same after you left."

Laura Lynne looks over at Sawyer and squeezes his hand back. "I am learning our parents' decisions have had lasting impacts on all of us. I always felt y'all were the lucky ones. Now, I am not so sure."

Sawyer nods, "We all have our own crosses to bear." They hit the base of the stairs. "Anything I should know before we go inside? Other than that Momma is there?"

"Just that everything worked out. There is no current crisis." Laura Lynne starts walking up the stairs with Sawyer beside her. Savannah and Beau are trailing behind. "There were human remains found by the slave quarters about two weeks ago. I refer to him as Dead Doe." This causes Sawyer to grin. "Uncle Gabe was arrested, but the charges dropped." They get to the top of the stairs. "We don't know who the Dead Doe is. It's still under investigation. Otherwise, it is business as usual. The kids and I leave for our homes tomorrow."

The door opens, and Pearl is standing there staring at Sawyer. She exclaims, "Well, look at what the cat drug in! Do my eyes deceive me, or is this Mr. Sawyer? As I live and breathe!" She comes forward and catches his hands. "Wondered what was takin' ya so long to join the festivities."

"Pearl, it's good to be home," Sawyer replies. He releases her hands, grabs her by the shoulders, and brings her in for a bear hug. "Missed you, girl."

Pearl laughs and swats at Sawyer. "Oh, get on with your own self!" She continues to laugh. "Now put me down and go say hi to your Momma. She will be glad to see you." Looking over Sawyer's shoulder, she sees Beau with the duffle. "Hand me that bag, Beau. I will take it to the master bedroom."

"There is no need for that, Pearl. My room is fine," Sawyer interjects.

Beau hands Pearl the bag, and Pearl explains, "Beau is using your old room. Besides, it's not your room anymore." She starts up the stairs to the second floor. "Be sure you say hello to my Momma too."

Pearl's mother, Queenie, all but raised the Beauregard children. She was much more than chief cook and bottle washer. She was their second mother. If a knee was scraped or you were hungry, you went to find Queenie, not Momma. Sawyer smiles. "I absolutely will."

"Come on. You can clean up after you see everyone and grab a plate to eat," says Laura Lynne, taking Sawyer's arm and steering him to the rear of the house.

The four of them head to the back porch. Victoria, Pearl's daughter, and the current chef at The Residence, has laid out a spread of light appetizers and desserts. She and Savannah have created a beautiful tablescape using some dishes and decorations stored in the dish pantry. Savannah discovered them the previous evening and fell in love with the dozens of plate sets, silver, crystal, and table linen.

"Look who I found walking up the entrance road," says Laura Lynne, entering the room. All eyes turn toward them.

Melanie gasps and places her hand over her mouth before exclaiming, "Sawyer!"

"Well, hello, young man. You are home." Gabe gets up from his chair and walks over, hand outstretched. "I told Laura Lynne not to call you, but I am so glad she didn't listen." Sawyer grabs his hand and comes in for a hug. "Good to see you, son."

"You too, Uncle Gabe, you, too." Gabe steps back, releases his hand, and pats Sawyer on the shoulder. "Go see your Momma."

Sawyer walks over to his mother, sitting in a chair, and squats in front of her. "Momma, I am home." She puts her hands on his cheeks and lays her forehead on his.

"It is where you have always belonged, young man. Time for you to assume your responsibilities."

Sawyer pulls back. "I am not gonna argue with you, Momma, not today. For now, I am glad to be back." Sawyer stands up and spots Queenie in her wheelchair, tears running down her face. "Queenie!" He goes straight to her and gathers her in a big hug. "How is the love of my life?" His eyes are searching for Pearl. Queenie is nothing but skin and bones, and her body is shaking.

His eyes catch Queenie's oldest son, Malcolm, who is the current purveyor of the farm. He took over for his father, Lincoln. Malcolm says softly, "Momma, this is Tripp." He pats Sawyer's arm. "He's come back from the war." He turns to Sawyer as he releases his mother. "Momma has cancer and dementia. She has good days and bad days. Today is a good day. A very good day."

Sawyer kisses her on the top of the head and squeezes her shoulder. "I bet these macaroons aren't nearly as good as the ones you made Queenie."

Laura Lynne laughs, "Don't bet on it. Victoria made them. She definitely has Queenie's touch in the kitchen."

"Where is Victoria?" asks Sawyer.

Pearl answers as she arrives on the back porch. "She is home today since it's her day off. She helped with the party prep yesterday and attended Miss Eileen's memorial. I will admit she is a better cook than Momma and I ever were."

"Come on, everyone, let's eat. I'm starved," Gabe says as he heads to the table to get things started. "Sawyer, you go first. It looks like you could use a few calories."

"I'm gonna go get cleaned up," Sawyer replies, "I'll be down in just a few minutes. Give the women a chance to fill their plates first."

"Please do. You smell like a goat," Laura Lynne says as she walks toward the buffet table.

"At least I don't look like one, baby girl," retorts Sawyer.

"Hmmph, says who?" Laura Lynne swats at Sawyer as he walks by, and he bumps her with his hip. They could be 12 years old again and waiting for supper to start.

Chuckling, Sawyer walks through the house to the grand entrance. The foyer has 20-foot-high ceilings and a twin staircase. Taking a deep breath, Sawyer lets it out slowly. God, seeing everyone at one time was not at all what he bargained for. He just wanted to get here and see Uncle Gabe, maybe Laura Lynne, if she was still here. Get his bearings. Not walk into a freakin' party, for God's sake. And he can't even have his own room. Glancing into his old bedroom as he hits the landing at the top of the stairs, he shakes his head. Maybe it was a good thing. Momma had made his bedroom into a shrine. There must be 100 trophies and awards on shelves and in trophy cases, not to mention his medals from the Army.

Sawyer quickly goes to the master bedroom and heads to the bathroom. He turns on the shower. He sees his shaving kit has been emptied and items placed in their appropriate places. He goes to the closet. His clothes are already hanging. Pearl has not only taken his duffel bag upstairs but unpacked it as well. He is surprised she didn't take the time to iron the wrinkles out of his button-downs and khakis. At least he had the sense to bring clothes other than his usual army fatigues. There is a certain dress code that is adhered to in the South and, specifically, at Tea Olive.

He disrobes and tosses the clothes into the hamper and his boots in the closet. The hot water feels like heaven. He lathers up and pays careful attention to his latest injury. A knife wound to his upper left arm, all muscle and clean, but it hurt like a mother when the medic pulled it out. Still made his stomach nauseous when he thinks about it. He is just getting too old for infantry duties. Another reason retirement seems to be the most appropriate course of action.

Sawyer doesn't really consider himself old. But seeing his nephew Beau and the proof he is pushing double nickels is staring him in the face. When Sawyer saw Beau walking towards him, he nearly tripped over himself. Beau is Sawyer's doppelganger. The exact version of him when he was Beau's age.

"Lord," Sawyer says under his breath, "I hope he doesn't make the same mistakes I did."

Turning off the water, Sawyer towels off and redresses his wound. He looks in the mirror and sees all the scars from battles too numerous to count. The damage to his body over the years has been making itself known. Most mornings, he wakes up so stiff that he has to move in stages. That is, if he sleeps at all. Sleep has been elusive for more years than he cares to count.

But he tells himself, "Enough stalling." He was a freakin' Colonel in the US Army; why would he want to experience the pain of his knife wound again rather than go back down and face his family? "Buck up, buttercup." He goes through his list, "Khakis on. Check. Button-down. Check. Sperrys on. Check." He is ready, and though he doesn't smell like a goat anymore, he does smell like lavender and lemons. He would need to ask about more manly-smelling soap.

2

Chapter Two

Summer 1985

Tripp sneaks down the stairs and goes to his father's study. Peering in, he sees his father sitting in his desk chair, his back to the entrance. He is cradling a glass of whiskey and looking out the windows, toward the river. Though at two o'clock in the morning, there is nothing but darkness to see.

Tripp clears his throat, "Dad?"

Without turning around, his father responds, "What is it, son?"

Sawyer takes a few tentative steps into the study, "What is going to happen to Laura Lynne?"

His question is met with silence.

He tries again, "She is coming back, right?"

Again, silence.

"Dad?"

Sawyer sighs, lifts the glass of whiskey to his lips and finishes the glass in one gulp. He turns the chair around to face Tripp, "What can you tell me about Jeremiah and Laura Lynne?"

"Not much, sir. The night of the auction, I caught Buck and Laura Lynne making out. I broke it up and brought Laura Lynne home. I told her to stay away from him. She said she would, but she was not happy about it. I had words with Buck the next day at school, and he told me he would stay away from my sister."

"I see. Define "making out," please."

Tripp looks down, slightly embarrassed, "They were kissing and Buck had his hands on Laura Lynne's butt. Cradling her against his crotch. That was all."

"And you are just telling me this now."

"Yes, sir."

Sawyer gets up from behind the desk and walks to the bar cart, refilling his whiskey glass. "You failed me son. You failed me and this family."

"Sir?"

Sawyer walks over to his oldest son and stares steadily into his eyes. At 6'2 they were eye level. "What was the one thing I told you was your job? Not only as a brother but as a man?"

"Protect my sisters. Protect all the women in the family."

"Your sister is now on a flight to your aunt's in Georgia because you failed to do the one thing I told you was the most important job you had in this family. Laura Lynne is ruined." Sawyer takes another sip of whiskey, "All because you failed to protect her from one of your best friends. Why didn't you tell me about Jeremiah?" Sawyer's voice begins to rise, "Before it got to this point? Where is your head? Your sense of duty and responsibility? For God's sake son, you were at school with them every day. It was your job!"

Tripp rubs his hands along his thighs, a sign he is agitated. "I'm sorry, Dad. I told them to stop the relationship. They told me they had. I didn't see them together anymore. I thought I had handled it."

"Fine job you did, son. Fine job."

Sawyer turns his back on Tripp and plops back into the leather chair, "Leave me alone. I think you have done enough damage for one day."

Sawyer feels the unshed tears in his eyes, his nose begins to tighten, he refuses to cry in front of his father. He leaves the room, and slowly walks up the stairs. At the landing, he is met by Avery.

"Tripp," Avery whispers, "What's going on?"

Tripp puts a finger over his lips and signals him to follow. Avery gets the message and follows Tripp to his room. He shuts the door.

"Hey, Tripp. You okay? I heard dad raise his voice. He never does that with you."

"He blames me for Laura Lynne's, umm, circumstances. Says I didn't protect her."

"Protect her how? What is going on? Nobody will tell me anything." Avery says as he sits down on the bed, watching Sawyer pace.

"And I'm not going to tell you either, but it's not good. I've never seen dad like that. And he's right, I didn't protect her."

"From who? And what?" asks Avery.

Sawyer stops pacing and walks over to Avery, "Listen Av, this isn't little kid stuff. I'm worried about Laura Lynne, like really worried." He sits down next to his brother, "The rumors are going to be brutal. People will be mean. Say nasty things. Don't believe any of it."

"Now I'm scared, Tripp. What aren't you telling me?"

"No reason to be scared, little man. Just want you prepared in case the gossip gets bad. Plenty of people in Venice been waiting for a chance to take the Beauregards down a peg or two. They will take their swipes."

"What about Laura Lynne? When is she coming home?"

"I don't know. Dad wouldn't tell me when I asked." Tripp looks at Avery with concern, "You gonna be okay?"

"Don't worry. I can hold my own." Avery gets up from the bed, "I realize I'm not the jock hero you are, but I have my own skills."

Tripp also stands up from the bed, "Avery, come to me if you need me." He holds up his pinkie finger, "Pinkie swear."

Avery holds up his pinkie and wraps it around Tripp's, "Pinkie swear."

The two brother's grin at each other, not realizing at that moment just how difficult the next months would be, and how their sister would no longer be a part of their family.

***

Present Day

By 4:00, it was time to see Queenie and Momma back to their respective nursing homes. Savannah is also worn out from the festivities and carrying her son, so she goes upstairs to rest. Beau and John, Tea Olive's foreman, take Momma back to the Pineview Assisted Living and Nursing Home. This leaves Sawyer, Laura Lynne, and Gabe to congregate in the study. Sawyer has been patiently waiting for an opportunity to find out why he was summoned to Tea Olive, though he has gleaned many details from the newspaper articles he read on the plane ride home. Now, he wants to hear what the paper did not divulge.

Gabe sips on a glass of bourbon, and Laura Lynne has unsweetened tea. Sawyer sticks with water. "Uncle Gabe, why don't you start, and then I will finish," says Laura Lynne.

Gabe puts his feet on the ottoman. "I guess the best place to start is the new garden excavation. Had a bit of unexpected money from a profitable investment I wanted to put back into the grounds. When your Daddy died, I spent the funds available at the time to update The Residence. I needed to do some work on the electric, plumbing, and roof and make it more livable for Melanie to keep her home as long as the Parkinson's would let her…well, anyway, it was finally time for me to play in the dirt. I found the old sketches for the original idea for the front garden. It led to the idea of a fountain as the centerpiece. You saw it on your way in, *Diana, the Huntress*." In the process of digging the irrigation, young Liam, a boy from town who helps me and John, came across bones."

Gabe shakes his head. "I should have called the sheriff right then and reported it. Instead, I covered it back up. I didn't want to desecrate a grave and figured it was probably remains from an animal." Taking a sip of bourbon, he continues. "One of the boys from the contractors I was using told tale about it at the brewery that night. Next thing I knew, the sheriff was here with a warrant to search the property. He also had a warrant for my arrest."

Laura Lynne picks up the tale, "Uncle Gabe called me, and I came down. I bailed him out and started doing some research. We can't figure out who the guy is. We do know it's a guy, 55 to 60, would have died around 1986 or as late as 1990." She looks up at Sawyer. "You don't have an idea, do you? Momma thought maybe a vagrant. Apparently, we had some here. Maybe one of Daddy's mistress's husbands or boyfriends?" Laura Lynne shakes her head.

"I can't think of anybody right now. Did we try missing persons?" Sawyer asks as he leans forward. "But I am confused why Uncle Gabe was arrested."

"Two words, my boy, two words...Chandler Monroe," Gabe explains.

The Monroes have had a beef with the Cooper/Beauregard family since Momma chose Daddy over Silas Monroe, Chandler's father.

Laura Lynne nods in agreement. "It didn't stick. He was released, and the charges dropped for lack of evidence."

"Two days in the Venice County Jail was plenty for me," says Gabe, "Though I did win $50 off Grady Cunningham. He is a terrible chess player."

Laura Lynne continues, "In the process of researching who the dead body might be, I spent hours going through old copies of the *Venice Gazette* newspapers. Came across some articles about abducted girls. They struck a chord with me. One thing led to another, and I discovered that Dr. Kenneth Butler was a serial rapist and pedophile. Bubba Westerman, our illustrious former sheriff, covered it up and blackmailed Dr. Goldbug to treat the girls and keep his mouth shut. All three were arrested Friday afternoon."

"Wait, you uncovered a pedophile ring by reading newspaper articles?" Sawyer looked incredulous.

Laura Lynne clears her throat and looks at her glass of tea. "It was a bit more than that. You see, I was able to put the pieces together because I was one of Dr. Butler's victims that summer of 1985. My testimony was the missing piece. The feds have been looking at Bubba for a while for other crimes, like money laundering and some type of real estate scam, even drugs. Anyway, when I showed Grady what I thought I had, it just spiraled from there."

"You were raped the summer of 1985 by Dr. Butler? That's why they sent you to Aunt Eileen's," Sawyer says, almost to himself.

"It's a rather long story. But basically, Momma and Daddy thought I was having sex with Buck." She looks at him. "You remember we had a crush on each other that summer?" He stares at her, shocked. "Anyway, they thought he had given me STDs. I told them it was not the truth, but nobody believed me. You were there, Sawyer; you saw how it was." She looks over at him. "The truth is I didn't figure it all out until many years later. I was in college by then."

"Oh my God, Laura Lynne. I am so sorry I didn't protect you better," Sawyer says as he reaches out and places his hands on her knees, gently rubbing them with his palms.

She smiles as she holds his hands. "You sound like Avery. Nothing you could have done." She gets serious. "He attacked 21 women in Venice, Wisteria, and Castille. They think he was still at it while he has lived in Boston." Laura Lynne says in frustration, "No telling how many lives he ruined."

Gabe chimes in, "There are several concerns moving forward you need to know about Sawyer. Things we need to consider as this investigation continues. First, Bubba Westerman is a snake and a weasel. He was also on your daddy's payroll." He holds up his hand. "Not mine, but he was on your daddy's." He readjusts himself in his seat and grabs a blanket to throw over his legs. "Second, there are some things from when your daddy was running Tea Olive that just don't add up. I have tried to figure out what he was into, but I can't and that has me worried."

"And Daddy and Uncle Gabe have been keeping Daddy's long-term mistress in high cotton with a monthly stipend." Laura Lynne rolls her eyes. "I met her, and she is a nasty bit of work. Blackmail money. She knows something, but I have no idea what. When I confronted her, I asked her to give me a tidbit of what she thought she knew. She told me you were the father of Victoria, Pearl's daughter."

Gabe and Laura Lynne watch as shock and then humor cross Sawyer's face. "Now, wouldn't that just be something? Can't say I have had the pleasure of knowing Pearl as more than a friend. Did you ask her?"

Laura Lynne grins. "Absolutely. She laughed so hard she doubled over. Though from the story, sounds like she wishes it were you. She did not go into detail, but Victoria's daddy sounds like a bad time in her life."

"Well, this mistress person lied," concludes Sawyer, "Maybe she is all bluster. I agree with your assessment, though. We stop the payments. Uncle Gabe?"

Gabe says, "I am willing. Just understand she may know something tangible. Something we don't want others to know about. Your father was up to something. I just don't know what she might know."

"We quit hiding and covering. We expose all our cards and see where the chips fall." Sawyer squeezes Laura Lynne's hands before releasing them and leaning back in his chair. "Laura Lynne?"

"Absolutely," she agrees, "We have to clean up the mess so the next generation can live without the fear of skeletons in the closet." She holds up a hand, "No pun intended. I can't imagine what she knows is anything worse than what I imagine. And my imagination is pretty amazing."

"You young people decide. The consequences will be yours to bear," Gabe says as he takes another slow sip of his bourbon.

"I know. I also know we have to protect the family, and circling the wagons makes the most sense. Too many loose ends, and Virginia Phillips is one of them," Laura Lynne replies.

"Is that her name? Virginia Phillips?" Sawyer rubs his eyes. "Does Momma know about her?"

Laura Lynne rolls her eyes again, "Everyone knows about her, Sawyer. We all just pretend she doesn't exist." She takes a long swig of tea. "Like we did growing up." Laura Lynne gets up from the couch. "Gentlemen, I am calling it a night. I heard Beau come in, and I want to spend some time with the kids before we turn in. They had to come to terms with a lot this weekend. I want to make sure they have time to ask me any more questions they might have."

"You're a good Momma, Laura Lynne," Gabe says as he looks over his bourbon and out the window, gazing into the fading sunlight outside.

"Sweeter words, Uncle Gabe, sweeter words." Laura Lynne rubs Sawyer's head and kisses his cheek as she walks by him. "I'm glad you're home. I plan to come back next month for a book club meeting. You still plan to be here?"

"I am here for the foreseeable future."

"Good, we will catch up more then." Laura Lynne walks to her Uncle Gabe. "I love you, and I am sorry I stayed away so long. I won't anymore."

"Glad to hear it. How about Beau and Savannah?" Gabe asks.

Laura Lynne laughs. "Are you kidding? Beau has been attached to your hip for three days. He loves it. I thought I wouldn't be able to drag Savannah out of the dish pantry. She has found her happy place."

"They are welcome anytime, Laura Lynne, with or without you. Tea Olive is for Coopers. It's their turn to enjoy the legacy we built."

Laura Lynne snaps her fingers. "Speaking of which, when I come back next month, can we talk about River Oaks? The kids and I have had some preliminary conversations, but I would like your buy-in before we move forward."

"Of course. This have to do with you wanting to build on Eileen's dream of using her assets to expand Tea Olive to its original size?" Gabe asks.

"Yes, yes, it does." Laura Lynne leans in for a kiss on top of Gabe's head. "Love you, good night."

"Good night," Gabe and Sawyer reply.

Laura Lynne leaves to go upstairs.

Sawyer looks at Gabe. "What's really got you worried that you aren't telling Laura Lynne?"

Gabe leans forward in his chair, cupping his bourbon with both hands. He glances over his shoulder and decreases the volume of his voice. "It has to do with this Bubba Westerman business with your father. I need to show you everything we have in order to understand what potential harm that man could do. I am not sure how best to approach this. I am not going to mislead you, Sawyer. Your father and the men before him were not exactly above board on all their dealings." Gabe sighs. "I have attempted to right as many wrongs as I can find. Since I took over, we have been above board on all aspects of Tea Olive and the business ventures we support, but I am not sure I can rectify some of the dealings. It has me worried."

"Good to know." Sawyer sits forward with his forearms propped on his thighs. "Listen, I didn't want to tell Laura Lynne yet, but I want you to know. I put in for retirement from the Army. I submitted my discharge paperwork before I left to come home."

Gabe is silent. He looks at his nephew studiously and with compassion. "You sure you are ready?"

"Momma's right. I need to step into my legacy and do what is expected of me."

Gabe tilts his chin contemplatively, "No, you don't. I can handle it for a few more years. And if you don't want it, we can determine who is the next rightful heir. Probably Avery."

"The truth is Uncle Gabe it's been time for a while now. My body is breaking down. I am tired and the last few years have been brutal. I have done my duty and done it as well as I could." Sawyer rakes his fingers through his short-cropped hair, "My biggest concern is adjusting to civilian life. Last time I was a civilian, I was 18 years old. That is a mighty long time ago."

"Nightmares?" Gabe served in Korea, only on one tour, but he understands.

"Nearly every night. Not to mention panic attacks and PTSD." He rubs his hands along his thighs. "I need time to heal and get my mind right. Plan a different future. Tea Olive is the perfect place."

"It always was for me, too."

The two men discuss family and business for another hour. Gabe slowly gets to his feet. "Time for me to go to bed. I am meeting with Malcolm in the morning to discuss the fields." He folds up the blanket and places it over the back of the rich, brown leather chair. "Why don't you join me?"

"How is Malcolm doing since he took over for his father?" asks Sawyer.

"He's turned in to a right good farmer." Gabe walks to the door. He works his way behind the couch and places his hand on Sawyer's shoulder. He gives it a squeeze. "Truth be told, not sure where we would be without him. He has a hand with the crops. He wants to try sweet potatoes as a crop rotation this year." Gabe walks toward the door. "We haven't done them in years. Could be he's right." Gabe gives one final wave. "Good night, Sawyer. I am glad you are home."

"Night, Uncle Gabe. See you in the morning."

It's not quite 10:00. The moon is out, and the cicadas are singing. Getting up from the couch, Sawyer walks around the study. Growing up, this study belonged to his father, but now he sees Gabe's footprint where his father's used to be. Sawyer pulls down books from the shelf, then he puts them back. He is restless. The call of the river is too much, and seeing no reason not to heed it, Sawyer walks to the mud room for a pair of boots. Gabe's fit just fine. Grabbing a flashlight and walking out the door, Sawyer starts down the path to the dock.

Tea Olive Plantation lies along one of the main tributaries of the Mississippi River. This waterway has always been the main transportation for the cotton crop. Its location has been instrumental as a water source and key to Tea Olive's continued success. It is also as pretty a place as you will ever see. It has long been believed by generations of Coopers that Tea Olive has mystical powers stemming from the indigenous people who lived along the river. Sawyer hopes these magical powers will help soothe his wounded body and soul. He sits on the dock. The moon is waning, and the air is thick. The breeze off the water is cool. The water temperature is still chilly. It's not quite May yet, so the water won't turn for another six weeks.

3

Chapter Three

Fall of 1985

It's the first day of school at Moseley Hall. Moseley Hall is the town's only private school, the school where those who can afford to send their children do so in hopes they will become lawyers and doctors. It is also Sawyer's senior year. Unfortunately, the rumor mill is grinding with gossip about Laura Lynne. Less than a month ago, his baby sister was sent to live with his Aunt Eileen. Most people assume she is pregnant; at least, that is what Grace, Laura Lynne's best friend, told him just this morning.

Sawyer has Chandler Monroe up against the locker with his forearm pressed against his windpipe. "Say it again, Chandler. You ass wipe. What are your thoughts about my little sister?" Nothing could make its way out of Chandler's mouth, including air.

Clayton "Clay" Newhouse, Sawyer's current best friend and the football team's wide receiver, grabs Sawyer by the shoulders.

"Let the prick go. Everybody knows he's a dick." Sawyer presses harder. "I said drop him!" Clay shouts as he pulls back on Sawyer's broad shoulders, causing him to stagger and lose his grip. Chandler starts gasping and gagging, leaning over with hands on his knees.

Sawyer leans down next to his ear. "One more word about my sister, or any other of my family members, and you can bet your ass I will finish what I started. Clay or not." Sawyer reinforces the threat with an elbow to the ear and causes Chandler to cry out. "Now go run home and tell your Momma, ass wipe." Sawyer hits the lockers with his fist. He looks at Clay and smiles. Clay knocks him on the shoulder, and the two of them head down the hall together. They fucking *hate* Chandler Monroe. He is a condescending prick. His father is now a judge and has been recently promoted from the DA's office. Chandler seems to think this somehow elevates his own personal status. Sawyer and Clay beg to disagree.

They make quite a pair, Sawyer and Clay: Sawyer, with his dark good looks, and Clay, a fair-haired god. The two became best buddies at the end of their junior year when Clay transferred from Pinckney Academy in Natchez. Clay's father was enticed to come to Venice by Sawyer's daddy, also a Sawyer. To keep things from getting confusing, the family and, well, the entire town call the youngest Sawyer "Tripp." He is the third Sawyer in the family. It's a Southern thing.

Clay's father is an IT genius. He worked for Xerox for years before he saw the potential in the computer industry and invested heavily in Microsoft. He capitalized on his idea to bring the tech industry to the farmer. Using computer technology, he can upgrade production by modernizing the farm equipment. Mr. Newhouse works as a consultant and is CEO and owner of Modern Farming LTD. When the Newhouse family came to town, his father placed the responsibility of making Clay feel welcome at Moseley Hall on Sawyer's plate.

It did not take long for Clay and Sawyer to become best friends. When the fallout from Laura Lynne's banishment from Tea Olive occurred, Clay stood by Sawyer's side. He was Sawyer's biggest supporter. "Bunch of pure breeds. Their families are too intertwined. Fucked with their brains and screwed up their genetics. Don't let them bother you," Clay responded after Buck Huger came nose to nose with Sawyer on the football field talking smack about Sawyer's Momma. A super low blow coming from one of his childhood friends and Laura Lynne's first kiss. Clay continued to be supportive, reassuring, "Why do you care what they say? Just keep throwing me the football. When we win all these games, that will shut 'em up."

Buck Huger has a right to be disgruntled with the Beauregard family. Buck and Laura Lynne were sweet on each other during her sophomore year. When Laura Lynne ended up in Dr. Goldbug's office with sexually transmitted diseases, their father automatically assumed Buck was responsible. Laura Lynne was adamant he was not, but Sawyer could not be dissuaded and confronted Buck's father. Robert Huger marched Buck to Dr. Goldbug's for testing after a sound beating, only to discover that Buck had tested negative across the board. Since then, Robert meticulously undermined Sawyer's business ventures and strategically removed Sawyer and Melanie from several prominent board positions. Social invitations had completely dried up. And, to make matters worse, Robert Huger had filed a lawsuit for defamation.

Sawyer took out all his anger and frustration on the football field, mostly against the opposing team. And, in the end, Clay was right. The boys have an amazing season, and the town rallies around as Moseley Hall wins game after game. Everything just seems to click on the field. Clay and Sawyer are unstoppable. It's like they have a sixth sense about each other on the field. They always know where the other is. They become more than friends. They become brothers. The gossip and rumors eventually die down, and Sawyer becomes the town's golden boy once again. Nevertheless, he is still a pariah at school. His friends from the last 17 years keep their distance. On the bright side, Sawyer's dad is somehow able to right the situation with the Huger family and make the impending lawsuit disappear.

Things at home are another matter. They are anything but getting better. Momma and Daddy are constantly at each other's throats. Daddy often slams doors and leaves town for Mobile. It's an open secret that Daddy has mistresses, but Sawyer thinks there is a special someone. Hence the constant "business" trips. Sawyer is left to pick up the pieces and be the man of the house. Avery is feeling the most impact of his father's neglect. Sawyer just keeps counting down the days until he is off to college and out of this emotional roller coaster.

Sawyer spends as much time as he can away from the house by spending the weekends with Clay or at the cabin. If that doesn't pan out, Sawyer heads to his Uncle Gabe's and bunks with him.

The trouble, if you can call it that, between him and Clay starts Christmas break. Clay has come over to The Residence to mess around and kill time. The football season is over. Much to the town's delight, the boys won the football state title for the first time since 1969. But basketball has not started, and the golden boys find they have time on their hands.

"Come on, Clay. Let's go hang out at the cabin," says Sawyer.

"Sure, man."

"Let me tell Queenie where we are going."

Sawyer walks to the kitchen, and Clay goes to the wet bar. He grabs a bottle of vodka and some lemons. After about 15 minutes, Sawyer comes out of the kitchen loaded down with a cooler and basket filled with Queenie's homemade sandwiches and desserts. Clay has a special fondness for Queenie's snickerdoodles.

At Clay's house, his mom makes all the meals and keeps the house. She said she wouldn't have a thing to do if she hired a maid and housekeeper. When he relays his mother's sentiment to Sawyer, Sawyer just laughs. "That's because your Momma's not from the South." Which is true. His mom is from the Midwest. She met his father at MIT. Both are brainiacs. His mother taught mathematics for years at his school. Now that he is grown and they have moved to Venice, his mom is applying to be a professor at the local community college.

"Come on, Tripp! Let's go!" Sawyer eyes the bottle of vodka and smiles. Clay winks.

"Here. Put it in the basket. Daddy won't care, but Momma would not be happy. Cocktails with dinner is one thing; shots are another." Clay snuggles the bottle and lemons amongst the many Tupperware containers.

"Good Lord! I think I want to marry Queenie," Clay exclaims.

Sawyer hits him with his shoulder. "I'll let you and Lincoln fight that one out. Since she's pregnant with her sixth kid, I am thinking you might lose that battle."

They both laugh and saunter out the back door off the porch and hustle to the farm truck. Every farm in Mississippi has one. It's generally a beat-up F-150 that is no longer streetworthy but works just fine on the farm. They hop in and drive toward the cabin, a very lofty term for the structure that's more a fishing shack than a cabin. It was built for fishing and hunting when the Cooper land traveled for another 2,000 acres in that direction. The land that was once all Cooper land is now shared between two families, the Hugers and the Cunninghams. Some ancestor had to sell the land, or maybe it was given away in marriage. Sawyer gets the generations all mixed up and honestly couldn't care less. That was more in his older sister Scarlet's wheelhouse.

Fifteen minutes later, Sawyer pulls up to the cabin. The boys unload, and Sawyer unlocks the door. It's not too bad. They haven't been out there since football season started four months ago. But during the summer months preceding, the fishing shack became their favorite place to hang out and unwind. "Come on, let's air it out and clean it up a little bit," says Sawyer.

"Yes, mom."

Sawyer laughs at the sarcasm, but he can't abide anything out of place. He prefers things neat, orderly, and clean. It is one of the reasons he is considering going to a military school for college instead of Ole Miss. His parents are pushing hard for him to play football for a Division I school and their alma mater. Sawyer knows he is good enough to make the team, but he would sit on the bench more than play. Good as he is, he is small time compared to the boys from the bigger schools of Jackson. The Citadel has been courting him pretty hard, thanks to his Uncle Gabe. He would get to play and probably start if he attended the much smaller school.

Clay opens the windows and grabs a broom while Sawyer unloads the groceries and wipes down the kitchen. He cracks open the vodka bottle and lines up a shot, one for him and one for Clay. Clay walks in with a dustpan in hand and says, "Shit, yeah." He heads straight for the counter and picks up the two small glasses. He hands one to Sawyer after he finishes slicing the lemon. "To the dream team." They clink and throw it back, sucking the lemon and laughing.

Neither Clay nor Sawyer are big drinkers. They prefer to stay in shape for their athletics. But they have the next two weeks off the playing field, and both agree to let loose for a bit. Sawyer, always the 'dad,' keeps things safe. No driving and no drinking in town. Keep it private and do it with people you trust. Today, as it has been all year, is just Clay and Sawyer. Both are usually very responsible drinkers.

"Come on! The cabin is clean enough. Let's go drop a line." Even in December, the weather is warm and sunny. It is perfect for fishing. The boys grab a sandwich and a pole. They meander out to the dock. They sit quietly, lost in their own thoughts. They occasionally talk about the future. Clay will likely follow in his parent's footsteps and go to MIT. He is fine joining his dad in the family business.

"Wish I was. It would make it much easier on me," says Sawyer as he baits his hook again.

Sawyer's plan for his life has been mapped out since birth. He will follow in his father's footsteps and run Tea Olive. He will protect the trust for future generations. But the problem is Sawyer doesn't want to stay in Venice, at least not yet. He wants to get out and see the world.

"I mean, one day, I want to live here. Just not right away. Dad can handle things here until I am ready, but of course, that would mean he would actually have to be here." Sawyer mutters the last part under his breath.

Clay knows all about his father's new paramour in Mobile. "Well, if you aren't here to do it, he won't have a choice." Clay looks over at Sawyer, "You got to do the right thing for you."

"Ha, easier said than done. You have no idea how difficult it is to be the oldest boy of both the Cooper and Beauregard families. I mean, Uncle Gabe and Aunt Eileen never had any kids. All the pressure is on us…me in particular."

"You're right. I don't get it. Truth be told, I wouldn't stay in this backwoods town if it weren't for Dad. You are about the only thing that makes it tolerable."

Sawyer looks over at Clay. "Really? You hate it that bad?"

He nods. "Yep, the people are cliquey. They have no tolerance for anyone different. Momma wants to go back to work because she doesn't have one friend here. Barely anyone will talk to us. Only reason they do is because they need Daddy's help." He shrugs his shoulders. "Make no mistake, as soon as they don't need him anymore, they will toss him aside. And us with him. Same thing was happening in Natchez. It's why we took the opportunity in Venice." Clay reels in his hook to recast his line. "Me, I plan to expand Daddy's business out West. I think I will try Oregon and California. Ya know, where people are more tolerant."

Sawyer stares at Clay. He has never heard Clay say one negative thing about Venice, school, or their friends. But it made a weird kind of sense. Honestly, if the Laura Lynne debacle had not happened last summer and ostracized Sawyer from his group of lifetime friends, he probably wouldn't have spent nearly as much time with Clay. He would have done what his daddy asked, but no more than that. Clay connected with Sawyer simply because he knew what it felt like to be an outcast.

"Screw 'em. Let's go have another shot. Fish aren't bitin' anyway," says Sawyer.

$$4$$

Chapter Four

The two young studs go into the cabin and turn on the radio to the basketball games. They sit at the kitchen counter and Sawyer pulls out some chips and dip. He uncaps a bottle of Coke. Clay sets up a round of shots. This time their toast is "Screw 'em," clink and drink.

Clay sets up another round. "This will be the last one for a while. Need to wash away our conversation. That shit got deep."

Sawyer nods in complete agreement. That shit did get deep. Sawyer sees Clay from a new perspective and truthfully admires him all the more.

"Stop looking at me so funny. I am still the same guy," says Clay.

"Are you? I had you cut out for the Southern life, not some hippie tree hugger. Makes me wonder if in ten years you're gonna have dreadlocks and roach clips in your hair?" Sawyer replies sarcastically.

"Hell, I just might. I always liked Bob Marley." They down their next shot. Sawyer sets up the chessboard. Gabe taught him to play, but Clay is a whiz. They spend the next few hours playing chess and listening to college basketball games. The boys devour Queenie's basket of food and drink plenty of soda with the occasional shot thrown in. It starts getting dark around 5:00. They sit on the porch and watch as the sun goes down. Sunsets are a gorgeous event on Tea Olive.

"If you want, we can spend the night out here. I just need to let the house know. They can call your parents." Sawyer gets up. "I think I will stay even if you go home. I don't want to face Momma right now. She will know I've been drinking."

"Sure. I'll stay. It beats listening to Mom and Dad discuss the latest brilliant computer design." He shakes his head. "I love my parents, but they look at me like some novelty. Both of them are super nerds. They have no idea what to do with a super jock kid."

Sawyer laughs and picks up the walkie-talkie. He makes sure it is positioned on the family channel and then beeps in. Pearl answers. Sawyer relays the plan. "Can you call the Newhouses and see if it's okay for Clay to stay?"

"Sure, back in a sec."

"What's the story with Pearl?" asks Clay.

"What do you mean? She's Queenie's oldest daughter. She has been helping out at The Residence since I can remember. Since she was little, she always came with Queenie when she came to work. She and her brother Malcolm did too, after he was born. We all just played together until Pearl started taking on chores with her mom. Malcolm did the same with Lincoln."

"And you think that shit is normal, don't you?"

"Well, it is normal for us." Sawyer takes a swig of Coke and makes a move on the chessboard.

Clay shakes his head and picks up his chess piece. He knocks down Sawyer's queen. "Check."

"What? Oh, shit, really?"

"Had you about five moves in, but you are getting much better." Clay gets out of his chair and starts pacing like a caged lion. The walkie-talkie crackles. "Tripp?"

Sawyer picks it up and presses the button. "Here, Pearl."

"Mrs. Newhouse says it is fine for Clay to stay, but Clay is not to forget y'all gettin' company tomorrow. Need you home by lunch." Clay nods.

"Got it, Pearl, thanks. Let Queenie know we are here."

She laughs. "She standin' right here." There is some static. "She wants to know if Malcolm needs to bring you more food before we head home."

"No, but thanks. There is plenty left. She packed enough for an entire weekend. Over and out." Sawyer turns off the walkie-talkie. Turning to Clay, he says, "Come on, let's go for a hike."

"Great. I need to move." They both grab their football hoodies and matching skull caps. They pull on their boots and head out the door. "Let's go to The Ridge."

The Ridge is what the locals call the little hill on the Cunningham place. It's the highest place around. Grady and his dad set up a fire barrel and some benches. It's a favorite place to hang out during the winter months. "Sounds good."

It takes them close to an hour to get up to the ridge. The alcohol throughout the day has started to take effect. Both are feeling pleasantly relaxed. They both plop into an Adirondack chair and stare at the moon. "Hey Clay, what did you mean about Pearl and Malcolm?"

"Nothin. Don't worry about it. Just talkin'," replies Clay.

Sawyer shakes his head, a mistake, as it takes a minute for his eyes to settle. "Jeez, no more alcohol for me tonight," Sawyer mutters. "I'm not mad. I just don't get what's not normal. Expand." Sawyer gesticulates with his hands. This causes Clay to clap his hands together and laugh at his whimsy.

"Lord Tripp, you trippin?" Then he laughs at his own joke. He cracks himself up. Sawyer stares at him as if he hasn't heard this at least a million times in his life. "Okay, okay." He clears his throat and leans back. "It's like the Civil Rights Movement never made it to your house or Venice in general. Man, people don't just work for one family, live on the property, and have their kids work after they are old enough to do chores. Sounds like slavery to me."

This causes Sawyer to swear. "Fuck you say? What are you talkin' about? We haven't had slaves in generations! Queenie and Lincoln are paid and get a place to live too."

"Do you hear yourself? They 'get a place to live.' Man, they earned that place." He looks at Sawyer. "Do Pearl and Malcolm get paid too?" This stops Sawyer's response in its tracks as he looks at Clay. "See, man? It's not normal. I bet the place they live comes out of their earnings. If not slavery, then maybe sharecroppers."

"You're pissin' me off, Clay! The Jacksons are like family. Been here since Grandma Birdie was alive and Momma was born."

"'Like' family, but they aren't, are they? And why is that Tripp? Do you think Pearl did that of her own free will? Hell no. I have actually talked to Pearl. She's pretty cool. She told me her family were slaves here at some point. She wants to go to school and get away from here. Quit serving and kowtowing to y'all. But her Momma can't handle the workload on her own anymore." He shakes his head. "And just so you know, Pearl and Malcolm have never been paid by y'all. Pearl says she does some odds and ends for some of the other houses. They pay her."

A knot forms in Sawyer's stomach. Clay is pointing out stuff he should have recognized himself. Pearl is "like a sister," but she isn't one. The truth is that Clay's right. And he doesn't like the picture he is painting. "You and Pearl got a thing?"

Clay stares at Sawyer. "Would it bother you if I did?" He holds up his hand and shakes his head. "Before you get all bent out of shape, the answer is no. Though, it's not because she is black. It's because she is not my type."

"And what type is that?" asks Sawyer.

"She is not a 'he,'" Clay answers, and then, realizing what he just let slip, he covers his hand over his mouth as if to stop the words.

Sawyer stares blankly in Clay's direction as if not understanding what Clay just said. Then, as if the words begin to sink in, Sawyer's entire body tenses before he shoots out of the chair and charges Clay. Clay takes the tackle seated in the Adirondack chair, and they both go flying backward. Clay hugs Sawyer to his chest and flips him on his back to hold him down.

"Cut it out!" Clay shouts.

Sawyer thrashes around. He tries to push Clay off of him.

"Stop it! You are goin' to hurt yourself!" says Clay.

After a few more failed attempts to untangle himself and take a swing at Clay, Sawyer relaxes. Clay is far superior at this than he is. He has spent years on the football field honing his skills. Sawyer just throws the ball and tries not to get tackled.

Clay asks, "If I let up on my hold, are you gonna punch me in the face?"

Sawyer shakes his head in the negative. Clay eases back but stays alert.

Sawyer could not land a physical punch, so he goes for a verbal one, "Christ man, how long you been a fag?" Sawyer asks with a sneer.

"Use that term again, and I will beat the ever-livin' shit out of you," Clay responds.

Holding his head in his hands, Sawyer tries to wrap his mind around what Clay is telling him. Then he asks, "Why are you tellin' me this?"

"I didn't mean to. It just sort of slipped out."

"Fuck off, Clay! I mean it! Fuck the hell off!." Clay puts his hands up and takes a few paces back. Then puts his hands on his hips, watching Sawyer warily. Sawyer pulls himself up off the ground and begins pacing back and forth. He walks over to the bushes and pukes. Sawyer empties his stomach of all the day's food and some of the drink. He stands upright and looks over at Clay. Clay has a Coke can in his coat pocket he pulls out. He walks over to the Adirondack chair and sets it back on its feet. He puts the can of soda on the chair arm and backs away.

Sawyer wipes his mouth with his handkerchief. He slowly walks over to the chair and picks up the Coke. He pops the top and takes a swig. Clay starts to talk, but Sawyer holds up his hand and shakes his head. "Give me a minute," he says.

Clay shrugs his shoulders and walks over to the fire barrel. He pulls out a stick and starts messing with the yard debris strewn around the campground.

"Okay, I'm ready now," Sawyer says as he swallows a sip of soda.

Clay doesn't turn around or even look at his best friend. He clears his throat and begins to talk quietly. "The correct term is homosexual or gay. Been this way my whole life. I can't remember ever feeling anything more for a girl than friendship." He glances over his shoulder and looks at Sawyer. "I have been biding my time through high school, waiting for college to start so I could get out of this backwoods state." He looks back at the barrel. "Then you came along, and all that changed."

"Man, you were my *friend*!" Sawyer shakes his head in disgust. "You're fuckin' everything up!"

Clay nods. "You *are* my friend. I thought I could play it that way and ride out my time. But I don't want to do that anymore." He turns fully around. "Shit, if anybody knew, I would be lynched or beat to death. I'm trusting you with my life."

Sawyer sees the truth in his statement. In fact, somewhere in Sawyer's muddled brain he remembers seeing an investigative report on television about a nurse in California that had her gay roommate killed to collect mortgage insurance, or some shit. Had his penis cut off to make it look like a hate crime. And that is in liberal California, nowhere near the ultra-conservative Bible Belt. Being a white gay man in Mississippi could most certainly result in death.

"What do you want from me?" Sawyer asks.

"Fuck!" Clay kicks the barrel and knocks it lopsided. "I don't want *anything*! I just want you to know." He sets the barrel to rights. "Forget it! Forget I said anything." He puts his hands in his pockets and starts walking.

Sawyer follows quietly. His mind is spinning. "Clay is gay. Clay is gay. Clay is gay," keeps repeating itself in his mind with each step. The walk back to the cabin is at a fast clip, but still takes close to 45 minutes. It's enough time for Sawyer's mind to settle, and honestly, he is fascinated. It's his first gay man, at least that he knows about. They arrive back at the cabin and Clay starts packing up.

Sawyer breaks the ice, "Come on. Let's go sit on the dock." Sawyer walks out the back door. "Too drunk to drive right now anyway." He grabs the vodka on the way out and takes a swig.

"Well, that's not going to help." Clay takes the bottle from Sawyer and takes a drink himself. The walk from The Ridge had allowed Sawyer a chance to calm down and to think. Clay has been by his side this entire year while his life has been in turmoil. He has warded off the gossip and innuendo thrown at Sawyer about his baby sister for the past six months. He has been protecting him on and off the field. Sawyer should give him a chance and at least listen.

They sit down in the chairs by the lake, sharing a bottle of vodka. "Why now? Why tonight?"

Clay grimaces. "Didn't mean to, man. Too much to drink. I thought I said the words in my head, not out loud. Then I saw your face and realized my mouth formed the words in my brain." He takes another swig. "Too late to turn back then." He looks out over the water. "Besides, I wanted you to know for a while. Felt dishonest, but, well, you know."

"Who else knows?" asks Sawyer.

"Just my mom and dad."

"They good with it?" Sawyer asks innocently. This causes Clay to belly laugh and slap his hand on the chair arm.

"Hell no! I came out to them my freshman year. Took them some time and a lot of talking to come around to acceptance. Shit. We even went to family counseling." He looks over at Sawyer. "Friend of my mom's from MIT." He gazes back over the water. "But they are cool with it now. Think the hardest part has been knowing they won't be grandparents. Well, that and realizing how hard my life will be being gay." He kicks the ground with his foot. "Be easier in California."

And it all began to make sense why Clay was so concerned with Pearl and Malcolm. He knew what prejudice looked and felt like, maybe not directly, but certainly indirectly.

"Kelly Sue?" Sawyer asks. Clay has been dating Kelly Sue since school started.

"No, she doesn't know. But we are just friends anyway. She and I put on a good show." He looks at Sawyer with a sideways glance.

"What? She's not a lesbo is she?" Sawyer asks, uncertain.

"Man, you got to do better with your slurs. First, I am a fag, and now Kelly Sue is a lesbo?" Sawyer looks at him for the first time, and Clay's eyes are wet and full of emotion. "No, she is not a lesbian. At least not that I know of, but she has big dreams. They don't include a husband and babies. At least not now. She wants to be a pediatrician."

Not surprising. Kelly Sue will be valedictorian of their class. Nobody else will even come close. It's rumored that she has a perfect score on the SAT. "So, you like kiss her and stuff?"

"What are you asking me here Tripp? I feel like I am on *20 Questions*." Clay says, taking another swig of vodka.

Sawyer shrugs and grabs the bottle out of Clay's hand for another swig himself. "I guess I just want to know how you know you aren't into girls. And like, how it works."

Clay gets up from his chair. He takes the vodka bottle and heads inside the cabin. "We need nourishment if we are going down that road. Come on. Let's eat while I talk. Tired of staring at the water so I don't have to look you in the eye."

Sawyer unsteadily gets to his feet. The vodka is doing the trick. It makes him forget all his worries. Now, he is just curious. "Like, have you done it with a dude, dude?" Sawyer laughs at his own joke.

"Christ!" Clay says, handing Sawyer a piece of bread. "Eat this and sit down." Sawyer reaches for the vodka. "And no more freakin' booze. You've had plenty." Clay snatches the bottle away and hides it under the counter. He turns on the sink and fills a glass with water. "Hydrate."

"Nope, not until you tell me if you have done the deed, man. Popped the cherry…with a dude, dude." Sawyer snickers.

Clay shoves the glass of water at him. "No, not yet." He starts pulling out food from the fridge and piling it on the counter. "Now drink!"

Sawyer complies. A deal is a deal. He finishes his glass and sets it down. He scrunches his nose. "Then how do you know you are gay?"

"I know, man."

"That's what I don't get. You've had sex with a girl but not a guy? And you are gay?" Sawyer spreads his hands on the counter and looks at them, as if seeing them for the first time. "I haven't had sex yet! How is this fair?"

Clay shakes his head and piles together a makeshift sandwich for Sawyer. "I have no idea why we are even having this conversation. You are not going to remember it in the morning." He puts the sandwich on a paper plate and slides it to Sawyer. "Eat." He starts making one for himself. "Yes, I tried to screw my way to being a heterosexual, and it didn't work. Plus, it wasn't fair to me or the girl."

Sawyer chews thoughtfully. "Think I will like it?"

Clay takes a bite of his sandwich. "You will freakin' love it. Why do you ask? Don't you like kissing Grace?" Sawyer has been dating Grace off and on this year, mostly off. She and Charlie had a fight, and she was using Sawyer to make him jealous.

"It's okay. But Grace is not a good judge. It's like kissing my sister. Besides, I don't really kiss her—more of a peck on the forehead kind of a deal. Couldn't do that to Charlie, man. Or Laura Lynne. She and Grace were best friends."

"Well, then, who do you kiss?" asks Clay.

Sawyer looks at his sandwich like it is the first time he has seen it. He scrunches his nose again. "I guess I don't kiss anyone, and no one kisses me." Sawyer begins to feel sorry for himself, then looks at Clay with hurt in his eyes. "Besides, the Beauregards are persona non grata these days. Nobody to go out with except you." Sawyer takes another bite of his sandwich, talking with his mouth full. "I didn't get one invitation this Christmas; sucks, man." He quietly adds, "It used to be the best time of the year." Sawyer starts to slide off his chair to the ground.

"Jeez, you are a lightweight, Tripp." Clay catches Sawyer on his way down to the ground and drags him to the bearskin rug by the fireplace. "You're too heavy, or I'm too drunk to get you on the couch," Clay says. He throws an afghan over Sawyer and puts a pillow from the couch under his head. "Sleep it off. We can talk tomorrow. Or..," he whispers to himself as he watches Sawyer pass out, "maybe you will forget I ever said anything."

5

Chapter Five

Present Day

The hour is late, and Sawyer takes his time walking to The Residence. He has high hopes tonight that the night terrors will cease, and he will be able to sleep. But Sawyer is not counting on it. Sleep these days is elusive at best. Trying to be as quiet as possible, Sawyer takes off his boots and walks across the hardwood floors in stocking feet. He takes extra care to avoid the step on the staircase that has the telltale creek. He starts to walk past Laura Lynne's room. The door is open, and she is busy at her computer. Sawyer leans on the doorframe and sticks his head in.

"How did it go with the kids?" he asks.

Laura Lynne takes off her readers and looks at the door. She smiles. Her big brother is as handsome as ever. Laura Lynne waves him in and motions for him to sit across from her. "Surprisingly well." She leans her head back and shuts her eyes. "It's like being on an emotional roller coaster, though. I feel like I just exposed this deep, dark hole to light for the first time in a long time. It feels good but not quite comfortable."

Sawyer sits down and puts his elbows on his knees. He teepees his hands, placing them under his chin. "I so get that metaphor." He winks at her. "By the way, baby girl, I read your book on the plane ride home." He looks her in the eye. "You could have told me how bad it got."

She brings her head back to center and opens her eyes. "Had to admit it to myself first." She laughs humorlessly. "Once I did that, I figured I may as well tell the world."

"Proud of you. It had to be tough. I personally don't do vulnerability," Sawyer replies.

Laura Lynne smiles and then turns serious. "Speaking of vulnerability...I want to talk to you about Scarlet."

Sawyer drops his head and rubs his eyes. "I meant to ask why she didn't come today. It seemed out of character." He snaps his fingers. "Oh! And what happened to Buck's parent's place? I walked through there today. It's deserted and falling apart."

"That is just it. Nobody will tell me much of anything. Scarlet engages with Uncle Gabe and the investigation one minute but disappears a day later, and nobody hears from her. Uncle Gabe called me because he couldn't reach Scarlet after his arrest." Laura Lynne leans forward. "There is something financial too. Like Momma had to step in and pay for the boys' school, or they would have been kicked out. That would have been fifteen years ago. Whatever is going on has been happening for some time."

"Buck Huger doesn't have money? No way! The land itself is worth millions! Or is it in foreclosure? Wait, wouldn't he have inherited his parents' money as the sole heir?"

"I have no clue. I just know there are land developers involved and a legal battle. Some company called Overpass Development Partners. Uncle Gabe told me he and some of the other farmers along the river sued them to stop development. It has worked so far." Laura Lynne leans in. "But get this, that is not even the most concerning thing." She whispers, "I had ice cream with Scarlet after Uncle Gabe's court appearance. She had bruises on her neck and arm. It looked like somebody had grabbed her. When I asked her about them, she said she ran into a shelf in the kitchen." Laura Lynne rolls her eyes. "I just don't believe it."

"Christ." Sawyer digs his thumbs into the corners of his eyes.

"Watch your mouth, Sawyer Avery Beauregard! Don't forget where you are! Uncle Gabe's liable to come in here with a switch if he hears you taking the Lord's name in vain." Laura Lynne grins as she leans back in her chair.

"Cut me some slack, Laura Lynne. I have been in the military for 40 years. I am not sure I know how to hold a conversation without using a swear word."

Laura Lynne swats at his leg, "Well, you better start remembering. The only thing that has changed here is the age of the people. Same rules apply." She starts giggling. "You should have seen Beau when Pearl started telling him what's what, just like Queenie used to do. He instantly fell in love. Savannah too."

Sawyer grins. "So, they will be back then?"

Laura Lynne nods. "Oh yes. As Beau so eloquently put it, 'It's like a piece of the puzzle was missing, and now I found it.' Tea Olive sure gets a handle around your heart. You won't be able to keep any of us away again."

Sawyer stands up and walks to Laura Lynne. He cups her face in his hands. "I hate what that monster took from you. And, consequently, what it took from us." He kisses the top of her head and starts to the door. "I'm back now, and I am not planning to go anywhere. I promise to watch out for the family and keep a special eye on Scarlet."

"And no secrets. Promise me, Sawyer. No more secrets."

He holds up his pinky, and Laura Lynne does the same. "I pinky swear." He starts down the hallway. "Night, baby girl."

Sawyer walks to the master bedroom, but not before checking on Savannah and Beau, who are both tucked up tight for the night. Uncle Gabe's door is closed, so Sawyer must content himself that he, too, is tucked up safe. Sawyer changes into his nightclothes, which consists of an army t-shirt and shorts. Sawyer spots his computer at his Momma's formal writing desk. As he sits in the very old, very small antique chair, he has a real fear he may snap the thing in two. He rolls his eyes. If he is going to claim the master bedroom, then new furniture is a necessity. He would deal with it in the morning. In the meantime, he pulls up his computer and checks his email.

Thankfully, there is little enough. He has a missive from his commanding officer checking on him. There are a few follow-up emails from his last mission, which he quickly returns with the required information. Before he closes the computer for the night, he Googles Tea Olive to see if there is any news linked to the name that he needs to be aware of. It's a habit he started years ago when he was overseas, just to keep tabs on news at home. Not surprisingly, there are several new links to articles about Gabe's arrest, the dead body, or Dead Doe as Laura Lynne has affectionately named him, and Gabe's subsequent release. Nothing that causes any real concern to Sawyer at this point. Sawyer is exhausted. It is time to try and get some sleep. Eye-balling the master bed, he can't help but think his parents had sex in this bed. Stupid, considering the bed is several generations old. Lots of Coopers had sex in this bed. Still, it makes him cringe.

He pulls back the comforter and climbs into the rose-colored sheets. This room is too feminine. It is no wonder Gabe chose Daddy's old rooms. There are a lot of negative things that can be said about Sawyer II. However, he had exquisite taste. He chose only the best, from the cut of his suits to the cigar case on his mahogany desk—only the finest and highest quality. Sawyer guessed the best word for his father is class. He just exuded class. Often referred to as Black Jack Bouvier, he was suave, debonair, and handsome—a real ladies' man.

Sawyer closes his eyes and tries to sleep. The morning cannot come soon enough. For Sawyer, the night is a place of nightmares and demons, panic, and anxiety. Sawyer prays Tea Olive will change all that.

***

"Shhhh! Beau, you are going to wake the whole house!" Savannah loudly whispers.

Sawyer opens his eyes and tries to figure out where he is. After years of waking up in different locations, Sawyer has learned to take a moment and assess, allowing his brain to remind him. He throws his legs over the side of the bed, pushing the pink sheets and flowered comforter off his long body. Jumping off the mattress, Sawyer quickly and stealthily moves across the hardwood floor to the bedroom door. He opens the door and peeks out. The hallway is dark, but he spots Savannah and Beau making their way down the stairs. There is light coming from the kitchen downstairs.

"Y'all okay?" Sawyer asks.

Savannah gives a little gasp and whirls around. "Lord, Uncle Sawyer! I didn't hear you. We didn't mean to wake you up! But Beau is about as quiet as an elephant." She starts heading down the stairs, carrying her suitcase. "We are fine. We have early flights out today."

Sawyer quickly goes to the stairs and grabs Savannah's suitcase. She smiles. Beau is already at the bottom of the stairs, having placed his suitcase by the door. He turns to go back up the stairs but stops when he sees Sawyer.

"I told her I would get it," Beau says.

Savannah sighs. "No. You took it from me and thought you could take both down the stairs at one time. Pearl is gonna skin your hide when she sees the dent you put in the wall."

"It's not a dent. It is just a scratch. And your suitcase is not balanced right. It made me lose my grip," Beau replies.

"Do you hear him, Uncle Sawyer? He is blaming the suitcase." Savannah carefully walks down the stairs. "But I still love him. Aggravating baby brother that he is. Life was much calmer before he came along."

Sawyer laughs. "Scarlet always said the same thing about me." He picks up the suitcase and takes the stairs with ease and agility. "Beau, please go help your sister. No falling down the stairs on my watch."

Savannah rolls her eyes. "I think I can navigate stairs."

"I don't know, sissy, that's a pretty big belly you are lugging about. Are you even able to see the stairs?" Beau asks, smiling.

"Stop pickin' you two! I smell coffee," Sawyer says as he places the suitcase next to Beau's at the front door.

Sawyer leaves his niece and nephew to their sibling volley of words and barbs to find the coffee. Laura Lynne is already up and dressed. Her hair is tied in a knot on top of her head. She has on large silver hoop earrings and a boho linen outfit with sandals. She pours hot water over a tea bag. Sawyer goes straight to the coffee pot and pours a mug. "You have some great kids, Laura Lynne."

"Thank you." She brings the mug to her lips for a sip of tea. "I think they are the best parts of me and Jimmy." She tears up a little. "Savannah is going to be a super mom. Way better than me. She already is."

Sawyer comes over and puts an arm around her shoulders. "Already miss them?" he asks.

Laura Lynne lays her head on her brother's shoulder and nods. "So much." He squeezes her close and then releases her as the two young people walk in.

Savannah immediately asks, "What's wrong? What happened now?"

Laura Lynne laughs and sniffles. "Nothing, honey. Sawyer and I are just talking about how wonderful y'all are and how much I am going to miss you." She puts down her mug and turns to the coffee pot. "Coffee?"

"Absolutely." Beau leans on the counter, looking at Sawyer. "Uncle Sawyer, Uncle Gabe showed me the books for the trust and Tea Olive. He walked me through the farm business and the other businesses in town the trust has invested in." He looks at the mug his mother handed him. "I was wondering if you would keep me in the loop, like, maybe let me help some?" He looks at Sawyer with hope and trepidation in his eyes.

"Once I get up to speed, certainly." Sawyer sips his coffee. "I am glad you are interested. When I was your age, I was far more interested in shooting things."

Beau smiles. "I like that too. But I love business and finance. Ready to put my degree to work. May as well see what I can do to help the family." He takes the mug of coffee from his mom. Laura Lynne beams.

"How about you, Savannah? Interested in money and finance?" asks Sawyer.

Savannah pours hot water over her tea bag—like mother, like daughter. "Well, more business. I heard Uncle Gabe talk about some of the businesses in town, like the bookstore. I have always had a passion for real estate and hospitality. Keep thinking I can do something with that." She smiles and rubs a hand over her belly. "Maybe I will after little man here makes an appearance."

Sawyer looks at Laura Lynne with a smile. She smiles back. "Let me think on it," Sawyer says, "In the military, I had online conference calls with my officers on a weekly basis. That way we all stayed on the same page. Maybe we need to consider something like that for the family." Sawyer shakes his head. "I need to think on it some more."

"Y'all need to get moving, or you will be late for your flights. It's still a long drive to the airport," Laura Lynne says as she pours coffee into a Yeti for Beau. She has a thermos of hot tea ready for Savannah. She puts everything in a plastic bag and starts around the corner of the kitchen island. "I packed egg sandwiches and some strawberries from Queenie's garden in here too."

Savannah and Beau look at each other and start laughing. Laura Lynne gets all huffy and says, "Once a mother, always a mother."

The four of them walk as a group to the front porch. Gabe is already outside, standing there in his overalls, waiting. Sawyer grabs the suitcases while Beau brings the car around.

"Come here, Savannah. I want to say goodbye to you and my great-great nephew," says Gabe. Savannah shyly walks over to Gabe as he asks, "Can I put my hands on your belly?" She nods. Gabe leans over and whispers to Nathaniel, "You were loved before we ever knew about you. Grow big and tall and strong. Never forget you are a

Cooper *and* a Beauregard. That means double the steel and double the love." He pats her tummy and looks up at her, smiling.

Savannah has tears in her eyes. "Stupid hormones." She holds Gabe's hands against her tummy. "Thanks, Uncle Gabe. I have loved getting to know you." She looks around the front porch and out to the gardens so lovingly tended. "I am going to miss this place."

Gabe leans forward and places his forehead on hers. "Not to worry. It will always be here for you. Come back whenever you want. Bring that young husband of yours. I want to meet Chris."

Beau pulls up at the base of the stairs in the convertible. Savannah rolls her eyes and looks at her mom. "At least this time, he didn't lower the roof. At least not yet."

Sawyer and Beau load the trunk as the other three make their way down the stairs to the car. Beau comes to stand beside Savannah. Laura Lynne comes in for the hug. "You two, be safe and smart. I love you with my whole heart."

Beau pets Laura Lynne's hair and wraps his long arms around his mom and sister. "Love you, Momma." He releases them and turns to Gabe and Sawyer. He shakes their hands. "Thank you. It was great to finally see this place and spend some time with y'all." Savannah releases her mom, and Laura Lynne gives her one final kiss on the head.

Gabe opens the passenger door, and Savannah slides in. Gabe looks at Beau, "Beau, you heard your mother. Be careful. Precious cargo."

"Yes, sir!" Doors slam shut, and the car starts down the driveway. Laura Lynne hurries to the top of the stairs. She turns around and starts waving. The windows to the convertible roll down, and the kids put their arms out and wave back. This goes on until the children are through the gate and down the road.

6

Chapter Six

Sawyer stands next to Laura Lynne, and Gabe asks, "What was all that?"

Laura Lynne wipes her eyes and blows her nose with Gabe's handkerchief. "Something we started doing when they were little and went to spend some time with Jimmy's parents. I would wave until they couldn't see me, and they would wave back. Silly, I know, but I never want them to look in the rearview mirror and see my back or, worse, me not be there. I will always be there, waving at them, encouraging them."

"That's a lot to expect from a wave," Sawyer says dryly.

Laura Lynne looks at her big brother. "Shut up. It's my wave."

Sawyer laughs, hooks his arm around her shoulder, and asks, "What time do you leave today?"

"As soon as I get packed up. My flight leaves at one. I like to get there in plenty of time. Nothing worse than thinking you might miss your flight. I prefer to travel stress-free." Laura Lynne puts her head on Sawyer's shoulder and pats his hand. Then, she disengages and walks in the house toward the stairs. "I will find you before I leave. It's going to take me a while to get everything packed."

Sawyer and Gabe nod as the two walk to the kitchen. Gabe asks, "Do you want me to top off your coffee?"

"Sure." Gabe pours more coffee into Sawyer's mug. "Mind if we sit on the back porch and watch the sunrise?" asks Sawyer.

"If you put on some clothes, that will be fine," says Gabe, giving him a critical look.

Sawyer looks down at himself. He is still in his T-shirt and shorts. Laughing, he starts for the door. "I have to dress for coffee on the porch. I am definitely back home." He climbs the stairs, and Sawyer sees Laura Lynne packing in her room. He pops his head in and states, "You were right. Uncle Gabe just sent me upstairs to get dressed for the day before I could join him for coffee."

"Told you. Welcome home." Sawyer slaps the door with his hands to leave and spots the scratch on the hallway wall Savannah was fussing about with Beau. And she was right; it *is* more than a scratch. It's a hole. From the looks of it, it was made from the suitcase's wheel. He sighs; he will have to get that fixed by a professional. One thing about these old houses is that going to Home Depot doesn't cut it. Sawyer adds that to his mental list of things to do.

Looking in his closet, Sawyer decides to change into work clothes. Unfortunately, his work has been in the army, so he has little more than army green and camouflage in his wardrobe. He chooses a pair of camouflage pants and a long-sleeved shirt. It is all he brought with him. Though, he did have enough foresight to pack the standard Southern Tuxedo of khakis, a button-down, a bowtie, and a navy-blue blazer. He is having the rest of his wardrobe shipped from the base.

For the last three years, Sawyer has been stationed in Washington, DC, at Ft. McNair. Not that his clothes from there will be very helpful here. A shopping trip is probably in order. He quickly makes the all-too-feminine bed, cleans up the bathroom, and double-times it to the back porch and Gabe. Sawyer is a master at keeping things clean and organized. But the frilly comforter and pink sheets need to go.

"Uncle Gabe," Sawyer says as he sits in the rocking chair next to his uncle, "Momma's pink linen and her tiny furniture have to go. I am scared to death to sit in the desk chair. It might collapse under me!"

Gabe laughs. "You notice I took your father's old rooms, right?" Then Gabe flicks his wrist, conveying his agreement. "Do whatever you need. But before you buy anything new, be sure to check with Pearl. There is plenty of furniture in the attic and the barn. You might find what you're looking for there. Linen too."

The two men watch the horizon, enjoying the sunrise. They discuss the weather and the year's cotton crop. Eventually, Laura Lynne joins them.

"Time for me to hit the road, y'all," Laura Lynne says.

Both men walk with her to the front door. Gabe takes her hands in his at the top of the porch stairs, much like he did Savannah's this morning. "Thank you for coming. I don't discount how difficult it was for you to come back. But I am glad you did." He leans his forehead against Laura Lynne's. "You come back next month for your book club. You hear?"

Laura Lynne takes a deep breath and leans back. "I'm glad you called me. It was time." She turns to Sawyer. "I want to say goodbye to Aunt Eileen and let her know I will be back. Can you put my stuff in the car for me?"

Sawyer replies, "I can. Do you want company?"

"No," she says, "I want to do it by myself. We were a team."

Sawyer loads up the car. Pearl and Victoria come to the front door as Laura Lynne returns.

"Okay, that does it," Laura Lynne sniffles, her throat choked with unshed tears. There are hugs all around. Then, hugging her big brother, Laura Lynne whispers into Sawyer's ear, "Take care of them, okay?"

Sawyer nods and gives her an extra squeeze to let her know he heard her. He releases his sister, walks her down the stairs, and helps her into her car. He shuts the door and says, "Be safe, baby girl."

Laura Lynne rolls down the window and sticks her hand out, waving at everyone as she drives away. Sawyer runs up to the top of the stairs, waving with all his might. Laura Lynne waves furiously and honks her horn as she disappears through the gates.

Pearl looks at Sawyer with a strange expression. "What was that all about? Quite the send-off." Sawyer laughs and shakes his head.

"Long story." He looks at Victoria. "Victoria, right?"

"Yes, sir," responds Victoria.

"Think you can work your magic in the kitchen for me and Uncle Gabe?" Sawyer asks. "I didn't get much supper last night; woke up hungry."

"Happy to. Any special requests?" Victoria asks.

"Whatever you make for Uncle Gabe works for me," Sawyer replies.

Victoria smiles. "Mr. Gabe likes a big breakfast himself. Easy enough to double the portions." She looks critically at Sawyer, seeing nothing but skin and bones. "They obviously don't feed you right in the Army. Don't worry, I think I can help fill you out some."

Victoria saunters back into the house and to her kitchen domain. Sawyer looks critically at himself before saying to Gabe, "I guess I am a bit scrawny."

"I wasn't going to say anything, son, but you look a bit the worse for wear. I imagine the nightmares don't help." Gabe places his hand on Sawyer's back, giving him a reassuring pat. "Victoria's cooking will help you gain weight, but maybe a project will help your mind. And more, I could use your help."

Gabe directs Sawyer's path toward the house's front sitting room. "Everything I need to show you is in the vault," Gabe says.

The vault is hidden behind the bookcase. One of the Cooper ancestors built a 6-foot by 10-foot room to store the family's valuables. Legend has it that the Cooper family children hid in the room during the Civil War when Sherman's men were marching through Mississippi. Eventually, the room was shored up with concrete and then steel, creating a huge vault with a tubular lock and its latest edition, the digital lock. Currently, the vault houses some of the more expensive or irreplaceable items of the Tea Olive Estate. There are heirlooms that include jewelry, antique guns, medals from various wars, a few gold bars, and an archive for important papers.

"Your father started keeping all the important files and papers in here," says Gabe. "Truth be told, I have not gone through them. Mostly because I would rather be in the garden." He opens the panel and disconnects the locks. The vault unlatches, and Gabe opens the door. With his arthritic finger, stained dark from all his years digging in the dirt, Gabe points to a corner on the far wall. "See that drawer over there in the corner? It's full of documents that need to be sorted."

Sawyer leans over and walks into the vault. As big as the vault is, Sawyer has to stoop to get inside and open the drawer. He grimaces as he takes a closer look. It's not one drawer; there are several. There are files and stacks of paper. "I see why you wanted to play with the flowers."

Gabe sighs. "Your father passed away unexpectedly. Then, he left me the trust and The Residence in the will. I never suspected he would do that; thought for certain it would go to you or Melanie." He looks at Sawyer. "We never spoke. Melanie can tell me nothing about the business side of things. I have basically had to figure this out as I go." He turns around and waits for Sawyer to exit before closing the vault door. "Gerald and his son Ace have been very helpful." Gerald and Ace Lally have been the family attorneys for several decades. "But as I mentioned, there is some money that is unaccounted for. Both in the debit and the credit column. Lally knows nothing." Uncle Gabe glances over his shoulder at his nephew. "Maybe you will have better luck."

The dinner bell rings. "Come on, let's eat. I like a big breakfast," says Gabe.

The two men walk to the dining room where the table is piled high with plates of biscuits and gravy, bacon, eggs, and grits. Sawyer can feel his mouth water as his stomach begins to rumble.

Gabe sits and quickly says grace before he begins to eat. Sawyer closes his eyes as he takes his first bite of biscuits and gravy. He is instantly transported back to the mornings of his childhood.

"Victoria cooks like her grandmother—only better. This is delicious," says Sawyer.

Gabe picks up the *Venice Gazette* newspaper carefully placed next to his breakfast plate, taking a sip of coffee. He replies, "She does. I am not sure how long she plans to stay with us, but I am taking full advantage of her culinary talents while she is here."

"She is leaving?" says Sawyer.

"Hmmph. I don't think I can keep her here once Queenie passes. She came two years ago to help out her mother and ended up in our kitchen. I know she has dreams of having her own place." He takes a bite of bacon, before rustling his newspaper open. "She definitely has the skill." Gabe hands a section of the *Gazette* to Sawyer. "You might be interested in the local goings-on."

Sawyer takes the paper. "Y'all still get the paper delivered? I didn't know they did that anymore."

"Tea Olive still receives a paper copy hand-delivered each Monday, Wednesday, and Friday," says Pearl as she refills the men's coffee mugs. "Though you are right, I don't know how much longer there will be a paper version. The *Gazette* sold a while back, and it is moving more and more toward an online-only version."

"Well, then they will lose one of their longest subscribers. I have no interest in sitting in front of the computer while I eat my breakfast," says Gabe. Gabe takes off his glasses and leans back in his chair. He has finished the last bite of his biscuit. He looks at Sawyer, tapping the earpiece of his reading glasses on the newspaper, pointing at a notice before saying, "Every fourth Thursday morning, the Board of the Venice Country Club meets. Your momma and I have been filling the seats since Scarlet and Buck stepped down, but I want you to start going in my place."

Sawyer is already shaking his head. "Not the country club type any-more, Uncle Gabe."

Gabe won't be dismissed. "Nonsense! You are both a Cooper and a Beauregard. Both your grandfathers were founding members of the club, and it is our duty to serve. It's time you take your rightful place."

Sawyer takes a sip of coffee to wash down the sausage gravy-laden biscuit. "Let Scarlet and Buck do it. It's more up their alley."

"Scarlet has her own reasons for no longer being on the board, though she has not shared them with me." He puts his glasses back on his nose. "Quit pawning off your responsibilities on your sister. She has carried the burden of this family alone for long enough." Standing, Gabe imparts his final word on the matter. "It's your turn, Sawyer. And it's an expectation." He holds up his hand. "At least for now, until the next generation is ready. The board is about more than member-ship, galas, and golf. It has a large philanthropy arm. It is important we give back to the community, and this is one way we do it. Besides, I am not asking. They meet next week. Put it on your calendar."

Sawyer sighs. He knows there is no arguing. He knew when he returned, there would be duties he preferred not to participate in. Besides, Gabe and his momma were getting old. The responsibilities need to be transferred. "Fine, but don't expect me to be a deacon at the church."

Gabe looks at him sternly. "You will one day be a deacon, just like all the men of the Cooper family." He starts walking toward the mud room. "Come on. We are to meet John and Malcolm out at the back field. You can drive the side by side."

Gabe slides on his mud boots, and the men stroll to the barn. The barn doubles as the garage and a storage shed. Gabe slaps Sawyer on the back. "Glad you are home. Now, if you will just stop shirking your responsibilities as head of the family."

"I am not head of the family yet. You and, well, Momma still hold that position."

"Only because you were not ready. But it's time, Sawyer." Sawyer looks over at his uncle with concern. He is 75 but still active and in excellent physical condition from all appearances.

"You're not sick, are you?" Sawyer asks.

Gabe smiles and shakes his head, "No, son. Just old."

They hop in the side-by-side, which is basically a juiced-up version of a golf cart made for rough terrain. Sawyer grins. He has always loved the farm's toys. "Come on, old man! Let's see what this amazing piece of engineering can do," Sawyer says as he jumps into the cart next to his uncle.

Smiling and laughing, the two men drive to the back field. At 2,000 acres of land, Tea Olive is divided by fields. Each field's location is its name, which is nothing clever but allows for a clear pinpoint of location. There is the back field, the front field, the east field, and the west field. The land that is used for living and harvesting is the dock, The Residence, and the garden. Not very original, but everyone knows what they mean and where they are.

John and Malcolm are waiting patiently in the back field when Gabe and Sawyer arrive. John is on his four-wheeler, and Malcolm is on one of the farm's tractors. Sawyer pulls up next to them and gets out of the side-by-side. He walks straight to Malcolm, his hand extended, and slaps him on the back. "Malcolm! We didn't get much time to talk yesterday. God, it's been forever. How are you?" Malcolm smiles and slaps him back. Sawyer looks over at John. "I saw you at The Residence yesterday and apologize for not properly introducing myself."

John reaches out his hand. "No problem. You were rightfully occupied with your family."

"Okay, get me up to speed here. What do I need to know?" asks Sawyer.

The next hour, the men discuss the plan for the field and the farm. This particular piece of land has not been cultivated in over ten years. "We have the equipment and the farmhands to do the work. I recommend we try our hand at organic Beauregard sweet potatoes," says Malcolm, "Lot of hoops to go through to make it official, but with the land being barren for so long, we have a unique opportunity." Malcolm looks at John for reinforcement. John nods in encouragement. Malcolm takes a deep breath and lets it out, then says what has been on his mind, "Truth is, I think we need to make the entire farm organic. It's what the young people want."

John agrees, "It's a risk, but I think we can mitigate it by starting with this field first. There are a few small farms in the area already making the transition to organic. We could be the first large operation to enter this market in lower Mississippi."

"And sweet potatoes are easy. Well, easier than cotton based on the research I have done," Malcolm continues.

Gabe has a thoughtful expression on his face, then says, "I have not considered organic for the farm. I have been doing organic for the kitchen gardens and the flower gardens for a while with limited success." He shakes his head. "I love the idea, but we have to have a successful crop. It is how we stay in business."

"Do we have a buyer?" Sawyer asks.

John nods, "I have a connection with a local buyer who works through a grant. The grant is to encourage organic methods of farming. He's an old army buddy of mine, Micah Hunter."

"Wait, you know Hunter? He was a captain under my command a few tours ago," Sawyer says with astonishment.

"Yes, sir. I was under his command in 1990 Desert Storm, US Army Infantry 5th Division." He shakes his head. "We were young and stupid, but somehow we survived. He was a second lieutenant then, fresh out of West Point."

"Small world, man." Sawyer looks at his uncle. "Micah is on the up and up. If he is involved, it's worth looking into." He looks at John and Malcolm. "I say we move forward. Uncle Gabe?"

"It's good your home Sawyer, otherwise I would have had a different response." He smiles and extends his hand to Malcolm, then John. "Looks like we are going into the organic farm business."

Handshakes and laughter all around. "I would like to see what you are thinking for the rest of the farm," Sawyer says to Malcolm.

"John is the business end of things, even has a PowerPoint. I'll stick to the plantin' and harvestin'," says Malcolm.

John holds up his hands as if in surrender. "Don't be humble, Malcolm. You have worked as hard as I have on this presentation. There is nothing easy about organic farming. The guidelines and rules are rigorous. Very different than what has always been done. Malcolm even took an organic farming course online to become certified." Malcolm is looking at the tips of his boots, obviously uncomfortable with praise. "All I did was find an organic buying connection."

"I would just as soon stay in the fields if y'all don't mind. John can give you the details," Malcolm replies. He looks up from his boots, shaking his head and smiling. "I am not gonna lie. I am pretty excited to try what I have learned. Fun to do something different after all these years."

Gabe slaps him on the back and points to the tractor. "Mind if I tag along? Let's see if you can teach an old dog new tricks."

"Hop on, Mr. Gabe. I was just getting ready to dig the field. Want a tractor of your own?" Malcom asks.

"You're dern right I do," Gabe says. He starts to follow Malcolm, shouting over his shoulder to Sawyer, "Tell Victoria where we are so she knows where to send lemonade and snacks when Liam gets here. He can help me on the tractor. It's time he learns." Waving over his shoulder at the two men. "You two talk shop. I am going to play in the dirt."

7

Chapter Seven

John and Sawyer watch them go. "I really hope one day I grow up to be your uncle," says John.

"Me, too." Sawyer turns toward his side-by-side. "Where to next?"

"Just follow me. I will show you what we have been up to."

The rest of the morning is spent going from one field to the next, discussing the farm. Sawyer and John are standing in the east field when the dinner bell rings three times, signaling that dinner is ready. "That is one sound I have truly missed. Come on. Pearl will tan our hide if we don't get dinner before it turns cold," says Sawyer.

"Yep, did that once, haven't done it again." Both men laugh. "You going to The Residence or the shed?" asks John.

"I'd rather eat at the shed and meet all the farmhands," Sawyer replies as he hops into his vehicle, "But I'm guessing my meal will be wherever Uncle Gabe eats."

"Normally, he takes his meals at the house. Not sure today, though; first time I have seen him plow a field," says John.

Sawyer stares at John in astonishment, "Really? He used to do it all the time. He worked with the field hands and oversaw all the cultivation and harvesting when we were growing up. Must have stopped when Daddy died, and he took over the business end of things." He shakes his head. "No wonder he is so anxious for me to learn the business. It's all making sense now."

John just shrugs his shoulders and holds up his hands, "I have no idea why he stopped. I never asked because I never knew he worked the land, other than his garden projects, of course." John straddles the four-wheeler and says, "Let's check the shed first."

Sure enough, Gabe and Malcolm are already there, digging in. Today's meal is shrimp po'boys, fresh strawberries, French fried potatoes, and plenty of lemonade and sweet tea. Pearl and Victoria are serving up large plates of food. There is a total of 20 people here today. Pearl signals Sawyer over. "Belly up to the trough." He holds out his hand for his plate. "Haven't seen Mr. Gabe this happy in a long time. Plowing a field? When I sent Liam out to the field as instructed with snacks and lemonade, he reported back that lunch would be at the shed today." She shakes her head. "Glad you are home."

Sawyer sees Gabe sitting at the head of the table. It won't be until harvest time that all the tables are full. He is holding court and having a grand time. He is obviously loved and respected. Sawyer smiles as he tells tales and spins yarns about previous harvests and family lore. He introduces Sawyer. "Everyone, meet my nephew, Sawyer Avery Beauregard III." Everyone nods hello. "He will be handling the business end of things moving forward." Gabe winks at Sawyer. "Might be news to him, but after today, don't see myself riding a desk for much longer."

Sawyer acknowledges the men with a dip of his chin and a friendly smile. He eats as his uncle resumes his storytelling. As he talks, Sawyer surveys the men surrounding the table. The hands range in age from 20 to 60. They're rugged and mostly unkempt. Working on farms is mainly seasonal work. Tea Olive has always kept a small group of farmhands year-round, then hired migrant farm workers as needed. In Sawyer's mind, this many people for current production seems excessive. Other than the new organic field, the harvest is planted. Not much to do other than the maintenance of the farm equipment, fences, and land. Sawyer decides he will need to speak with his uncle about labor and labor costs. But for now, Sawyer feels the best course of action is to just take everything in and absorb the current status quo. There will be plenty of time for him to draw his own conclusions. And Sawyer knows, for all his talk of loving the field, Gabe is a shrewd businessman.

After lunch, Gabe and the rest of the staff return to their perspective jobs. Sawyer plans to start culling through the documents in the vault. It has to be done, so he may as well get at it. Storing the side-by-side in the barn, he spots the door to the storage area in the loft. He takes a side trip up the stairs to see if he can find any appropriate furniture for the master suite. Over the generations, as the matriarchs of The Residence have changed, the décor has also changed. That which no longer suits goes to the barn loft or the attic for storage. Nothing is ever sold. The occasional pieces are given to family members or donated as auction items for the country club's charity events. The loft is a treasure trove of antiques, some outdated and no longer usable, but most of them in excellent condition.

Sawyer walks through the maze of furniture and rugs. He finally locates some heavier pieces from his grandfather Poppy Cooper's old rooms, the rooms his father took over and now Gabe is residing in. The Cooper men are all big men, so the furniture is built to fit their frames. He wanders through the stacks and boxes, seeing trunks and old steamer luggage. Sawyer shakes his head. Proper inventory and organizing needs to be done by someone who knows antiques. Maybe Scarlet can help him. She majored in Literature and Art History at Ole Miss.

Feeling better about his potential for a decent night's sleep, or at least lying awake in a bed more suited, Sawyer walks back to the house. In his mind, organizing the estate paperwork is the best way to wrap his arms around the immense responsibility. He shakes his head at the magnitude of the project. Knocking off the dirt from his boots and removing them before walking inside, he takes a minute to pour a glass of sweet, iced tea before getting started. He takes a big gulp and smiles as the taste of home assails his senses. Nothing sends him back to his childhood quicker than sweet tea. And nobody in the world makes it like it is made in the South. He knows from experience.

The papers in the vault are in a make-shift file cabinet. Sawyer hunts around the house for a bag to put them in, settling on a backpack he finds in the entry hall closet. Stuffing it full, he takes the contents to the dining room and unloads. He walks back to the vault for the next batch. It takes seven more trips before the paperwork is cleared. Sawyer locks the vault and returns to the dining room to begin separating the papers. The table, which seats 12, is full of stacks of paper. Sawyer is dismayed by the mess as his brain and body prefer things neat and tidy. These papers are neither.

With no clear understanding of where to begin, he decides to pick a pile and start sorting. Sitting down, he searches his pockets for his reading glasses and sighs as he puts them on. His need for reading glasses was the first sign he might need to consider retirement. His age was beginning to impact his performance, much to his chagrin.

Sawyer is still sitting, hunched over the dining room table, when Gabe arrives from the fields, dirty, tired, and happy. He leans on the door jam and surveys the papers strewn all over the room.

"It's a mess, isn't it?" asks Gabe.

Sawyer looks up and takes off his glasses. He rubs his eyes before replying. "This stuff dates back to the Civil War, maybe even before. It's 150 years worth of business documents, letters, deeds." He rustles around for a minute, spots what he is looking for, and holds it up. "There is even a bill of sale for a plow dated 1876." He shakes his head. "I decided to start by putting the documents in three categories: active, inactive, and archival."

"Let me get cleaned up, and I will come and help you," says Gabe.

Sawyer shakes his head negatively. "No, I want to do it. Honestly, I have learned a lot in the last few hours. It's basically a history of the farm." Sawyer stands up. "Though I haven't found anything from the 21st century yet." He walks to the end of the table and grabs another stack. "I told Victoria we would eat on the porch. I hope you don't mind." He waves his hand. "I will figure out a system and eventually get this all cleaned up."

"No rush. It is just the two of us. Dining on the porch works just fine."

Gabe goes upstairs to shower and dress for dinner. Sawyer again unclicks the readers at the bridge of his nose and lets the glasses hang around his neck. He rubs his eyes and checks his watch. It's nearly 6 pm. He gives a mighty stretch and decides a shower sounds perfect. He rubs his arm. He needs to change the dressing for his knife wound anyway.

As he enters his room, he sees his laptop and decides to fire it up. He makes a list of things he needs to purchase in town. He will make a trip tomorrow. Tracking his trunk and a couple of boxes he sent to Tea Olive, he notes the arrival will be on Friday. Refusing to check his email, he closes the laptop and begins to disrobe on his way to the shower. Fifteen minutes later he is dressed in his one pair of khakis and button-down shirt. It will have to do until Friday.

Sawyer meets his uncle on the back porch. Gabe is behind the bar making a cocktail. "Can I make you something?"

"Don't do much more than the occasional beer anymore. I think I will stick with Victoria's sweet tea."

Saying nothing, Gabe pours Sawyer's tea and walks over to the twin rocking chairs. "Join me?" asks Gabe.

Sawyer sits down and accepts the tea from his uncle. He takes a long drink as Gabe watches him intently. Sipping his cocktail, Gabe asks, "You ready to talk about it, son?"

Sawyer has never been able to get anything past his uncle. He sighs. "Not really. But I have learned the booze don't help. Seen too many good men drink themselves to death." He starts to rock his chair back and forth. "Could easily be me. Don't want to start because I am afraid I might never stop."

Gabe nods. "When you are ready, then." Gabe also begins to gently rock his chair back and forth. The two men sit in companionable silence, sipping their drinks and looking over the fields. Finally, Gabe breaks the silence, "You got one of those newfangled phones? Haven't heard from Laura Lynne or the kids yet."

"No, and I don't want one." He puts down his tea. "Don't worry, she'll call. It was a long day for all of them." Sawyer gets up. "I am going to forage for supper. I'm starving."

"Won't have to go far. Victoria will have it all laid out, with heating instructions." He waves Sawyer along before pushing himself out of his chair. "I'll join you. Most nights, I just eat at the kitchen island. Makes clean up easier." They meander to the kitchen together and walk through the swinging door.

"Uncle Gabe, you good with me using Poppy Coop's old furniture in the master? I saw his desk, the bed, and the dresser today in the barn storage. I think it better suits me and my Cooper height."

"Take what you want." Gabe sits at the counter. "What is on the menu tonight?

Sawyer glances at the handwritten note attached to the hood of the stove. "Seared pork chops, Brussels sprouts, macaroni and cheese, key lime pie for dessert." Sawyer looks at the stove and re-reads the instructions. "Looks like it is heat and eat." Sawyer starts the stove and slides all the containers into the oven. Sawyer sets the timer. "Ready in 12 minutes." Sawyer leans against the counter, waiting for the meal to heat. "I think I will head into town tomorrow. Mind if I take your car? I probably need to think about buying one. I haven't had a car since my last deployment to DC."

"Use your Momma's. Her Caddy is still in good running condition."

"It's pink."

Gabe laughs. "You're man enough to..." The phone rings, and Gabe hops off the stool to pick it up. "Hello?" He listens. "So glad, sweetheart...Me too...Love you too, baby girl." He turns toward Sawyer after he hangs the receiver on the hook. "Everyone is safe at home. Beau hit a few delays, but everyone is home safe and sound."

"Glad to hear it." The buzzer rings, and Sawyer pulls everything out of the oven. "Let's eat as I try to convince you how a pink Cadillac does not fare well for my first impression in town."

Gabe laughs again as he bellies up to the island. "Nonsense, everyone will know who you are in that car. Has Beauregard written all over it."

"It screams Lady Beauregard. And no offense to the older generation of women out there, including my momma. But I am not a pink Caddy kinda man." He takes a bite of his pork chop and chews. "I have never had a pork chop that melts in your mouth." He sighs, cuts another piece, and puts it in his mouth. "God, this is good."

"Watch your mouth, young man! No using the Lord's name in vain in this house." Sawyer grimaces; Laura Lynne had warned him. "And stop talking with your mouth full. I realize you have been in the military for most of your life, but it is no reason to lose all your manners." Gabe puts a bite of Victoria's pork chop in his mouth. His shoulders sag, and he closes his eyes. "But you are right, mighty fine vittles."

After dinner, the two men convene to the study to watch television and catch up on the golf and baseball news. For the second time that night, the phone rings. Sawyer glances at his uncle before answering it. Gabe just shrugs his shoulders before saying, "I have no idea who it would be this late. Why don't you answer it and find out?"

Getting up, Sawyer walks to the desk and picks up the phone. "Hello? Tea Olive Plantation."

There is silence on the other end, then, "Tripp? Is that you?"

"It is…and from the sound of the voice, I must be talking to my old friend Grady Cunningham," Sawyer answers.

"Laura Lynne said she had called you when shit went down with Mr. Gabe. Didn't realize you were back in town quite yet."

"Arrived yesterday. Laura Lynne and the kids headed out this morning." He looks at Gabe. "You need to talk to my uncle?"

"Well, that depends. You here to stay, or are you headed off again?"

"Here to stay. I put in my retirement papers before I left. I think it's time for me to focus on my family duties."

"Bout time, man. Missed you around here. And this shit with the dead body's got the DA," Grady's voice is decidedly derisive, "All in an uproar. Hence the reason for the call. Just wanted to give you a head's up the investigation is hot and heavy. It appears your uncle is still in the crosshairs. As well as various members of your family, including yourself." Grady is silent. "Anything you want to tell me about?"

"Like I killed a man when I was a teenager? Hell, no, Grady. My killing years didn't start 'til I was sanctioned by the military." Sawyer begins to pace. "Listen, I will be in town tomorrow. Any chance we could meet? You can bring me up to speed?"

"Absolutely. Meet me at the *Gazette*. I will bring the coffee."

"As in the *Venice Gazette* offices on Main Street? Why there?"

"You will see when you get there. Besides, too many ears at the station. If we go to the Magnolia Café, you will be bombarded by well-meaning fans, flocking to shake hands with the town's golden child. Our very own prodigal son," Grady says with chagrin.

"Please. I haven't been that since senior year and only because we won state. Nobody remembers that sh...stuff," Sawyer says, glancing at his uncle.

"Hell, they don't! Plus, a war hero to boot. Besides, Moseley hasn't won state since 1986. Though we came close when Trey was a senior." Trey is Grady's nephew and Grace's son.

Sawyer stills and quietly responds, "I am nobody's hero, Grady." He clears his throat. "What time in the morning?"

"Hey man, sorry if I touched a sore spot." Sawyer says nothing. "Wasn't intentional. How about 9?"

"Sure. I will be the one in the pink Cadillac." He rolls his eyes.

Grady laughs. "Got it, see you then." He starts to hang up, then changes his mind. "Glad you are back in town."

"Thanks, bye, man."

Gabe has been listening to Sawyer's end of the conversation. "What was young Grady Cunningham calling about? Couldn't have been good."

"He just wanted us to know the investigation into Dead Doe is heating up again. I am meeting him in the morning." Walking around the desk, Sawyer makes a detour toward the back door. "I think I will take a walk out to the dock."

Gabe closes his eyes and puts his hands on his chest. "I surely do not care for that. I surely do not." He sighs. "But I am curious who the poor fellow is. Though most recently, I am thinking he is a vagrant. Melanie seems to align with that train of thought as well."

"Hopefully, we will find out soon and lay all the speculation to rest." Sawyer opens the back door and walks out on the porch. The air is cool, and there is a breeze blowing—a perfect night to clear his head and think about the impact Dead Doe might have on the family. The call with Grady shook him more than he cares to admit. A war hero? If Grady only knew the truth. Sawyer picks up the pace and starts to jog. He works up a sweat in his khakis and button-down shirt. He hits the dock and leans over his knees. He tries to swallow the bile his thoughts are causing. Standing up, he put his hands on his hips. He points his chin to the sky and closes his eyes. Sawyer takes a deep breath. He can feel the anxiety attack making its way to his chest cavity, squeezing his heart and closing his throat.

8

Chapter Eight

2 0 years ago 2003

Sawyer unfolds the letter he keeps tucked away in his breast pocket. He likes to read it before he goes into the field, especially when the mission is expected to be dangerous. Sawyer rubs the paper between his fingers. The texture alone sends his senses back to his childhood. He remembers sitting at the big Resolute Desk in his father's study, where Sawyer II completed his correspondence using his engraved Crane cotton stationery. It's the same stationery Sawyer is currently holding. The yearning to return home has become more and more insistent. Ten years is long enough to sow his oats, to mature, to come to terms with his chosen destiny. He feels more ready to embrace the path laid out for him since birth, maybe settle down and have a family.

Every year since Sawyer had been in the military and moved from station to station, country to country, battle to battle, he received a quarterly package from Tea Olive. No matter where he was, the Tea Olive box always found its way to him as if by magic. The package was filled with Southern delights: pecans, macaroons, snickerdoodles, sweet potato bread, Delta Pride soda, and fresh socks and underwear. The bounty is the talk of the squadron when it arrives, and Sawyer is a generous gifter of the contents. Well, all except the sweet potato bread, his favorite.

Three years ago, in addition to the regular large box of goodies, there was a letter for him from his father. The two had barely spoken since that long-ago night his senior year of high school. Sawyer carefully flattens the creases of the stationery with his hand before turning it over to read the contents once again.

Dear Son,

I am not a perfect man. Far from it.

But you are my son, and I miss you. This distance between us is my fault.

I know that now. I know that my actions and the actions of your mother have torn apart this family to a place where I fear it is irretrievably lost. I sit here, staring at the river and thinking to myself, "Where did it all go wrong?" And I know the answer, though I struggle to admit it, even to myself. My failings as a husband and then as a father all culminated in the summer of 1985. My pride got in the way of my children. You told me as much, and you were right.

I have no excuses. I was raised by an amazing man. Your Grandfather Beauregard, Grampy, was a man of integrity and intellect. You remind me so much of him, more so than you do of me, and for that, I am eternally grateful. I failed my children. I didn't protect them. I didn't stand up for them. I didn't, God forgive me, believe them. I couldn't admit then and can barely admit now that the one who messed up was me.

I should have been a better father, a better man, to you all.

I cannot right the wrongs of the past, but in this millennium, as I swear before God and write to you, I will do my best to right the many wrongs I have done.

But, I am afraid I may fail yet again. I am a weak man.

If I do, if I cannot make right what I have made wrong, I need you to do it for me. Take care of your sisters and your brother; stand up for them the way you did for Avery. Stand beside them the way you did for Laura Lynne. And Scarlet, well, she is a lone wolf. Be there when she needs you.

Don't do what I did. Don't let pride be your downfall.

I need you to stay alive. Fight whatever battle you need to wage with yourself and the war, but you come back to Tea Olive. If not for me, for yourself and your siblings. You come back and make it what it should have been, what it once was. I know you will succeed where I have failed.

You are a better man, an honorable man.

Sawyer Avery Beauregard, II

His old man is right, it's time for him to head back home.

His thoughts are interrupted as the blare of the camp horn signals that Sawyer and his troop need to be ready to move in 15 minutes. He quickly folds the letter and tucks it back into the frayed envelope, securing it into his breast pocket. If he dies today, he wants it on his person. He wants his father to know he has heard his apology, he has accepted it as such, and he plans to come back.

Sawyer enters his tent and watches as his men ready for deployment. They were headed into enemy territory, and all of them were well aware of the potential danger. The men were eerily quiet as they focused on their preparations. Sawyer walks to each man, shoring up the ranks by offering words of encouragement or a slap on the back.

The tent empties, and the men load up into the caravan.

The Battle of Baghdad is underway. It is a large-scale urban battle the US military is waging in an effort to displace Hussein from his seat of power. Phase II, the initial siege, had high casualties, but there was progress.

SSG Sawyer Beauregard, "Tom," and his unit are set to deploy for Phase III: the assault. The plan is to conduct breach operations and maintain command and sustainment of forces. Then, they'll establish a foothold.

Sawyer and his unit have been hand-picked as the tip of the sword. His unit is the first squad to breach the stronghold. Sawyer and ten members of his two fire teams are moving during the initial breach. Another squad within his higher echelon platoon will be in the second wave. Their job is to provide clean up and protection.

Sawyer looks over his squad. He is the oldest by far. He prefers to stay "boots on the ground" and not behind a desk, though his commander would like him there. His second in-command, Brady, is barely 24 and is on his second tour. Brady hails from Brooklyn and is street-smart and tough. He received his nickname, Dodger, during basic training. "Dodger, you and your fire team have the right. I will take the left with the boys of the second fire team." Dodger nods. He is all intensity and little talk. "Meet you in the middle." They knock knuckles. Both go in their respective directions.

Sawyer has a bad feeling in his stomach about this mission. His "hinky bell," as his Aunt Eileen would call it, hippie guru that she is. Well, it is ringing loudly. However, orders are orders. And his squad is ready. Young, and green, certainly, but Sawyer and Dodger, his senior fire team leader, run a tight ship. There is nothing more to do but pray and raid.

Sawyer and his squad slowly and methodically make their way through the local security. All pretty basic stuff. Nothing unexpected. Dodger's team does the same. They meet up with no casualties though one of Dodger's boys, Cameron, "Red," has an eye injury from some dust debris. The second wave is already secure in their positions.

"Don't get cocky. We aren't done yet." Sawyer throws up a hand signal, and everyone surges forward, guns at the ready. They slowly pick off potential threats. And then their cover is blown. Hussein's forces unleash their fire power. Dodger dives and rolls, taking his team with him. Sawyer does the same. Sawyer is shouting commands, his radio crackling. The shit has hit the fan. Now, it is time for the real work. Dodger signals. He and his team are making their way into a building and onto the roof. Sawyer acknowledges. He will do the same on the adjacent building. He radios for airpower. He inserts the coordinates into the computer. One of his boys is hit. He has a leg wound.

Sawyer scrambles over the debris to take a look. It is not horrible. Jason, 'Doc,' wraps him up and doses him a with numbing agent. After receiving a thumbs-up, everyone is on the move again. There is a fire show on top of Dodger's building. He and his team have breached the roof. Sawyer signals his team to speed up. They need to get to the rooftop to help Dodger.

Word comes through the radio. Air power is here. The coordinates are once again confirmed by Sawyer. Dodger acknowledges. The bomb is dropped. Sawyer sees it as if in slow motion. The bomb is a direct hit on Dodger's building. Sawyer screams, but it's too late. The rooftop is demolished, along with Dodger and his team.

"Tom! Tom! Come on, man. Shake it off! Shit is hitting the fan. We need you," Doc screams in Sawyer's face. Doc grabs Sawyer's shoulders and gives him a good shake. "Get us the fuck out of here!"

Sawyer explodes into action, pushing Doc off of him. He starts shouting commands. The air raid continues with Sawyer's squad methodically clearing buildings, rounding up enemy soldiers, protecting civilians. The second wave of U.S. military has arrived and provides additional support by completing the tactical maneuvers Dodger and his team would have been performing had they not just perished. With the demolition of the building and the expert shooting of his team, Sawyer can establish a stronghold in this little downtrodden town in the middle of nowhere. Phase III is officially over.

In the aftermath of the siege, Sawyer discovers that unbeknownst to everyone, the building where Dodger and his team chose to climb was the local stronghold. Its demolition also caused the demise of the Hussein radicals in the area. The team later located an arsenal of weapons in the basement, all military grade. The mission is considered a success, and Sawyer is awarded a Bronze Star.

But Sawyer caused the death of Dodger and his team. Dodger was the oldest soldier in the team, and he was only 24. The mission is reviewed by the military board and Sawyer is cleared of any wrongdoing. He receives a commendation and a bump in rank.

This is the beginning of Sawyer's nightmares and depression. The overwhelming sense of guilt burrows deep into Sawyer. He did all the right things. He attended all the funerals. He wrote to the widows, the girlfriends, and the mothers. He signs up for another tour. Penance he supposes for his role in cutting the lives of his squad short. Survivor's guilt. Hell, he even does therapy, not that it seems to help.

Neither does drinking, or whoring, or exercise, or anything. Time. Time is the only thing that makes things bearable. Sawyer is able to tuck it away into the recesses of his mind during the day hours. It is at night when he no longer has a say over what his mind chooses to remember and replay, that he suffers the most.

9

Chapter Nine

Present Day

Sawyer wakes up with a start. He sits straight up, having tossed his bedclothes off the bed. He has a pillow in his hand as if to be used as a weapon. A cry of "No!" dies at the back of his throat. He is sweating, and his breathing is quick and heavy. The nightmare ends as he shakes off the demons, placing his head in the pillow he holds. It is back. The dream he has been able to tuck away for short periods of time. He knows why. Sitting on the dock, reliving his failure, and Grady's "war hero" comment were the catalysts. He knows what to expect, too. First, the nightmares, then the depression, along with the guilt and shame. The soul-crushing guilt.

His best line of defense is to get up and get moving. He dons his running outfit and walks downstairs. He moves quietly and quickly. After so many years as an athlete and soldier, his morning exercise routine has always included fitness. Now, it's more for his mental health. He starts out at a light jog toward the dock, then veers to the left, deciding to see the farm. If he is going to run all this someday, he needs to see what will be involved. He knows only what his father taught him before he left for college. Growing up on Tea Olive, he would often join his uncle in the fields, riding with him on the tractor. He understands what it takes to make a farm like this successful, but he just doesn't know how to do it.

As he runs, he takes in the fields of cotton. The green stalks are beginning to explode from the ground. The fields will be white come October. Harvest time is exciting and beautiful. It never snows in Mississippi, but when all the fields are white with balls of cotton ready to be plucked, it is as beautiful as fresh snow. And more profitable. He rounds the corner of the newly plowed field and spots John standing with his hands on his hips. He looks at the rows while chewing on a blade of grass. Sawyer jogs up beside him.

"Hey John, field looks good." Sawyer is not even panting, though he has a sheen of sweat glistening on his chiseled face and prominent cheekbones. He has run over two miles.

John smiles. "Today is planting day. We are running a tad behind schedule, but I think we can still make it before planting season is completely over." He looks at Sawyer. "Enjoying your run?"

Sawyer laughs. "Hard to quit the habit after all these years. I figured I could do two things at once." He shakes his head. "Been too long since I have been involved with the farm. I have a lot to learn."

"You're lucky. You got a really great place here. Mr. Gabe is a hell of a guy."

"What's your story, John?" Sawyer leans over and reaches for a blade of grass. He, too, puts it between his teeth.

"Not much to speak of. I joined the military right out of high school—one of the few legal options available to me. College wasn't in the cards. Did a few tours. Retired. Spent a few years dabbling in this and that. I ended up working as a field hand at Cotton Mill. Grady told me about the Tea Olive job. I interviewed with Mr. Gabe, and he gave me the opportunity. Now, I'm here."

Sawyer nods. "Wife? Children?"

"No to both. Not much family left either." John gazes at him. "You lookin' for a reference?"

Sawyer claps him on the back. "No, man. Just figuring out who is who and what is what." Sawyer spits out his piece of grass. "Besides, if I needed one, I would just call Micah."

"Fair enough."

"Listen, I am headed into town today. Laura Lynne told me what you did for her, how you stayed up all night when shit was going down with Bubba Westerman, how you kept watch over the house and my family." A look of disbelief and anger crosses Sawyer's stunning features. "Still hard to believe. I spent plenty of time in Bubba's jail cell, waiting on Daddy to come get me. Breaks my heart what he allowed to happen to Laura Lynne." Sawyer shakes his head. "Anyway, I would appreciate the continued back up while I am home. I am meeting with Grady in town today. He called last night. Said things are heating back up again." Sawyer looks around the field and then back to John. "If you could look out for things while I am not on the premises, I would sure appreciate it."

"Lookin' out after Mr. Gabe is no hardship. I love and respect that man and would consider it an honor. I will keep an eye out."

"Thanks, man." Sawyer smiles and waves as he walks backward. He picks up his pace. "See ya later." He runs back to the trail he was running on before veering off to speak with John. He estimates he has another 30 minutes before breakfast. Time enough to see a second field.

Sawyer allows his stride and pace to increase. He begins to run as his muscles loosen and his brain clears. He runs along the field, then the river. He passes Queenie's house and waves at one of the girls in the garden. Queenie and her husband, Lincoln, have six children between them. Over the years, the Jackson family has added many grandchildren and great-grandchildren. Sawyer has forgotten who has remained in Venice and who has moved away. But seeing Queenie at Aunt Eileen's celebration was heartbreaking. She has always been there, and the idea of her impending death strikes close to his heart. She has been one of the few constants in Sawyer's life, there since he arrived on this earth.

Sawyer makes the entire loop around the west fields and circles back to The Residence. He decreases his pace and begins to walk. The run has done its job, ridding him of the remnants of last night's nightmare. Running always has a soothing effect on his mental state. Ready now to face the world, Sawyer kicks off his shoes at the back door of the mud room and walks into the kitchen. The kitchen smells like heaven. He saunters over to Victoria, who is busy flipping pancakes on the griddle. "Victoria, I have never asked a woman this before. You are the first, but will you marry me?"

Victoria laughs. She looks over her shoulder after she expertly ladles the next batch of pancake mix onto the griddle. "You just love me for my cookin'."

"Damn right." Sawyer moves to get a glass out of the cabinet when an apple hits him square in the middle of his back. "What the hell…," and turning another apple hits him square in the chest. He looks up. Gabe is standing at the island reaching for an orange as he's all out of apples.

"Young man, you will *clean up* your language in this house. I let it slide yesterday, but no more. You will be a gentleman while you live under my roof. I will not put up with your ugly mouth, and neither will Victoria and Pearl." He points his finger at Sawyer. "I *know* you know better; now *do* better." He turns toward Victoria. "My apologies for this miscreatin's behavior, Victoria. If you don't want him to eat your pancakes, I don't blame you." He turns his eye back to Sawyer. "Don't care how old you are, son. Do it again, and I swear I will take a switch to you."

Sawyer hangs his head, a smile on his lips. "Yes, sir."

"Humphh! Go get cleaned up and meet me on the porch."

"Yes, sir." Sawyer turns back for his glass and fills it with water. He walks past Victoria and says quietly. "Sorry if I offended you." She smiles at her pancakes and keeps her back to Gabe and Sawyer. She makes no comment. Gabe stares at him. "I'm going, I'm going!"

Sawyer is dressed and ready for the day 20 minutes later. He meets Gabe on the back porch, who has already eaten. "What is your plan for the day, Sawyer? Still headed into town?"

Sawyer sits at the table and piles his plate high with pancakes and strawberry syrup. "Yes, sir. I am meeting Grady. I have some errands to run. Do you need me to get anything for you?"

"No, but check with Victoria before you leave. She likes to get our coffee from Magnolia Café. Haven't done that in a while. She is probably a bit low." He places his thumbs on his suspender straps and leans back on his heels. "Anything for me before you go?"

Sawyer chews and swallows. "Just a question. What happened to Twin Oaks? I walked through there on my way here, and the house was all but falling down. The property is a mess."

"I need to sit down for this conversation." Gabe pulls back the chair he had recently vacated and sits back down. He crosses his legs and wrinkles his forehead. "Well, that is a conundrum. A few years ago, Buck up and sold the entire 1,500 acres to an outside developer, company called Overpass Development. Not sure how much he got for it, but it put things in quite an uproar. I tried to speak with him and Scarlet about it, but neither of them would discuss the decision. What was so appalling, to my way of thinking, was not offering it to me for purchase. If they needed the money, I am sure we could have come up with a reasonable plan for payment. Keep it in the family, you know, for Robert and Cooper." Robert and Cooper are Scarlet's two boys. Gabe clears his throat. "From a personal standpoint, I noticed around the same time that Scarlet and Buck dropped out of things. Melanie and I didn't see Scarlet for months." He allows his eyes to gaze out the window toward the water. "Got right worried. Then we caught wind that the developer was planning to divert the river. He wanted to create retaining ponds and tidal creeks." Gabe looks back at Sawyer. Sawyer has finished eating and is sipping his coffee. He is listening intently.

"Divert the river?"

"Yep, caused quite a stir. As you are well aware, the river is life for the plantations. The impact to Tea Olive, not to mention the surrounding plantations and farms, would be detrimental." Shaking his head, Gabe continues, "The farmers and even some of the city folk ended up banding together and hiring a lawyer to stop the construction. Not exactly sure what language they used, but basically, Lally alleges the plan is illegal, and the judge put a stop to all construction until a judgment was reached. Litigation ensued, and the developer fought us up until about six months ago. Rumor has it, the developer has fallen on hard times."

"Any idea who the developer is?"

"Oh yes, name's Jacob Tinsley—some city slicker from Chicago of all places. Grady always thought Overpass Development was a front. Who knows? He could be right."

"What about Scarlet and Buck? What is the situation there? Laura Lynne mentioned she had some concerns."

"Scarlet is tight-lipped about the situation. She takes care of me and your momma, for the most part. But I agree, something has happened. She won't talk to me. I have tried a few times. I know Laura Lynne did, too, when she was here, but she didn't have much luck either. You were always her favorite. Maybe you could speak with her."

Sawyer continues, as if not hearing Gabe's last statement, "Laura Lynne mentioned finances? Something about Momma footing the bill for Moseley for the boys?"

"Really? Well, if she did, she didn't tell me. You might ask Melanie. Now that you are home and planning to stay, Melanie might start confiding in you." Gabe clears his throat. "God knows that woman would vex any man's soul, but she is your momma. You need to go and see her regardless." Gabe looks pointedly at Sawyer. "And your sister."

Sawyer nods as he finishes his coffee. "I will, but not today. Momma would not appreciate seeing me two days wearing the exact same outfit. Plus, I have a full day today. But you're right. You're also right about a lot of other things. It's just going to take me some time. I could ask for some patience from you."

"You aren't going to get it. I don't have much time left on this earth, and it became all too apparent yesterday I want to spend those years doing what I love: farming the land."

Sawyer sighs. It had been worth a try. "Understood. See you at supper tonight?"

"Of course. 6:00 sharp."

Sawyer stands and starts picking up the dishes and cleaning the table. "Have fun playing in the dirt."

"That's my plan, son; that is my plan." Gabe takes the back porch steps and walks to the barn, anxious to start his day.

"Oh, Mr. Sawyer, there is no need for you to clean up breakfast dishes! You have plenty to do without adding responsibilities."

"Victoria, I can certainly bring my plate into the kitchen on my way through the house." Victoria gives him an odd look. "Unless you prefer me not too?"

"Well, the truth is, Mr. Gabe and I have a system. He stays out of my kitchen, and I stay out of his gardens."

"And you want me to do the same?" She smiles and takes the plates. "Okay, a man knows when he is not wanted…and I certainly don't want to do anything to mess up your cooking!"

"Are you always so amiable?"

"Just used to taking orders, I guess." Then he asks, "You need me to get coffee?"

"No, Momma took care of it last week. But thanks."

"Where is Pearl?" asks Sawyer.

"Today is her half day. We share the job of watching Grandma Queenie amongst everyone who lives here. Today is Momma's morning. She will be in later this afternoon. Drive safe."

Chapter Ten

Sawyer follows Gabe out of the mud room and walks toward the barn. Gabe drives off in the side-by-side, waving as he heads toward the back pasture. He is happy as a clam. With a grimace, Sawyer is less than pleased to see the pink Cadillac. Gabe has removed the cover and placed the keys on the hood. It is as embarrassing as it has ever been. Sawyer shrugs his shoulders in resignation as he slides into the driver's seat. He adjusts the seat to fit his 6'4" frame. The car starts with a purr. Sawyer puts the pink monstrosity in reverse and backs out of the barn. He rolls down the window and puts his arm out as he cranks up the tunes and sings along with Motley Crue.

He passes the turn-off to the old chapel and the family cemetery. He probably needs to go and see his father's grave. The list in his head just keeps getting longer. He has to keep reminding himself he has plenty of time to get everything done, but for some reason, he has an unexplained sense of urgency.

Shaking his head, he mutters to himself, "Not sure about this retirement shit."

He comes into town and, unlike Sunday when he arrived, the main street is bustling. With new eyes, he sees all the updates and changes that have occurred since he was here for his father's funeral five years ago. He vividly remembers the call from his mother. He was between assignments and temporarily back in DC when his assistant interrupted a meeting for him to answer an urgent phone call from Mississippi. His momma was stoic as always, almost without emotion. His father had died of a massive stroke. He needed to come home and assume his responsibilities.

Sawyer still finds it hard to believe his father is no longer only a phone call away. Seeing him in that casket, still robust and muscular, haunts Sawyer. His father, with all his shortcomings, is still one of Sawyer's heroes. He never missed a football or basketball game. He taught him how to ride a horse and a bike, drive tractors and cars, fish, shoot, and drive a boat. Hell, he had even talked to him about girls and gave him his first pack of condoms. They spoke regularly over the years, Sawyer's constant connection to home. His dad was a good father. He was just not a good husband. Reconciling that had taken Sawyer a long time, but in the end, he considered his father an honorable but flawed man. This was later confirmed when the will was read. The plantation and house, the managing of the trust, had been placed with Gabe, much to his mother's dismay. But, in Sawyer's eyes, it was the best gift he could have given to both him and his uncle.

The Cooper family trust should have gone to the oldest Cooper son, Gabe, in the first place. Instead, when Poppy Coop died, he willed it to his son-in-law, Sawyer's father. At the time, his father tried to right the wrong, but Gabe refused, saying, "You were always more of a son to him than I was. Besides, eventually, Tripp will be the heir." So, when Sawyer II died, and Gabe received the trust, Sawyer felt it more than justified. And it gave Sawyer time. With Gabe inheriting it, Sawyer was freed to live his own life a bit longer before being burdened with family responsibility. Sawyer liked to think his father was giving him an opportunity to come to terms with his fate.

Neither here nor there now. The five years were what he needed to be ready to come home. He felt in his soul that this was the final move of his life. He is back home at Tea Olive to stay. Sawyer pulls into the *Gazette* parking area and parks the Cadillac. He unfolds from the front seat and notes how busy the little downtown area is for nine on a Tuesday. He recognizes some of the business names from his uncle's ledger. Sawyer figures that, at some point, he should stop by and meet the owners. But right now, he needs to meet with Grady.

He opens the front door to a tinkle and spots a grey-haired lady dressed in a matching lime green dress and cardigan. She looks up from her computer and smiles. "Sawyer Beauregard! Grady told me to expect you this morning."

A smile breaks over Sawyer's face, "Miss Wright? Is that you? Didn't you try and teach me English in high school?"

"I absolutely did! And call me Mary! I retired last year and am working here now. Not that that entails much. Opening and closing mostly, now that everything is online. Laura Lynne tells me you have retired and are here to stay."

"Wow, the grapevine still works well around here. Yes, that is my plan."

"Not the grapevine. I am no gossip." Mary takes her reading glasses a little further down her nose and peers over them as she did when she reprimanded him in class. "Laura Lynne told me in confidence. I certainly have not blabbed it to the local gossip mill."

"My apologies," Sawyer says with a slight bow, "I did not know you and Laura Lynne were that close."

"Well, the last couple of weeks she worked in here trying to do some research on the corpse y'all found at Tea Olive, Mr. Dead Doe. I helped her, and we figured out we worked well together. She asked if I minded doing some research for her. You know, to help her with her books. We speak regularly."

As Sawyer is about to answer, there is a tinkle at the front door. Turning around, Sawyer sees his old buddy, Grady. He is decked out in his sheriff's uniform and completely bald, but otherwise, the same guy Sawyer spent endless hours with growing up. Grady extends his hand and comes in for a side hug. He slaps him on the back. "Tri..Sawyer now, sorry. Going to take some getting used to. Good to see you, man. It is really good to see you."

Sawyer closes his eyes as he embraces Grady. There is just nothing better than a good friend. "Hey man, thanks for all you did for Laura Lynne and Uncle Gabe. Mean that."

Grady steps back. "Glad I could help. Sorry, I didn't help when we were kids."

Shaking his head in agreement, Sawyer concedes, "I feel the same." He rubs his hands on his thighs, a habit he picked up when he was quarterback before he would run a play. "Can you get me caught up on the investigation?"

"Yep." Grady turns toward Mary. "Mary, can we use Laura Lynne's old office."

"Sure. I will let y'all know if anyone comes by." She winks. "I have become quite good at all this espionage."

Chuckling, Grady snags the coffee he brought with him off the counter and hands Sawyer a steaming cup. He leads him back behind the front desk. They weave through the front office to the back corner office. Grady shuts the door behind him and takes a seat. He waves for Sawyer to do the same.

"What do you know so far?" asks Grady.

Sawyer recounts Laura Lynne's version of events, then looks at Grady. "What does she not know that I need to know?"

"First, that Dr. Butler is one sick son of a bitch. From what the feds tell me, he has been molesting girls for years here and all the time he has been in Boston. They are working on his computer now but have already found plenty of porn, including children. Quite the racquet going, and just like here, he had some 'help' keeping his hobby from being discovered." Shaking his head, Grady continues, "He is being extradited here, initially. Then will face charges in Boston. He lawyered up immediately and is not talking."

"What is Laura Lynne's part in all this?"

"Well, right now, nothing. It all depends on whether there is a hearing or not. Everyone would like to keep the victims out of the courtroom, but it just may not be possible. And truthfully, based on what has been found, it could take years before the case sees the inside of a courtroom. Dr. Butler's got money. His wife's family has an entire law firm at their beck and call. We just have to wait and see how this all plays out."

"But for now, she is in the clear?"

Grady nods in agreement. "For now. But no promises, Sawyer. This is big. Very big. Laura Lynne is the lynchpin that puts everything together."

"Okay, we will deal with that when we have to. What about Bubba Westerman? Uncle Gabe has some concerns there."

Grady leans over and lowers his voice, "He has a right to be. Hell, I have some major concerns myself. He's been on my daddy's payroll for as long as I can remember. For all I know, he still pays the man." He leans back again in his chair. "He was sheriff for 40 years. He probably has intel on the entire town. There is no telling what secrets he is hiding. I have been wondering if it would be better if he just kept them to himself."

Sawyer nods in agreement. "Uncle Gabe seems to think the same. Listen, what can you tell me about this land development deal with Buck's property? Do you know anything about that?"

"Only what my daddy tells me. I guess you know that he and some of the other landowners put a stop to the development?" Sawyer nods. "Well, what nobody can figure out, and what Buck and even Scarlet won't tell us, is why they sold it in the first place. From the rumor mill, they got pennies for the property. It caused a real mess as it drove all the land values down, and not just a little. Our property devalued a staggering sum, according to my real estate agent sister. Not that it matters since we will never sell the land."

Sawyer stares at him blankly, trying to take it all in. "That makes no sense. The land and house should have gotten top dollar. It's prime real estate and fertile farmland."

"Well, if you can figure it out, let me know." Grady clears his throat. "There is another thing about Scarlet, Buck, and the boys.

Some of it is rumor, but I know some of it is fact. And, if you and I didn't go way back, I wouldn't be telling you. But I know if we were in each other's shoes, you would tell me if something were up with Grace and her family." He clears his throat again.

"What is it, Grady? Just spit it out."

"Well, it's about Bobby." Scarlet and Buck's oldest son, Robert Taylor Huger. "Bobby had some run-ins as a teenager, same as we did growing up—crap like underage drinking, smoking weed, that kind of thing. None of us thought much of it. Buck would come and get him from the station. He and his buddies were in and out on a regular basis."

Sawyer smiles. "Sounds like old times."

Grady returns the smile. "And it was, and definitely how we treated it. Slap on the hand and send them home with a parent." Grady sobers. "Bobby went off to Ole Miss, and it seems his drug habit picked up considerably." He sighs. "I know for a fact that he has been in and out of rehab multiple times. Last I heard, he was using again."

"Really?" Sawyer had no idea. Being away from home and off to various missions, he has not been around for his nephews' growing-up years. "Is he living around here somewhere?"

"No, last I heard he was in the Midwest somewhere, Illinois, Indiana, Iowa….some 'I' state." Grady raises his eyebrow. "The rumor mill is that they sold the property to pay for his rehab stints, or drug habit. Nobody knows for sure, but that is the assumption."

"Okay, okay. I gotta wrap my head around this. Laura Lynne mentioned Scarlet has been acting distant. She even noticed some bruising on her neck and arm and asked me to keep an eye out."

"Really? Well, nothing I have ever noticed, but then Scarlet and Buck are rarely seen around town anymore. Other than helping out your mom and uncle, Scarlet stays away. This past couple of weeks while your uncle was battling this thing in court is the most I have seen her since your father passed."

Sawyer stands up and starts pacing. "I don't like this. Not one bit."

"It gets better. Laura Lynne told you about your dad's mistress. Virginia Phillips?" Sawyer stops pacing and faces Grady. "Well, when all this stuff with Dead Doe was going down, I went to Mobile to see her. Laura Lynne recommended I follow up on some questions we had for her. Laura Lynne had already been by to see her, and she told me something was off. She could not put her finger on it but thought she was holding out on her. Like she knew something but didn't say what she knew."

"Yeah."

"The place was empty. No signs of her. Did a little digging. No information on her before she met your father some 35 years ago." Sawyer turns to look at him. "And I can't find any trace of her. Not even the house. The house is listed under a corporation name. Grace did some digging for Laura Lynne and shared what she learned. The property is owned by a company called Green Acres. I think it might be a front for someone or something else."

"She may have gotten a new name when she got out of the business. Laura Lynne told me this Ginny woman was an escort. That's how Daddy met her. So, changing her name would make sense. But up and disappearing..." Sawyer gazes at Grady. "You think she got spooked, don't you? Like she knows something, and maybe Laura Lynne is right?"

"Only thing I can think of. The question of the hour is what?" He shrugs his shoulders. "I have to agree with Laura Lynne. Something is definitely off there.

Sawyer collapses in the chair, "I need to tell you my father has been sending her blackmail money for years. He even has a separate account he used to pay her outside of the trust. We agreed as a family to stop the money. It may not have been the smartest move, but neither Laura Lynne nor I are interested in hiding. We would rather fight. My understanding is Laura Lynne told Ginny something exactly like that when she was there."

"Blackmail? So...she knows something."

"Or maybe Daddy thought she knew something and was willing to pay to keep her quiet. We are not sure how reliable her information is. Laura Lynne got her to tell her one of her secrets, which ended up being a complete fabrication." Sawyer leans against the doorframe. "Anything else, Grady? You are just a fountain of fun information this morning."

"Well, yes, there is one more thing," says Grady. "I have not seen Buck Huger in years. If you remember, he did not attend your father's funeral either. Years, Sawyer. Like maybe ten." He leans forward, his forearms on his knees. "I just thought you should know."

"Really? I don't even know what to say to that...where is he?"

"From what I can tell, he spends his time in Biloxi."

"Gambling? Maybe that is what happened to the money?" Sawyer rubs his eyes with his thumb and forefinger. "This conversation has been less than fun, Grady. Anything else?"

Grady gets up and picks up his hat. He looks Sawyer in the eye. "You call me. For anything. Anytime. I don't have a clue what is going on with your family, but it all started when your uncle found that dead body. Seems to me that if you can solve that puzzle, the rest might make some sense."

Sawyer closes his eyes and pinches his nose. "It does seem to all stem from that summer in '85, doesn't it?" Sawyer puts his hands on his knees and pushes himself off the doorframe to follow Grady. He passes Mary as she sits at the computer at the front desk. "Thank you, Mary, for letting us meet up here."

Mary turns on her stool, smiling as she peers over her glasses. "Never a hardship to have such handsome men around. Happy to help. Feel free to use the offices anytime you need. I enjoy the company."

"Ma'am." Grady smiles as he and Sawyer walk out the door to their cars. "What are your plans for the day?"

"Right now, I am getting some more coffee. Then, when I feel like it, I am going to buy myself a new car. Preferably something that is not pink." He frowns as he looks at the Cadillac. "Have a few errands, but mostly I need to get back to Tea Olive. I have been gone too long."

Grady nods. "Understood. Once you get your feet under you, Prissa and I would love to have you come over for supper. I could invite Charlie and Grace, be like old times."

Sawyer nods as Grady unlocks the car door and slides into the driver's seat. "Sounds good." Sawyer gives a wave. "Thanks, Grady, I owe you one."

"Nah, let's call it even. I owe you for my shitty treatment of you your senior year." Grady closes the door and backs out. Sawyer takes a deep breath and closes his eyes. He lets it out, slow and steady. It feels so good he does it again. He will try anything to settle all the information Grady just imparted. Lord, he needs more coffee.

11

Chapter Eleven

Sawyer strolls down the main drag to Magnolia Café. This was the hang-out when he was a kid. Back then, it was more of a diner. It was open 24 hours a day and was *the* place for Mosely students to hang out. Now, it's a fancy coffee and sandwich shop. It is still owned by the Gaillards, as Sawyer noted on Gabe's ledger. And it looks like Sawyer has timed his arrival well. The morning crowd is gone, and the lunch crowd hasn't yet started. Sawyer makes his way through the outside dining area without incident. When he opens the café doors, he is met with air conditioning and the stares of a dozen locals.

Sawyer nods and smiles as he makes his way up to the counter to order.

"Welcome to Magnolia Café! What can I get for you today?" The barista is a teenage girl with rainbow-colored hair and a ring in her eyebrow. She's sporting overalls and a tie-dyed t-shirt. The name on her badge says Amanda.

"Just a regular cup of joe, Amanda. Black and the largest one you have."

"Got it. Name, please."

"Sawyer Beauregard."

She smiles. "Hey, wait a minute! Are you related to Miss Laura Lynne? She came to my play at Moseley Hall and my mom's book club. She is great. I love her."

"Yep, I am her big brother."

Rainbow-haired Amanda looks up and winks, whispering to Sawyer, "Now I know why conversations stopped when you walked in the door." She turns toward the coffee maker. "Just stand over by the end of the counter, and I will have it out to you momentarily."

"Tripp Beauregard, as I live and breathe." Sawyer turns toward the voice, low and seductive. Husky, like she had one too many packs of cigarettes. And from the looks of her, she probably had.

"Well, if it isn't Beth Ann Bodeen. What brings you into town today?" Beth Ann is currently wearing a too-tight pencil skirt and sweater with boots. She is all pink and, to Sawyer's eyes, looks like sin. The outfit does nothing to conceal her assets.

"I work over at the police station these days. I like to get the boys a mid-morning snack." She looks at Amanda. "Mandy, the usual, please."

"Yes, ma'am."

"You here for a while? Liam told me you were back in town."

Sawyer registers the connection; young Liam helps out at the farm with Gabe and John. "Is Liam your boy?"

"Sure enough. He's the best thing I ever did. He was devastated when he found those old bones out at Tea Olive. He felt like he started the whole thing with your uncle."

Mandy leans over the counter and hands Sawyer his coffee. Sawyer nods his thanks and takes the lid off his cup. He blows gently on the coffee. "He's a fine young man. I met him yesterday." And he could not be more opposite of his momma. He is a country boy down to his buzz cut and overalls. And skinny as a string bean.

"He loves working at Tea Olive. Mr. Gabe's real good to him."

"Glad to hear it. Plenty of work to keep him busy."

"Miss Beth Ann, orders up."

"Thanks, Mandy." Beth Ann picks up the order. "Tripp, walk me to the door?"

"Of course."

Sawyer and Beth Ann walk through the front door and down the walkway. "Listen, it's none of my business, but I dearly love Mr. Gabe, and he's good to my boy." She keeps walking toward the sheriff's office. "But the sheriff's office is buzzing with all the stuff happening at your place. Not gonna lie, it's the biggest news to hit Venice since you won state in 1986." She stops and turns to look at Sawyer. She blows a piece of bleach-blonde hair out of her eyes. "I would watch my back if I were you. That asshole Chandler's got a real hard-on for you."

"Nothing new there, Beth Ann. He and I have been at each other since the day we were born."

"Yeah, but then he was just a pissant on the gridiron. Now, he has the law behind him. And a grudge."

Sawyer smiles. "Thanks for the heads up, Beth Ann, and for getting me out of Magnolia Café." Sawyer turns around. "Did the eye daggers make a hole in my shirt?"

Beth Ann laughs her rowdy, bodacious laugh. "No holes, but might see a knife or two sticking out of your back. You Beauregards sure do make a scene when you come to town. Never seen anything like it." She starts down the street. "Now mind yourself, Tripp. Plenty of people here like to see you and your kin take a mighty tumble off your pedestal."

Sawyer waves at her as she makes her way down the street. Beth Ann Bodeen was the sexiest thing on this side of the Mason Dixon when they were younger. She didn't go to Moseley Hall, from the wrong side of the tracks, but she played a starring role in many a boy's teenage fantasies, especially in that cheerleading outfit. And, if you believe the locker room gossip, she was hot as a firecracker between the sheets. Not that Sawyer ever found out. His momma would have skinned him alive if he had wandered over those tracks.

Shaking off his reminisces, Sawyer takes a sip of his coffee and decides it's as good a time as any to stop into some of the businesses and shops he saw on the Tea Olive ledgers. Wheelbarrow Books, which is attached to the Magnolia Café, seems like a good place to start. From the outside, it's eclectic and creative. The window display is artistic. Front and center as a monthly feature is Laura Lynne's book, *The Bluebird Diaries*. Sawyer feels a touch of pride for his little sister's success.

He walks in. He realizes he is still holding his cup of coffee, so he turns around to walk back out when he hears a voice from the back. "Welcome to Wheelbarrow Books! Can I help you with something?"

"Well, yes. But, first, let me get rid of this coffee."

"Oh, no need for that. Coffee is not a problem. In fact, it's often a necessity to enjoy a good book." This sprite of a woman holds out her hand. "Hi, I am Diane. The owner and operator of Wheelbarrow Books."

Sawyer shakes her hand. "Sawyer Beauregard."

"Sort of guessed you were a Beauregard. You have your daddy's good looks."

"You knew my dad?"

"Sure, he was the one that helped me establish Wheelbarrow Books. The Beauregard men have been very good to me and Mandy. Helped us through some tough times." Diane reminds Sawyer of someone. She has this ethereal look to her, sort of whimsy and strong. She has on flowing garments and smells of the woods, like a sprite or a fairy. She is gorgeous, but not in a classical sense. They begin to walk toward the back of the store toward a cozy corner with plush chocolate- colored chairs, a small circular table with a lamp designed out of books, and footstools in deep purple. There were even two throw pillows of hunter green. The perfect corner to curl up with a book.

"How long have you been open?"

Diane takes a seat and waves at Sawyer to join her. "Well, Mandy is 17 this year, so close to 15 years. We moved here after my husband was killed in Iraq. I needed a fresh start. We had been stationed in Biloxi, and with no family to speak of, this is where I ended up." Diane looks at him. "My turn. Laura Lynne is a favorite of mine, both as an author and as a new friend. She told me you were coming to town. Is this visit social or business?

Sawyer leans back in the plush chair and is enamored with this woman. Aunt Eileen, that is who she reminds him of. And he loved his Aunt Eileen. Not at all surprising that she and Laura Lynne would connect, considering that Laura Lynne had spent several years living with Eileen. "Well, Diane, a little of both. I just arrived in town a couple of days ago with the intention of taking over some of the business side of Tea Olive's interests. But mainly, I am just stopping in to take a look around. See what's what."

Diane nods. "Got it. Feel free to look around. Maybe buy a book or two."

"Wait a minute. Quick question. Mandy? Is that your daughter? The rainbow-haired barista next door?"

She starts to laugh. "Yes! That is my girl. She does love to make a statement." Diane gets a faraway look in her eye. "The older she gets, the more she looks like her father, and the more she acts like him. He was a dreamer."

"Really? That's surprising. I have been active military for 35 years, not too many dreamers in the ranks."

She gets quiet, thinking back. "I know, but we were broke. Mandy was on the way. We had no insurance and no feasible way to earn any money. Couldn't live on love alone. Thomas enlisted and didn't even tell me. Next thing I know, he is in basic training." She looks at him. "He hated it, but he loved me. Loved Mandy even though he never met her."

"I'm sorry. I did not mean to bring up such a sad memory."

"No, it's good. Thomas was a good man. He deserves to be remembered." Diane looks at him. "I am just sorry it was a nasty war that took him. It took out his whole squad. He didn't even make it a full year." She smiles. "Nice to talk to someone who understands what it means to be military." Diane stands up. "I am glad you came by today. Come by anytime. And bring your coffee." She walks away, heading to the back office. Sawyer is certain it's to dry her eyes, which had welled up with tears as she spoke.

Sawyer lets himself watch her walk away. What an intriguing woman, confident, beautiful, and smart. He suddenly wants to know more about her and to his surprise, he feels alive for the first time in months. Hell, maybe years. He smiles to himself. Yep, he will definitely be back.

12

Chapter Twelve

Spring 1986

Things between Sawyer and Clay are no longer the same. After that night in the cabin during Christmas break, Sawyer has a hard time reconciling the fact his best buddy is gay. He isn't sure how he feels about it. He knows he should feel repelled. It's a sin after all. But in truth he is more curious than anything.

Basketball season is winding down, and baseball season is heating up. He has already declared his intent to join the Citadel in the fall, dispelling his parents' hopes for another of their protégé to follow in their footsteps at Ole Miss. And though his father and Buck's parents have somehow reconciled their feud, most of Sawyer's longtime friends are still keeping their distance. Sawyer cannot wait to get the hell out of high school.

"Mr. Tripp, you about ready?" Queenie is at the door, standing in the hallway hovering.

"Yep, just need to get this bowtie straight. Don't worry, Queenie. I won't keep Momma waiting."

"It's your big night tonight. I know you will come home with a pile of awards." She begins to walk down the hallway. "I'll let your Momma know you on time."

"Thanks, Queenie," Sawyer calls out as he pulls on his navy-blue blazer and slides into his new dark brown dress shoes. They pinch a bit, but nothing a few wears won't take care of. One last glance at the mirror and Sawyer follows Queenie down the stairs.

"Son, join me in the study." Sawyer's daddy, Sawyer II, is in similar attire to his son. He is holding a glass of bourbon. "I have something to give you while we wait on your mother."

"Yes, sir." Sawyer joins his father. The room is his father's sanctuary. It's done up in dark brown hues; the study is a man's paradise, soothing in color with plush leather furniture. The left side of the room is dominated by an antique desk dating back to the original owner of Tea Olive, Dean Nathaniel Cooper. The room exudes wealth, class, and masculine elegance. Sawyer's father is standing next to the bar set, pouring a small drink of bourbon for Tripp. He tops off his own.

"I know it's been a difficult year for our family, but you have done a remarkable job, son. You made the grades, you won a state championship, and you have stayed out of trouble. Even got a nice scholarship for the Citadel. I wanted you to know I am proud of you." Sawyer II hands Sawyer a small box wrapped in dark brown paper with a gold bow.

Sawyer takes the box. "Thank you, sir."

"Go ahead and open it. I think you might be able to use it tonight."

Sawyer unties the bow and tears the paper, opening the jeweler's box he has seen dozens of times in the family safe. He knows what it is, and his eyes begin to dampen. He looks at his father. Seeing Sawyer's glistening eyes, Sawyer II chokes up. "You've earned them, son." Taking the box from his hands, his daddy hands Sawyer his handkerchief. "Let me help you."

Sawyer holds out his arm. His father removes his cuff links and exchanges them for the family heirloom. The cuff links date back to the 1880s. Sawyer's father wore these cufflinks for years. They were a gift to him on his wedding day from his new father-in-law, Poppy Cooper. The cufflinks are solid gold rose cut and engraved with a star. At the center of the star is a diamond.

"Thought I wouldn't see these until my wedding day." Sawyer stares at his sleeve before looking up at his father.

"Probably should have waited, you're right. But it's been a traumatic year all the way around, and I want to celebrate my son's accomplishments." Sawyer II clears his throat. He hands Sawyer a glass of bourbon and picks up his own. "To my amazing son, to an amazing future. You stand on the shoulders of the Cooper and Beauregard men who have come before you. Never forget your destiny, son." The glasses clink. "Cheers."

"What do we have here?" Sawyer's mom appears in the doorway. She is dressed as the lady of Tea Olive Plantation in a navy-blue lace overlay cocktail-length dress and navy pumps. Pearls adorn her ears and throat.

"You look beautiful, Momma."

"Thank you, and you are mighty handsome." She glances at her husband. "You look just like your father did at that age." She walks over to Sawyer and adjusts his tie. Then she pats his chest. Her eye catches his sleeve. "Those look perfect on you."

"I know what they mean to both of you. And I know you are worried that I don't plan to come back to Tea Olive and take my rightful place. But I will. I just want to do other things first."

"We know, son." Sawyer claps his hand on his son's back. "Tonight is a night of celebration, not rehashing old arguments. You have made up your mind, and your mother and I have agreed to accept you are a man with his own right to make a future for himself." He looks at Melanie. "Where's Avery?"

"I asked him to bring the car around. He should be out front. Are we ready?"

"Ladies first." Melanie smiles at her husband. It's the first smile Sawyer has seen between his parents since last summer when Sawyer's whole world seemed to blow up. It gives him hope.

Outside the front door, Avery is sitting in the front seat of the Rolls Royce and grinning from ear to ear. At 14 years old, he is the youngest and the family goof ball. He is also the most spoiled by his momma. Sawyer II smiles. "Slide out from behind the wheel, Avery. Let your old man drive."

Avery gets out of the driver's seat but not before giving the horn a good honk, much to his mother's chagrin. Sawyer tweaks his brother's ear as they slide into the back seat. "You are an idgit."

"Y'all have a fine time this evening, Mr. and Mrs. Beauregard. Lincoln and I will keep an eye on things until you get back." Queenie helps Melanie into the front seat.

"Thank you, Queenie. We won't be terribly late," Melanie replies.

The awards banquet is held at the Venice Country Club. As soon as they arrive, Avery dashes out to hang with his buddies while Sawyer and his parents make their way to the bar. Procuring a glass of champagne for Melanie, Sawyer II decides to continue with his bourbon. Tonight's event is more of a cocktail party than an award assembly, but it also helps to raise funds for the school. The funds flow freer if the patrons are liquored up.

Sawyer's mom and dad are pulled into a conversation by the headmaster and his wife, leaving Sawyer on his own. He nods at several of his classmates, but everyone keeps their distance. Nothing new here. He is used to the leper role by now. His eyes are searching the crowd for Clay. He spots him over in the corner, talking with his parents. He walks in that direction.

"Good evening, Mr. and Mrs. Newhouse. Mrs. Newhouse, you look lovely." Sawyer air kisses Mrs. Newhouse's cheek and shakes hands with Clay's father.

"Thank you, Tripp. Where are your parents?"

"They got roped into a discussion with Headmaster Kolensky." Sawyer waves his bourbon in the general direction of his parents, making his cuff links take center stage. Before Mrs. Newhouse can ask about them, the seating bell rings. Sawyer, being both a Beauregard and a Cooper and the grandson of two of the founding members of the club, excuses himself to make his way to the Founder's table.

The Founder's table is located on an elevated platform that looks over the 18th green. The table is reserved for the five founding families of Venice Country Club. The table seats Hugers, Cunninghams, and Monroes, in addition to the Beauregards and Coopers. There is a sixth family, the Whites, who are considered ad hoc members of the board of trustees. They do not have voting privileges but are the first family to join the country club and, therefore, have the right to sit at the table. They are not in attendance this evening since they are on a European trip, celebrating their empty nest. Their daughter Rachele graduated with Scarlet the previous year.

Everyone takes their assigned seats. Headmaster Kolensky begins the evening with his welcome address. The event takes close to three hours as the awards are presented for academic, athletic, musical, citizenship, and leadership for the high school students. Sawyer settles in his seat between his father and mother. And, as he did every year, Sawyer sweeps the athletic and leadership categories, taking home a total of six awards. He is the "town son" once again.

"Dad, Clay didn't get an award. What's going on?" Sawyer leans over to whisper in his dad's ear. The families at his table are all smiles. Seems like all the issues and concerns from the past year have disappeared—evaporated as if they never existed. Buck and Charlie pat him on the back and invite him out to the ridge to celebrate. Sawyer hasn't been to the ridge since he and Clay were there at Christmas. And he hasn't been invited by his childhood friends since last summer.

"Later, son. Go congratulate your friends. Get y'all's pictures taken. It's your last night like this for a while. Go ahead and enjoy it."

Sawyer gets up from the table and scans the room for Clay and his parents. He can't find them in the crush of people. Sawyer is pulled from one person to the next. He is congratulated, receives pats on the back, and has his picture taken at least 100 times. He is even propositioned by Candy Westerman, the sheriff's daughter. At least he is pretty certain that is what she was suggesting when she mentioned meeting him on Cotton Mill Road. It felt really good to be a part of the in-crowd again.

Eventually, Sawyer circles back around to his parents. His mom is beaming. Apparently, her place in society had been re-established tonight as well. She snuggles up under his arm and gives him a kiss on the cheek. "Well done, son. Well done."

"Hey, Mrs. Beauregard, okay if Buck and I steal Tripp for the rest of the night? Some of the guys are going to the Ridge. Grace's dad said it's fine." Charlie puts his arm around Tripp and pretends to hit him in the stomach.

"Not before you boys speak to Headmaster Kolensky. But yes. Y'all have fun and be careful." The boys walk away. "Tripp! Find your father, and let him know."

"Yes, ma'am," Sawyer replies. As they get out of earshot of his mom, Sawyer whispers, "What the hell, Charlie? Y'all treated me like a pariah for the past year, and all of a sudden, I am your best friend again? What gives? And where is Clay?"

"That fag? Who the hell cares," says Buck, who has procured a bottle of bourbon from the bar and stashes it in his coat pocket. "Come on, let's go have some fun."

Sawyer stares at them. These guys have been his best friends his entire life. "Y'all go on to the Ridge without me. I will catch up later. I want to talk to my father."

"What? Why?"

Sawyer ignores his boyhood friends and walks toward the club's smoking parlor and gaming room. It's where all the fathers go after any event. He knew he would find his father smoking a cigar and sipping a bourbon. Sawyer walks into the crowded quarters. Men stop him for congratulations and well wishes. Many are regaling him with feats from their own youth. Finally, Sawyer spots his father near the French doors. He is talking to Mr. Gaillard.

"Dad, can we talk?" Sawyer is out of breath, and his anxiety is obvious.

"Son, don't be rude. Harvey and I are discussing business. Can it wait?"

"No, it can't wait." Sawyer looks at Mr. Gaillard. "My apologies, sir."

"Looks like y'all have some business to take care of, Sawyer. How about we catch up another time?"

Sawyer II nods as Harvey walks off. He grabs Sawyer by the upper arm and propels him out the doors to the porch. He nods at people and takes Sawyer to a secluded spot. "Just what is so important that you needed to interrupt a deal Harvey and I have been working on for weeks? This better be good."

"What the hell is going on, Dad? For months we have been freaking pariahs to this town, and all of a sudden, tonight, I am winning awards. Hell, I am even being invited to the Ridge by guys who haven't spoken to me in a year. Not to mention being glad-handed by every man in the place. I was even asked out to Cotton Mill Road!" Sawyer spits out the last, wiping his mouth, "And what about Clay? Why didn't he get any awards? Dad, they gave wimpy Chandler Monroe the Best Wide Receiver? Who are we kidding?"

Sawyer II's shoulders sag, and his voice lowers as he puts a hand on Sawyer's shoulder. "Look, I know Clay was done wrong, but we can't have a man of his character winning awards. He does not represent the values that is Moseley Hall."

"What does that mean? Clay is a standup guy, and he has been a good friend to me. Hell, my best friend this year."

Sawyer II looks at his son with a concerned expression, "Son, do you have something to tell me?"

"Tell you? About what? Clay?" Looking at his father, Sawyer puts it all together. Somehow, they found out about Clay or suspected it. "Dad, no...there's nothing to tell."

Sawyer II's eyes are laser beam sharp, and he looks less than convinced. "Son, you need to tell me if something happened with you two. Y'all have been awfully close these last nine months."

"You all but threw us together, Dad! It was your idea for us to become friends. What were your words exactly? 'Make sure he feels welcome and show him what Venice has to offer.'" Sawyer shakes his head and starts walking away.

His father calls after him. Sawyer ignores him. He has to find Clay and figure out what is going on.

He goes out of the back exit of the club and begins walking toward town. Clay lives in the historical section. Sawyer stops at the gas station and scrounges in his pocket for a quarter. Using the pay phone, Sawyer calls the Newhouse residence. Clay's mom picks up.

"May I speak with Clay, Mrs. Newhouse?"

"I am not sure that is a good idea, Tripp." Her voice is husky and sounds like she has been crying.

"Listen, I need to talk to him, please. Just tell him to come get me at Pickett's. Please!" The line goes dead.

"Crap!" Sawyer paces up and down the sidewalk, trying to figure out what to do. He could call again, but it probably wouldn't do any good. "Whatever." Sawyer goes into Pickett's and walks to the Beer Cave. He grabs a 12-pack and pays for it at the counter. They don't even ask for identification, not that there is any need. Everyone in town knows Sawyer. Hell, he's the town son, right?

Sawyer walks over to the dumpsters and breaks open the beer. He guzzles his first can. He opens the second and stands with the can to his lips as Clay pulls up in his Ford Mustang. "Get in and bring the beer," Clay says, pulling up.

Sawyer grabs his 12-pack and sits in the front seat. Clay takes off. "You good man?" asks Sawyer.

"Hell, no, I'm not good!" Clay has the windows rolled down, and he turns up the radio. The music is blaring, and his tires spin as he exits Pickett's parking lot. He yells, "Give me a beer!" over the radio.

Sawyer hands him the one he just opened, then fishes out another one for himself. He leans back in the passenger seat and lets the wind blow through his hair and clear his brain. He finishes his second beer.

Before fishing out his third, he realizes Clay is pushing 80 as he exits town. This is not good. He turns down the volume of the radio.

"Head to my house. Let's go to the cabin. Take Cotton Mill and go in through the back."

Clay doesn't acknowledge him. He just turns the music back to blast and finishes his beer, tossing it in the back seat. He holds out his hand for another one. Sawyer holds it out of reach. "Not until you freakin' *slow down!*" Clay guns the engine, and then his entire body begins to shake. He slows down, way down, and Sawyer realizes his shakes are tears. Clay is sobbing. Once again, Sawyer turns down the radio. "Pull over, buddy. Let's not make this horrible night any worse."

Clay shakes his head and takes a deep breath. He wipes his face on his sleeve. "No, man, I'm good."

Riding in silence, they make the fifteen-minute drive without further incident. Clay puts the car in park. "Hey, man, I'm not staying; just wanted to make sure you got home."

Sawyer is having none of it. He leans over and takes the keys. "You are staying, at least until I know you will make it home safe." He stays seated in the car seat. "What the hell happened tonight?"

"Don't tell me you don't know! Hell, it was your old man who orchestrated this shit show. And he got his golden boy back in the process. Now, give me my fucking keys!" Clay reaches over and starts hitting Sawyer, punching him and grabbing for the keys. Sawyer punches back and begins wrestling him. The whole time, Clay yells at him. He calls him every foul name and word in his vocabulary. Sawyer changes tactics and goes into defense mode. He wards off the blows until, finally, Clay wears himself out. He is crying again, sobbing into the steering wheel.

"Come on, Clay. Let's go sit on the dock." Sawyer gets out. He grabs the beer and goes into the cabin. He doesn't even check to see if Clay is following. Sawyer turns on a light and drops the beer on the counter. He takes off his blazer and shoes, then pulls off his tie. He carefully removes the cufflinks and places them in a saucer on the counter.

Rolling up the sleeves of his shirt, he goes to the snack drawer. He rummages until he finds a bag of pretzels. He grabs a few beers before putting the rest in the fridge. Clay comes in the front door as Sawyer walks out the back. "Make yourself comfortable. Feel free to grab some beer."

A few minutes later, they are sitting on the dock with their feet hanging in the water. Both are sipping their beer. "You ready to talk, man? I have no clue what happened at the club tonight."

Clay is quiet. So quiet. Sawyer figures he will never speak. Finally, Clay says, "It happened after the dinner bell rang. We were headed to our seats when Coach Freidman pulled my father aside. My dad has not told me exactly what happened, but I pretty much figured it out. Dad came back to Mom and me. He was furious and pale. Told us we were leaving. I would not be receiving any awards. He was pushing us out of the club. I have never seen my father so pissed."

Clay takes a deep breath and wipes at his eyes. He takes another swig of beer. "Friedman told my dad they knew I was a homo and there would be no awards. There would be no more coming back to school. And no graduation ceremony. If we went quietly, I would still graduate. If not, I would be expelled, and an interview with Ron Adams would be granted as a feature story in the *Venice Gazette* about his 'star' wide receiver."

"Shit. How did they find out?"

Clay is silent. "Apparently from your father. And the only people who know are my mother and father, my therapist. And you." Clay looks at Sawyer with accusation in his eyes.

"It wasn't me! I swear, Clay! I would never do that to you." Sawyer sidles over to Clay on the dock and leans into him. He places his mouth on Clay's mouth and kisses him. He whispers, "It wasn't me, Clay. I swear."

Clay pulls back, startled. He looks at Sawyer with trepidation. "What are you doing?" Then, as if something inside of him long contained has been released, Clay comes in for a hard kiss. Their teeth and lips clash. Their tongues mingle. The taste is exquisite. Clay is holding Sawyer's head between his hands as he pulls back. "Are you absolutely certain?"

"Yes, absolutely certain. If you are leaving tomorrow, I want to know."

They make their way into the cabin, holding hands and stopping frequently to touch and taste. Clay lights a fire. The two hurt and broken boys go about discovering themselves and each other. It changes them both. Forever.

13

Chapter Thirteen

Present Day

Sawyer parks the pink Cadillac in the barn. He places his head on the steering wheel and takes a deep breath. The car is loaded down with packages and boxes after an afternoon of shopping. It's his absolute least favorite chore, but after all these years in the military moving from base to base, he is an expert. He lifts his head and shakes off his temperament. It is nobody's fault but his own. He chose the life of a vagabond soldier. Now that it is time to put down roots, he finds himself struggling to cope with the myriad of details. However, one thing he can resolve right now to make himself immediately more comfortable is to change out his mother's antique, frail, and frilly bedroom furniture.

He exits his vehicle and goes to the bunkhouse, where he entices a few farmhands to help him move furniture. The furniture is heavy, and the task takes much longer than expected, but by suppertime, Sawyer has a room full of manly furniture. Though he still has pink walls. That will need to wait for another day.

"Thanks, guys. Here." Sawyer hands each of the five men a crisp 100-dollar bill. "Appreciate the help."

Delighted with the boon, Greg, a young man in his mid-20s, replies, "Anytime, Mr. Beauregard. Anytime. And I mean that."

"Please, call me Sawyer. My uncle deserves and expects the Mister, but I don't. If Sawyer doesn't suit, feel free to come up with something else. But Mr. Beauregard has never fit." He slaps Greg on the back and thanks the men again as they walk back to the bunkhouse.

Sawyer enters the study and sees freshly brewed tea sitting on the beverage cart. He pours himself a glass with chagrin. He really wants something stronger, but after breaking the habit of his younger years, he knows alcohol will only ease stress for a short time.

Instead, he fixes his gaze on the stack of papers littering his uncle's desk. He rifles through several stacks before he comes across what he is looking for. He cross-references the document with the ledger from 1986. It's not there. Well, he found some of the missing money. Hell, he has found a significant amount of missing money. Now, where did it go?

Sawyer clicks on the computer and starts accessing bank records. He calls one of his contacts in DC. Within 15 minutes, he has the information he is looking for, and it nearly breaks his heart. He sits in the desk chair and remains there, his mind swirling back to those last days in high school. To the award ceremony and Clay. The cabin. He is still sitting there when Gabe arrives some 30 minutes later.

"Sawyer, is everything okay?" Gabe is at the bar, pouring himself his evening drink. Tonight, it looks like vodka and water.

"I don't know Uncle Gabe. But I think I found some of the missing money."

Gabe walks over to the desk with his drink in hand. "Okay, how bad is it?"

"I am not really sure. It looks like a half-million-dollar payoff to Headmaster Kolensky in 1986." Sawyer shows him the document from the trust withdrawing the money. Then, he confirms the withdrawal recipient with the numbered account and the ledger. "I was able to look up the numbered account and reach out to one of my buddies in DC. The account is closed now, but he was able to trace it back to Kolensky."

Gabe looks over the documents. "Any ideas why?" He rustles a few pages on the desk as he leans over and taps the ledger. "500,000 dollars is a lot of money now, but in 1986, it was a monstrous sum. It's not possible your father had that available in liquid assets. The trust would have been the only source for such a large payment. And I was never notified. I doubt Eileen was, either. Melanie probably knows."

Sawyer puts his head in his hands. "I think I might know why." He looks up with tears in his eyes. "Hush money."

"To keep quiet about Laura Lynne?" Gabe shakes his head. "Would he stoop that low?"

"Well, I hadn't thought about Laura Lynne. I guess it could be her. But I think it was actually me, or more specifically, my best friend from senior year, Clay Newhouse."

"What about Clay Newhouse?"

Sawyer jumps up, startling his uncle. "Can we talk about this outside? Maybe take a walk to the dock?"

Gabe nods his head. "Of course. Grab your drink. It's mighty hot out there still."

Sawyer all but runs out the back door. His uncle trails at a considerably slower pace. Sawyer makes it to the oak tree before realizing his uncle cannot keep up. He slows his pace and circles back toward the house. His mind is whirling from what he thinks he has uncovered.

"Son, can we bring it down to a gentle stroll? I have been out in the fields all day. My bones are tired."

"Yes, yes, of course. I'm sorry."

"No need to apologize. I know you got something you are trying to work out." He pats him on the shoulder. "You ready to tell me now?"

Sawyer takes a deep breath and recounts his memory from the awards ceremony, leaving out the night at the cabin—no need to freak his uncle completely out.

His uncle is silent. He stops in his tracks. Sawyer pulls up short. Gabe responds, "And you don't know how he knew?"

"No, I never told."

They continue to mosey back to the house. "Listen, Uncle Gabe. One last thing before we go in. Do you know if Kolensky is still alive? I'd like to have a few words with him."

"I have no idea. I know he is not in the area. Retired not too long after Avery graduated, I think."

"Okay. I think I might spend some time over the next few days checking up on him. A good place to start might be the *Gazette*. I can get Miss Wright on it." Sawyer chuckles. "That woman is one piece of work."

"So was her momma. She was a firecracker." He smiles. "Come on, let's have some supper. I'm starving."

"Speaking of firecrackers, what can you tell me about the owner of Wheelbarrow Books?"

Gabe casts a sly glance over at his nephew. "Met our Diane now, did ya? Mighty sharp lady. She had a tough go of it, but she has made a good life here for herself and Mandy." He meanders up the steps. "Why do you ask?"

"I think I might be ready to see some fireworks. It's been a while for me."

Gabe turns toward the kitchen. "For her too, son. So, if you decide you want to make a purchase, start with the sparklers. And if you hurt her, I will personally tan your hide."

"Yes, sir."

Dinner is meatloaf and garlic potatoes; thank you, Victoria! And the two men eat in relative quiet, each lost in their own thoughts. "You okay, Uncle Gabe?" Sawyer stands to clear the porch table. "If it's all right, I think I want to turn in a bit early. Play on the computer a bit. See if I can find anything out about Kolensky."

"I'm fine, son, just fine. Probably watch a little TV."

"Call me if you need me." As Sawyer turns away from the table, he says, "I love you, Uncle Gabe."

"I love you too. Night now."

***

Waking up, Sawyer lays still for just a moment, taking in the sounds of the plantation. The cicadas are still singing, and from the light shining through the window, he knows the moon is high and full. Closing his eyes, he wills himself back to sleep. It doesn't work. He gets up and checks his clock, and it is 4 AM. Shocked, he checks again. He has been asleep for six hours. Maybe his uncle is right; maybe Tea Olive is a healing place. Or maybe it's sleeping in a bed that fits his large frame. Either way, he is grateful for the first good sleep he has had in more months than he cares to admit. After a quick stop in the bathroom, Sawyer puts on his running gear. Might as well start his day with a run.

As Sawyer begins his jog, he finds himself headed toward Cotton Mill Road and the Ridge. So much of his teenage years were spent there. First, with Grady and Buck as boys, then the gang of friends from Moseley, and finally, just him and Clay his senior year. He has not been back since his high school graduation. It seems like it is time to face some of his demons. Perhaps that was the only way to fully heal or to understand what events have led to his current situation. His need to move endlessly. His lack of any valuable relationships, family or otherwise. Sawyer begins to believe it all stems from the time he was in high school.

The Ridge is as it has always been. The rickety seating has been replaced with more sturdy Adirondack chairs and a picnic table. There is even a fire pit to replace the steel barrel. The spot is well used, and Sawyer hopes Grady and Grace's children have continued the tradition of celebrating and hanging out at the Ridge. Seeing no reason to stay, Sawyer circles the seating area and jogs back across the property toward the back section of Tea Olive. Coming up on the small creek, he sees John on the dock sipping a cup of coffee. Sawyer waves, and John lifts his coffee cup in acknowledgment.

John calls out, "Thought I heard someone come by a bit ago and assumed it was you. Interested in some coffee?"

"Ummm, sure."

"Head around front, and I will meet you at the door."

As Sawyer approaches, he notices John is armed with a shotgun as he enters the back door of his cabin. Sawyer also notices the work that has been done on the cabin. It's no longer a shack held together by redneck ingenuity. John apparently knows what he is doing when it comes to carpentry and engineering. Sawyer says admiringly, "You've done a lot of work on the place. It looks better than I ever remember it."

"I enjoy using my hands. Settles my mind in the evening." John ushers him into the kitchen. "Consider it my form of running."

Sawyer gives a low whistle. The kitchen has been updated into a chic, urban-inspired venue. The cabinets are refurbished, and the wooden countertops are replaced with granite. The light fixtures add a sleek accent in wrought iron. Running his hand along the counters, Sawyer continues, "Wow, this is great. Looks much different than the last time I was here."

"Thanks. The kitchen was the first fix. I just finished up the bathroom if you want to have a look. Figured it would be the most work intensive, and I was right." He works on a coffee machine that looks like it belongs at Magnolia Café. "How do you like your coffee?"

"Black? Hell, I don't know. Make me what you are having." Sawyer walks down the hallway toward the bathroom while John gets a mug from the cabinet. Sawyer opens the bathroom door and is surprised by the spaciousness and the luxury of the formerly sparse room. The colors of browns, blacks, and grays reflect the kitchen. Sawyer takes a closer look and realizes the bathroom has been extended to include a closet from the adjoining room.

"This is fabulous. I remember this bathroom was nothing more than a toilet, sink, and shower head with a drain in the center of the room. It didn't even have a shower curtain."

John stands in the doorway and extends a coffee mug to Sawyer. "It stayed that way the first year. But it was worth the wait. In my old age, I enjoy a hot shower at the end of the day. May as well be in a bathroom with some amenities." John points to a switch on the wall. "I put down heated tiles and towel racks. Don't tell the guys. I don't want them to think I am a sissy."

Sawyer laughs as he sips his coffee. "Your secret is safe with me. And your coffee is delicious. What other talents do you have that I don't know about?"

The two men walk through the house to stand on the front porch. "Sawyer, there is one thing I should probably tell you. I don't mention it often, but with your request for my help yesterday, well…you know, watchin' over the place and all." He points to a rifle propped up against the porch railing. "You should know. I was Special Forces, and I have a hand with a gun. I'm an expert sharpshooter. And I don't miss."

Sawyer nods thoughtfully. He should have guessed it the first time he met John. "What's your kill rate? Never mind, none of my business." Handing his mug back to John, Sawyer slaps him on the shoulder. "Need to finish my morning run. Thanks for the cup of joe."

"Anytime. And Sawyer? I got your back. For some reason, I think you are going to need it."

"Thanks, man." Sawyer waves as he jogs away from the cabin. He circles the rest of the farm. He covers the fields he did not see on yesterday's run. He waves at the occasional farmhand as he passes by. He hopes word gets out that he is in the fields each morning overseeing operations. From what he has seen since he returned, his uncle is not holding them accountable to a full day's work. He will need to speak with him about allowing John to take the reins. Accountability and productivity over the past couple of months have been slacking.

Sawyer brings his jog down to a walk. He puts his hands on his hips as he walks up the drive to the plantation house. Gabe is standing on the front porch, pacing. He spots Sawyer and comes to a stop. Sawyer can tell from his body language that he is upset. Sawyer picks up his pace and comes to stand at the base of The Residence's stately entrance.

"Uncle Gabe? You okay? What's up?"

"Nothing earth shattering. I just got to thinkin' last night, about your friend Clay and the missing money." Gabe walks down the porch stairs as he talks, "Come on, let's go the barn, I need to add some oil to Jolene's engine before the day gets too far ahead of me. Forgot yesterday."

Sawyer walks in step with his uncle, "What about Clay?"

"Yes, right. Well, do you know how to get in touch with him? Might be worth asking him what he knows. In a round-about sort of way." Gabe opens the barn door, "It occurred to me that a man as bright as his father wouldn't let this go, I doubt Clay would have either. I know I wouldn't have, not if he were my son."

Sawyer props himself against the barn door watching as Gabe uncaps the oil and walks over to Jolene, his latest love, the side by side off road vehicle. He works the lid off the engine and pours the oil. "So, you're awful quiet. You don't think it's a good idea?"

"No, it's not that. I just haven't seen or spoken to him since senior year." Sawyer pushes himself off the door and walks toward Jolene, "But you are right. His dad wouldn't have let this go without knowing what happened. I'll look into it."

Gabe finishes with Jolene, closing her lid, "Come on. I'm starving. All this talking has worked up an appetite. Pearl and Victoria are probably wondering what happened to us."

Sawyer opens the barn door and plows into young Liam. "Whoa! What have we here? Liam? What are you doing here? Isn't it a school day?"

"Yes, sir. It is. I just need to get my bike. I left it here over the weekend."

"By all means. Didn't mean to run you over."

"No problem, sir. But I need to hurry. Momma's in the car waiting. She is already mad I am making her late for work."

Sawyer looks up and sees Beth Ann Bodeen sitting in a silver Toyota Camry. He waves as Liam comes racing out of the barn, pushing his bicycle. Beth Ann pops the trunk, and Sawyer walks over to help Liam load the bike. "Good morning, Beth Ann."

"Good morning. Sorry about all this. Not sure how he thought he was going to get back and forth to school without his bike." Beth Ann rolls her eyes and gives a half-grin.

"It's no problem." Sawyer responds.

Liam slams the trunk shut and hops into the front seat.

"Y'all have a good rest of the day," Sawyer says.

Beth Ann waves and executes a quick y-turn, honking her horn as she speeds down the driveway. Gabe comes over and stands next to Sawyer, saying, "It is truly a mystery how that woman has turned out as well as she has. And is raising such a good kid."

"Why do you say that?" asks Sawyer.

"She had it rough growing up. She and her sister. Her father was a piece of work. He raised those two girls on his own. Well, he and the cadre of women who were in and out of his house. Their momma left when they were little."

"Y'all plannin' to eat this morning?" Pearl stands in the mudroom doorway with her hands on her hips and dishtowel thrown over her shoulder. "Thought I was gonna have to send out a search party for you two." She whips the towel off her shoulder. "Come on! Breakfast is getting cold."

With a grin at each other, Sawyer and Gabe turn toward the house. Each feeling like this revelation from the past is a turning point both in their relationship and for the future.

14

Chapter Fourteen

Sawyer sits at his computer. He promised his uncle he would follow up with Clay, but he loathes taking this step. For Sawyer, this chapter of his life ended a long time ago. He is not interested in revisiting this area of his past. For years, he struggled with his sexual identity. All his other relationships have been with women. And not because of some mixed-up guilt shit from his church upbringing. Which, he has to admit, was his initial desire to seek out women. No, Clay has been the only man. And in his mind, will be the only man.

"Well, shit," Sawyer mutters as he Googles Clay's name: Clayton Samson Newhouse. His LinkedIn profile immediately pops up. Sawyer clicks on the link. Clay's picture and bio appear on the page. He is the current CEO and part-owner of Modern Farming. The company's location is in Oregon. There is no personal information available. Sawyer clicks on the contact information and sends an email. He notes the company phone number but decides against calling him. His email is brief. "Clay, your old friend Tripp from Venice, MS. Would like to catch up. Please send me an email if interested. I will come to you. Hope all is well."

With that done, Sawyer decides to Google his old headmaster, Mr. Kolensky. For the life of him, he cannot remember the man's first name. The Google search is fruitless. Who would know? Sawyer considers asking Grady but decides against it. He is law enforcement, after all. Besides, this needs to stay in the family. It is times like these that he wishes he had a cell phone. Instead, he walks into the hallway to use the house phone and looks at the list of phone numbers lying beside the phone. He calls Scarlet. She picks up on the second ring.

"Scarlet, it's Sawyer. I need to pick your brain."

"Well, hello, wayward brother. I heard you were in town. No, 'How are you? It's been forever?' I see. Straight to the point. Okay, what can I do for you?" Scarlet is curt.

"Sorry, sorry! I have a lot on my brain. We really do need to have coffee or lunch together. I need to catch you up on a few things. And I need an ally. We were always good at that growing up."

Scarlet's tone softens with a sigh. "Yes, we were always each other's best advocate. Is everything okay?"

"For now, yes. But the day is young." He chuckles. "Listen, do you remember Headmaster Kolensky from Moseley Hall when we were there? I am trying to figure out if he is alive. I tried to Google him, but I don't have a first name."

"Elijah Kolensky. I really don't know if he is still alive. It has been years since I have seen any of the family. When his wife, Edith, died, his daughters moved him to be closer to them. Their oldest, Sabrina? You might remember her. She was at school when we were, but she didn't hang in our crowd. Super geeky. Anyway, she is a high-powered attorney in Atlanta, last I heard. I think that may be where they ended up, but I am not sure."

"Hmmm. Maybe I can figure out where he is using his daughter's name. Sabrina Kolensky, an attorney in Atlanta, should narrow the search. Did she ever marry?"

"Not to my knowledge. Scuttlebutt was she moved to Atlanta because she was hired by a professional athlete who was in some deep trouble. Some basketball player who was accused of killing his wife. Don't know how true that is, but though our grapevine in Venice is often not exactly correct, it is also rarely wrong."

"Anything else you can tell me?"

There is silence on the other end for a moment. "Not that I can think of right now. I want to ask why you need this information, but it probably needs to wait until we see each other. Right?"

"Yes. The sooner, the better. I can meet you somewhere, or you can come over. Just me and Uncle Gabe around here these days."

"How about you meet me at the "Whistle Stop B and B" in Wisteria? It is quiet and secluded. Does today work? Maybe 4 PM?"

"Ummm, sure. Wisteria?"

"Yeah, I know the owners. They have a bar area open to the public. You will see it when you get there. And Sawyer? Do me a favor, and don't tell Uncle Gabe or Momma you are coming today. Let's keep this between us."

"Scarlet, are you okay? This seems very cloak and dagger."

"I am perfectly fine, Sawyer. I just don't see where we should concern them with this." The switch from soft and kind to curt and defensive throws Sawyer off his game.

"Whoa! Sure. Didn't mean to hit a sore spot. 4:00 at the Whistle Stop. Got it."

"Very good." Scarlet hangs up before Sawyer has a chance to say goodbye. He looks at the phone in his hand, wondering what went sideways in the conversation. Seems Laura Lynne had a right to be concerned about Scarlet. Something is definitely off.

Sawyer returns to his laptop and searches "Sabrina Kolensky of Atlanta." Sure enough, she has a LinkedIn as well. Sawyer sends her a message requesting her father's information. With nothing more to do, Sawyer closes his laptop and walks downstairs. He finds his uncle lacing up his work boots.

"You going to the fields?"

"Yes. I didn't sleep well last night and thought maybe plowing some dirt would shake off the cobwebs." He looks at Sawyer. "What's on your mind?"

"I want to propose a change. Up for the discussion?"

Gabe puts his booted foot on the ground and stands up. "Sure. Walk and talk?" Nodding, Sawyer joins Gabe in his walk to the tractor. "What's on your mind?"

Sawyer clears his throat. "Well, the last several days, I have noticed on my runs the lack of work being completed by the field hands. Seems like a lot of them are just lulling the days away. Doubt too many have put in a hard day's work since I have been here. Longer probably."

"Go on."

"I want to put John in charge of the hands. I realize this will displace Roger, but I think Roger's past his prime. The young guys are taking advantage."

"You are probably right. Problem is Roger has been good to us. He needs the money too. He's supervised the harvesting and planting for what? Some 30 years or more. Done good work."

"I know. I considered that. What if we gave him a severance package? Something we can agree on. And generous. I would like to consider the same option with all the guys over 65. What do you think?"

Gabe slaps Sawyer on the back. "I think it is time for me to vacate my role as executor of the trust."

"Uncle Gabe! That is not what I was implying! I simply..."

"No, no. It's time. And honestly, it would be a relief to me. I want to keep my hand in the pot. Maybe as a consultant? Isn't that the term they use these days? And spend the rest of my time with Malcolm in the fields." Gabe stops to look at his nephew and asks, "What do you think? Do you accept?"

Sawyer looks at Gabe, then turns his gaze to the farm and The Residence. He is home for good. He knows it now. "If you are ready, then yes. I am ready too."

"Now, son, this means for good. No more gallivanting around the world. To run this place and earn the trust, you have to be here all the time."

"I know. I am tired of living like a vagabond. I am ready to take on my legacy. And, uncle, I know the sacrifices it entails."

"Good. I will call Gerald in the morning. Get the paperwork started to transfer the trust. And as far as John and Roger, you do what you think is best. I support you. Truth be told, the old guys will probably be grateful." The men are at the tractors, and Gabe begins climbing up. "Proud of you, son. It is a big relief to see you step into your rightful spot. You do this old man proud."

"Don't get too carried away. I still have a lot to learn. I expect you to teach me."

Gabe tilts his chin in acknowledgment and turns on the tractor. Over the roar of the noise, he shouts, "John is working in the back fields today if you want to find him now." Gabe puts the tractor in gear and starts rolling out to the field.

Under his breath, Sawyer murmurs, "Well, that is not how I expected that conversation to go. Ready or not, here I come."

Sawyer decides his first duty as the new executor of the trust is to stop by the bunkhouse and see what is going on there. At nearly 10:00 in the morning, the building should be empty. He hops on one of the four-wheelers and takes off toward the building. The bunkhouse is large and can house up to fifty men. It was built in the 40s and, over the years, has been updated to allow for better facilities. Pulling up, Sawyer notes four men sitting on the front porch playing cards. He walks over. The men are laughing as they play a round of poker. From the looks of them and the smell, they have been at this for quite some time.

"How you boys doin' this morning? Who's winning?"

Either too inebriated to notice, or this is a normal form of entertainment, none of the men catch Sawyer's tone. It is the same one he used in the military when one of his officers was out of line.

"Froggy here is up a couple hundred," says a scraggly-looking guy. Sawyer estimates him to be somewhere around 40, though he could have been 25. It is hard to tell with all the grime, not to mention the rode hard put away wet look.

"Good for you, Froggy. Where might I find Roger?" asks Sawyer.

The scraggly guy answers again, this time talking around his cigarette. "Hell, if I know. Said something as he left. Old guy always talking about somethin' nobody listens to."

Sawyer assesses the situation and decides the best strategy of attack is to secure backup for when he kicks these sorry oafs off his property. He starts his four-wheeler back up as the four men happily continue with their game, oblivious.

Sawyer finds John in the back field as expected. He parks the four-wheeler and walks over to John. "Hey Colonel, what's up?"

"I have a proposition for you. And then I need your help."

"You need me to shoot someone?"

Laughing, Sawyer's face splits into a huge smile. "Not yet. But depending on how you answer, your gun might sure enough be needed." He turns serious. "John, as of this morning, the running of Tea Olive and the family's businesses have been handed over to me. I want to make some immediate changes, and I need a good, solid team around me to make it happen. I want you to be on that team."

"What will happen to Mr. Gabe? I owe him a lot."

If Sawyer had any doubts about John's character, that one sentence dispelled them. "He will stay on as a consultant. He plans to work the fields with Malcolm. He will stay at The Residence, of course." He looks at John, "I'd like you to step into Roger's spot. Take on leading the fieldhands. We can work together to determine an equitable salary."

"And Roger? How does he feel about this?"

"I haven't spoken to Roger. But I am guessing he will be as relieved as Uncle Gabe to step aside from his duties. I haven't really thought this completely through, but I would like to offer severance packages to those who are loyal workers. Get rid of the slackers. Keep the ones who show initiative. It is time for an overhaul."

John walks to the fence post and gets a piece of straw to put between his teeth, contemplating. Finally, he turns to Sawyer. "Micah tells me you are a good man. One of the best. I trust his judgment more than my own." John walks over and shakes Sawyer's hand, "Looks like you got yourself a new foreman."

"Great. Let's grab Malcolm and head to the bunkhouse. I just came from there. Four guys are sitting on the porch playing poker. Some dude named Froggy is winning. Time to clean house."

"Then we need Malcolm for sure. And I need my rifle. Wherever Froggy is, you will find his best mate Freddie. Freddie and Froggy are hardcore bad guys. I haven't seen them work one full day since they got here. This won't be easy. They've a good thing goin'."

"Thanks for the warning. You get your gun, and I will get Malcolm. Let's meet back at the trailhead."

The two men nod and go their separate directions. Sawyer swings up next to Malcolm who is working in the organic sweet potato field. Malcolm turns off his tractor at Sawyer's signal.

"You interested in a little trouble this morning?" asks Sawyer.

"What you got in mind?"

"Time to get rid of the riff-raff. You know Froggy and Freddie? Currently playing poker at the bunkhouse? Today they get their walking papers."

"Hell ya! Those boys nothin' but trouble. What do you need from me?"

"Not sure, mostly just your presence. John will meet us there. He's bringing his rifle," says Sawyer.

Malcolm reaches into his tractor and pulls out a baseball bat. "I keep this with me just in case. You never know what you might find in these fields."

"Bring it along." Sawyer scoots forward on the four-wheeler. "Hop on. Let's go have some fun."

With a war whoop, the two men meet John at the trailhead. Leaving their vehicles, the three men walk to the bunkhouse. Froggy and his friends are sitting exactly as Sawyer left them an hour ago.

"Hey, boys. Froggy still winning?"

"Hell no! I'm up by 100." Grinning, the scraggly dude, whom Sawyer assumes is Freddie and the ringleader, looks over at Sawyer. His demeanor instantly changes when he sees John with his rifle to Sawyer's left and Malcolm to his right. Freddie scoots his chair back and leans on two legs. "Well, well. What do we have here?"

"Your pink slip. Time for you boys to pack up and move on. I don't want any trouble," says Sawyer.

"Oh, you do? Well, I don't think so. I really like it here," Freddie responds.

"I'm sure you do. Real nice place we have here. Takes a lot of work to keep it up. Work you boys haven't been doing," says Sawyer.

"Roger seems happy enough. Just ask him," Froggy interjects.

"I don't need to ask Roger," Sawyer says calmly. "You see, John here is the new foreman, and he agrees with me. Time for you boys to go. You've had your fun. Got paid plenty to play your poker. Fun is done. I will give you ten minutes to pack your bags and head on. If you are not gone, then well, the three of us will happily escort you off the premises." Sawyer looks at his watch. "Clocks ticking."

Freddie drops his chair to the porch, and with a smoothness that surprises even Sawyer, John pulls his rifle to his shoulder and has it aimed at Freddie's chest. "Freddie, I suggest you drop that weapon in your hand. Slow and easy. That goes for you too, Froggy. One move, and I shoot. And it will be a pleasure. I heard what you did to Roger. Trust me when I tell you I don't miss."

Sawyer sees them now. Both men have a gun in their hand. Sawyer kicks himself for not arming up before confronting the men. A mistake he won't make again. John holsters the bullet and has his finger on the trigger. He is completely focused. There is no mistake he has done this before. Freddie raises his hands nice and slow. He signals Froggy to do the same.

"No need to get hostile. But I think the Colonel here is making a big mistake. You see, if we were to leave, there might be a bit of trouble, if you know what I mean. Hate to see anything happen to your family. Fine folks."

Sawyer bounds up the stairs and across the porch, he hears a rifle shot and sees Freddie's gun go flying as he tackles the fieldhand. He straddles Freddie and begins pummeling his face. Malcolm is right behind him, taking his bat to whoever gets close. John is methodically shooting his rifle over their heads, peppering the bunkhouse's porch roof. With a final punch, Sawyer hears the jawbone of Freddie break and the man passes out. Freddie didn't have a chance to throw his first punch.

"Who's next? Come on, you cowards! You come onto my property, are treated well, and try to threaten my family? Your ten minutes are up!" Sawyer stands above Freddie and kicks him in the side. "Take your buddy and get the hell out of here. Get out of Venice. There is no place for you here. And if you show your ugly asses anywhere near my family, my land, or me, I will finish what I started. *Are we clear?*"

Sawyer walks off the porch and stands watch as Malcolm pushes the other three off the porch. Froggy, holding his hand, goes to the truck parked to the side of the bunkhouse and backs up toward the porch. The other two men lift a groaning and heavy Freddie off the porch and into the bed of the truck. John has his rifle trained on Froggy the entire time.

Sawyer saunters over to the driver's side of the truck. Froggy has his window down and stares straight ahead. "Froggy is it? One last word of advice. Go far away and never look back."

"I got stuff in there. And I want my money."

"You lost that chance when you pulled your gun on me. Stupid prick move. You might want to find better friends, Froggy. And a better name. Makes you sound like a boy going through puberty. Christ, find some integrity." He slaps the side of the truck as he steps back. Froggy shoots him a bird as he barrels off down the road.

15

Chapter Fifteen

"Want me to take off his finger?" John asks as he lowers his weapon. "Y'all okay?"

Malcolm smiles and laughs, "Most fun I've had in ages. There are a few more we might want to oust while we're at it. They've been sucking up money and air for quite a while. Roger is too scared to do anything." He looks at John. "What exactly happened to him that got him so scared?"

"Not worth repeatin'," says John as he looks at Malcolm. "Well, let's go find the others. Get them gone too."

"Think you will need me? If not, I want to find Roger. He deserves to know from me what is happening," says Sawyer.

The three look at each other with alarm as, in unison, they hear the dinner bell ringing loudly and repeatedly. "Shit! Come on!" The bell doesn't stop as Sawyer jumps on his four-wheeler, and Malcolm scrambles on behind him as he makes his way toward The Residence. Sawyer sees people running from all directions as he takes the dirt road, going as fast as he can toward the clanging bell and whatever trouble lies ahead.

Pearl stands at the bell ringing with all her might as Sawyer whips around the back of the house. "It's Mr.Gabe! He needs help! I don't know what...just *go!*"

Sawyer slams to a stop. "Malcolm, stay here with the women! Pearl knows where the guns are and *call Grady!*"

Malcolm gets off the four-by-four with his bat in hand to help his sister. Sawyer takes off down the back path toward the west field, with John following closely. The farm truck is hot on their heels as Sawyer careens down the field to the lone tractor standing at the edge of the field. He cannot see his uncle. Sawyer's heart stops as he scans the field, looking for signs of life. John shouts and points toward the left. Sawyer's gaze darts in that direction. To his relief, he sees Gabe standing near the grove of trees. His heart begins to beat at a normal pace when his brain registers his uncle is still alive.

Turning off the engine, he comes to an abrupt stop in front of Gabe. Sawyer sees blood coming from a wound on his head, and Gabe is cradling his chest and left arm. "Uncle Gabe! What happened? Who hurt you?"

Sawyer rushes to his uncle in time for Gabe's frail body to sag in his arms. He leans close to his uncle's mouth and hears him whisper, "I'm okay. Need help though."

"Are you sure? Who hurt you?"

Roger is next to Sawyer and his uncle. John has his rifle at the ready, using the farm truck as a shield. He's protecting the men, unsure of where the threat lies.

Roger is talking animatedly, "It was some of Freddie's buddies out in the fields. Some sort of signal on the phones. They came after me, but I shot one of them in the leg and another one in the shoulder before they turned tail. Not sure who was out here with Mr. Gabe. I figured he was next when I heard the bell ringing. What in the hell happened?"

"Later. Uncle Gabe?" Sawyer's voice is gentle as he steers his uncle toward the truck. "Come on. Let's get you home. See what's what. Can you walk?"

Gabe nods as he takes his first step and then crumples in Sawyer's arms. "Shit!" Sawyer turns his body and gently scoops one arm under his uncle's legs. Securing him against his chest as he walks to the passenger's side of the truck. "Roger, drive me to the house. John, jump in the back. Counting on you to keep us safe."

"Already there, boss," John says, moving toward the truck bed.

"Roger, you have your walkie-talkie for the house?" Receiving his acknowledgment, Sawyer begins barking orders. "Call The Residence, tell them to call an ambulance…"

"No! No ambulance. Dr. Treelove," wheezes Gabe.

Unwilling to argue with his uncle, Sawyer concedes. "Call Dr. Treelove. Then, have them call the nursing home and make sure Momma is safe. Also, have them check my sisters and brother. I don't know what just happened, but I need to know everyone is safe." Sawyer hears sirens in the distance and prays Grady is nearby.

Roger is still talking in the walkie-talkie when he pulls up to the house. John jumps from the bed of the truck and walks in front of Sawyer as Sawyer gently exits the truck. Sawyer cradles his uncle to his chest and walks through the back porch to the study. He carefully places his uncle on the couch as Pearl and Victoria meet them.

"Sawyer, what is going on? Dr. Treelove is on the way. Your Momma is fine. I can't reach your brother and sisters."

Sawyer looks at Pearl and grabs her by the shoulders. "Pearl, take care of my uncle. Where is your brother?"

"He's standing guard on the front porch. Why? What's the matter?"

Sawyer walks to the front porch and sees Malcolm fully armed. "Malcolm, go to your mother's house and check on Queenie. Make sure your family is okay. I have no idea what is going on, but I don't like it." He takes Malcolm's arm. "Your family is as much a part of Tea Olive as we are. Go!"

"You watch my kin, Sawyer. Don't let anything happen to them."

"I won't. I swear."

Malcolm runs down the front porch toward the back of the house. Sawyer sees him driving the farm truck, taking off down the fields as the sheriff's car pulls up. Grady rolls down his window. "What's going on Sawyer?"

"Go check the fields, Grady. John and I have the house. Roger shot two men out in the east field. Not sure if they are still there. Malcolm is fully armed and headed to his house to check on his family. Radio whomever the hell you need to and make sure he is not harmed." Sawyer paces back and forth. "I have no idea about the rest of the hands. I don't even know who to begin looking for. Wait."

Sawyer walks to the front door and shouts inside, "Roger! Come here."

Roger appears at the front entrance with his firearm at the ready. "Yes, Colonel."

"Go with Grady's man and see if you can locate the rest of the workers. You are the only one who knows them. Make sure they're safe."

Roger nods and walks to the sheriff's car. Grady gives orders, and the two men drive toward the fields. "I called Dad. He has armed men on the Cotton Mill side, where our property meets yours. You're vulnerable around the Twin Oaks side. I sent a cruiser to assess the situation. What in the hell happened, Sawyer?"

"I don't know exactly. Come inside, Grady. I don't like us exposed. My uncle has been hurt."

"How bad?"

"I have no idea. He won't let me call an ambulance. He insisted we call Treelove, so we're waiting on him now. Uncle Gabe is in the study." As soon as the two men arrive at the study, John leaves his post.

John nods. "I am going to scope the perimeter and then find an eagle's nest. I have the walkie-talkie. Call if you need me".

"Thanks, John. I wish I knew what was going on," says Sawyer.

"Me, too," John replies.

Pearl holds Gabe's hand and talks softly to him. She looks up at Sawyer and says, "He's resting. The cut on his head is not too bad. It's his ribs. I think he has a few cracked ones. He says he was kicked by one of the farmhands. Guy by the name of Greg."

"Son of a bitch! I just met him yesterday!" Sawyer exclaims, "He helped me move furniture from the barn to my room."

"I will still take a strap to you, young man. Watch your foul mouth." The quiet statement is music to Sawyer's ears as he looks at his uncle. Gabe's eyes are open. The hazel irises are the prettiest Sawyer has ever seen.

"Yes, sir. You scared the life out of me," says Sawyer, lowering his voice.

"Just a scratch. Thanks to Pearl. She saved the day. Her and her bell."

Pearl smiles. She scoots off the chair, "Victoria is on the way with some coffee for both of you. Dr. Treelove will be around shortly."

"Did you hear from Malcolm? Or my siblings?" asks Sawyer.

"Malcolm called, and all is well at home. My brother George is on the way with his sons to stay for the duration. Malcolm is coming back this way. Laura Lynne and Avery responded to the text. They are fine. But they want to know what is going on. No word on Scarlet."

"Pearl, thank you. Sounds like maybe things are beginning to settle down."

"Let's hope so. I don't think my arm can take ringing that bell again anytime soon!" And with that, she leaves. Grady walks into the study carrying a tray loaded with coffee and sandwiches.

"Here! Let me take that. Good Lord, who is she planning to feed?" asks Sawyer.

"Well, not Mr. Gabe. Strict instructions not to let him eat in case he needs to get an X-ray or something. Victoria is in the kitchen cooking up a storm. I think it is her way of burning off nervous energy. I was not going to turn down her cookin'. Best in the county." He winks at Gabe. "Don't you tell my momma I said so!"

Sawyer takes a sandwich, sits down across from his uncle, and takes a bite. He didn't realize how hungry he was. He looks at the clock and sees it is nearly 1:00 already. Well past lunchtime. He swallows and then says, "I think this story starts with me." Sawyer recounts his morning conversation with his uncle, the subsequent firing of the four fieldhands, and the ensuing brawl. "Then Pearl starts ringing the bell like crazy. We knew it was something bad. She hadn't rung the bell like that since Scarlet set the kitchen on fire when she was seven."

"How well do you know these men, Mr. Gabe?" asks Grady.

"They came on maybe six, eight months ago. Started out fine, but then they were slacking off. Talked to Roger about it, and he said he would handle it. Honestly, that is all I know. The last couple of months, I have been working on my own projects, and then, there is Dead Doe. Roger will know more."

Sawyer looks at his uncle and asks, "What happened to you?"

"I was working in the field. Had the tractor running nicely. Two of the fieldhands waved at me. Greg and Stacey. I slowed the tractor down and picked up the walkie-talkie. I figured something must be going on. I couldn't reach anyone, so I switched the dial to the house line and radioed Pearl. She picked up. They must have seen me with the walkie-talkie because they started running toward me and jumped up on either side of the tractor. Greg pulled me down. That is when I hit my head. I had enough time before they reached me to tell Pearl to send help. I think I shouted 9-1-1! Stacey took the tractor keys out of the ignition and threw them somewhere. Greg pulled me a few feet away when they heard the bell ringing. He said some choice words to express his anger, then kicked me solidly in the stomach before they took off." Gabe signals Sawyer for some more brandy. "I got myself to rights. Sort of dragged myself over to the grove of trees."

"He was standing there when I got there," says Sawyer.

"I saw them boys tear down the front drive. And when Mr. Gabe called, I just knew something was wrong." Pearl is standing in the doorway, listening. "And when Mr. Gabe screamed '9-1-1!' the only thing I could think to do was ring the bell."

"And I called the sheriff's department while Momma was ringing the bell." Victoria walks around the corner with a plate of cookies. "I just checked my phone. It was 11:46."

"Have both of you been listening the entire time?" asks Sawyer.

"Of course. This involves all of us," says Pearl.

"You're right. It does. And everyone is safe and accounted for but Scarlet. Any ideas where she might be?" asks Sawyer.

"No, no clue," Pearl replies.

Glancing at the clock, it suddenly dawns on Sawyer that she is probably on her way to Wisteria to meet him. Crap! As nonchalantly as possible, Sawyer gets a couple of sandwiches and cookies. "I am going to take these out to John. He deserves this and more. Glad he was on our side today."

Sawyer walks out the backdoor and can't spot John's roost anywhere. He whistles. John whistles back and emerges from behind one of the azalea bushes, almost in full bloom. "All quiet out here, Colonel. Any word?"

Sawyer updates John on the current situation. "Listen, I have a favor to ask. I was supposed to meet my sister Scarlet today at 4:00. It's a little B and B in Wisteria called the Whistle Stop. I can't reach her, and I can't go out there either. Do you mind driving over there and telling her what is going on? Discreetly."

"Sure. I know the place. Great couple who owns it. How much of this do you want her to know?"

"All of it. Once I know where the rest of the fieldhands are, I will feel better. I don't want to leave until all souls are accounted for. Hopefully, Malcolm is helping Roger with that."

John takes the sandwiches and cookies. "I need a vehicle. I left the four-by-four out in the field with yours. My truck is back at the cabin. And I am not driving the pink Caddy."

For the first time in hours, Sawyer cracks a smile. "Take Uncle Gabe's Mercedes. That should be manly enough for you. Keys are in the lockbox." Sawyer steps closer to John and leans forward slightly.

"And, John. The minute you see her, please have her text Pearl." He slaps John on the arm. "Thanks, man. For all of it. Laura Lynne told me I could count on you in a crunch. She was right."

"My pleasure, Colonel. Like I said earlier, Mr. Gabe's been mighty good to me."

16

Chapter Sixteen

John goes to the barn, and Sawyer sees the sheriff's car coming back to the house. Roger is not with him. Sawyer waits while the young man parks the vehicle and gets out. "Where's Roger?"

Smiling with the face of an angel, the kid is no more than 20 years old, he reports back. "Left him out in the west field. He wanted to look around a bit more. I didn't see the harm in it."

Sawyer's alarm bells go off. He looks at the kid and starts barking orders. "Get Grady and tell him to meet me there. Give me your keys." He kicks himself for letting John go to Wisteria and leaving before all this, whatever it is, is completely resolved.

"Sir..." The young deputy stands, gawking as Sawyer takes his keys from his hand and jumps into the cruiser. He shouts, "Tell Grady!" as he slams the door shut. He finds the sirens and turns them on as he takes off across the yard to the fields. It takes him less than five minutes to get there, and he immediately realizes he is too late. Roger's lifeless body is hanging from the front right tire of the tractor Gabe was driving. The two four-wheelers are nowhere to be seen.

"Shit, shit, shit!" Sawyer hits the steering wheel before he stops and parks the car. He glances in his rearview mirror and sees Grady barreling down the dirt road in his momma's pink Cadillac. He is pissed. He pulls up beside Sawyer and parks. Before he can blast Sawyer for stealing his car, he sees Roger strung up. It is as close to a lynching as Grady has ever seen.

Both men exit the vehicles, and Sawyer hands Grady the radio. Grady calls it in and then looks at Sawyer. "Why did they kill Roger?"

"Well, we have to figure he knew too much. About something. This whole thing reeks. I have been thinking about it. The excess numbers of men, the proximity to the abandoned Twin Oaks, the synchronicity of today's attack. This was planned. Almost like a contingency plan. And I think Roger knew or was somehow involved."

Grady's radio cackles to life. Grady squeezes the button and says, "Grady here. What's up?"

"Pearl wants Mr. Beauregard back at the house. Dr. Treelove just arrived."

Grady holds his hand out and gestures toward the pink Caddy. "Your chariot awaits. And Sawyer, if you ever steal my deputy's vehicle again, I will personally arrest you. Friend or no friend."

Sawyer grins. "That boy nearly wet his pants when I charged after him for the keys to the car. He can't be more than twelve. Aren't there any men who want to work with you?"

Grady sighs. "He is Prissa's baby sister's son. Fresh out of the academy. Green. He's a good enough kid, but this will mess him up some, so go easy on him. The department will do a thorough investigation of his conduct, and it won't be pretty."

Grady and Sawyer hear the sirens coming in their direction. It sounds like the entire fire department, an ambulance, and the sheriff's department are on the way. Truthfully, Sawyer is glad for the additional manpower. Two thousand acres is a lot of territory to cover. There are plenty of places to hide. "Sawyer, before you go. Malcolm is at the bunkhouse with some of the men. You might want to stop and see them. We need to talk to all of them, so don't let them leave."

"Will do. Thanks, Grady. Glad you're here."

Sawyer gets into the Cadillac with a sigh. What a day. He decides to check on the men before going to the main house. Maybe he can learn something. He pulls up, and the bunkhouse looks deserted. Malcolm comes to the door. He is still fully armed. "Hey, Sawyer. I found some of the men. Not too many, though. From the sounds of things, I think Roger was into something. Maybe over his head."

"I have to agree. I just found his body strung over Uncle Gabe's tractor. He was gutted like a pig and hanging from a wheel. Whatever he knew or did went with him to the grave."

"Roger is dead?" Malcolm asks.

"I'm afraid so," says Sawyer as he climbs the stairs to the bunkhouse. He can't believe he was here just a few hours ago. It seems like a lifetime. "Let me talk to the men. Tell them what's going on. The sheriff's office will want to speak with them and find out details."

Sawyer walks into the bunkhouse. There are ten men sitting around the kitchen table. Sawyer recognizes a few of the older hands, but most of the guys are new faces. "Everybody okay? Anybody hurt? I have a doctor at the house, so now is the time to tell me if you need his services."

"Jake there sliced up his hand pretty good on the barbed wire fence. Probably needs stitches." The man speaking stands up and extends his hand to Sawyer. "Colonel. Lance Gilbert."

Sawyer shakes his hand. "Thanks, Lance. Anybody else?"

There is silence at the table. Sawyer pulls up a chair and tells the men of the day's events. He decides not to leave anything out. At this point, he cares more about their safety than he does the gossip mill. When he is done, Lance kind of raises his hand in question. "What is it, Lance?"

"I have been a hand here on and off for twenty years. I questioned Roger about why he was hiring so many people, and he told me to mind my own business. Funny thing was, lot of them seemed to work the night shift. It wasn't until you got here that the men started working in the day. Though, I didn't see too many of them in the field. I asked Roger where they went all the time. He told me Mr. Gabe had them working on a special project."

The other field hands nod in agreement, each adding their version of the same story. Finally, the talk seemed to die down. "Listen, I need to ask y'all to stick around. At least until the sheriff gets done speaking to you. Once all that is completed, if you want to move on to another farm, I will write you a check for what you are owed and ask no questions. Those of you who choose to stay, well, there will be plenty of work over the coming weeks."

Sawyer excuses himself and goes back out on the porch, with Malcolm following behind him. "Thanks, Malcolm, for all you did. It's been a hell of a day."

"It certainly has. It certainly has."

Sawyer walks down the stairs. "Can you bring Jake over to the house and let the doc take a look at his hand? I'll have Victoria make up some food and send it back over. Lance seems like a good man. If you agree, let him watch the boys for a while. Leave him the walkie-talkie. I'm not sure when you can leave, but as soon as you can, I know you want to get home."

"Naw, not really. My brother and his boys can handle it. I think you probably need me more here," Malcolm replies.

"You're probably right." Sawyer looks over the fields and turns back to his old friend. "Thanks again, Malcolm. I'll see you back at the house."

Sawyer drives the Cadillac back to the barn and parks. As he walks to the back porch and up the steps, Sawyer turns around to see if he can spot the cars in the west field. He can't see them, but he can hear them. He hopes they aren't tearing up the fields too badly. Then, shaking his head at his callousness, he goes to check on his uncle.

Sawyer goes into the study as the doctor is closing his bag. "Vincent, this is my nephew. Sawyer, this is Dr. Vincent Treelove. He tells me I am fit enough to stay home."

Dr. Treelove smiles at Sawyer. Sawyer is surprised at how young he is. But then, anyone under 50 seems young to Sawyer these days. "Mr. Gabe, be honest. What I said, Mr. Sawyer, is that he is able to stay home as long he follows my instructions. The bang on his head is the biggest concern. I doctored the cut, but a head injury can be fatal.

Any signs and symptoms, blurry vision, confusion, swelling, or fever, he needs to go to the hospital immediately. His ribs are bruised. Nothing appears to be broken. Without an X-ray, I can't be sure."

"I'm good, Doc. No X-rays necessary."

"You are stubborn as a mule. But he's right. Even if cracked, there is nothing to do but wait for them to heal. So, for now, I am comfortable leaving him home. He will heal better here anyway." Vincent looks at Sawyer. "Anything I can do for you?"

Sawyer looks down at himself for the first time. He has blood and dirt down the front of him. "The blood is my uncle's. I am not hurt. But there is a field hand, name of Jake. He sliced his hand pretty good. Malcolm is bringing him by for you to take a look if you don't mind."

"Don't mind a bit. Okay, if I just leave my stuff set up here?"

Gabe slowly moves to stand. He has been sitting at the edge of the sofa for his examination. "I plan to take a shower and change. Maybe have some coffee and food. Now that I have the green light, Victoria can feed me." He looks over his shoulder as he walks gingerly toward the downstairs guest bed and bathroom. "Sawyer, run upstairs and grab some clothes for me, please."

Pearl materializes at the door once again. "I got him Sawyer. Why don't you go take a shower yourself? It's going to be a long night."

"I think I will. Listen, can Victoria rustle up some food for the farmhands? There are ten of them in the bunkhouse. Malcolm and Jake can take it over there when they are done with the doc here."

"I don't think it will be a problem. Oh, and before I forget, Scarlet texted that she is fine. She received the information you sent? Said thank you, and she would be in touch."

"Great! Everyone is accounted for. I think I will take that shower, Pearl."

Sawyer goes upstairs to his room. He strips to his waist and looks at his knife wound. It is open again. He walks to his intercom and buzzes downstairs. "Doc, do you mind coming to my room? Think I could use your services." Without waiting for a reply, Sawyer walks to the head of the stairs. Dr. Treelove sees him and begins his ascent.

Laughing, Dr. Treelove says, "I thought God himself needed my services. Don't think I have ever been to a house with an actual intercom. I guess you probably need one here. How many square feet do y'all have?"

"Nobody knows for sure, but a rough estimate is 15,000. Many of the rooms are closed off. The whole house has not been in use since I was a child." Sawyer turns in the hallway, exposing his left side to Dr. Treelove. "Got this knife wound a week or so back, thought it was healing nicely, but I think maybe I tore it open again. Take a look?"

"A knife wound? Okay, is there somewhere with better lighting?" Sawyer simply walks over to the wall and flips on a switch. The entryway's chandelier lights up the space. Vincent gazes with awe at the glass fixture. "Wow. Just wow. I have heard all about it, but this is the first time I have ever seen it. It's gorgeous." Tearing his eyes away from the 19th-century Russian masterpiece, he focuses on Sawyer's arm.

The chandelier is another one of Grandma Birdie's treasures from her European tour. Sawyer looks at it with fresh eyes. He has never known the entryway to have any other fixture, so he is always surprised when visitors are awestruck by his home. "Ouch. That stings a bit."

"I imagine so." He places gauze on the wound and stands up straight. "You need an antibiotic and stitches. Any allergies I should know about?"

"None, Doc. You carry all that in your little bag?"

"And my car. I am what is nowadays called a concierge physician. I basically do house calls. It is a new thing they are trying out in rural areas as a way to keep people cared for and out of the hospital." He dabs some alcohol around Sawyer's wound and injects lidocaine to numb the area. "We can do this standing, but it may be more comfortable for you to lie down."

"Standing is fine, Doc. Just do what you have to do."

"I see stubborn as a mule is a familial trait."

Sawyer grins as Vincent stitches up his arm. "Truer words were never spoken. Wait until you meet my mother."

"I know your mother quite well, in fact. Fine woman. Mr. Gabe became my patient through her." Vincent tapes up the gauze and retrieves his bag. He pulls out a vial and syringe. "Giving you a dose of Rocephin. If it continues to be red and swollen, or you start having a fever, call me. We don't want you to get a nasty infection. But this should do it." He looks expectantly at Sawyer. Sawyer sighs and drops his drawers, exposing his right hip. Vincent is quick and efficient. "All done. Try to keep the gauze dry." He hands a box of saran wrap to Sawyer. "Here, I will show you the first time then you can do it yourself." Vincent rolls the saran wrap around his arm and over his dressing.

"Handy. Thanks."

"Nothing to it. Knife wounds are usually something I have to report. Can I take it from you that this has already been completed?"

"You can. Military issued."

"Very good then. Now, to find this Jake fella. I must say our first meeting has been quite entertaining, at least from a medical standpoint," Vincent says jokingly.

"Glad I could brighten your day, Doc. Feel free to snag a cookie from the kitchen. Victoria has been cooking and baking all day."

Vincent smiles and packs up his case walking slowly down the staircase while keeping his eyes on Grandma Birdie's chandelier. Sawyer walks back to his room and turns on the shower. He likes Vincent. Quirky but calm. Nothing today rattled him. Sawyer likes that in a man, especially given his previous employment.

The hot water from the shower feels divine. Sawyer closes his eyes and lets the grime and blood wash off him and swirl down the drain. He reaches for his soap bar and inhales the scent of sandalwood and patchouli, another one of his recent purchases. He takes the time to wash his hair. Stepping out of the shower, he sees himself in the mirror. Not bad for a man approaching double nickels.

He hears the intercom cackling and walks into his bedroom. "Sawyer, the state police are here. Mr. Gabe asked me to call Mr. Lally and he is also on the way. Can you come down and deal with this, please?" asks Pearl.

"On the way." Reprieve over, Sawyer quickly dresses and double-times the stairs. He comes into the kitchen where Pearl and Victoria are busily making plates of food. "Where are they?"

"I was not letting them into this house until you could deal with them. I told them to wait on the porch and that is where they are." She points toward the front of the house. "The front porch."

Sawyer does an about-face and walks to the front door. He girds his loins and every other part of him before opening the door. He hears the front gate ringing. "Pearl, can you get that?"

"Absolutely not! It's reporters. They arrived about the time you went upstairs. They can stay outside the gate. None of their business what's going on here." Sawyer rolls his eyes. Great, reporters.

17

Chapter Seventeen

Sawyer sits down on the back porch with his gun next to him. The house has been asleep for hours, but Sawyer stands guard against any unwanted guests. He has a distinct feeling he has not seen the last of Freddie and his gang. Until those boys are behind bars, Sawyer imagines he will not have a restful night's sleep. He gets up and paces the circumference of the house once again. He can see a glow of light from the west field. He knows it's from the crime scene. A police officer is standing guard until forensics has completed their work. They won't arrive until the morning.

He circles to the left side of the house and looks toward the horizon toward the Jackson's homestead. Pearl and Victoria left with Malcolm a few hours ago. Sawyer smiles as he remembers the conversation with Pearl. He and his uncle were sitting on the back porch, rocking, when the two women came out.

"Sawyer, Mr. Gabe. Victoria and I are heading home. Malcolm is coming to get us. Y'all need anything before we leave?"

"No. We are good," says Sawyer, "Thank you for everything. I don't know what we would have done without your bell ringing. You saved the day." Sawyer stands up from his chair. "Why don't y'all take tomorrow off? Y'all worked plenty hard today. No need to come back tomorrow."

Sawyer can almost feel Pearl rolling her eyes. "Me and Victoria will be here as usual." Malcolm pulls around in the farm truck, and the two women walk down the stairs.

Sawyer escorts them to the vehicle and walks over to the driver's side while they climb in the truck. "How are you holding up, Malcolm? The boys all right in the bunkhouse?"

"Just fine. The deputy and police officers took everyone's statements and then told them they could leave. All ten decided to stay. I gave them assignments for the morning. I haven't seen John since this afternoon, so took it upon myself. I figure it's better if their hands are busy. Plenty of work in the fields." He looks over toward the back porch. "How is Mr. Gabe?"

"Sore and tired. Sad about Roger. They worked together for a long time and were good friends."

"Any ideas what this was all about?" asks Malcolm.

"Just speculation. There are no true leads. Nobody has seen or heard from Freddie and his gang. Uncle Gabe seems to think they have headed for the hills. I think not. I think they're still close by."

"Hmm. Well, let me get the women home. I plan to sleep out at the bunkhouse with the men. Stay close by in case you need me."

"Thanks, Malcolm. I appreciate it." He lightly pats Pearl on the arm and gives her a gentle smile. She rubs the top of his hand in acknowledgment. "Have a good night."

Sawyer picks up his pace and rounds the front of the house. There are plenty of places to hide in his uncle's garden. He takes a stroll around the azalea bushes, shining his green light as he scans the area. Seeing nothing, he continues on his walk. He goes to the right side of the house and gazes at the horizon toward the cabin and John. John was a lifesaver today, though his errand to see Scarlet took much longer than expected. He had tried to keep the information from his uncle, but the man is not stupid.

He scans the yard, where the light from the house turns into darkness. He hears a whistle. He smiles and returns the sound. Sawyer watches as John emerges from the darkness. "Hey, Colonel. I wanted to check in before I went to the cabin. All well here?"

"Where the hell have you been? You should have been home hours ago. Did everything with Scarlet go okay?" Sawyer asks with concern.

"Well, the telling took a lot longer than expected. She was visibly upset. I didn't want to leave her there alone, so I hung around until I thought it was safe for her to drive. Then I followed her back to her house. I watched her turn into her driveway just to be on the safe side."

Sawyer goes into the yard. Scarlet is not an overly emotional person. "Upset how?"

"Just crying and stuff. I don't know. Something seemed to be bothering her. She was shocked to see me instead of you. I don't know Sawyer. I just thought I better stick around until I knew she was all right. You might want to check on her yourself."

"Okay, thank you. Sorry for snapping at you. I appreciate all you've done today. Tomorrow is bound to be equally taxing. We both need to get some sleep. You good at the cabin? Malcolm is staying at the bunkhouse tonight. I am sure there is room for you too, if you prefer."

"No. I like my space. Besides, it is smarter for me to be on that side of Tea Olive. I'll know if anyone gets too close."

Sawyer holds out his hand for a handshake. John grabs it. "Thanks again, man. Really. I owe you one."

"Let's call it even. Have a good night." He indicates the walkie-talkie on his hip. "You keep in touch, and I will do the same." Sawyer watches as John walks into the darkness toward his little cabin in the woods. Twenty minutes later, Sawyer receives an "Arrived. All clear. Over and out" from John.

Completing the circle, Sawyer watches as the horizon begins to lighten. "Hello to the house!" Sawyer turns toward the voice and sees Malcolm approaching. "Good morning! Sleep any?"

Sawyer indicates his gun and shakes his head in the negative. "No, man. My gut is telling me this is not over, but it was quiet last night. How about you?"

"Caught a few winks. Want me to keep watch for a while? I don't mind. I left Lance at the bunkhouse. He knows to keep the boys in line."

"If you don't mind, I'm going to take you up on the offer. I checked on Uncle Gabe about two hours ago. He's sleeping soundly. I want to let him sleep as long as he can. Today is bound to be another long one. I need a run and a shower before the day gets away from me. Plus, it has the added benefit of helping me clear my head."

"Got ya covered. I will be here when you return."

Sawyer quickly changes into his running shoes and exchanges his rifle for a handgun. He straps a chest halter over his shirt and secures his gun. Last night, Sawyer went into the vault and did a thorough inventory of the guns. He was amazed at the collection and took all the best pieces. He found boxes upon boxes of ammunition. It was as if his father had been preparing for war. Sawyer appreciated his foresight.

Sawyer begins his trek around the perimeter of the farm. It is a six-mile run but can be double that amount if Sawyer takes all the trails. Sawyer figures this is as good a way as any to look for Freddie and his gang. Or, at the very least, determine where the gaps in his security are. Grady's comment about Twin Oaks made him start thinking about his vulnerability on that side of the farm. The Cunningham's estate runs along Cotton Mill Road and bumps up next to Tea Olive. The river runs along the back of the property. There is a long steel fence and security along the front of the property. But now, with Twin Oaks abandoned, the property line that separates the two estates is no longer secure. The only people in that direction are the Jacksons, but their place is closer to the river, leaving acres of unsecured space.

Sawyer runs down the drive toward the front gate. He is pleased with the level of security. He is not so pleased to see a few reporters' vans. To avoid any chance of a meet-up, he veers to the right and cuts across the property behind the tree line. Once clear, he resumes his run along the fence, checking for any possible breaches. All appears secure.

He takes another right and runs along the property line until he reaches the area he perceives as the most vulnerable. At one point in the very distant past, there was a stone wall erected between the two plantations. Over the years, the stone wall had eroded and not been rebuilt. The remnants are clearly visible. As Sawyer scans the wall line, he sees the two four-wheelers that were missing from the west field irretrievably stuck in a ditch. The two drivers had attempted to escape over the embedded rock and were unsuccessful.

Upon closer inspection, Sawyer notes what appears to be a blood trail. He hops the low-slung wall and follows it for about 100 yards. It abruptly stops. From the track marks, Sawyer surmises the two were picked up in a vehicle.

Sawyer returns the way he came and continues his run. He sees nothing else of note until he makes it to the west field. There, cordoned off and under a tent, is Gabe's tractor and Roger's body. Grady sips coffee and talks to the new sheriff when he spots Sawyer and waves him over. "Sawyer, allow me to introduce you to the sheriff. He took over after Bubba Westerman. Jerry Thomas, meet Sawyer Avery Beauregard III. Sawyer, Jerry Thomas." The two men shake hands.

"Sorry, it is under these circumstances, Sawyer", Jerry says. "Your family is certainly getting their share of hard times these days."

"Nice to meet you, Jerry. And, yes, we are. Any word on Freddie and his gang?" asks Sawyer.

"Nothing. We've checked all the local potential hang-outs and have an APB out for his truck. Some of your boys were able to give a good description, and one even remembered the license plate. It was an ego plate "IISNBR1."' Grady answers and shakes his head in amazement at the stupidity of some folks.

"Listen. Last night, you got me thinking, Grady, about the vulnerabilities on the farm," Sawyer says. "This morning, I decided to check the perimeter, and you were right. I found one of the escape routes. You know that ditch we used to play in as boys near the old stone wall along Twin Oaks' side? You remember where we would meet up with Buck?"

"I do. If you follow the path, it leads you to the main drive. Or it used to. Not too sure now." Grady looks curiously at Sawyer. "Not too many people would know about that spot. What makes you think these two farmhands did?"

"Found the two missing four-wheelers stuck in the gully. There's a trail of blood. I followed it about 100 yards, and it stops. Figure someone picked them up in a vehicle. There are tire tracks. Probably worth a look."

Jerry presses the button on his shoulder radio. "Beth Ann? Send Buddy over to Tea Olive. Has the CSI team arrived yet?"

Beth Ann's voice crackles over the radio, "Estimated arrival is 0800. Buddy has been dispatched. Over and out."

Jerry checks his watch. "That gives us about 15 minutes. You mind showing me this place?" With a sigh Sawyer realizes his run for the day is over. He climbs in the sheriff's car and directs him to the four-wheelers. The sheriff walks around several times, then points in the direction of Twin Oaks. "The main house is down this path?"

Grady responds, "Merriwether. Yes. It's a good walk, though."

"Merriwether, right. I can't get used to people naming their houses." Jerry says. "We drove through the area several times last night. There were no signs of vehicles or people present, but that doesn't mean much. Need a search warrant to enter the house." He presses the button on his shoulder set again. "Beth Ann, get Chandler Monroe on the line. I need a search warrant." He looks at Sawyer. "What are you thinking?"

Sawyer shrugs. "Drugs. Gambling. Prostitution. Could be any number of things, but drugs make the most sense. Drop off the drugs along the river. Transport to Merriwether, which is now abandoned and in litigation. Break the drugs up and repackage them. Sell to the drug dealers." Sawyer stands with hands on hips. "It's brilliant. And way above Freddie's brain capacity. No way he could pull this off. He's just a lackey."

Sawyer watches as the front gate opens and several vehicles enter, including Buddy. Jerry walks to the drive and flags Buddy down as the rest of the caravan make their way to the west field. Buddy parks the car and gets out, walking with Jerry to come face-to-face with Sawyer. He has none of the bluster he displayed yesterday. He takes his hat off, his eyes downcast. "Colonel Beauregard, my sincerest apologies for yesterday's debacle."

"Look at me when you speak, Deputy." Sawyer crosses his arms in front of his chest as Buddy glances nervously at Jerry. Jerry stands to the side and says nothing. Buddy squares his shoulders and lifts his eyes to Sawyer, repeating his earlier apology. Sawyer holds out his hand, and Buddy grasps it like a lifeline. "We all make mistakes, son. It's what we do with them that matters. There was no way of knowing Roger would be killed in that field." He slaps him on the arm. "And I am sorry I stole your car."

Sawyer departs, allowing the two men to cordon off the new crime scene site and work on their search warrant. Sawyer decides to sprint to the house in an effort to get a bit more of a workout in. Malcolm is probably wondering where in the hell he is. When Sawyer rounds the back of the house, he sees not Malcolm but John standing sentry. "Everything okay, Colonel?"

"Yeah. Where's Malcolm?"

"He went to fetch Pearl and Victoria. He asked me to stand watch until you got back. Did you find out anything new?"

Sawyer tells John about the four-wheelers and his suppositions about drug smuggling.

John responds, "Could be. Could also be sex trafficking. Could be both, as they both work the same way. Supply and demand."

"I sure hope not. Listen, thanks for keeping an eye out. I can handle it from here. What are your plans for the day?"

"I want to vet the farmhands who are still here. Maybe we can talk later this afternoon about my recommendations there. Also, I thought it might be worth tossing the bunks of the men who disappeared yesterday. Might find something. That work?"

"I should have thought of that yesterday. Let me know what you find. I'm getting a shower." Sawyer looks over his shoulder as he walks up the porch steps. Pearl and Victoria get out of the farm truck, and John jumps in the back. The two men wave as they drive away. "Good morning, ladies!"

"Morning. How are you? And Mr. Gabe?" asks Victoria.

"I need coffee. Not sure about my uncle. He was not up when I left this morning. How about y'all?" Sawyer hasn't moved from the porch step. Pearl marches up the stairs around him obviously ready to work.

"Had a right fine time last night with the house full. Momma enjoyed the extra company. But honestly, I was ready to be here. Too many men in too small a house. Reminded me of my growing-up years. Testosterone everywhere," Pearl huffs as she walks into the house.

Victoria starts laughing. "Momma is just mad because the boys used all the toilet paper, and nobody thought to buy anymore. She liked to have a fit." Pearl pops her head back around the porch door.

"What sane man uses the last of the toilet paper and doesn't go and get some more, *knowing* there are women in the house? Idiot boys." She goes back into the house as Sawyer and Victoria look at each other and then burst out laughing.

"Come on, Victoria. Let me help you with your packages. This idiot boy needs a shower."

The rest of the day creates a routine for the week. Sawyer would keep watch at night, ensuring his uncle's and his safety. Malcolm would relieve him in the morning so that he could take his run and scope out the property. When Sawyer returned, John would be standing sentry and Malcolm would arrive with Pearl and Victoria. Gabe was sore but mobile. He spent his time resting and taking short walks through his gardens. In the early afternoon, Sawyer would retire to his room to catch a bit of shut-eye. Then, he would do it all over again.

By Saturday, the crime scenes were secured, and the forensics was completed. Roger was hauled off to the morgue. Grady stopped by every day with word on the investigation. Nothing much had happened. The search warrant was unable to be executed as they lacked probable cause. Freddie and his gang had not been located yet. The four-wheelers were dusted for prints and returned to their rightful place in the barn. And tossing the contents of the bunkhouse turned out to be of little value. Much to everyone's frustration, the case was rapidly growing cold.

On Saturday afternoon, Sawyer goes to the kitchen, where Pearl and Victoria are busy cooking for the family and the remaining farmhands. "Ladies, tomorrow is Sunday. Let's all take a break. There is really nothing more to be done at this point. Agreed?"

"You get no argument from me. Glad to see everyone pull out and things get back to some semblance of normal," says Pearl.

Victoria nods her head in agreement. "I will make a tomato pie for your supper tonight, but you're out of coffee. I need to make a run to town and pick up a few things." She begins taking off her apron.

"Just make a list, and I'll get it. Give me a chance to see what gossip is brewing at the Café," said Sawyer.

"If you're going, stop at Wheelbarrow Books and pick up Mr. Gabe's order. Diane called yesterday to let us know she had his books. She heard about his accident and offered to bring them by. This will save her the trip."

"Got it. Anything else just put it on the list. Then, finish up here and go home."

"What about Mr. Gabe? I don't want to leave him alone."

Gabe barks from the doorway, "Y'all are nothing but a bunch of worrywarts! I'm fine. In fact, I plan to take the side-by-side out and check on John and the boys. Feeling fit as a fiddle."

"There you have it, ladies. The men can handle it." Sawyer winks at Pearl. "At least temporarily."

Pearl pulls the dishcloth off her shoulder and swats Sawyer with it. "Get on with your own self! Ain't got time for your nonsense, now."

Sawyer follows Gabe to the mudroom and watches as he puts on his boots. Sawyer hands him the rifle propped up by the door. "I know you can take care of yourself, but I want you armed when you're outside." He pulls a walkie-talkie from his back pocket. "And with communication. At all times. Promise me."

"Not a hard promise to make. Planned to ask you for both. I'm no fool, Sawyer. I won't ever be unprepared in the fields again." He opens the door and walks outside with Sawyer on his heels. "The rest of the boys armed?"

"Just Malcolm, John, and Lance are carrying. The rest have knives and other types of weapons. But they're all staying close together for now. They should be in the east field today." Sawyer watches as his uncle climbs into the side-by-side. "I almost lost you once; let's not have a repeat."

"Don't you worry about me, son. You're the one going to town today. I suggest you watch your back."

Sawyer slaps the hood a few times and steps back as his uncle starts the engine. "Probably very sound advice." He waves as his uncle drives away.

18

Chapter Eighteen

Sawyer drives off the GMC lot in a brand-new Yukon, fully loaded. He'll need to arrange for someone to pick up his momma's pink Cadillac, but Sawyer promises himself it will not be him. He smiles as he runs his hands along the steering wheel. Sawyer has not owned a car in 15 years. Today, he splurged and could not be happier with his purchase. And it has the added bonus of making him feel considerably less conspicuous than he did when he drove into town this morning.

He parks his new car at Wheelbarrow Books and walks through the front door to the sound of wind chimes announcing his entrance. Diane and Mandy are standing at the counter. Sawyer waves as he walks to the back of the shop. He appreciates the smell of patchouli and the two beautiful women who greet him.

"Sawyer! It's good to see you. How is Mr. Gabe?" asks Diane.

"Right as rain and ready for some new literature. Pearl mentioned you have an order for my uncle," answers Sawyer.

"Mandy darling, can you go to the back and pick up Mr. Gabe's order? It should be near the front," says Diane.

"Sure, Mom. Be right back," says Mandy.

"I told Pearl I was happy to bring the books by the house. It was no trouble," says Diane

"It was a good excuse to leave for a few hours. We have been hunkered down for the last couple of days. Good to have a break."

"I bet. I heard through the grapevine y'all had a bit of trouble out your way. Seems like y'all can't seem to get away from it. If there is ever anything I can do to help, just please let me know." Mandy returns to the counter with a stack of books. "Thanks, love."

"You can come have a cup of coffee with me." Sawyer is as surprised as she is by his invitation.

"Umm, well, Saturday is usually pretty busy…" Diane stammers and blushes. She looks for help from her daughter.

"Don't look at me. I think you should go." Mandy pointedly looks around the empty store. "I think I can handle the crowd."

"Well, okay…if you're sure." Diane walks from behind the counter, and Sawyer is struck by her womanly curves and ethereal quality. She has a Stevie Nicks air about her. Sawyer has always been a Fleetwood Mac fan.

Sawyer steps to the side, "After you." He places his hand at the base of her spine. He feels the immediate shiver that runs through her back. How very interesting. It appears he is not the only one feeling the vibes here. He follows her through the side doors and into the back room of the café.

He has forgotten the two buildings connected.

Sawyer feels the stares and hears the whispered comments as they make their way to the front of the café. Sawyer takes Diane's hand. She starts but does not immediately jerk away. He leans down and whispers in her ear. "Forgive my forwardness, but I have a plan to create new gossip for the grapevine. A diversion of sorts."

To his surprise and delight, Diane moves her head slightly and allows her lips to brush his unshaven cheek. "An excellent strategy. I bet you are a good chess player. Ever beat your uncle?"

Laughing and smiling as he pulls her closer, he answers, "Not yet."

"Me either. I do have hope, though."

He brushes his mouth along her ear and feels her shiver as he whispers intimately, "It's always good to have a dream." He pulls back and, breaking contact, ushers her to the front counter. He smiles to himself as he glances at the currently teepeed zipper of his pants. Definitely feeling the vibes.

"Sawyer? What would you like?" Diane asks.

"Whatever. You choose. I normally get black."

She gives him a flirty look and glances down where his eyes were only moments ago. The seductive look on her face nearly brings him to his knees. "Gretta, we will have two Espresso Con Panna. Thanks."

"I'll have it right up. Y'all go ahead and have a seat. I'll bring it to you," replies the ever- efficient Gretta.

Diane shows Sawyer to an intimate corner for two. It looks like a reading nook in Wheelbarrow Books. "Mandy and I designed this space. Mrs. Gaillard loved our concept in the bookstore and asked us to do the same for her." She looks around. "I love to come here and see where people sit. Most of the time, the book nooks are being used."

Sawyer can't take his eyes off Diane's expressive face. She glances his way and laughs. "You're staring."

"You are fascinating." Gretta appears carrying two cups of espresso. "Thank you, Gretta." With a wink to Diane, she smiles and flounces away.

"Gretta is best friends with Mandy. If I know my daughter, and I do, she is texting furiously. And as a warning, we are probably getting our picture taken by Gretta."

Without looking up from his espresso cup, which has a pretty whipped cream topper, Sawyer smirks. "By more than Gretta, if I had to guess. You're sitting with the currently notorious Beauregard prodigal son who has not one but two dead bodies unaccounted for on his property. You're going to get a reputation."

"Considering this is the first coffee date I've had since my husband died, feels like that could be a good time."

"Are the men around here dumb and blind?" asks Sawyer.

"I take that as a compliment. No, neither. I have just not been interested." She sips her espresso. "Until now." Her comments are without guile. Sawyer appreciates her straightforward approach. "What about you? Currently dating?"

"No. And to clear the air, I haven't been in a serious relationship in years. I have gone out from time to time. I enjoy the company of women. But to your question, the answer is no." Sawyer takes a sip of espresso and continues. "I think all that is about to change, though. You up for dinner? Say tomorrow night. You and Mandy can be my guests at Tea Olive. Uncle Gabe would love to see you both."

"Sawyer, are we still putting on a show, or is this a real invitation?" Diane relaxes back into the comfy chair in their book nook.

"I quit playing the minute you held my hand. The invitation stands."

"Then we accept. Or at least I do. My daughter's social calendar is much more robust than my own."

"Why don't you have her bring a date? Or a friend? Plenty of space at the table. Besides, it might be more fun for her if she has someone her age. Right now, Uncle Gabe and I are bachin' it together. Be fun to have some young people around." He reaches across the table and pushes some of the hair that has fallen out of her bun away from her eyes. He tucks it behind her ear. "But no pressure."

Diane's cheeks turn pink, and her eyes smolder. She clears her throat. "This is new territory for me. I meant it when I said I have not been with a man, or a woman, for that matter, since my husband died 13 years ago. I have no idea what I am doing."

"That makes two of us. Why don't we figure it out together? It'll be fun. And I promise, your reputation is safe with me."

"I doubt that. I seriously do."

Sawyer turns the conversation to a safer subject—one less likely to cause his dick to explode. He asks her about her bookstore, and Diane's entire demeanor lights up. She regales him with tales of customers, author signings, and competition with the internet. She glances at her phone. "I'm sorry. It's Mandy. The store is busy, and she needs help. I need to go." She stands up, and he does the same. He catches her hands in his.

"This has been lovely, Diane. Come by tomorrow night at 6. Casual attire. Bring Mandy."

She hesitates and then leans in for a brief hug, kissing his cheek as she pulls away. "I feel like a crazy teenager. I'm trusting you, Sawyer. We will be there." He watches her leave and glances at his watch. He and Diane have been at the Café for over an hour. He has one more errand to run before he goes back home. It's probably fruitless, but he figures it is worth a try.

He decides to walk to the sheriff's department and leaves his new truck parked in the now-packed parking lot of Wheelbarrow Books. The walk is only a few blocks. It gives him some time to enjoy the shops along Main Street. He is pleasantly surprised by the revitalization efforts. He walks into the sheriff's department, and it takes a moment to recognize the place has not changed much. His butt used to warm that very bench sitting across from the front desk, waiting for his father to pick him up after a night of revelry.

He walks up to the desk and rings the bell. To his surprise, Grady comes out of his office at the sound. "Sawyer! What are you doing here? Is everything all right?"

"Everything's fine. Wasn't sure I would see you here today, but decided to take a chance. I have a favor. It's a big one."

"Come on back. I am one of the only ones here today. Pulled the short straw." Grady sits behind his desk, and Sawyer sits across from him.

"How difficult would it be for me to talk to Bubba Westerman?"

Grady leans back in his chair and steeples his fingers. "It could be arranged. Of course, he would have to be willing. Surprisingly, he has not lawyered up yet, though he is not talking. What do you hope to gain?"

Sawyer leans forward and props his elbows on his knees. "I don't know. He and my father were pretty tight. Certainly not socially, but he was on Daddy's payroll for years. Hell, your daddy's too. But I think it was for more than keeping you and me out of that jail cell behind you."

"He knows more than he is sayin'. We all know that. Mostly because the man is not talking. Period."

"Where y'all got him housed? Laura Lynne mentioned Jackson at one point. Is he still there?"

"Yeah. You know, Sawyer, you could play this another way. You could go on visitor's day and surprise him. It might be a better play than a more formal arrangement. I know he's allowed visitors. Candy has been to see him a time or two."

Sawyer looks at him quizzically, and Grady clarifies, "My wife is good friends with Candy. This arrest has really torn her world apart. She tells her things." With a grin, Grady tips his head to the side. "Like she just called to tell me you had a date with our resident free-spirit bookstore owner, the fairy-sprite Diane." Grady laughs at Sawyer's expression. "Well played, buddy. Well played."

"What can you tell me about her, Grady? There's something about her. When we got done with coffee, I was so hard I could barely walk."

Grady's grin widens. "She does have that effect on men. Though, she has never shown any interest in any of the locals. At least from what I know. Super nice lady. She arrived here some time ago with her two-year-old from Biloxi. Her husband had been killed in Iraq, and she wanted a fresh start. Grace kind of took her under her wing. She found her a rental, helped her get a job at the Magnolia Café, arranged for babysitting, that kind of thing. Your father gave her seed money for Wheelbarrow Books. Prissa goes to her book club every month. She wouldn't miss it. It's like a religion." Grady asks contemplatively, "You thinking about tapping that keg?"

"It has certainly crossed my mind."

Grady lets out a laugh and then gets serious. "Man, I wish you the best. But it is my duty to warn you if you mess with her in any way,

I will have to kill you. My sister will make me. And you know Grace; she is mean when she's protective." Grady signals Sawyer to follow him to the window. Grady cracks the blind for a better view. "You see all those cars at her shop? Those are all her mother hens checking on their baby chick. Word went out she was having coffee with a big bad rooster." He clicks it shut. "I wish you luck."

"It was just coffee. And she and Mandy are coming for dinner tomorrow night."

Grady slaps him on the arm. "And so it begins. This will be fun to watch." Grady follows Sawyer as he walks to the front of the office. "In all seriousness, she's a great woman. You couldn't do better."

"It was just coffee."

"Keep telling yourself that. With Prissa, it was just dinner and a movie. Let me know what happens with the Bubba visit. Maybe you're right. Maybe he will talk to you. It's definitely worth a try."

Sawyer gives Grady his military email address. "It's encrypted. Send me what you can on Bubba."

"You got it. Good to see you. And, keep in touch. Lot going on at your place these days."

"Hell, I didn't even ask. Any word on Freddie and his gang?"

"Women do make you forget your troubles, don't they?" He walks with Sawyer outside. "We found the truck abandoned at a mall in Castille. But no sign. Looks like they had help." He looks around the parking lot. "Where is the pink Caddy?"

"At the GMC parking lot. I almost traded it in when I bought my Yukon, but I couldn't do that to Momma." Sawyer starts walking back toward the bookstore. "Bye, Grady. Thanks for everything."

It dawns on Sawyer as he approaches the bookstore parking lot that he forgot to get his uncle's book order. Heeding Grady's advice, Sawyer directs his steps to his Yukon and makes a hasty retreat back to Tea Olive. No need for the rooster to go into the hen house.

19

Chapter Nineteen

Much to Sawyer's relief, Gabe agrees that Sawyer should remain home while he goes to church. Leaving Tea Olive unattended, even for a couple of hours, did not sit well with either of them. Although he was not pleased his uncle insisted on driving himself, he knew better than to argue. It would only make Gabe double down. Sawyer's stubbornness is not isolated only to himself in this family.

Sawyer waves to Gabe from the front door as he drives his Mercedes down the drive. As old as he is, Gabe is sharp-witted and in good health. After his father's sudden and unexpected passing, Sawyer's own mortality began to set in. Shaking off his musings, Sawyer walks to the study, where he has set up his laptop. Since his uncle's beating in the field, Sawyer has slowly been taking over areas of the house that traditionally go with the title of executor. The study is sacrosanct for the men. Without comment, Gabe moved his personal belongings to the smaller space outside his rooms on the downstairs level.

Pulling up his email, Sawyer sees a missive from Grady. In it, he gives details about Bubba's visiting hours and recommendations on the best times to go, etc. The next available time is this upcoming Wednesday. Sawyer plans to go and see what shakes loose. There is another email from General Williamson checking on him. Sawyer sends back a banal response and then asks him to make sure his retirement papers are submitted. He will definitely not be returning. Finally, he checks his LinkedIn messages and sees that Sabrina Kolensky from Atlanta has replied. It reads:

Sawyer! What an unexpected surprise. Please accept my condolences regarding your father. I did not know him well, but my father always had a glowing respect for him. We are both sorry for your loss.

As far as your request to see my father is concerned, he would love the company. He is in the advanced stages of kidney disease, and his mind is a bit questionable at times. He currently resides at Peachtree Downs Skilled Nursing Home. You simply need to set a time to see him. I have provided the information below.

If I can be of any assistance on this matter, please let me know.

Moseley Saints Forever,

Sabrina

Sawyer pulls up the address on Google Maps and is pleased to see it's less than two hours from River Oaks. Although River Oaks is ultimately Laura Lynne's property and estate, the Cooper Trust has been managing it since Eileen's death. Sawyer hasn't been to River Oaks since he was a child. He may as well see what the current situation is while he is visiting with Elijah Kolensky. Kill two birds with one stone.

Sawyer checks his watch. Gabe won't be home from church for another hour. Sawyer holsters his firearm and collects a rifle. He radios John about his whereabouts. John acknowledges. Sawyer has gotten in the habit of using John as his backup—a 'buddy' of sorts. Gabe made an excellent choice when he hired John.

Because the house is empty, Sawyer walks to the property line between Twin Oaks and Tea Olive; no need to stray too far from The Residence. He is in the habit of checking the property several times a day, but so far, he has seen no signs of any trespassers or movement. But, after the chaos of the past week, Sawyer doesn't want to take any chances.

He stealthily walks through the wooded area, avoiding the roots and sticker bushes. As he approaches the low-hung and broken portion of the stone wall, Sawyer spots movement. He immediately crouches behind a tree. His military training kicks in, and his movements are nothing but reflex. Sawyer glances around the tree and sees two men in camouflage hot-footing it over the wall. He pulls back. Gingerly, he pulls his radio out and turns down the volume. "John, I have a situation. Need backup. Location of stuck four-wheelers." Hearing his affirmative response, Sawyer unsnaps his holster and lies down on his belly. He scoots forward, placing the rifle site to his eye. He recognizes one of the men, Jake. He's the kid who sliced his hand on the barbed wire fence. He can't see the other one clearly.

He decides not to intervene and instead watches them unload bags and toss them over the wall. Jake high-fives the other man. The second man jumps over the stone wall. Sawyer catches sight of John in his peripheral vision. He signals him to stay with the second man while he follows Jake. John signals understanding.

Sawyer realizes the two men have unloaded a wheelbarrow. Jake makes his way back toward the bunkhouse, pushing it in front of him. He walks down the path Sawyer takes every day to check the perimeter. Jake does not seem concerned, humming and making plenty of noise on his journey. Sawyer sees John climb over the stone fence. Sawyer continues to follow Jake at a distance, watching as he stows the wheelbarrow and his camouflage jumpsuit in a pile of debris. He covers it with foliage branches and pulls out a cigarette. He sits on a stump to smoke and then pulls out his phone and texts. The reply he receives must be a good one since he smiles when he gets it.

Sawyer decides now is as good a time as any to make his presence known. He carefully makes his way back to the path and then stands upright. He barges through the underbrush into the field where Jake is sitting, well, was sitting. "Hey, Jake! What are you doing out here?" Sawyer walks over and picks up the cigarette Jake has dropped on the ground. "Be careful there, buddy. Good way to catch the place on fire." Sawyer hands him the butt end. Jake nervously takes it.

"Colonel! You scared the shit out of me. What're ya doin' out here?"

"Could ask you the same thing, but I think I already know the answer."

Jake recovers some of his cool. "Yeah, having a smoke before you freaked me out."

Sawyer walks toward the pile of debris and lifts off the branches, keeping Jake in his site the entire time. "After you met your buddy. Want to explain yourself?"

Jake turns to take off and runs directly into John. John pushes him off, and Jake stumbles, falling to the ground. He covers his head and starts cowering, crying. "Don't hurt me. They made me do it."

"Who are they, Jake?" asks Sawyer.

"Freddie and Froggy. I swear. I got nothin' to do with it. Nothin'."

"Who was the guy at the Twin Oaks wall?" John has his gun trained to the ground, but Sawyer has no doubt that he is primed to use it if necessary.

"I don't know. I never saw the guy before today. I didn't even get a clear look at his face. He had on a hoodie and sunglasses. You saw him, man," Jake whines.

"I don't believe you, Jake." Sawyer walks over and pulls him up by the armpit. "Stop your whimpering. I'm not going to hurt you. Come on. Be a man." Sawyer propels him toward the house in time to see his uncle pulling in the driveway. To his surprise, he sees another car following closely behind him. As they get closer, he sees it is Charlie and Grace.

Charlie rolls down the window. "Need some help, Sawyer?"

"Yeah! Call your brother-in-law and tell him to come over. I have some trash that needs to be hauled off," Sawyer calls out.

Charlie leans back in the car and talks to Grace. She has the phone to her ear and is talking to Grady. "He'll be right over."

Gabe parks his car and quietly joins Sawyer and John. He has obviously overheard Sawyer and Charlie's conversation. He looks at Jake, cowering and sniveling. "Jake, what's going on here?" Sawyer begins to answer, but Gabe interrupts. "I'd like to hear it from Jake. He and I go back a-ways." Sawyer clams up and releases Jake's arm, taking a step back. Charlie gets out of his car and signals Grace to drive to the house. She slides across the truck seat and takes the wheel, driving away. Sawyer hands Charlie his handgun.

"Jake?" prods Gabe.

"I didn't know what to do. God, can I have a cigarette?" asks Jake nervously.

"Sure, when you are done explaining what just happened," says Sawyer.

Jake takes a deep breath. "Last night, me and a couple of boys went to the 'Under the Moon Saloon.' Met a girl who was into me, ya know?" He looks at John for confirmation. He gives a slight nod. "So, I stuck around after the boys left. She was just playin' me, man. She went to the ladies' room, and Freddie and Froggy came and sat next to me at the bar. Told me they had a job for me. I didn't want to do it. Told me if I didn't things would get bad for me. Threatened me with a knife."

He gulps. "I didn't know what to do. It seemed easy enough. Haul these bags they had stowed in one of the old slave cabins to the drop off point. Guy would meet me there. Look at nothing and say nothing. I never saw the girl again, either." He wipes at his nose. "Can I have that cigarette now?"

John tosses him his pack of cigarettes, and Jake fumbles to pull one out and light it.

"And how did you slice your hand. I'm not believing your barbed wire story," Sawyer asks.

"It was! I swear! I heard the bell ringing and started to run. Thought I could help out. Then saw Roger shoot Greg and Stacy. I turned the other way and hightailed it straight into the barbed wire fence. Nearly took out my eye. I hid until Malcolm found me. You can ask him. I swear."

Gabe looks him in the eye until Jake looks away. "What was in the bags, son? I know you looked."

He hesitates before answering. "What the hell? I'm probably dead anyway." He looks at Gabe, "Heroin. Enough to supply the entire state of Mississippi. There were eight duffle bags each carrying 40, maybe 50 bricks."

Charlie gives a low whistle. "What is that? Like 10 million on the street."

Sawyer shakes his head. "I have no idea. Chri…" Sawyer sees his uncle's stern look and changes his epitaph… "Crap. Thank God, Grady is here. He can take over." He looks at Charlie. "You can handle things here? I want to take John to the slave quarters and scout around."

"Ain't nothin' there," Jake mumbles.

"I prefer to see for myself. Which one was it?" asks Sawyer.

Jake takes another drag of his cigarette. "The one where they found the dead guy. With the yellow tape."

"Grady and I can manage here. Y'all go ahead," Charlie says.

Sawyer nods and starts to walk off, but not before Charlie indicates with a glance that he will watch over Gabe. Grady saunters over. He arrived in his deputy car still wearing church clothes. Sawyer lets Gabe and Charlie get him up to speed.

"John, what did you see?" Sawyer asks.

"Couldn't make out the features of the second guy, but he was white. Had a dark beard, maybe 30 to 35 years old. He was skinny but strong. He carried those duffle bags by himself. I followed him maybe 50 meters. He seemed to know his way around pretty good. Like real comfortable."

"Did you see any vehicles?"

"No. I didn't see or hear anybody else."

"Think Twin Oaks is a base of operations?"

"Could be or could just be a layover. Colonel, slow down. Let me scout out the left, you take the right. No need to barge into what we don't know."

Sawyer is surprised by his own carelessness. John is right. "Thanks, man. Brain is preoccupied." The two men break off and a few minutes later meet up on the other side. The coast is clear. "Come on, let's look around. Try not to disturb anything."

Sawyer walks to the cabin cordoned off by the police where Dead Doe was found. Almost a month ago now. He is looking at the lock when John comes to stand beside him. Sawyer says, "Lock is new. Wonder how long the stash has been in there? Could explain the increase in tension with all the police swarming after Dead Doe was found. It would have been difficult for them to get the heroin without arousing suspicion. Bad luck."

Sawyer and John raise their guns at the sound of a stick breaking, ready to shoot. Grady walks through with his arms up. "Whoa! Just me. Sorry. Should have made my presence known. Find anything?"

Sawyer shows him the lock. "Not one of ours. We were wondering if it was here when you found Dead Doe."

"No idea. We can check the pictures of the scene though. There should be some of the cabin itself. Might tell us something," says Grady.

"Learn anything from Jake?" asks John.

"My gut tells me he's not involved. I think he was a weak link Freddie could play and he did. He had to figure out a way to move the merchandise. Jake was an easy target. I have Buddy taking him in. State boys are on their way. Jerry's working on a search warrant for Twin Oaks. He doubts it will be approved with what we have."

"John might be able to help out with that. John?" John relays his experience with the second man.

Grady radios in the information. "I need to wait here until backup arrives. John, if you could stay, I would appreciate it." Grady looks at Sawyer. "You go on back to The Residence. Gonna be a lot of people here shortly."

Sawyer sighs. "Not sure why I thought coming home would be tranquil and serene." With a chuckle, he continues, "And maybe even boring."

The next few hours are a blur as the sheriff and his deputies arrive. Next, the state police. Finally, CSI is here once again. Nobody is happy to be there on this beautiful Sunday afternoon. Grace has taken over the kitchen, fixing sandwiches and fruit. She serves sweet tea and cookies as if she is hosting a garden party instead of a crime scene.

Sawyer, John, Gabe, and Charlie are on the front porch watching everything unfold. Finally, Sawyer says, "Charlie, not that I don't love having you and Grace here, but why are you here?"

Charlie snickers. "Grace's idea. She wanted to make sure you had everything you needed for your date tonight. She was worried about you cookin' dinner. It bein' Sunday and all."

"Oh Lord! I forgot. Diane and Mandy are supposed to come over at 6. I should cancel."

"You will do no such thing!" Grace comes out on the front porch with another plate of food. "That woman hasn't had a date since she has been a widow. You will not cancel. Besides, I already have a dinner menu planned."

"I'm not sure it's such a good idea. I can postpone. And just so you know, I am perfectly capable of cooking a meal. Not as good as Victoria's food but edible."

"You have a date with Diane? Hmmm, decided to light that firework, did ya?" Gabe says. "Grace is right. Let them come. We could use a distraction."

Sawyer knows better than to argue with the two of them. Besides, he would like to see Diane and spend some time with her. He looks at the line of cars in the drive. Lovely first impression.

"All right, all right. But don't make it too fancy, Grace. Just something simple. It's a *date*." He places heavy emphasis on the word date. "Not a marriage proposal."

"Just leave it to me." She turns around and leaves the men to their plate of sandwiches and talk.

"I do love that woman. Especially when she's fired up." Charlie digs into his ham and cheese.

"From what I've seen of her, that's all the time," John comments dryly. Charlie chokes on his sandwich while the other three men start laughing.

"Truer words, my man. Truer words," Charlie concedes.

"What has you men smiling and laughing while I am working my butt off on this lovely Sunday afternoon?" Grady walks up the steps and grabs a sandwich. "Wouldn't have anything to do with my sister, would it?"

"Yep, it surely would. I have a new respect for you, Grady. Being her little brother. And I thought Scarlet was a fireball," replies Sawyer.

"She still scares me to death." The men laugh and cut up while they demolish the sandwich tray.

Wiping his mouth, Gabe asks what everyone wants to know, "You learn anything yet, Grady?"

Grady sighs. "The state boys are executing a search warrant of the dwellings on Twin Oaks, including Merriwether. Hopefully, that will turn something up. The assumption is Freddie and his gang were meeting a boat on the river to unload the heroin. They would store it here on the farm until they could transport it safely. But we don't know for certain. The unknown is who is getting it on the other side."

Gabe shakes his head. "I feel so stupid. I can't believe all this has been going on under my nose."

"Don't feel bad, Mr. Gabe. This is a high-end operation," Grady reassures him. "Well-thought-out and someone who knows the inner workings of both your farm and Twin Oaks. Maybe a farmhand who has worked both farms and learned the ropes. Who knows?"

"I hate knowing Roger was involved in this mess. Has anyone come forward to claim his body? I don't think he had any family. As far as I know, Tea Olive was his family," says Gabe.

"I don't know, sir. I can find out for you," says Grady.

Gabe stands up from this chair. "You do that, young man. If nobody claims him, I will take care of it." He shuffles toward the front door. "I'm going to the study and watch some golf. Excuse me."

He disappears through the door. Grady looks at Sawyer and says, "This has hit him hard."

"I know. He thinks he failed somehow. I get it. It will take him some time. Once we nail the bastards, he will feel better, I think. I know I will," Sawyer replies.

Grady's radio cackles. "Gotta run. We'll catch up later. Good luck on the date!"

Charlie stands up. "I'm going to collect Grace and get her out of your hair."

Sawyer laughs. "I appreciate that more than you will ever know. But, man, thanks. I was glad you were here today." Charlie squeezes his shoulder as he walks by leaving John and Sawyer together on the front porch.

"John, I know I've asked a lot of you today. But do you mind checking on the Jacksons? Let them know what's going on. I know Queenie has her sons and grandson there, but I would rather they know firsthand what's happening." He checks his watch. It's close to 4. "They should be home from church by now."

"Sure, Colonel. Malcolm went home Saturday, but do you want him back at the bunkhouse?"

"No, let him stay home. Lance can handle it. What do you think about making him your number two man?"

"I agree. I've always liked him. No bullshit and that goes a long way with me."

"Okay. Let's pray things slow down by tomorrow. I'll meet you at the cabin once Malcolm and the ladies get here tomorrow. We can talk employees and business."

"See you then." John walks toward the barn and a few minutes later Sawyer sees him in the farm truck making his way through the back fields.

20

Chapter Twenty

Sawyer walks down the porch steps dressed in his new khakis and button down. He opens the passenger door for Mandy. She giggles as she gets out. "Thanks Mr. Sawyer." She gives him an exuberant hug. "Thanks for the invite! Mr. Gabe is one of my favorite people."

"I have it on good authority you are also one of his. He has the chess board out and ready for a lesson." He steps away and ruffles her hair. Sawyer watches as Diane comes around the car. "Sorry about the police cars. It's been quite a day."

"So I heard." She smiles. "Grace called."

"Well, then. No need for explanations. Come on in, ladies. Let me show y'all my home." He guides the ladies up the stairs and into the entrance. He turns on the chandelier. Every vase has fresh flowers, curtesy of Grace.

"Wow, it *is* gorgeous. I've been told, of course, but the actual experience is stunning. The staircase is divine. I bet y'all had a grand time torturing your momma by sliding down that rail," says Diane.

"What child could possibly resist? Come on, Uncle Gabe is waiting for us in the study."

Gabe stands at the bar cart. He walks forward and embraces Diane and then Mandy. "Welcome to Tea Olive. Can I get you a drink?"

"Just a tea please. I need to drive home," says Diane.

"She doesn't *need* to drive home. She just doesn't trust me to do it." Mandy looks at her mother. "I didn't even scratch the car."

"No, you just ran a stop sign and nearly caused poor Mr. Gaillard to die of a heart attack. Not to mention your mother." Diane looks at Mandy. "We are not discussing this again. Final word."

Gabe says, "Here, Mandy, have a tea. Diane, maybe you can bring Mandy over to the house during the daylight hours, and I can teach her in the farm truck. Did it with all my nieces and nephews. There's plenty of space to roam around in and no stop signs."

"Really, Mr. Gabe? Momma, can I? Please," Mandy begs.

"It's an awfully kind offer. We will see," says Diane.

The house phone rings, and Sawyer excuses himself to answer, "Hello."

"Sawyer, it's Grady. The search warrant is completed. I wanted you to know we did not find anybody there, but it's definitely been used as a base of operations. Looks like they've been breaking up the heroin and remixing it for sale on the streets. Whoever was in there fled in a hurry and left all the equipment. Like they knew we were coming. But at least we have some new leads to follow."

"Thanks for the update, Grady. I assume you have men posted there for tonight?"

"Yeah. You can rest easy. And enjoy your date. Bye, man." Grady disconnects, and Sawyer walks back into the study.

"Sorry for the interruption." Sawyer relays the conversation he and Grady had to his uncle and guests. "Happy to put that aside for a bit. Anybody ready for supper?"

The group walks to the dining room, where Grace set the table earlier—simple, casual, but classy. Only the basic fork, spoon, and knife as opposed to the full table setting his mother used for every meal. Sawyer pulls out a chair for Diane, and Gabe does the same for Mandy. Once everyone is seated, Sawyer brings the bowl of chicken bog and fresh rosemary bread from the kitchen and places it on the table.

Gabe smiles in anticipation. "Grace outdid herself. Smells like her momma's secret recipe."

Sawyer places the fresh salad on the table, and after blessing the food, everyone digs in. The conversation is lively, and Sawyer enjoys Diane's diverse background of knowledge on a myriad of topics. Her daughter is equally insightful. A dessert of fresh fruit with a light syrup concludes the meal.

Gabe stands up and winks at Mandy. "Sawyer, Mandy and I have the dishes. Why don't you and Diane walk to the river?" Without waiting for an answer, Gabe picks up his dish. "Come on, young lady, let's do the work so I can teach you the Sicilian Defense."

Sawyer looks to Diane. "Think we just got outmaneuvered by a pro. Come on. Let's take a walk."

He escorts her off the back porch and to the path leading to the river. "You have a lovely daughter, Diane." He smiles. "Her mother is not too bad either."

Diane gives him a flirty smile. "She's great. My biggest joy and accomplishment. I have loved raising her. But I'm looking forward to the next phase of my life. Being a mom is fabulous. Being a single mom is tough. She will be off to school in two years. She has her eye on SCAD. She is talented enough."

"What about you? What will you do when she goes to school?"

"Stay here. I love the life I've created. And nobody is more surprised by this than me!" She laughs. "Growing up I was certain I would be a fortune teller on the pier in Santa Monica moving from place to place. You know, a nomad." She looks over at him as she slides her hand into his and snuggles up against his arm. "What about you?"

He clasps her hand back, delighted by her initiative. "I always knew my life would lead me back to Tea Olive." He stops and pulls her around to face him. They are standing under the oak tree, the moon shining bright. "I sent an email to General Williamson this morning telling him to push through my retirement. I'm not returning. I'm here to stay." He takes her other hand in his and pulls her close. "I'm going to kiss you now, unless you tell me otherwise."

Saying nothing, she tilts her head back and leans forward. It's all the invitation Sawyer needs. He gently kisses her lips, licking the seam of her lips with his tongue. Her lips immediately part, inviting him in. Releasing her hands, Sawyer wraps his arms around her, drawing her tight against his chest. She does not shy away from his embrace. Instead, she snuggles in closer and murmurs softly into his mouth. With a groan, he releases her mouth and puts his head on her shoulder, breathing in the exotic smell of her. He kisses the nape of her neck before leaning back and gently taking her hand. The two are silent as they walk down the path to the river.

They have made it to the dock, and Sawyer places his back against the railing and spreads his legs, pulling her in and keeping his hands on her hips. She looks at his lips with a serious expression on her face before kissing him once again. Sawyer allows her to lead this time. When she pulls back, they are both breathless. She smiles. "That's the first kiss I have had from a man since Thomas died. I don't think I allowed myself to realize how much I missed it. And you are an excellent kisser."

Diane turns around and leans her back against his chest. He wraps his arms around her, and she grabs his forearm with her hands.

Diane gazes up and down the river. "It's beautiful out here."

He kisses the back of her head. "Yes. I've always loved it. Charlie and I spent hours on the river. I need to get the boat out. *Miss Melanie.* Perhaps that can be our next 'date.'"

"*Miss Melanie?*"

"Yeah, it was my dad's baby. He named her after Momma."

"I can't wait." Diane starts to pull away from Sawyer's chest. He immediately pulls her back tight and snuggles her neck. Laughing, Diane gently slaps his arm. "Come on, we need to get back. The longer we stay, the more questions Mandy will have for the ride back."

Reluctantly Sawyer releases her and stands upright. He grabs her hand as they walk the way they came. "I meant what I said Diane. I want a second date. Doesn't have to be on the boat."

She smiles as she looks over at him. "You're getting no argument from me. And the boat sounds great. I love the river."

They enter the back door, flush and laughing. "Looks like y'all had a good time. How was the river?" asks Gabe.

Mandy stares wide-eyed at her mother, the chess game forgotten. She blinks a couple of times. Diane looks at her questioningly.

"It is lovely, Mr. Gabe. You have a great place here." Diane walks over and rubs her daughter's head. "You okay, sweetheart?"

Mandy swallows. "What? Yeah, fine. I just don't think I have ever seen you so, well, happy. It looks good on you, Mom."

Startled, Diane glances at Sawyer. He shrugs his shoulders and hides his grin.

Diane says, "Well, I am happy. It was a lovely evening. One I'm sorry to see end. But end it must. You have school tomorrow, young lady."

With a cheeky grin, Mandy holds out her hand. "Why don't you let me drive? That way I can be super happy too."

"Not on your life, kiddo. Come on."

Diane and Mandy say their goodbyes as the two men follow them out the front door and down the porch stairs. Gabe opens the passenger door for Mandy, and Sawyer walks around to the driver's side. He leans down as Diane slides into her seat. "Listen, I am not sure how soon I can get back to town. There's a lot going on around here. And I need to make a trip to Jackson. But when I get back, let's plan to take the boat out." Looking at Mandy, he winks and then startles both women when he kisses Diane on the lips. "Call me when you get home. With all that's going on, I need to know you're safe." Staring into Diane's eyes, he says, "You can close your mouth, Mandy. Might catch a fly." He laughs as he shuts the door. The two men wave as the Toyota zips down the drive.

Gabe slaps Sawyer on the back. "You got it bad don't ya boy?" Sawyer doesn't acknowledge. "Why are you planning a trip to Jackson?"

With his hands on his hips, Sawyer looks at his uncle. "I plan to visit Bubba Westerman. I'm hopin' he will tell me something. He and Daddy were pretty tight. Want to come with me?"

"I do, but it's probably not a good idea."

"Why not?" asks Sawyer.

"Well, the last time we spoke I threatened him. He wasn't too happy," Gabe replies.

"Threatened him how? And why?"

"He expected me to continue funding his 'campaign' as your father did for so many years. When he realized I had no plans to continue your father's installments, he attempted to intimidate me. So, I threatened him."

"Threatened him? How?"

"With the truth." Gabe puts his hands in his pockets. "Don't ask; you don't want to know." He changes the subject. "Listen, while I have you for a minute. I called Lally today, and he's drawing up the papers for the transfer of the trust. He'll come by tomorrow with the paperwork." He clasps Sawyer's shoulder in his grasp. "I appreciate you taking this now. You're doing me a favor."

And that was all it took. Any reservations Sawyer might have had came to a screeching halt at those words. His uncle needed him to take over. Grasping his hand, Sawyer replies, "I won't let you down."

"I know that, son."

Sawyer stands up and embraces his uncle. Sawyer lets the tears flow. It has been a long journey back home—back to his legacy.

21

Chapter Twenty-One

"I'm sorry I didn't call you sooner. It's been a hell of a few days, Laura Lynne." Sawyer sits at his desk in the study, fielding phone calls from his siblings. First, it was Avery who was calm about the entire situation. Laura Lynne is hot.

"Sawyer, I freakin' wake up this morning to a front-page article about the murder and subsequent suspicion of drug smuggling on the..." Sawyer hears her clicking on her computer. "'Quaint, southern plantation known as Tea Olive located in Venice, Mississippi.' Please explain."

Sawyer recounts his version of events from ousting Freddie and his gang, Roger's murder, and the drug operation that has apparently been running through Tea Olive. "I am packing my bags. I will be there by tomorrow afternoon."

"Laura Lynne! There's no need for that. We're fine here. And exactly what do you plan to do? Write about them?"

"Don't you get smart with me, big brother! I can shoot a gun almost as well as you. Besides, Uncle Gabe doesn't need to be alone, and I can't imagine you can stay at the plantation 24/7."

"He's not alone. Ever. John is here, and Malcolm is close by. Pearl and Victoria are also here practically every day. It's a regular Mardi Gras parade at Tea Olive."

"You mentioned everyone but Scarlet. Where is she?" asks Laura Lynne.

"I haven't heard from her since John met her in Wisteria. He made sure she got home safe, but otherwise nothing." Sawyer chooses not to disclose John's unsettling feelings about his interaction with Scarlet.

"And Momma? What is your plan there?"

Sawyer takes a deep breath. Laura Lynne's got him on this one. He has not been by to see their mother since he arrived. "I honestly don't have one. I'm trying to avoid that particular battle."

"Hmmmph. Fine. I won't drop everything and come this minute. But I did talk to Diane and confirmed the book club a week from this Thursday. So, plan on me next Wednesday." She clacks some more on her computer. "And for God's sake, pick up the damn phone and call me the next time someone is killed or some other God-awful thing happens. I don't want to read about in the damn paper!" She hangs up the phone. Almost immediately the study phone rings again. He sees it's Laura Lynne. He picks it up and holds the receiver away from his ear, "And buy a damn smart phone so we can reach you!" She hangs up again.

"Which of my lovely nieces was that? Or was it my sister?" Gabe stands in the study doorway in his overalls sipping a mug of hot coffee.

Sawyer drops his head in his hands. "Laura Lynne. She sure is feisty. I don't remember her being quite so...sassy."

Gabe laughs. "Sassy. Now there is a word to describe the Cooper women." Gabe comes in and sits across the desk from Sawyer. "What are your plans for today?"

"Mostly doing what I'm doing right now. I want to finish going through the files and trying to organize the paperwork. I don't want to stray too far from the farm. Too much going on. Why? Do you need me today?"

"No. I was just curious." Gabe looks at his overalls. "I am going to work in the kitchen garden. I plan to stay close as well. What about the boys? What's your plan there?"

Sawyer picks up the two-way radio he has on the desk. "I just called John and Malcolm. They will both be here shortly for us to make a plan. I don't want anyone alone in the fields."

Gabe pushes himself out of the chair. "I'll let you be and tell Victoria to plan on four for breakfast." He pauses on the way to the door, looking over his shoulder. "Oh, and don't forget, Lally will be by later this afternoon with the trust paperwork."

Sawyer nods as the phone rings again. He grimaces. "Hello. Tea Olive Plantation." He pauses a moment and then grins. "Speak of the devil. My uncle and I were just talking about you. What can I do for you, Ace?"

"Hey, Sawyer. Listen, Dad just brought me all the paperwork to transition the trust over to you," says Ace, "I just want to verify a few things with you. Is now a good time?"

"Fine." The two men discuss the trust, Sawyer answers one question after another. Finally, Ace finished his questions. "Ace, before you hang up, can you do me a big favor? I would do it myself, but I don't want to leave Tea Olive right now."

"Sure. At your service. What do you need?"

With a heavy sigh Sawyer acquiesces to technology. "A smartphone. I have no idea what I might need, but something simple. Laura Lynne nearly bit my ear off this morning when she called me. And once I quit needling her, I realized she has a point. With all that is going on, we need to be reachable."

"No problem. I'll bring it when I come out this evening. Expect me around 5."

Sawyer hears John and Malcolm come in. Pearl is not pleased her brother has his muddy boots on in her clean kitchen. Sawyer smiles. Family.

Sawyer signals the two men into the study as he hangs up the phone with Ace Lally. "Hey. Thanks for coming in this morning. I just have a few things on my mind and want to be sure we are all in agreement." He looks at the two men. "First and foremost, I'm giving each of you a 20% raise. I plan to reorganize the way we structure the business end of the farm, including the pay structure. But I will start with salary adjustments." He looks at them as they nod agreement. "Second, the men. John, you and I planned to release some of the older guys, but I think we need to wait a while. I don't know who we can trust and making new hires does not seem smart. Thoughts?"

"I agree. Safety has to be the first priority. Malcolm?"

"I know the men who are left. They are all old-timers. Been with us for at least three or four seasons. Most of them much longer. I think we can trust them."

"Okay. I don't want anyone, including you two to be out in the fields alone or unarmed. I have plenty of guns and ammo, so let's make sure everyone has what they need. Y'all figure out a schedule and let's include around the clock night watch. The sheriff's department is currently staked out at Twin Oaks, but I don't know how long they will be there. I don't want the plantation unguarded."

For the next hour the three men strategize how to best manage the farm with the few men they have left. Pearl's voice comes over the intercom. "Y'all come get your breakfast before it gets cold. Pancakes need to be eaten hot!" The three men adjourn the meeting and go fill their plates and bellies with Victoria's cuisine.

By midafternoon, Sawyer feels like he has a better handle on the current status of the business and the trust. He sent a message to Beau, asking him to review the current business structure for Tea Olive and to give him suggestions. Beau is quick to respond and sets up a time to meet via Teams. Sawyer grimaces. He has never been a fan of office work or conference calls. He gets up from the desk and begins pacing. He missed his morning run.

"Hey, Pearl. I want to go for a run, you gonna be around for a bit? I don't want to leave Uncle Gabe here by himself. But God's honest truth, I need to get away from that computer screen."

"Sure. Go on." She holds up a swatch of paint. "What do you think about this one for your room?" Sawyer glances at the deep, dark blue in her hand. "It's called Gentleman's Gray."

"It looks blue." He walks closer. "I like it though. Anything is better than the current rose situation."

"I will take care of it. I figured it was a good time since Mr. Gabe is using the downstairs bedroom while he recuperates. You can sleep in his rooms until the work is done."

"Listen, Pearl. Be careful who you have in the house right now. Only people you know and trust. You understand?"

"Loud and clear. Now go run off some of that energy. Your bouncing around and pacing is distracting the rest of us trying to work."

Without any argument, Sawyer changes into his running gear and straps on his holster. He decides to take his regular route, circling the plantation. He gets no further than the property line at Twin Oaks before he jumps the low stone wall and makes his way to the main house. Nobody stops him. He sees Grady and Jerry standing by their cars, thumbs in their belt buckles. They are in a deep discussion.

"Hey Grady! Sheriff. Hoping you've got some news you can share with me."

Grady looks at the sheriff before receiving a shrug and a nod. Grady shows Sawyer a picture on his phone. It's a Confederate flag with two machine guns crossed in an "X" with the letters MRM above the guns. "Ever seen this before?"

Sawyer takes the phone for a closer look. He hands it back to Grady and says, "No. What is it?"

"It's a gang symbol for the Mississippi Rebel Mafia." Grady tilts his head toward the house. "Found it all over the walls in there. Along with enough drug paraphernalia to indicate whoever is behind this has been set up here for quite a while."

"No leads?" asks Sawyer.

Grady looks at Jerry as he answers, "Not locally. The feds have been watching these guys for some time. They're all over the South. Each gang has an initial for their state. So, the Georgia gang would call themselves GRM. But the gang symbol, the flag, and the guns stay the same. MRM is fairly new to the scene."

"Any local suspects? Besides Freddie and Froggy? I don't see them having enough brain power to accomplish something of this magnitude," Sawyer hypothesizes.

"No, we think somebody from out of state. Perhaps a Mafia Lieutenant. But we're just guessing," says Jerry.

"Anything on the bearded guy John and I saw with Jake?"

"No. And Jake says he never met him or saw him before. I tend to believe him. The boy slept like an angel in the cell last night. Excuse me just a minute." Jerry walks off to talk with one of the crime scene technicians.

"Listen, Grady. I got to thinking on my way over here that you might want to vet the Cotton Mill employees. Make sure they're legit."

"Way ahead of you. Charlie thought the same thing. He and Dad are meeting with each of the men today. Seeing what they can find out and getting rid of any questionables. But thanks."

"I should have suspected Charlie would be on it." Sawyer leans over to whisper, "Anything else I should know?"

Grady whispers back, "There has to be someone local. Someone who knows the terrain, the way the farms work, and knows the river. Somebody who grew up around here seems to be the safest bet." He steps back and clears his throat, slapping him on the shoulder. "How was the date last night?"

Jerry comes up beside the two men and asks, "What date? Oh, you mean the one where the lovely Diane ate chicken bog and broke rosemary bread before being escorted out to the river for a bit of lip-locking with the town golden boy and prodigal son?"

Sawyer looks at the grinning faces of the two men and says, "I will be forever fascinated by the grapevine of this town." Sawyer starts to jog away, turning to run backward as he replies, "It was as amazing as reported." He turns back around with a salute. "Later, fellas."

Sawyer finishes the rest of his run without incident. John and Malcolm have things in hand and running smoothly. When Sawyer returns to The Residence, Ace is waiting patiently on the front porch, eating macaroons and drinking sweet tea. "Sorry, Ace. The time got away from me. Give me a moment to clean up."

Smiling and popping another macaroon into his beefy jowls, he replies, "No problem. Take your time. It's never a burden to eat Victoria's macaroons."

Sawyer runs into Gabe on his way out to the front porch. He is cleaned up for supper. "Be done in a sec."

Sawyer double times it to his room and jumps in the shower before he notices all his toiletries are missing. He shrugs, allowing the water to rinse away the worst of the sweat and grime. He wraps the towel around his waist and walks to the chifforobe. His clothes are missing. Then he notices the furniture has been moved away from the walls and is covered in plastic. "For God's sake." Sawyer walks out in the hallway and marches into his uncles' rooms nearly colliding with Diane. "Whoa!"

Diane grabs hold of Sawyer's bare shoulders as he crushes her to his chest, the two tumbling to the floor. Sawyer protects Diane with his body, allowing his back to take the brunt of the fall. Diane hastily pushes herself up on his chest. "Oh! Are you okay? Sawyer?"

Sawyer puts up a finger. He had the wind knocked out of him not to mention the shooting pain emanating from his healing knife wound. Diane looks at him with amusement and interest. "Fine." Sawyer lays his head on the floor. "What are you doing up here?"

Diane picks up the bag from the floor. "I brought your uncle his books. I forgot them yesterday. He asked me to bring them to his rooms." She looks around. "These are his rooms, right? The ones you showed us on the tour yesterday."

"Yes, these are his. Long story." Sawyer brushes the hair that came loose from Diane's bun away from her eyes, cupping her face. "Come here." Not one to not take advantage of an opportunity, Sawyer draws Diane in for a long, slow kiss. As she responds enthusiastically, Sawyer deepens the kiss and rolls over putting Diane on her back. He cups her buttock with his right hand, drawing her closer to his center. Both gasping as contact with the juncture of her thighs is made. "Christ."

He smiles down at her flushed cheeks and he kisses her eyes. "You okay? I didn't mean for all that to happen."

"I'm glad it did." She kisses him soundly before scootching herself into a seated position, pulling her skirt back around her legs. "When can we do it again?"

Sawyer chuckles and grins, getting up from the floor. "When I have more time. Ace and Uncle Gabe are waiting for me." He extends his hand. She grasps it as he pulls her off the floor. She steps back, gazing at his nakedness. She looks at him as an artist would view a painting. And he can tell that she likes what she sees. "But we will finish this."

"I certainly hope so." She scoops up the bag of books and places them on the bed. She glances at Sawyer one last time before she walks out the door.

"Hot damn." Sawyer takes another quick shower, this time ice cold before finding his clothes and getting dressed. He is still twitching from his encounter with Diane when he walks outside.

"I thought we were going to have to send the troops in, Sawyer. What have you been up to?" Gabe glances at Sawyer and looks down the drive at Diane's car as it leaves. "Have anything to do with the lovely Diane?"

Smiling from ear to ear, Sawyer responds, "Absolutely."

Ace chuckles. "They do make you forget your schedule, don't they?"

"Huh?" Sawyer glances absently at Ace's grinning face. Gabe starts to laugh and claps his hands together.

"Come on, son. We need your John Hancock. Pearl and John said they would be witnesses. Call them out, will you, Sawyer?"

Laughing at Sawyer's quizzical expression, Ace pops out of his chair. "Have a seat man, looks like you need it. I'll get Pearl and John. Maybe I can snag another macaroon while I am in there."

Sawyer sits down and puts his head in his hands, combing the hair on his head back.

"No need to tell me what happened in there with Diane. I already know what's got you so befuddled."

He smiles as he looks at his uncle. "She's pretty great, isn't she? I want to see her again. Take some time with her. But with all this craziness...and I don't want to leave you alone."

"God will open up that door if you are meant to walk through it. You ready to stop acting like a love- struck teenager now so we can get this business with the trust done? Ace has been out here for an hour eating all the macaroons. He didn't leave me but one and I nearly had to snag that out of his mouth before he demolished it."

"Sorry. I didn't mean to get distracted."

"Not a bit of worry. Fine way to spend an afternoon." He grins at his nephew.

Sawyer bursts out laughing. "Mighty fine."

"Come on, let's go inside. It could be hours before Ace gets out of that kitchen."

22

Chapter Twenty- Two

It took a couple of days, but the mechanizations of Tea Olive were back at full tilt, the farm operating on its normal schedule. Sawyer felt he could safely venture off the farm for a few hours.

"You stay close to The Residence, Uncle Gabe. I will be back by late this afternoon." Sawyer puts the Yukon in reverse. "You sure I can't convince you to come with me?"

"No. I am fine here. Quit your worrying. Things have been quiet the last two days. I don't expect today will be any different," Gabe replies.

"Okay. I will do my best to be back before Doc Vincent comes around today. I want to hear for myself how you're doing."

"You're worse than both of your sisters and your momma combined." Gabe steps back from the car window and leans back on his heels. He has his thumbs wrapped around the straps of his overalls. "Go on now. You don't want to miss visiting hours."

Sawyer nods and rolls up his window. Today is the day he meets Bubba Westerman face-to-face. Or at least, will try to. Sawyer has no idea of what type of reception he may receive. He may get no further than the waiting room. Sawyer's phone rings and scares the life out of him. He nearly runs off the road as the Bluetooth rings loudly in the car. He fumbles to answer it while trying to decrease the volume.

"Hello?"

"Sawyer? What are you doing?" asks the voice on the other end.

"Answering the damn phone. Give me a second. I need to turn down the volume." Sawyer finds the buttons on his steering wheel and makes some adjustments. "Okay. Better. Scarlet, is that you?"

"Yes. I got your voice messages. Sounds like you had quite a weekend. Any updates?"

Sawyer gives her the latest before springing his current plan on her. "Now, I am headed to Jackson County Jail to see Bubba Westerman."

"Bubba? Why? You think he knows about the drug smuggling? Or Dead Doe?"

"I don't know what he knows, and that's the problem. He's not telling anyone anything. I imagine he knows plenty. I guess you know he was on Daddy's payroll for years. I found it in the ledger as 'campaign donations.' Funny thing though, he received them annually, not just on campaign years."

"And you have no idea what this money bought?"

"Well, it kept me and Avery out of jail a few times. But other than that, I can't imagine. I really think it was something pretty benign, like 'look the other way' money. I can't find anything illegal, but I suspect there were some borderline practices going on when he was in charge. Stuff Dad kept off the books."

"I know he employed illegal immigrants to work the farm, but then so did Buck's daddy. It was pretty common. Nothing else comes to mind."

"Well, if anything does, just send me a text. Laura Lynne convinced me to get a phone, so you can reach me at this number any time." Thinking about his conversation with John, Sawyer decides to probe. It is, after all, a little brother's prerogative. "Scarlet. What is going on with you? I can't reach you. You're never around. I haven't seen you since I've been home." His voice is one of compassion. "What's going on, Sissy?"

"Nothing. Nothing is going on. Besides, you're the one who ditched me in Wisteria. I swear! You and Laura Lynne are gone for years leaving me to care for Momma and Daddy, not to mention Uncle Gabe. I take a breather, and y'all act like I have deserted the family! I haven't! I just need a break. And it's your turn!"

Sawyer is silent as he listens to her heavy breathing. Then replies, "From your reaction, I beg to disagree. Something is definitely up. When you're ready to talk about it, let me know. And Scarlet? There is a place for you at Tea Olive anytime you want it." He pauses. "Or need it."

The phone goes dead.

Sawyer considers the conversation with Scarlet for the remainder of the drive. His sister has always been high-strung, but this seems over the top. He shelves his concerns about Scarlet as he navigates the multi-step process for attaining entry to the correctional facility. He registers his name and the inmate he wishes to see. Sawyer has a moment of levity when he sees that Bubba's given name is Bradford. It just does not fit the bald, fat, tobacco-chewing, unkempt man. It's too refined.

Sawyer waits another 20 minutes before he is called back to the visitor's area. Instead of the glass partitioned cubicle with a telephone to speak, Sawyer is in a room of tables and benches with snack machines. He walks over to the coffee machine and gets two cups. He looks at the small table and bench, all bolted to the floor. He sits down as the prisoners in their khaki scrub sets and plastic shoes come through the door. If Bubba is surprised to see Sawyer, he doesn't show it. He sits across from Sawyer and reaches for the coffee.

"Thanks. I heard you were back and wondered if you might come by to see me."

Sawyer is taken aback by the statement. Bubba is behaving almost as if he knew Sawyer would be coming for a visit. Weird. Shaking off the niggle in the back of his mind, Sawyer cuts to the chase. "Then, you won't be surprised why I'm here."

"Nah, you want to know what I know. Everybody does. Gonna tell you what I tell them, go fuck yourself."

"Mighty big talk from where you're sitting. I had a nice long talk with my uncle, you might want to reconsider your stance."

He looks at Sawyer from across the table and for the first time, Sawyer realizes Bubba Westerman is nobody's fool. The look in his eyes is one of shrewdness and intellect. "Nah. I have plenty on your uncle. And your old man. We're at what you might call a stalemate."

"Maybe a deal then? I recently became the executor of the trust. What would it take to make you talk?"

Laughing uproariously, Bubba spreads his hands. "Not money. I got plenty. Now, if you can get me out of here."

"I don't have that kind of leverage, and even if I did, I wouldn't use it."

"Then we got nothin' more to discuss."

Sawyer leans over the table and gets up close and personal with Bubba and his bad breath. His tone is menacing. "You're lucky I haven't had you killed. What you let happen to my baby sister? You are one sick, demented son of a bitch. She was friends with your daughter!" He leans back with a nasty grin.

Bubba's eyes show the first hint of regret. " I am real sorry about Laura Lynne. That should have never happened. I took care of the problem after Doc Goldbug called. Like to have killed him myself."

Sawyer looks sick to his stomach. What a vile and repugnant excuse for a human being. "I'd say you owe us one, or more specifically, Laura Lynne."

Sawyer sits back down across from Bubba Westerman and his oily, gray face. It is obvious prison has not been kind to Bubba. He has dropped a considerable amount of weight, and his skin hangs under his arms. He taps his fingers in a rhythmic cadence.

"The truth is I know nothing about your corpse. I have no clue who the man is or where he came from. Nobody was more surprised than me when he appeared."

"Bullshit," Sawyer responds.

Bubba holds out his hands. "It's the God's honest truth. But I might have some information on your current dealings out at Tea Olive, which might be more to your liking."

Saying nothing, Sawyer waits for him to continue.

"About six or seven months ago, a gang started running drugs up and down the river. I don't know who, only that the person who is in charge is from around here. A local. I have it on good authority he is smart and mean with it. Like cold. Kill a man as quick as look at him." He clears his throat. "That deal with Roger? I think it sounds like this guy." He whispers low, "And those boys you're lookin' for? Dealt with them in the past, also local. If they are holed up somewhere, it is going to be close by. They haven't gone far. Have Grady check out some of the old haunts; he will know where to look."

"Give me a name, Bubba."

Bubba laughs out loud. "Haven't got one, and even if I did, I wouldn't tell you. I have to stay alive in here. Whoever this guy is, he's connected. No way he could pull off this type of operation without financial backing. And who has that type of money around Venice, MS? You know as well as I do the list is short, and they all belong to the Venice Country Club." The buzzer rings, and Bubba begins to stand. "Consider us even, now. My regards to your family."

Sawyer stays seated as he watches Bubba walk away. Bubba always treated him well when he was growing up, keeping him out of trouble and out of jail. To some degree and to Sawyer's eternal regret, he looked up to the man. Now, seeing him with a man's eyes, no longer that of a rebellious teenager, he sees what he should have seen all along. He's a snake, coiled and ready to strike if prodded.

Sawyer gets out of his seat and walks away, sick to his stomach. With a heavy heart, Sawyer calls Laura Lynne. He knows he has to tell her what he just learned. It is her right to know.

"Hey, big brother! What's up? Not another dead body, I hope," Laura Lynne cheerfully answers the phone.

"My, you are in good spirits. I hope what I have to say doesn't bring you down. Gray around today?"

Laura Lynne gets instantly serious. "Yes, he's here. You want me to get him?"

"I just met with Bubba Westerman."

"Oh, God. Okay, go ahead. I can handle it," says Laura Lynne.

Sawyer relays his conversation with Bubba to his little sister. "The son of a bitch knew. All I can surmise is there was an understanding that Dr. Butler would keep his habit with those from less fortunate circumstances than ours. The weak and vulnerable. Those who could not fight back. He crossed a line with you."

Laura Lynne is silent, allowing the feelings to wash through her. She clears her throat. "I'm not really sure how all this makes me feel. Validated in some ways. Nauseous in others. Sawyer, they had an understanding. Bubba turned a blind eye. Why? He has girls of his own."

"I mentioned that. Money is the only thing I can fathom. Being paid for his silence, maybe. I think that's what Daddy was doing too." Sawyer taps the steering wheel. "Did you know his name is Bradford?"

"Are you saying he wanted to be a part of the good ol' boy club? So, he tries to buy his way in? Never works, you are born to it or you marry into it. He was nothing more than their lackey, paid to do a job."

"And he never got what he wanted," says Sawyer. "I plan to talk to Grady and get his thoughts. See if anything Bubba told me pans out—like locating Freddy and his gang."

"Well, we already know about my skeletons. And he didn't know anything about Dead Doe? That's surprising, I would think he would. But he did seem to know about the drug running. I find all this a bit hard to take in."

"Don't be so trusting, Laura Lynne. He could be lying through his teeth. Oh, and another thing. Remember how you told me you thought Dad's mistress knew you were coming?" Laura Lynne murmurs her acknowledgment. "Well, it was the same with me today.

Bubba was not at all surprised to see me. Nobody but Grady and Uncle Gabe knew I was coming. It was weird."

The line is silent.

"Laura Lynne, are you okay? You're awfully quiet," Sawyer asks compassionately.

Laura Lynne's voice is quiet but strong, "I feel validated, Sawyer. Every suspicion I had was right. There is joy in knowing I'm not crazy." She is quiet for another moment as if gathering her thoughts. "For some reason, this feels almost like closure of some sort. Plus, I can add it to my book."

"Your book? The one Mary is helping you with?" Sawyer asks.

"Yes. I decided to write it, sort of Truman Capote style. This will make a nice ending."

"Laura Lynne, it's not over yet. There is still a potential for a trial."

"It *is* over for me, and for now, that's all that matters." She turns practical, ready to move on from the conversation. "Listen, I need to go. Thanks for telling me. And don't forget, I will be there soon for book club. I heard your date with Diane was wonderful. Not trying to pry, but if you two want to take some time away while I'm there, I am happy to watch over Uncle Gabe and Tea Olive."

"You talked to Diane?" Sawyer asks, obviously miffed.

"Of course. She is my friend. In fact, she was my friend first. But currently you are top of the list for her affections. Whatever you did, keep it up. She likes you. Listen, I really do need to run. Gray is getting ready to leave, and I want to tell him about Bubba before he goes. Be safe and careful. Love you." She hangs up the phone.

23

Chapter Twenty-Three

Sawyer smiles as he enters Tea Olive's gates. He slows down to take in the blooming azalea bushes, the dogwoods with their pink and white flowers, the daffodils nodding their yellow heads in the soft breeze. Sawyer rolls down his window and stops the car. He looks over the expanse of front gardens to the majestic plantation house he once again calls home. From this distance he can barely see the large gas lanterns on either side of the ornate front door. The lanterns stay lit 24 hours a day, their firelight dancing. They stand sentry to The Residence, always ready to welcome friends and family alike.

Sawyer shakes his head at his fanciful turn of thought. At one time, he thought he might be a writer himself. He majored in literature at the Citadel, falling in love with the old bards and playwrights. His classmates used to tease him mercilessly, but Sawyer didn't care. Back then, he considered himself a Renaissance man and would visit Charleston's open mic nights, listening to the brave souls willing to share their work. He loved it. Of course, this was before war tore his soul out. Maybe, just maybe, he was beginning to find the self he had lost on the battlefield. There is certainly no more beautiful place to be in spring than Tea Olive.

Sawyer notes Dr. Truelove's car as he drives toward the barn. Perfect timing. Sawyer hastily makes his way to the house and into the study. Vincent is playing chess with his uncle. And losing. He looks up as Sawyer enters. "Thank God you're here. Your uncle is knocking my

199

socks off in chess. I was hoping you would get here before I needed to go. I want to speak to you in private, if I may."

"If it is about me, I want to hear it," says Gabe as he knocks down Vincent's king. "Checkmate."

Vincent looks at the board with a frown, "Seriously? I should lie and tell you I am talking all about you, but that would go against my ethical standards as a doctor." Vincent smiles reassuringly. "It's not about you, Mr. Gabe. I gave you a clean bill of health. It is Sawyer I need to see."

"Sure, Doc," says Sawyer, "Let's go to the front room."

Vincent follows Sawyer to the sitting room. The doctor walks around the room, gazing at the antiques and the artwork. "Stunning. I minored in art history. Your home is a treasure trove."

"Art history? You surprise me. You are quite the polymath. I'll give you a tour sometime, or a better person would be my uncle or Scarlet. They both know more than I do about our family history." He sits down on one of the wingback chairs. "What can I do for you?"

"How is the wound? I'm happy to look at it while I am here."

Sawyer just lifts his shirt up and leans forward. The wound is no longer dressed and is healing nicely. "Whatever you shot me up with seems to have done the trick."

"Yes, it does." The doctor sits across from Sawyer. "You want to talk to me about the nightmares?"

"Not really. But I am curious why you think I have nightmares," says Sawyer.

"You don't hide them very well. You want to talk about it?"

Sawyer sighs as he gets up from the chair and starts to pace. "It's always the same nightmare. It happened a long time ago. I lost some good men and a good buddy. I was cleared of any wrong doing. I even got a promotion. But I know those men died because of me, and it haunts me. Most of them were just kids."

Vincent listens quietly and then asks, "You take anything to help?"

"Honestly, I've been down that road. I don't want to go down it again. I prefer to figure this out on my own, but I appreciate the offer." Sawyer stares out the window while he talks. He looks over his shoulder. "Did my Uncle Gabe ask you to check on me?"

Vincent nods. "He did. He said he hears you almost every night, tossing and turning. Sometimes you cry out, sometimes you scream. It has him concerned."

"Damn," Sawyer thinks. He thought he was doing a better job at hiding his nightmares. Sawyer speaks up, "I'll talk to him. And if things get to a place where I think I need help, I'm not afraid to ask for it."

Vincent hands him a piece of paper with an address on it. "You might try the veteran's support group. I know the man who facilitates it. It might do you some good to know you're not alone."

Sawyer takes the sheet of paper, knowing he won't go. He is a loner and sharing his troubles with strangers is not in his makeup. He shakes Vincent's hand. "Thanks. I'll think about it."

On his way out, Vincent asks Sawyer, "If you were serious about the tour of the house, I would love to take you up on it. Your uncle has my number."

"Sure, Doc. We'll plan it. Maybe we can include a meal. Victoria is quite the cook."

"An offer I look forward to. Thank you, Sawyer. Can you please tell Mr. Gabe I'm leaving? I need to get to my next appointment. Also, as you heard, your uncle is cleared physically. He is still sore, but the bruising is down, and there seems to be no long-term effects. He can do whatever he feels up to trying."

"That's good news. Very good news. Thanks."

The two men shake hands and part ways. Sawyer watches as Vincent climbs into his Wagoneer. He hears his uncle come up behind him. "Why didn't you just ask me about my night terrors?"

Gabe shrugs his shoulders. "I figured if you wanted me to know, you would tell me."

"How about we grab a drink, and I'll tell you the story. It's not like it's all that unique to me. I'm sure you have heard it a hundred times from other vets."

Gabe squeezes his shoulder. "Sounds like a great idea." He glances at his wrist to check the time. "I could use a brandy."

For the next hour, Sawyer recounts the events of that long-ago mission. He tells Gabe about Dodger, the other boys, his part in the explosion, the subsequent investigation, and the promotion. The guilt he felt for being awarded a medal for his role. His uncle listens quietly as he sips his brandy. Finally, Sawyer has nothing more to say. He looks to his uncle. "I can't erase the images from my head at night. They sneak up on me."

Nodding, Gabe looks into his brandy as he speaks. "Bad situation. All of it. War generally is. What I found for myself was the opposite of what I wanted to do. I embraced this part of myself instead of trying to get rid of it. You can't get rid of the demons. You have to make peace with them." He looks at Sawyer. "What if you were the one killed instead of Dodger? Would you want Dodger to be eaten up with nightmares for the rest of his life? My guess is he would be livid with you. He knew the consequences of the mission going in, just like you. He died with honor. Your nightmares take that away in a sense."

"Survivor's guilt is my best friend." He's quiet for a moment. "Embrace the demons. Well, I haven't tried that yet. I just do my best to forget."

"Whatever happened to Dodger's wife and son?" asks Gabe.

"I have no idea. I would think his boy would be like 30 by now."

"Maybe you should find out. It might be some of the closure you need."

Ready to change the subject, Sawyer latches on to Gabe's segue. "Speaking of closure, I did see Bubba today."

"Wondered what happened in Jackson. This seemed more important, though."

Sawyer recounts his conversation with Bubba and his call to Laura Lynne. "He swears he doesn't know anything about Dead Doe. And I don't know how accurate the information was about Freddie and his gang. I plan to talk to Grady tonight. We are to meet at the Ridge around 9 PM.

"How did Laura Lynne take the news?" asks Gabe.

"Remarkably well. She felt validated. She said she already knew the truth, but it felt really good for Bubba to admit his complicity. Her only question is why he would allow a predator in Venice. I told her money."

"Power and money. A heady combination."

"While we are on difficult topics, I spoke to Scarlet today. She doesn't seem herself, not that I know exactly what that is anymore…as she pointed out. I just can't shake the feeling she is avoiding me…and you, for that matter."

"Scarlet is a tough one to figure. She keeps things close to the vest. She normally comes by once a week and checks on me. The same with your momma. I guess since you and Laura Lynne have been here, she hasn't found it necessary. I am sure she appreciates the break."

Sawyer shrugs, "Maybe. What can you tell me about Buck? I was afraid to ask Scarlet."

"Not much. I haven't seen him in years. He and Scarlet seem to live separate lives since the boys left home. I've never asked, and she has never mentioned it. I didn't want to pry."

The two sit in companionable silence. Rocking in their chairs, both lost in their own thoughts. Eventually, Sawyer gets up. "I'm going to heat up some dinner. Can I get you anything?"

"No, son. You go ahead. I want to sit here a bit and watch the sunset. I'll get something later."

Sawyer walks closer to his uncle and looks at him with concern. "You sure you're okay? I can cancel with Grady tonight."

Gabe pats the hand Sawyer has placed on his shoulder. "I'm fine. This is just thinking time for me. When I am here alone in the evenings, this is my usual schedule. I enjoy watching the day settle."

"Love you, Uncle Gabe."

"I know. I love you too."

Sawyer eats supper while watching spring practice training for the Atlanta Braves. He's been a fan since his Aunt Eileen took him to a game when he was ten years old. As if sparking a connection, Sawyer snaps his fingers and pulls out his new phone. He texts Laura Lynne, asking if he can go to River Oaks while she is here visiting. Perhaps he can convince Diane to join him; he could mix business with pleasure. Sawyer grins as he sees her response, "Sure. I'll arrange. Send dates."

Sawyer looks at his watch and decides to walk to the Ridge. He has plenty of time. He picks up the walkie-talkie radio and finds Gabe in the kitchen, heating up dinner. "I'm headed out. Please stay close to home and keep a weapon close by while I'm gone."

Gabe gives him a steely-eyed gaze. "I can handle myself, son. Quit acting like you are the only one with any sense in this house."

"Sorry. I know, I know. I'm leaving." Sawyer arms himself and then radio's Malcolm and John with his plans.

John answers. "Roger that, Colonel. See you when you come my direction."

"Roger."

Sawyer slides his radio into his back pocket after hearing from Malcolm. He is pleased with the two men and the team they are creating. John and Malcolm both bring different abilities to the work making them a well-rounded team. But they are going to need more help. If all goes according to the plan Sawyer has been creating, Malcolm and John will lead a team of their own. But, first, he needs to meet with Grady. There is unfinished business that needs to be handled: Dead Doe and Bubba Westerman. Not to mention Freddy and the gang.

"Hello to the house!" Sawyer hollers as he approaches John's cabin.

John comes out the front door with two cups of coffee. Sawyer smiles as he joins him on the front porch. "Thanks, man." He takes a sip. "As good as Magnolia Café." He puts his hip against the porch railing and sits, palming his coffee cup. "What did you want to see me about?"

"I want to ask your permission before I step into your family business," says John.

"Ask away."

John clears his throat. It is the first time Sawyer has seen him nervous. He is intrigued. "If you agree, I'd like to keep an eye on your sister, Scarlet." He looks at Sawyer with concern. "I can't shake this feeling she is in trouble of some sort."

Sawyer lifts his mug to his lips and takes a swallow of coffee. He closes his eyes to savor the nutty flavor. "Of all the things I thought you might tell me, this is not one of them." He looks at John contemplatively. "We're all worried about her. I agree something is off, but you think there is trouble? How? Or maybe the better question is what trouble?"

"I can't put my finger on it. That day at the B and B, she was nervous and jumpy looking over my shoulder at the door the entire time like she was waiting for someone. And not in a welcoming way. With fear." He shakes his head. "I just sensed it. And God's honest truth, I trust my gut. It's saved me more times than I care to count."

Sawyer holds up his hand in acceptance. "I understand. My gut tells me Scarlet is not herself. I agree. How would you keep an eye on her? She lives some 30 minutes away."

"Well, I thought about that. It would require me being away from the farm some, but with the boys providing security now, I think you could spare me now and again." He gives a sheepish grin. "And I know how to watch without being seen. The army trained me well. I can do it, and she won't know. Neither will anyone else."

Sawyer stands up from the porch railing and throws the dregs of his coffee into the yard. "You have my permission. And if you find anything, I trust you will let me know."

"Yes, sir." John shakes Sawyer's hand.

"No more sir. Makes me feel like I am in the army again. My name is Sawyer, use it."

Now, John's grin takes over his entire face. "Then, it may not sit well to know the boys have started calling you Colonel. It seems to have stuck."

Sawyer grins, "That's fine, just no more 'sirs.'"

"Got it, Colonel."

Sawyer flicks the universal sign of 'kiss my ass' to John as he leaves to continue his trek toward the Ridge. He hears John chuckling as he walks away. Sawyer trusts John's instincts when it comes to Scarlet, mostly because they mirror his own. Hopefully, they are both wrong, but Sawyer doubts it.

Sawyer makes the final ascent to the small ridge and sees a small fire burning in the fire pit. Grady is already there and currently poking the fire with a stick. Some things men never grow out of. "Hey, Grady. Thanks for meeting me."

Grady smiles as he stands up. Sawyer appreciates the man Grady has become. He is several years younger than Sawyer and Charlie, but since he was Grace's brother, he was always with them. He looks like his mother, whereas Grace looks like their father. He has the height and breadth of his old man, though. No doubt he grew up on a farm. "No problem. I figured it was serious."

Sawyer nods and tells Grady about his conversation with Bubba. Grady rubs his chin. "So, he thinks local too?" He looks at Sawyer. "For all his faults, Bubba Westerman knows the people of Venice. He could be on to something. Can you tell me the specific words he used when he told you to tell me where to look for Freddie?"

Sawyer thinks for a moment. "He just said the boys were local and to check the regular haunts. That you would know where to look."

"He used the word 'haunts'?"

Sawyer reviews the conversation in his mind. "Yes, he specifically used that word. Why, what does it mean?"

"I think he is referring to the old Laurel House. The main house is gone, but there are plenty of buildings around the property. Most are old and falling down, but we sometimes find squatters."

"And haunts?"

"Every Halloween, the kids would scare themselves silly by running up to the Laurel House and touching the door. The kids swear there is a ghost who lives there. I did it myself when I was a kid and almost wet my pants. Don't tell me you didn't go?"

"Nope, wasn't a thing for me, though I have heard the rumors." Sawyer walks to the fire and pokes around the flames with a stick.

Grady walks over and mimics Sawyer's movements. "Not to change the subject, but I heard back from the coroner on your Dead Doe. They have narrowed the window on the time and cause of death." Grady tosses his stick in the fire. "Blunt force trauma to the head on or about 1991."

"Wow, how can they be that accurate?" asks Sawyer.

"Something about the body decomposition and the items they found with the body."

"Well, that clears me and Laura Lynne. We weren't here during those years. Just leaves the rest of the family. And the Jacksons, for that matter." He looks at Grady. "Any suspects?"

"Sure. A super long list. You named most of them. But until we can identify the body, we don't have much to go on. I will tell you Chandler is pulling out all the stops. He's submitted a request for familial DNA tracking, which generally takes at least a year. He's attempting to fast-track it."

Sawyer sighs. "No surprise there, Grady." Sawyer holds out his hand, and Grady shakes it. "Thanks, man. I can't tell you how glad I am to have you on our side." He smiles, "Go back to your family,

Grady. It's getting late. I'll take care of the fire. I think I might sit here for awhile and let it die down. Let my mind clear."

"Anytime, brother. Anytime."

Sawyer watches as Grady walks down the path toward Cotton Mill. He sits down on one of the chairs and closes his eyes. Just for a minute, just long enough to settle his mind and concentrate on the next steps.

24

Chapter Twenty-Four

Spring 1986

Tripp wakes up in the cabin and knows instantly he is alone. He pulls on a pair of sweatpants to walk into the kitchen. There is a pot of coffee brewing and a note on the counter. Sawyer picks it up, knowing it is a note from Clay saying goodbye:

Tripp,

Last night was incredibly special, and I loved being with you. And yet I knew, even as we were together, it wasn't right for either of us. I know my path. I know my future. Yours is not with me.

'I shall be telling this with a sigh
Somewhere ages and ages hence:
Two roads diverged in a wood, and I-
I took the one less traveled by,
And that has made all the difference.'

Clay

Sawyer read the note again. Of course, Clay would say goodbye with Robert Frost. Sawyer leaves the note on the counter and pours a cup of coffee. He takes it to the back door and out on the dock. He is unbelievably calm, considering the events of the previous night. He took a male lover. Never did the thought even cross his mind until Clay's revelation at Christmas. And as if a siren song, the lyrics of this melody kept bringing him back. Back to the idea of loving Clay in this way, of experiencing this emotion with someone he implicitly trusted.

Or was it just a pity fuck? Did he feel so bad for Clay that he tried to make things right by giving him his virginity?

Sawyer shakes his head and goes back to the cabin. He takes a lighter from the drawer and burns Clay's note. He can't chance someone finding it, learning what he did last night. Sawyer can't imagine sharing this type of intimacy with any other man. He knows, as Clay knew, that his path would be different than the one Clay chooses. His will be the path well-worn with time and tradition.

Sawyer walks to the bathroom and turns on the shower with its stingy spray. He shucks his drawers and stands under the hot water, allowing the tears to fall as he rinses the remnants of his time with Clay down the drain.

When he arrives back at the main house, he walks into the study and finds his father sitting at his desk working. Sawyer tosses the two cuff links on the paper his father is studying. His father glances up and then leans back in his chair, removing his readers. "What is this?"

"I don't want them, Dad. Whatever happened last night, whatever deal you made, I want nothing to do with it. You sold out my friend. He didn't deserve it, and neither did I."

"You don't know what you're talking about, son. You should be thrilled with the turn of events. You have done nothing but complain for the past year about your friends. Last night, you were one of them again."

"No, thanks. I can't be so easily bribed." He gestures to the cuff links. "That was all these were. Nothing but a bribe to keep me in line." He hangs his head. "You know this past year has been awful. You are right about that. And through it all, I thought we could weather the storm as a family. Instead, you all but disappear, Mom hides in her rooms, and Scarlet never comes home from school. Y'all have left Avery and me to fend for ourselves. Thank God for Queenie, or we would likely have starved to death."

"You watch your tone with me, young man!" Sawyer's father stands from his chair and leans over his desk, his weight on his hands. "I did what needed to be done for the sake of this family."

"Bullshit! You did what you had to do to save your own ass!" Sawyer leans over the desk and is face to face with his old man. "Don't worry, Dad. I won't tell. It's too embarrassing and disgusting. Not to mention shameful." He stands up and gives one last parting shot. "But you need to stick around, take care of Avery because, after graduation, I'm outta here. I have no intention of returning." He walks to the door. "You have lost three of us, Dad. Maybe you can salvage Avery."

"Don't you walk away from me, young man! You have no right..."

Sawyer does not hear the rest of the sentence. He goes to his room and packs his bags, throwing them into the back of the farm truck. He drives over to the cabin and unloads his luggage. School is over in three short weeks. He can hardly wait.

***

Present Day

Sawyer looks out the window and sees his uncle working in the flower gardens. Smiling, Sawyer puts down the papers in his hands and decides to join him before going into town. His Teams meeting with Beau had been productive, and Sawyer felt he had a good start to their new business plan. Beau recommended a way to ensure health care insurance for the farmhands, which was nothing less than brilliant. Well, it will be if he can pull it off. He hopes to share the idea with Diane if he can convince her to join him in Twin Rivers for the weekend.

"Playing with your flowers before the rain?" Sawyer asks.

Gabe stands up from his stooped position. He is holding roses in one hand and clippers in the other. "I want to get the good blooms off before the storm hits. Looks like it could be a soaker." He tosses the roses in the basket at his feet. It is overflowing with spring flowers. "Pearl can freshen up the vases." He looks Sawyer over. "Dressed kind of nice to be in the garden."

Sawyer pulls the lapel of his jacket down and tugs at the sleeves. "This, old man, is not for the garden. I'm going to town and plan to sweep our fairy bookstore owner off her feet."

"Ohhh, the fabulous Diane." Gabe reaches into his basket and pulls out a selection of fresh blooms. He hands them to Sawyer. "You don't want to go empty-handed."

Sawyer takes the offered flowers and smiles. "Thanks, Uncle Gabe, you are a charmer." He starts to walk away. "I won't be long. John and Malcolm are here."

"Wait." Sawyer turns around, and Gabe hands him another bouquet of flowers. "This one is for Melanie." Sawyer starts to protest. "Son, I don't want to hear it. She is your mother. She deserves to know what is happening in her own family. Besides, she may know something about the Kolensky payoff."

Gabe has a valid point. And Sawyer has been avoiding his mother since the day he came back to Venice, mostly out of guilt. He has not been a very good son over the years, avoiding her as a way of preventing the inevitable conversation about coming back to the farm and taking over his legacy. Since he has done just that, avoiding her should no longer be an issue. "You're right." He sighs and looks at his watch. "I'll be back in time for supper."

Chuckling, Gabe turns back to his flowers and spots Liam riding up the driveway on his bike. "Oh, good! Liam is back." He waves as the boy rides by. "He's been on an overnight field trip with his science club. I can't wait to hear about the space museum."

"It's fascinating his momma is Beth Ann Bodeen."

"Maybe not as fascinating as you may think. Underneath all that pink is a pretty smart woman. Men just get distracted by her curves." Gabe starts snipping more flowers. "Quit stalling. The flowers are going to wilt. Put them in water before you go. There are mason jars in the barn."

Shaking his head, Sawyer walks to the barn and nods to Liam as he darts past him to the gardens. "Hi, Colonel!" Sawyer watches as Liam joins Gabe at the flowers, talking a mile a minute. Gabe puts a hand on Liam's shoulder and steers him to the bench, listening intently. Sawyer is glad Liam has a Gabe in his life. In Sawyer's eyes, there is no better role model.

Sawyer finds the mason jars and fills the bottles with water at the sink. He cuts the stems and places the flowers in the jar at varying heights. Spotting some twine, he wraps a loop around the rim and ties a bow. He carefully places the mason jars in a box and puts the box in his Yukon. All he can think is that women are a lot of damn work. Exasperated, he revs the engine and heads to town, windows down and Motley Crue pounding through the speakers.

He goes to the bookstore first. He hasn't seen Diane since their interlude in his uncle's bedroom three days ago. He parks and walks around to the passenger's side to get the vase of flowers. He opens the door and leans over, fighting with the box and spilling water from the jar. Frustrated, he slams the door shut and nearly drops the arrangement when he sees Diane standing there smirking. "Those for me?"

"Christ, woman! You have a way of sneaking up on a person." Regaining his composure, he holds out the jar of flowers. "Yes, these are for you."

"From your gardens? They're beautiful." Her eyes soften, and her smirk becomes a smile. She takes the jar from him and unable to resist, she buries her face in the bouquet. "Thank you, Sawyer." She walks over to him and lifts her face for a kiss. He obliges.

"Come on in. I saw you pull up as I was getting ready to close for the evening. I'm glad you stopped by."

Sawyer follows her in, placing his hand at the small of her back in the way he knows she likes. She smiles over her shoulder. "I'm sorry I haven't been by to see you before today."

"No need to apologize. You warned me. Let's just enjoy the time we have together." She puts the mason jar on the counter and turns the lock on the front door. She pulls Sawyer into the book stacks and places her arms around his neck. He gathers her close. "Now, kiss me for real."

Sawyer swoops in for the kiss, running his hands along her back. Their lips lock and immediately their tongues begin their seductive dance. Diane raises up on her toes, increasing the pressure and allowing her breasts to press fully against his chest. She runs her fingers through his hair as he cups her buttocks, lifting her against his zipper. She murmurs as he runs his lips along her neck, gently nibbling at her ear. "Diane, I don't want to take you in the book stacks, but if we don't slow down that's what's going to happen."

"I know, I know." She holds on tight, and he does the same. Their breathing labored. "You just taste so good."

Sawyer lifts his head and lightly kisses her lips. "I know, so do you." They stand in the stacks, looking into each other's eyes, lost in their own little world. Finally, Sawyer clears his throat and takes her hand as they untangle themselves. "I have a proposition for you."

"Oh? Do tell."

"Next weekend, I have to go to Atlanta for a meeting. While I am there, I'll be staying at River Oaks. I want you to join me."

She releases his hand and takes a step back, leaning against the bookcase. "What's River Oaks?"

"It used to be my Aunt Eileen's horse farm. Now, it's more of an animal shelter for rescues. The main house is a rental. Laura Lynne is considering selling the place, and I'd like to see it before we make any decisions."

"I see." She looks at him with longing. "I really want to go, but I don't see how I can. I need to watch Mandy, and there is the store."

"Mandy can stay at Tea Olive. I already cleared it with Laura Lynne and Uncle Gabe. They would love to have her. Is there someone who can cover for you at the store?"

"Maybe. I don't know. I've never had a day off."

Sawyer grabs both her hands, "What? Are you serious? What do you do when you get sick?"

"I don't know. I don't get sick. Ever. Mandy either."

Sawyer lifts her hands to his lips, he gently kisses the knuckles, nipping at her fingertips. "No pressure, Diane. I want you there, but I understand if you can't come." He drops her hands from his mouth but continues to hold them. "Just let me know. I'll buy the tickets and make all the arrangements."

She nods and walks into his space, placing her head on his chest. "Let me talk to Mandy, and then I'll let you know." She looks up and smiles. "Thank you for the flowers."

"Uncle Gabe's idea. And a very good one." He glances at his watch. "Listen, I need to go. I have to see my mother, and I want to get there before the supper starts."

"Okay, one last kiss before you go?"

"Absolutely." Sawyer kisses her thoroughly. "Okay woman, you're going to make me miss my mother. Not that I mind." He pulls her around, her back to his front. He places his chin on her head and takes a deep breath. "But as Uncle Gabe told me earlier, I can no longer shirk this responsibility."

"I like your mother. I always have."

"Really? Well, that is good to hear. She is a formidable woman, most people are intimidated by her," Sawyer remarks.

Diane shrugs, leaning fully into his embrace. "I think she has had to be. I get that." She snuggles and gives his arm a squeeze, kissing his wrist before disengaging. "Come on. I will walk you out. It is time to lock up anyway."

Sawyer watches as Diane turns out the lights and locks the doors. Grady is right, she is like a fairy or maybe a sprite. She has this ethereal peace about her that is a balm to Sawyer's ragged psyche. Simply being in her presence, watching her perform mundane everyday tasks causes a contentment he has never experienced. It is definitely addictive. But then, so are her kisses.

"Call me when you make up your mind. You have my number?"

"I do. Enjoy your mom." Sawyer grimaces as he steps back from her Camry and watches as she backs out of the parking lot. With a car honk and a wave, Diane disappears down the road. Sawyer climbs into his Yukon and drives the short distance to his mother's assisted living facility. He straightens his jacket and brushes his pants. Taking the bouquet of flowers, Sawyer walks into the home. He is greeted by a bubbly woman named Daphne.

"Her room is down the hall and to the left. You can't miss it." Daphne leans close and whispers, "Be sure you knock. Mrs. Beauregard is a great believer in formality." She rolls her eyes and scrunches her nose.

"Thanks for the tip." Sawyer walks down the hall, his very presence causing a stir amongst the residents. He's surprised by the number of people he recognizes. The names on the door tags are like a who's who of Venice society. He comes to his mother's room and knocks on the door. After a few moments he hears her grant entry.

He opens the door and walks into her room. She is fully dressed for dinner and sitting in a dusty rose wingback chair. "Hi Momma. I brought you some flowers."

"Thank you. You can put them on the entry table, Sawyer." She looks at the flowers skeptically. "Though perhaps a new vase would be appropriate."

Sawyer rolls his eyes. Of course, she wants a different vase; a mason jar is not going to suit Melanie. He glances around the room. The room could easily have been one of Melanie's rooms at The Residence. The space has been outfitted with antiques, artwork, and a chandelier hanging from the ceiling. The walls are a dusty rose with sage green accents—a lady's parlor of sorts.

"Yes, well, perhaps you can find something more appropriate." He walks back to his mother and takes a seat across from her. "How are you doing, Momma?"

"I think it's a better place to start for me to ask you the same question." She gives him a look only mothers can bestow upon their wayward sons. "How are you doing? And even more importantly, what is going on at Tea Olive? I've heard gossip from these crows, but I would prefer to hear the truth from you." She thumps her cane on the ground. "Please proceed."

"Yes, ma'am." Sawyer starts at the beginning, laying out the events at Tea Olive over the past two weeks. He ends up with Gabe transferring the trust to his name, making his legacy official. A gleam enters her eye when he reveals his plan to stay in Venice, for Tea Olive to remain his home.

"So, you've decided to embrace what you have so handily avoided all these years."

"Yes ma'am. I know you are pleased."

"And this upsets you? Me being pleased? Or is it more that your father and I were right all along? You cannot run from your birthright, no matter how fast or how hard. Nobody understands that better than me."

"You, Mother?"

She looks around at her quarters before setting her steely gaze on her oldest son. "Yes, me! I have had no choices, no free will. Only expectations and demands. There was no running from them. Where would I go? It fell to me to marry well and produce heirs. I did what was expected of me. Now, it is your turn."

"Did you not want to be a wife and mother? A society woman?"

Melanie sighs. "It doesn't matter what I wanted. I was all but trapped. Gabe had a falling out with Papa. And Eileen, well, we knew from the time she was little she would be unable to produce any children. It was my responsibility. What point would there have been to shirk it? To what end?" She straightens her skirt.

"What would you have done if you had choices?"

She gazes out the window and speaks softly, "I would have liked to be an academic. I loved school, and I was good at it. Maybe a professor teaching art history or literature." Her voice becomes stronger. "It doesn't matter now."

Sawyer leans forward and grasps her hands. "I'm sorry. I didn't know." He squeezes her hands. "Momma, I have a few questions I need to ask you about Daddy. Some stuff I found in the books. Think you can help me?"

"Of course, what do you want to know?"

"That spring of 1986, right before I graduated from Moseley. You remember the awards banquet?" She nods. "There was a transaction of $500,000 to Headmaster Kolensky the week prior. What can you tell me about it?"

"A half million dollars? No, that number is not right. We did give him a donation, but it was $50,000, not $500,000."

"What was the donation for?" asks Sawyer.

She looks steadily in her son's eyes, not batting an eyelash. "You already know the answer. To have Clay removed from the school quietly and discreetly. If his proclivities had been made public, you would have been ruined. Your father and I discussed it and came to the same conclusion. He had to go."

He did know the answer. But hearing it from his mother, so briskly eliminating any perceived threat to her son, still gives him a jolt.

She continues, "But the amount we agreed on was $50,000. It was not trust money. It was Beauregard money. We never touched the trust for these *delicate* matters."

"I take it to mean bribes and blackmail when you use the term 'delicate'?"

"Don't be crude, Sawyer. Sometimes, business matters require grease to skid the wheels. But we would never jeopardize the trust," Melanie replies.

"Would there have been $500,000 in the Beauregard holdings?"

"Oh, yes. As the only child, your father inherited all the Beauregard assets. We agreed to place the land and businesses in the trust, but all liquid assets were never included. Have you not seen the separate bank account? Gabe should have shown them to you."

"Not yet." Sawyer rubs the tops of his thighs with his hand—his tell. His mother notices. Sawyer asks, "Is there anything else I might need to know, Momma? Like who Dead Doe is? Or maybe why drugs are being run through our property?"

"Certainly not. Do you have any ideas?"

He glances at his mother. Sawyer says, "If you are asking whether it was me, the answer is no. Dead Doe was killed in or around 1991; I was enlisted and off to my first war then. It couldn't have been me." He gets up from his seat. "As far as the drugs are concerned, it is a fairly new operation but well-established long before I came home." He walks over to his mother. "Can I escort you to dinner?"

She smiles, and he can see glimpses of her regal beauty, a glimmer of the young girl who captivated his father's heart. "I would like that, son. Perhaps as we walk, you can tell me about your date with the bookstore owner. I hear she dined at Tea Olive."

Thirty minutes later, and a myriad of handshakes and reminisces about the glory days of his high school football career, Sawyer extricates himself from the dining hall. His discussion with his mother still swirls around in his brain. Something she said lands on the tip of his brain, not quite filling in a missing link. He just can't place it yet.

He contemplates the missing $450,000. His mother's version of events makes the most sense. $50,000 is much more in line with a bribe for a headmaster of a tiny backwoods private school. So where is the missing money? According to his army buddy, the amount deposited into the Kolensky's account was $500,000. And what about the Beauregard money account his mother referenced? He only knows of one account, the one Ginny Phillips was being paid out of, but it was his father's private account.

He pulls into Tea Olive before realizing he never asked about Bubba Westerman. Parking the Yukon in the barn, Sawyer throws his keys in the lock box and looks at his mother's prized pink Cadillac. He shakes his head. A teacher? He just can't picture it. He moves Liam's bike out of the doorway and makes his way to the mud room. He kicks off his shoes and takes off his jacket, unbuttoning his shirt and sleeves as he makes his way up the stairs. He hears Gabe call, "Sawyer! Is that you?"

"Yes, sir." Sawyer changes direction and heads to the study. Gabe and John play chess while Liam sits at the desk reading. "Uncle Gabe. I'm sorry that I'm late. I got held up in the dining hall at Momma's."

"No problem. We saved some supper for you." Uncle Gabe looks at Sawyer's grim face. "We can talk later. You have time to grab a shower."

Sawyer goes upstairs, and his eye falls on his old room. He goes into the shrine his mother created, noting his letterman jacket has been placed in a shadow box and hangs above his mantelpiece like a piece of art. He has mixed emotions when he sees his trophies, medals, ribbons, and awards. There is a part of him that basks in the glory of his achievements. He had, after all, worked very hard to reach them. And, up until his senior year of high school, he loved every minute of his time on the field and with his teammates. His coaches helped mold him into the man he has become. One, he hoped, played fair, didn't cheat, was a team player, and was an exceptional leader on and off the field. It is not until this moment, standing in the middle of his shrine of a room, that he realizes his mother basked in his success as much as he did. Perhaps more. And, probably, his father too. As he leaves the room, he makes a note to himself to ask Pearl to box it all up and put it in storage. Maybe add a fresh coat of paint to the room too. Time for a fresh start.

He makes haste in the shower, his stomach growling. He puts on his new khaki pants and shirt, all neatly pressed courtesy of Pearl. As he comes down the stairs, he hears his uncle in the kitchen. "Sawyer! In the kitchen."

Sawyer walks through the swinging doors, and his uncle is bent over the stove, stirring something in a pot, something that smells wonderful. "Shrimp boil," Gabe says with a smile, "With Pearl's brothers and nephews staying at Queenie's, Victoria is making family favorites. And we get the benefit. Sit down at the island. You can tell me what your momma had to say. I'll slice some of the rosemary bread."

Sawyer goes to the refrigerator and pours a glass of unsweet tea. "What happened to John and Liam?"

"I sent them home. We need privacy for this conversation. Don't worry, it was getting late anyway. John will take Liam home. Now, tell me about what Melanie had to say." Sawyer recounts his mother's version of events from 1986.

"$50,000 makes more sense than half a million. Maybe we got the number wrong?" asks Gabe.

"I thought about that, and I'll double-check. But I feel confident about the number." He looks to his uncle as he dishes out the stew into a bowl. "What about the Beauregard account? Do you know anything about that one?"

Gabe shakes his head. "No, but it makes sense there would be a separate account. Maybe it is in your mother's name?"

"I didn't ask, but that doesn't make sense either. She would have received it when Daddy died. She would've been notified." Sawyer tucks into the shrimp boil, savoring the smell and taste of home. "Honestly, I have more questions than answers. I am hoping to get some of them solved next week when I go visit Headmaster Kolensky."

"You're going to Atlanta then?"

"I'd like to. I spoke with Laura Lynne, and she's arranged for me to stay at River Oaks while I'm there." He gives his uncle a sly glance. "That is if you are willing to have a house full of women while I'm gone." His uncle raises an eyebrow. "Laura Lynne said she would watch Mandy for a few days if I wanted to take her mother with me."

Gabe gives a low whistle. "You sure about this? Aren't you moving awfully quick for a lifelong bachelor?" He looks at Sawyer in all seriousness. "Don't hurt her, son."

"I don't plan to. Worried she will hurt me, though. I don't know, Uncle Gabe; she feels like she could be the one I've been waiting for." Sawyer wipes his mouth and throws down his napkin. "I always thought marriage would be out of the equation for me, but maybe I just needed the right woman. I don't know. Feels different this time."

"You know I would love for Mandy to spend the weekend here at Tea Olive. Just know if you do this, you're making a commitment. One you won't easily be able to walk away from. It is not honorable to hurt a mother and her daughter."

"I know. I know." Sawyer pushes away from the island. "No offense Uncle Gabe, but I stay out of your love life. I'm asking you do the same for me." He gives him the eye.

Gabe throws up his hands. "Point taken. Butting out."

"Now let's see if we can find the missing $450,000.00."

25

Chapter Twenty-Five

Over the next several days, The Residence takes on a frenzy of activity in preparation for guests arriving. Laura Lynne is scheduled to arrive on Wednesday, and Mandy will be arriving after school on Friday. Much to Sawyer's delight and also, if he admits it to himself, trepidation, Diane has agreed to accompany him on his trip to Atlanta.

"Pearl, it's not that big of a deal. Laura Lynne has no expectations, and Mandy is a teenager. I am sure pizza and Netflix will satisfy her."

Pearl gives Sawyer a blank stare before succinctly putting him in his place. "I don't tell you how to play soldier; don't tell me how to run The Residence." She walks past him up the stairs. "By the way, while you're gone, I will have your rooms painted. Your new one and your old one. Gonna repair that hole in the wall your nephew made while he was here." She huffs. "Imagine you fools thought I wouldn't notice. And before you say anything else to get you on my bad side, I am using Bill Gates for the work. Only Bill."

Sawyer smiles. Tea Olive has used Bill for years to renovate and update the house. He is one of the few contractors that Sawyer trusts. With a shake of his head, Sawyer continues down the stairs. Bill is a friend of Gabe's, which puts him in his 70s. "Don't let him fall and break a hip."

"Hmmph!"

"What did you do to get her all riled up?" Gabe asks as he stands at the kitchen entrance, a biscuit in his hand.

"I suggested she not go to a lot of fuss about our guests," Sawyer says.

Gabe lets out a belly laugh. "Son, you ought to know better by now. Pearl has standards." He puts the rest of his biscuit in his mouth and brushes his hands. "What time does Laura Lynne arrive?"

"She texted she would arrive at the house before suppertime. She hopes Victoria will make her a tomato pie. I told her it was a bit early for tomatoes," he says while he enters the kitchen with his uncle, hoping to snag a biscuit.

"Not for my greenhouse. I got a bushel of them. Don't you worry, Mr. Sawyer, I'll make sure Laura Lynne is fed." Victoria slaps a ball of dough on the counter and starts kneading it with vigor, obviously peeved.

"I never suggested…" starts Sawyer. Victoria looks at him with the same baleful look her mother gave him on the stairs not five minutes ago. "Fine! Fine! I'm going." He grabs a biscuit and motions for Gabe to follow him.

"What is up with the Jackson women today? I can't seem to do anything right," says Sawyer.

"They want to impress your future stepdaughter," says Gabe.

Sawyer juggles his biscuit and almost drops it. "My what?"

Gabe chuckles and slaps him on the back. "Don't say I didn't warn you." Gabe continues to chuckle as he heads out the back porch, Sawyer staring at his back. "Good morning, John! You here to see me?"

Jonh replies, "No, sir. The Colonel if he is available."

"Yep, go right inside. He's probably still standing in the hallway," says Gabe.

John walks through the back porch door, careful not to bring in any dirt from outdoors. Pearl would ring his neck with company coming and all. "Colonel, you got a minute?" He takes a closer look. "You okay? You look a bit pale."

"What? Yeah, I'm fine. Just realized what a mess I started when I invited Diane to Atlanta this weekend," says Sawyer.

"I heard you were planning on asking her to marry you." John starts to laugh. "I see you figured it out too."

"Women. I swear." Brushing his hands off, he walks toward John. "What can I do for you?"

"I wanted to talk to you a minute about that special project," John says.

"Special project?" Seeing John's pointed expression, Sawyer realizes he's talking about Scarlet. "Sure, let's head to the barn. We can talk and walk at the same time."

Sawyer meets John at the base of the porch stairs. "What's up?"

"That's just it. I have no idea what is going on at her house, but something certainly is." He turns to face Sawyer. "You know that bed and breakfast I met her at the day you asked me to?" Sawyer nods. "Well, she goes there every day, twice a day." Sawyer stops walking and looks toward John. "I went in after she left one morning and asked about her. She's going by the name Annie." He looks Sawyer in the eye. "She is their housekeeper."

"What?"

"Apparently, she also sells them the soaps and detergents she makes." Sawyer looks at him blankly. "Those salt scrubs and soaps you have at The Residence? Those are hers."

"Really? I had no idea. She works as a cleaning lady? Under an assumed name? Why?"

"No clue. According to the woman at the front desk, she is well-liked and does a great job. She's been working there for about six months." Sawyer hasn't moved. "I thought you should know."

Sawyer shakes his head. "Anything else?"

"I have been watching the house when I can. Someone is there with her, but keeps weird hours. I have yet to see him or her."

"Probably her husband, Buck. I haven't seen him since my return. Or heard anything about him. I will check with Grady and Charlie. Maybe they can give me some more information." Sawyer shakes his head. "A cleaning lady? That is hard to believe. Do you think she is safe?"

John shrugs. "She appears to be."

"Well, it explains why she is not around much. My gut tells me to let it be as long as she is safe. She's a grown woman; it is none of our business. If she wants me to know, she will tell me." Sawyer smacks him on the shoulder. "Thanks for looking out for her, though."

"No problem."

"You gonna be around this weekend? Laura Lynne will be here with Diane's daughter. Things seem to have died down over the past week, but I would feel better about leaving if I knew you were here."

"I got you covered. I wouldn't want you to miss out on your engagement shindig."

"Cut me some slack, would you? Uncle Gabe is giving me plenty of grief. Not to mention Pearl and Victoria."

John laughs as he walks away.

Sawyer jumps into his Yukon and takes a drive into town. Lally called yesterday and invited him in for a meeting. He would not disclose what the meeting was about, but Sawyer assumes it must be trust business.

Sawyer arrives at the Law Offices of Lally & Lally. Father and son greet him at the door. "Sawyer, come into my office. I have coffee and doughnuts waiting." Sawyer follows Garfield into his office and takes a seat. Ace pours a cup of coffee and hands it to Sawyer.

Garfield continues, "I got a call a few days ago from Jackson Correctional. Yesterday, I went to visit Bubba as his attorney. I am here speaking to you today as his attorney." He nods to his son. "Ace has been taking over the operations of the trust and working with Tea Olive for the past year. We have made the transition official. I will no longer represent you and your uncle. I want there to be no issue with representation." He sips his coffee. "Do you agree, Sawyer? If not, we can figure out another way around this situation."

Sawyer is quiet for a moment, thinking through the implications. "Do you want to represent Bubba Westerman?"

"Unfortunately, I already did that years ago. When I first got started and took any client that came my way, I provided legal counsel regarding family law. I am his legal counsel of record—a fact I had forgotten until we met yesterday," Garfield explains.

Sawyer looks to Ace. "You up for all this? Right now, my families' affairs are pretty complicated. They will probably stay that way for a while. Now is the time to back out if you aren't interested."

"No, my family and yours go back a long way. And it has been good for both of us. I would like to stick around. Besides, your family is never boring," says Ace.

"You have no idea." Sawyer contemplates his options and sees very few alternatives. He likes Ace, and he is honest. "All right, Ace. Looks like it's you and me." He takes a bite of doughnut and closes his eyes as the sugar hits his system. "Listen, while I am here, can you tell me anything about Buck Huger? I haven't seen him around."

"Dad probably knows more than I do," Ace replies, "He and his father never used us or any of the local attorneys for any business or personal stuff. I approached Buck once, hoping to land him when his parents died. He told me he was sticking with his guy, a distant relation, maybe a second cousin. I dropped it after that." Ace looks at his father. "Dad?"

"The Huger family has been here almost as long as the Coopers," Garfield begins, "Though they did not come into their wealth until the Civil War. They were blockade runners. The family made their money selling their bounty to those who could afford it. It was after that that his family acquired Twin Oaks. They grew cotton, same as everybody else. It wasn't until Robert, Buck's father, began running the farm that they began playing in the stock market. Robert had a hand with numbers and spent less and less time with the farming operations, instead gambling on the stock market, with considerable gains from my understanding."

"So why did they sell Twin Oaks?" Sawyer asks.

"I have always assumed it was because Buck was not as good at the stock market as his father. I really don't know," says Garfield.

"Hmmmm," Sawyer says as he gets up from the chair and holds out his hand to shake Garfield's hand. "I appreciate all your help."

"I'll walk you out." Ace follows Sawyer out of the room to the large foyer. "Anything I need to know?"

Sawyer looks at him quizzically. "How did you know?"

Ace laughs and slaps him on the back, "I'm a lawyer. I read people for a living. Something my father said bothered you. What was it?"

"Where is Buck in all this? Laura Lynne and I have been worried about Scarlet. She's not acting normal, at least not the normal we are familiar with. And I just found out today that she is working as a cleaning lady."

This comment stops Ace in his tracks. "Why on earth? If she needs money, wouldn't she just come to you or Mr. Gabe?"

Sawyer shakes his head. "I've been thinking about that, and I don't think so. When she married Buck, Daddy gave Scarlet her share of the trust. Legally, she has no claim on the trust. Knowing my sister, she has too much pride to ask for a handout." Sawyer puts his hands in his pockets and leans back on his heels. "Listen, can you do some digging around? See what you can find out about Buck and maybe their finances? I'm not sure what I am looking for, but it all seems fishy."

"Sure, I will see what I can find," Ace replies.

"Oh, and Ace, keep our discussion about my sister between us, will you? I don't want to embarrass Scarlet."

"Of course."

"Thanks, man. I'm gone for a few days, but Laura Lynne comes in this afternoon. If you need anything, give her a call."

Ace grins. "Have fun in Atlanta. Give Diane my regards."

Sawyer grimaces. "You know too?"

Ace laughs. "Are you kidding? My wife has been talking about it nonstop. Very juicy gossip."

Sawyer rolls his eyes as he opens the front door, for the first time wondering what he was thinking when he thought his private life might remain that way. What a joke. He glances at his phone as he walks toward his car. It's a text from Grady's reading. "Urgent. Saw your car at Lally's. When done, meet me at G."

Sawyer wonders, "Christ. Now what?" He turns his steps from the parking lot to Main Street. He may as well enjoy the beautiful day while it lasts.

He enters the Gazette front door, the bell tinkling. Mary is sitting at the front desk, absorbed in a novel. She looks over her glasses at Sawyer. "Good morning, Sawyer. He's in Laura Lynne's old office."

"Thank you, Mary. You look especially lovely today. I like the peach color on you."

She smiles and winks at him. "You are in a particularly good mood this morning. Wouldn't have anything to do with your trip this weekend?"

Deciding against exhibiting his frustration, Sawyer grins and smacks his hand on the counter. "It absolutely does." Then he leans closer to her. "Any clue what Grady wants?"

"None, but from his demeanor, I don't think it's good. He looked pretty shook up," says Mary.

"Got it. Thanks."

Sawyer makes his way to the back office. Grady paces with his hat in hand, sporting his sheriff's uniform. "Hey, Grady, what's up?" asks Sawyer.

Grady stops pacing. "Buddy, you may want to sit down for this. It's not good."

Sawyer does not argue. He sits in the office chair. "Okay, Grady. Give it to me."

Grady sits in the chair across from Sawyer, his elbows on his knees, twirling his hat between his hands. "It has to do with Laura Lynne and her...rape."

Sawyer is silent, letting Grady put his words together. He is quiet for a long time. Finally, he clears his throat. "There is just no easy way to tell you this. So, I am just going to tell you. There were multiple perpetrators, not just Dr. Butler."

Sawyer stares blindly at Grady as he continues. "The prosecutor was suspicious after discussing Laura Lynne's case with a doctor who specializes in sexually transmitted infections. So, she confronted him with her information, and he confirmed he and another man molested her that night."

Calmly, Sawyer asks. "What other man?"

Grady throws up his hands. "Your guess is as good as any. He's not talking."

Sawyer jumps up. "Fifteen minutes, Grady. Give me fifteen minutes with that son of a bitch, and I will give you all the information you need. Then, I will kill him."

"Stand in line. I already expressed the same sentiment to the prosecutor. Not that she disagrees. She is something else. Her name is Sadie Crawford, and I like her. She's good, and she doesn't take any shit."

"Well, that is something." Sawyer's expression turns from anger to pain. "Does Laura Lynne know?"

"Not yet. I thought it might be best if you told her. Sadie called me with the information. Apparently, you and I are on a list Laura Lynne provided to Sadie giving her permission to share information on her case. Today, I really wish I were not on that list."

"Dear God..." Sawyer rubs his temples and squeezes the bridge of his nose. "I hate this."

Grady stands up and gives Sawyer a pat on the shoulder. "I know, man. But I think its best if she hears it from you."

"Grady, man. I haven't been much of a brother to my sisters, especially Laura Lynne. I walked away and didn't look back. What do I do? How do I fix this?"

"Looks to me like you are fixing things right now. You're here. But you can't leave again. They need you; be there for them." He puts his hat back on. "What time does Laura Lynne come in today?"

"This afternoon. Around 3."

"One word of advice. Don't sit on this. Tell her right away. She'll be pissed if you wait and then be mad at you for not telling her straight away. Take it from me," Grady says with a wry grin.

"Grace?"

"Yeah, we have had our fair share of brother-sister shit. Nothing like this, but she has been plenty mad at me over the years, mostly for keeping stuff from her. I think of it as protecting her; she thinks I don't think she is strong enough to handle it. Or, as she has often told me, 'I am not a child. I don't need protecting.'" He smiles. "She is always right. She handles things better than me."

"Thanks, buddy. I'm glad you were the one to tell me."

"Here if you need me." Grady checks his watch. "Listen, are you okay? I gotta run." Sawyer nods. Grady continues, "Thank Mary for me. I'm going out the back door."

Grady walks out of the office with a brief wave. Sawyer drops back in his chair and hangs his head. He hopes Grady is right because right now, Sawyer is not handling this news well at all. He feels a hand on his shoulder.

"You all right, Sawyer? Can I get you anything?" Mary asks quietly.

"Mary, have you ever thought the world was handing you more than you could deal with? Like just one more thing and you were going to go crazy?"

Mary turns matter-of-fact. "Of course, all the time. It's called life, and the more you engage with it, the more you deal with. Add love and relationships into it, and it can get tricky."

He looks up questioningly. "Why do you do it? I'd rather just keep to myself."

"How did that fair for you Sawyer? Not to put too fine a point on it, but you seem pretty lonely to me. People make things complicated, that is for certain. But they also make life worth living. Take it from an old spinster like me. Stop hiding and start living. You moving here is a step in the right direction. And taking up with Diane is another one," says Mary.

"She's pretty great, isn't she?"

"Absolutely. She would probably like it if you stopped by and said hello before you leave town. That big-ass Yukon you drive is hard to miss. I'm sure she knows you're in town."

Sawyer's jaw drops. Never in a million years would he ever suspect his old English teacher would ever cuss. "Miss Mary! Watch your mouth!"

She laughs like a schoolgirl. "Trying it out. Ron thinks it's sexy."

At that Sawyer jumps up. "Thanks for letting me meet with Grady. Talk with you later."

Her giggle turns into a full-blown bawdy laugh. "Thought that might get you movin'. Now, go see Diane. Tell her how much you're looking forward to this weekend. It will perk you up."

Sawyer hightails it out the door, the bell jingling behind him. Mary is right about one thing: the idea of seeing Diane does perk him right up. He walks down Main Street toward the bookstore, texting her as he walks, "meet me for coffee in 10?" Her response is immediate and affirmative.

As he walks into the Magnolia Café, he is assailed by the smell of fresh coffee and the curious stares of patrons. Since his return, he has gotten used to the constant scrutiny from the townsfolk. They are too Southern to be rude to his face, but he knows his trips to town and the current situation at Tea Olive have the town talking. About him. And his family. He nods to several people but does not engage in conversation.

As he walks toward the counter, he sees Diane coming through the back door. She walks up to him and smiles, lifting her head for a kiss. He obliges, taking his time to savor her scent and taste. "Glad you stopped by. I've missed seeing you." Diane places her head on his chest before stepping back. Sawyer keeps his arms loosely around her waist.

"You too. And I'm sorry. It has been busy getting everything in place for the weekend."

"No apology necessary." She slides her arm around his waist and turns toward the counter. "Good morning, Gladys, the usual for me." Diane looks at Sawyer. "What do you want?"

"Surprise me."

Diane smiles and orders him a lavender latte. "Come on; let's sit down. Gladys will call when it's ready." She glances at her watch. "I only have 20 minutes before the shop opens." They walk hand in hand to a cozy corner. "Now, what brings you to town today?"

"Business. I had to meet with Lally. We can talk about it later." He smiles as he reaches for her hand. "Are you ready for the weekend?"

"I am. Nervous, but ready."

He chuckles. "Me too. I didn't think I would be, but I am." He turns serious, "And Diane, nothing has to happen. I have no expectations. Mostly, I just want to get to know you better." He looks pointedly around the café. "Without all these prying eyes."

She breathes a big sigh. "I am so glad to hear that." She looks at him intently. "This matters. Us. Much more than it should. I think you ought to know that before going in."

He gently kisses her hand. "I know. It matters that much to me too. I don't know why; it just does."

Their intimate moment is interrupted by Gladys calling Diane to the counter. Sawyer waves her down while he collects their drinks. He hands Diane a chai latte and places his cup on the small table. "Do you have the store covered while we are gone?"

"You mean Laura Lynne hasn't told you?" Diane sips at her tea. "She and Mandy are going to work the store on Saturday. She seems pretty excited about it. I think she has even convinced Miss Mary to help her."

"Really? That's great. Laura Lynne will love that, and I bet she will be good at it." His look turns to one of concern. "But it does expose her to reporters and the like. I don't know."

"She said you would say that, so she already roped Grady into security detail. Plus, Gray is going to be here too."

"Wait, what? Nobody tells me anything."

"Relax, it just happened this morning. With all that's going on and you leaving for the weekend, Gray thought it wise to tag along. He sounds like a pretty protective husband. And from Laura Lynne's experiences, I would say he has cause to be. Anyway, he's joining her for the weekend."

"I am not mad, just surprised. How do you know more about my family than I do?" She glances at his phone knowingly. "What have I missed?"

"About 15 phone calls and 20 texts. She gave up and started calling me. I answer," Diane replies.

"Yeah. Well, I hate this thing. I can't get used to people having access to me all the time. It stays in a drawer at the house most of the time. I only pull it out when I come to town."

"I don't want to sound like a nagging wife, but you need to be available. Your family has a lot going on, and you are the center for them right now. Being available is part of the deal." She looks over her steaming cup of tea at the consternation on his handsome face. "Don't be angry."

"I'm not. It's just harder to be the head of this family than I thought. Running the farm? Deciding on organic versus traditional farming methods? Revamping the business side of things? All that's simple. Relationships and caring are the hard part. I am not sure I am up to the task."

"I would say you're doing a fine job. Just keep that phone on you and answer it when someone calls. At least for now." She grins. "We can put a sexy ringtone on it. Maybe 'The Army Song?'"

"More like 'Taps,'" says Sawyer.

She slaps his knee. "It's not that bad. Cheer up. This weekend, we are going away, and you are going to get laid. It's gonna be great."

"God woman, I think I love you," he says cheekily.

She turns serious, "I think I love you too. And it scares me to death."

26

Chapter Twenty-Six

June 1986

"Back here Avery!" Tripp calls out from his spot on the dock. He has a line in the water, pretending to fish. Mostly, he is thinking about graduation and planning his future.

Avery slams out the back door of the fishing cabin, beer in hand, "Hey bro! Mind if I join you?"

Tripp eyes the beer can. Avery is fifteen years old now and coming into his Beauregard height. He plays all the customary sports at Moseley Hall, Tripp had watched him when his own schedule allowed it. He was pretty good. But what he excelled at and what Tripp hated, was public speaking. He had run for and won president of his class and Vice President of the Student Council. Pretty big deal considering he is just now a sophomore.

"Well, well Mr. President. What brings you out my way?" asks Sawyer.

"Need a break from the Residence. Its brutal there. And quiet. Never knew a place could be so quiet. It's like a mausoleum."

"You could stay out here with me. Or, after graduation tomorrow you can have the place all to yourself."

Avery takes a drink of beer from his can, "So, you're really gonna do it? Leave for Charleston." He grimaces, "Was hoping I could convince you otherwise. We could work in the fields together, one last time. Uncle Gabe needs the help."

Tripp raises an eyebrow, "Uncle Gabe tell you that?"

Sitting down on the dock, his legs dangling over the edge, Avery sighs, "Hell no, man. I just want you to stay." He looks over the water, "I don't want to be here by myself until I have to be." Another swig of beer, "Laura Lynne called last night. She's not coming home. That means if you go, well, it's just me."

"I can't stay, Av."

Avery looks over his shoulder at his older brother, the one person he has always looked up to and who has never let him down, until now. "That's simply not true. You can stay. You are choosing not to. I want to know why. Why are you choosing Charleston over Tea Olive? What happened between you and dad?"

"Let's just say we let each other down," Tripp replies, reeling in his fishing line.

"Hmmph. Shit answer."

"Well, it's the only answer you are gonna get. And by the way, when did you start drinking beer?" Tripp asks.

Avery looks at his can, "Give me a break. You know how it is at Moseley."

"I do, that's why I'm asking." Tripp hooks a grasshopper to the end of his line and casts his line again, "Be careful, it can get you into a lot of trouble. A beer here and there is fine, hang with your friends, but never get drunk. Ever. You hear me?"

Avery doesn't respond. Tripp can feel him rolling his eyes.

"Avery! Do you hear me?"

"Yeah, yeah. Whatever." He looks over his shoulder, "Stop changing the subject. Tell me why you are leaving now instead of waiting. I don't know man, it's like I'm being left here to fend for myself."

Tripp puts down his rod and walks over to Avery, sitting on the dock next to him. "I know. It's absolutely not fair to you. I hate it."

"Then don't leave. Wait until the fall."

"I could, I guess. But then what? I am leaving, regardless. It won't change anything. You have your friends, right? They're not going anywhere." Tripp replies, referring to Avery's childhood, long-term friends Stratton, Noah, and Walker.

"I know. I know. They stuck by me this year." He looks at Tripp, "Your friends were shit. At least you had Clay."

"Yeah, it was a shit year. For sure."

"I'm not gonna change your mind, am I?" Avery asks.

"No little bro, you're not. I have a plan and I'm gonna get out of here for a while. I need a break and I want to sow a few oats before I have to hunker down at the Citadel. I'm told knob year is hell."

All the sudden, the fishing line takes off. Tripp's pole darts across the dock and as one, Tripp and Avery lunge for it. Avery gets it first and with a wild laugh and a grin, starts reeling the fish in.

"Whoo, hoo! We snagged a big un," says Avery.

"Be gentle, Avery. Let him tire himself out. That fishing line is as old as the cabin. You don't want it to break."

Avery looks at his brother, "You are such a mom. I got this."

And, he did.

***

Present Day

Laura Lynne and Gray arrive at The Residence in the late afternoon. They pull up to the front porch driving a bright red Jeep Gladiator. Sawyer, Gabe, and Pearl greet them as they climb out of the car.

"It never gets old, this place." Laura Lynne walks up to Gabe and gives him a hug. She turns to Pearl and does the same.

"Laura Lynne! What in the world did you bring? You are only here for a few days," Sawyer says as he helps Gray unload the car.

"Don't get her started, Sawyer. It's best just to keep your mouth closed and smile. Not wise to get between a woman and her luggage," Gray stage whispers to Sawyer. "Might keep that in mind for your weekend dalliance."

Sawyer smiles and slaps Gray on the back. "Good to see you, man. It has been too long."

"It has." Gray lowers his voice, "Listen, did I see armed men walking the property?"

Sawyer nods. "Yes. We can talk later."

"Just be sure you include me in those talks," Laura Lynne calls from the top of the stairs.

"Woman has ears like an owl," Gray mutters, then louder says, "Don't you know that women are supposed to be seen and not heard?"

Laura Lynne looks at Pearl, and the two start to laugh, "Not these women!"

"Come on, y'all. Stop your bantering now. Victoria set up a nice cheese tray on the back porch for your arrival," says Gabe.

Sawyer and Gray come up the stairs loaded down with luggage.

"If y'all can just take that to Laura Lynne's room?" asks Pearl.

Gabe and Laura Lynne follow Pearl to the back porch as the men lumber up the stairs. Sawyer takes the opportunity to speak privately with Gray. "The armed watchmen you mentioned?" Gray nods. "They are patrolling 24/7 and will continue while I'm gone. John will be here all weekend and will handle the details, but let's you and me take some time this evening so I can show you what's what."

"Sounds good. Been pretty quiet since Roger was killed and the drug running was discovered?"

"Yes, for now. But I don't trust it. I wouldn't be going to Atlanta this weekend if I didn't think it was important." Sawyer puts down his bags and then walks to the window seat. Sawyer runs his hand along the curtain, remembering how Laura Lynne would sit here as a girl and gaze out the window, writing in her journal. "Listen, Gray. I have some news for Laura Lynne." He turns to face Gray. "It's bad news. It's gonna shake her up. I'm still shook up."

Gray turns away from his luggage to face Sawyer, his eyes alert. "What type of news?"

"News about Kenneth Butler. Do you want me to tell you first?"

"No. As bad as I want to know, it's not how Laura Lynne and I do things. We face the hard together." He walks toward the door, his pace slow. "Best we do it straight away. Give her time to come to grips with whatever you have to say." As if to himself, he quietly continues, "Your sister, she is stronger than you think—a true steel magnolia."

"My mother and sister are the same. At least they used to be." Sawyer walks behind Gray to the door. "Come on, let's get this over with."

The two men walk down the stairs and out to the back porch. Gabe and Laura Lynne are laughing and talking about the plane ride and Gray negotiating for the Jeep. Laura Lynne looks at her husband as he walks through the door and immediately sits up straight. "What is it? What happened?"

Gray comes over to sit next to her. "I don't know yet, honey. But Sawyer has some news about Dr. Butler he needs to tell us. I told him we would hear it together."

Laura Lynne looks expectantly at her brother. Sawyer looks her in the eye, not flinching from the pain he is about to inflict. But he's unwilling to cause her more pain by prolonging the inevitable. "Grady stopped me in town today. He had a call from the prosecutor. What is her name? Katie?"

"Sadie. Sadie Crawford," Laura Lynne replies.

"Yes, Sadie. She notified him that she had spoken with Kenneth Butler and had confirmation regarding some inconsistencies she and the medical consultant discovered in the medical files." He takes a deep breath. "There was more than one person who molested you that night. According to Kenneth Butler, there was another abuser."

Laura Lynne's face turns pale. Gray grips her hand. At the news, he scootches closer to his wife on the settee, wrapping his free arm around her shoulders.

She rasps. "Who? Who was it?"

"The bastard would not reveal a name."

Gabe watches the unfolding of events, his focus on his niece. He is so stunned that he does not even correct Sawyer on his language. Tears stream down Laura Lynne's cheeks, unchecked. Gabe hands her his handkerchief, and she mindlessly takes it from him, grasping it in her hands.

"What else?" asks Gray.

Sawyer holds up his hands. "That is all I know." His eyes have not left his sister's face. He watches as if from some depth of her being she pulls out from herself a strength only women possess. She turns matter-of-fact, wiping her eyes and blowing her nose. She pats Gray's hand, signaling for him to release it. He reluctantly complies. She stands and walks over to Sawyer giving him a hug. He holds on tight.

"Thank you for telling me," she whispers in his ear. She pulls away and walks toward the porch stairs. Without looking behind her, she says, "I need a moment. I'm going to my thinking tree." She turns her head slightly over her shoulder, "Gray, can you join me in about ten minutes?"

"Why don't I come with you?" Gray stands up and takes a step toward his wife. His pain for her palpable.

"No. Please. I just need a few minutes to myself." She finally meets his eye. "I'm okay. I promise."

"Okay, love. Ten minutes," Gray agrees.

She walks down the stairs, and as she turns the corner of the house, she takes off, running down the path.

"She used to do that when she was little, and she got in trouble," Gabe says, "It's why we called it her 'thinking tree.' She would climb up into the branches and sit with her back against the trunk. Sawyer finally found her there the first time she got a spanking for backtalking Melanie. We had searched for her for what seemed like hours. Couldn't find her. She liked to scare us to death." Gabe clears his throat, wiping his eyes. "When Sawyer asked her why she was up there, she said, 'I was thinkin'.'"

"I remember that. I was with Daddy when he found her," replies Sawyer.

Gray is quiet the whole time the two men talk, staring down the path Laura Lynne had taken. Gabe gets up from his chair, walks to

Gray's side, and puts his hand on his shoulder. "There are a lot of things that can be said about my sister Melanie, most of them not good. But one thing she did do right was raise strong, resilient girls." He gives Gray a bit of a push. "Go on, son. I would say the ten minutes is up."

Gray doesn't wait for a second invitation; he bounds across the porch and down the stairs to find his wife and offer what comfort he can.

"Uncle Gabe, did I do the right thing?" Sawyer asks.

Gabe has his hands in his pockets, rocking back on his heels looking toward the trail Gray just took. "Yes. You did. Hard as it was, it was the right thing." He looks over at Sawyer. "Son, you have my permission to kill that man if you ever get the chance. Or better yet, let me do it."

Sawyer looks at his uncle with surprise. Gabe is the most compassionate, calm, and gentle man he has ever met. The idea of him killing anyone, even as evil as Kenneth Butler is surprising.

"What? You think I can't hate that son of a bitch as much as the next guy? You're wrong. It is one thing to be evil; it's another to mess with my family. Never forget I have as much of my father's blood in me as my mother's."

Sawyer clears his throat and asks, "Want a drink?"

"More than my next breath."

Laura Lynne and Gray arrive back at the porch some thirty minutes later. Laura Lynne's eyes are puffy and red from crying, but she puts on a brave smile for her uncle and brother. Gray is very protective of his wife, keeping her hand in his as they climb the stairs. Laura Lynne leans into her husband and whispers to him. He nods and with obvious reluctance, releases his wife's hand. Laura Lynne walks over to her brother who is sipping a whiskey. His eyes are sad. She leans over to give him a big hug and he stands up, enveloping her in his arms.

"I am so sorry I hurt you," says Sawyer.

"You didn't hurt me. Dr. Butler did. And I realize it doesn't change anything, really. I think the worst part is the not knowing. Who else was there? I need to process the whole thing, but for now I want to enjoy my weekend. Can we put it aside? At least for a little bit?"

"Whatever you want. I love you, baby girl," Sawyer says as he holds her close.

"I know. I love you to."

Sawyer moves his mouth close to her ear and whispers, "But I *fucking* hate Ken *fucking* Butler."

She smiles a watery smile. "Me too."

The evening is subdued. Gray and Laura Lynne retire to their rooms early. Pearl brought a dinner tray to them and reported back to the men that the two lovebirds were snuggled in the bed binge watching *Madam Secretary*. "From the looks of Laura Lynne, I don't think she will be awake long. Poor thing looks worn out."

"You heard?" Sawyer asks.

"Well, of course! How else do you expect me to see to everyone's needs if I don't know what's going on around here? And, let me tell you, if I get the chance, I am taking Momma's iron skillet to that man's head *after* I remove his manhood with my oyster knife!" She looks at Sawyer. "That night, when your momma sent her to your Aunt Eileen's? I keep thinking we should have done something more."

Sawyer nods his head in agreement. "I know. Me too."

"Nothing the two of you could have done," says Gabe.

Sawyer disagrees, "You weren't there. Momma was a whirling dervish. Poor Laura Lynne was silently crying."

"Miss Melanie was throwing clothes around, demanding I help her pack, screaming at my momma. She was hysterical. I look back at it, and at the time, I was confused. It wasn't until later, when Momma explained what happened, that I realized I should have done more to protect my friend," Pearl says thoughtfully.

Sawyer concedes, "That is the thing, though. I always felt the same. But the truth is we were..."

"Powerless." Laura Lynne completes the sentence as she approaches.

Pearl jumps up from the rocking chair where she had sat down when Sawyer started to tell his story. "Oh, Laura Lynne! I'm sorry. We weren't talking behind your back."

Laura Lynne gives a small smile. "I know, Pearl. I heard most of the conversation." She perches on the porch railing across from the trio. "I don't want y'all to feel bad. We were just children. Nothing any of us could do." She looks at Pearl, then at Sawyer. "Truth is, when Momma and Daddy came to visit me in River Oaks that fall, I could have come back. I chose not to."

Sawyer gets up and walks to Laura Lynne, grasping her hands. "That's not true. Avery told me about that trip. And their ultimatum. You would have been a prisoner here."

"Yes, that's true. But I could have come home. It wasn't until I came back last month that I realized I had made the right choice. The right choice for me, and at the time, for Momma and Daddy." Sawyer starts to interject again, and Laura Lynne squeezes his hands and continues, "Please, let it go."

Tears run down Pearl's face, and she brushes them away when Laura Lynne looks at her. Laura Lynne gets off the railing and walks back to the door, but before going through it, she glances over her shoulder, "Y'all were my heroes that night. Especially you, Sawyer, you never left my side, just like you promised." She glances at Pearl. "I left my dishes in the kitchen. Thank you for dinner. Goodnight."

"Goodnight," says Pearl. She looks at Gabe and Sawyer, "If y'all are good, I'm going home." Without waiting for a reply, she follows Laura Lynne through the porch door, obviously still upset.

Sawyer looks at Gabe, who is quietly rocking in his chair. "Think I should go in and see what's what?"

"No, son. Let them talk. You will just get in the way."

"Good, because I have no idea what I would say."

"What's between Pearl and Laura Lynne is beyond words. They were like sisters growing up. You rarely saw one without the other." He looks at Sawyer. "Son, you can't fix everything. I know that is your instinct, but neither of those women would appreciate you butting in." He shakes his head. "You got some learnin' to do when it comes to women."

Sawyer chuckles, "And what makes you an expert on women?"

"I grew up in a house full of them. Fascinating creatures."

By the next morning, everyone seems to be in better spirits. Laura Lynne is up and out the door before Sawyer gets out for his morning run. He finds Gray in the barn messing with Tea Olive's fishing boat, *Miss Melanie*. Sawyer greets him, "Good morning, how is Laura Lynne doing?"

Gray turns around from the boat, "She's good. Resilient. Strongest woman I know." He glides his hand down the side of the boat. "How about you? Thought I heard you last night. Bad dreams?"

"Sorry, man. Just some shit I am working through. Army crap. But I am good." Sawyer walks over to the boat, hiding his embarrassment. "She's a beaut isn't she?"

"She sure is. Classic. Does she run?" asks Gray.

"No, and I haven't had time to work on her. She hasn't been used in years. She may need a complete overhaul," replies Sawyer.

"Mind if I play with her a bit while I'm here? Fishing off the dock is great, but being on the river would be a blast."

"No, please. Go right ahead. If you could get it running, we could add river patrol to our watch route. Right now, we just have the john boat. It's no match for the river, though. But *Miss Melanie*? She cuts through the water like a hot knife through butter."

"What year is she?" asks Gray.

"She's a 1970 Chris Craft and my Daddy's pride and joy. Bought it for his and Momma's wedding anniversary."

"You don't see this type of craftsmanship anymore. And I am not gonna lie, I love a wooden boat. Classy."

"Daddy was that." Sawyer looks at the man who married his baby sister. There is no doubt he loves Laura Lynne. "My daddy would have liked you."

"Really? You think so? An 'ol country boy like me?" asks Gray.

"Underneath my father's good looks and his way with women, he was nothing more than a country boy himself."

"Laura Lynne doesn't talk about him much," Gray replies.

Sawyer takes a seat on the stool, "Well, I'm not surprised. He and Laura Lynne were thick as thieves. He doted on her. I think because she was a lot like him—a dreamer. She looks like our mother, but she has Daddy's personality." He looks at his hands. "When all this shit happened that summer of '85, I think she expected Momma's reaction. But she never expected Daddy to turn on her. I think that hurt her more than anything."

Sawyer gets up and walks over to Gray, his hand outstretched. Gray shakes it. "Thanks, man. For looking out for Laura Lynne. She deserves a good guy in her life. Looks like she found one."

"Thanks, man. I appreciate you making me feel like a part of the family." He grins sheepishly. "And though she does not talk about her father, she does have plenty to say about you. She's really glad you are back home."

"Surprisingly, so am I. Listen, I want to get my run in before it's time for breakfast. Feel free to have a hand with the boat. If you want to take her on as a project, I would sure appreciate it."

"Wow. I would love the chance. Might take more of an expert than myself, though."

"There is a good boat mechanic in town. Go ahead and do whatever needs doing. Just have them bill Tea Olive."

Grinning like a schoolboy and rubbing his hands together, Gray laughs. "You got yourself a deal."

Sawyer smiles as he trots out the door, happy he has someone else dealing with the long list of to-dos he wants to complete on the farm. There is just so much that has lain dormant over the last many years.

From his conversations with Gabe, it sounded like his mother and father were just doing the minimum to keep things running for the last ten years or so. Gabe mentioned the mess he inherited and the amount of time it had taken to get things unraveled and in order. Sawyer has a long way to go before Tea Olive is back to the level of operation it was during his youth. His mind is churning through the projects he hopes to complete over the upcoming months when he spots Malcolm in the organic sweet potato field.

"Malcolm, how's it going?"

"Hey, Colonel. Just checking it out now. Want to join me?"

Sawyer sighs; he is going to miss his run again. And he hated that Gray had heard him during the night. The night terrors still managed to creep in every once in a while, though, as a whole, he felt like he was doing better. Sharing a bed with Diane this weekend could be trickier than he thought. Shaking his head as if to dispel his uncertainty, Sawyer joins Malcolm to discuss the Beauregard sweet potato project.

27

Chapter Twenty-Seven

"Sawyer, just have them spend the night here tonight! Besides, this way, Mandy doesn't have to get herself off to school alone in the morning."

Laura Lynne sits at the kitchen island, enjoying a cup of tea and discussing the book club event with Pearl, when Sawyer comes in from the fields. He immediately goes to the refrigerator for tea and a plate of chicken and waffles, which are leftovers from the morning's breakfast.

He shovels in a bite and closes his eyes, savoring the sweet and hearty bite, "I don't know, Laura Lynne. Seems awkward."

Laura Lynne rolls her eyes. "I think you should consider it. Be easier for everyone all around." She grins over her tea. "Besides, I already texted Diane and invited them. She said she is going to check with you."

Sawyer glares at her. "Laura Lynne, I love you with my whole heart, but stay out of my personal life. This is difficult enough without you butting in!"

"But what are little sister's for but to butt in? And anyway, it will make the transition for Mandy easier if she has her mom with her on the first night. Help her get settled." Then, seeing how upset Sawyer was by the idea, she makes a hasty retreat. "I'm sorry. I overstepped. I can make an excuse."

Sighing, Sawyer puts down his plate of food and guzzles some tea. Christ. He had just spent the last four hours ensuring there were no holes in the security measures he had taken, checking fences and shoring up areas of weakness. He was already on edge about leaving in the first place.

"No. Don't do that. It's too late now. But I mean it, Laura Lynne, stay out of Diane and my relationship. If you can even call it that yet."

"You're right. I apologize. I mean it. Even though, in this particular instance, I *am* right."

It is Sawyer's turn to roll his eyes. "Pearl, is it too much trouble?"

Pearl shakes her head, "The rooms are ready."

"Rooms?" He looks between the two women. "How long have you been planning this?"

Laura Lynne gets up from the counter. "Long enough to make the weekend a special one for Mandy. I can't wait to get my hands on a teenage girl again. Girl time!" Laura Lynne goes to the sink to wash out her teacup. "By the way, thanks for giving Gray free reign on *Miss Melanie*. I imagine by the time you get back, he will have it seaworthy."

"I sure hope so. And, no thanks necessary. I appreciate the help." He closes his eyes as he leans against the counter. "Truth is, the place is in need of a lot of work. Every time I turn around, there are more and more projects that need attention. Hard to prioritize." He looks at Pearl. "What can you tell me about the last years Daddy ran Tea Olive?"

Pearl leans her forearms on the kitchen island. "It was pretty bad. He did his best to maintain it, but his mind was failing. Miss Melanie did most of the business side of things, and thankfully, Mr. Gabe was here to do the farming, but a lot of things were left unaddressed. I did what I could to help." She spreads her hands. "I even reached out to Scarlet for some support, but she had her hands busy with her own problems. Just figured we needed to keep things running as best we could."

"How bad was his mind, Pearl?" Laura Lynne asks.

"It hit him mostly at night. They call it sundowner's syndrome. When the sun goes down, the confusion starts. There was a nurse with him at night since he couldn't be left alone. He would wander off. It was as if his mind would go back to when he was a young man. He talked like he was 30, maybe 40 years old, and it was 1975 again. Wasn't unusual for him to think I was my momma."

"I didn't realize..." Laura Lynne whispers.

"Oh, Miss Melanie didn't want any of you to know how bad it got. She didn't want him to end up in the hospital or a nursing home. Then, one evening, he wandered off. The nurse had not arrived yet, and he got past Miss Melanie. We found him at the dock, looking as alert and with it as I had seen him in, well at least a year. He thanked me for all my years here, for looking after the family. How he regretted his actions had torn up the family. How he should have been a stronger father. A better husband." Pearl's eyes are distant as she remembers. "Then, he told me how much he loved the land and Tea Olive. And the river. He never wanted to live or be anywhere but here. He patted me on the shoulder and walked back to the house." She pushes back off the counter. "He died that night."

"I should have been here," says Sawyer.

"We all should have been here." Laura Lynne shakes her head. "I'm sorry you had to deal with all this without us. Honestly, though, I thought Scarlet was around more. She called to tell me when y'all hired the nurse. But I guess I just assumed it was her who was handling Momma and Daddy."

"All that is water under the bridge," says Pearl, "It has been over five years since Mr. Sawyer died. Mr. Gabe, he has been able to do a lot, but Sawyer's right. There's a lot of stuff needs doin'."

"Okay, Pearl. Make a list and let's start getting it done. Might make sense to hire someone to do all the housework, so you can run The Residence. And, Beau and I have been reviewing salaries and job duties. He made some recommendations that I think will be a benefit to everyone. But first things first, you and Victoria deserve a raise."

"And a bonus," Laura Lynne interjects.

"And a bonus. You and your daughter are too valuable to our family and this farm to not be properly compensated. Let's start with a 20% increase, and then, we'll go from there," says Sawyer.

Pearl sits on the stool. "Thank you. I'm not going to argue. I deserve it and so does Victoria." She grins sheepishly. "I can take that request off my list."

Sawyer and Laura Lynne look at each other and laugh. "Of course, you already have a list!"

Pearl jumps off of her stool and whips the dish towel off her shoulder, swinging it in first Sawyer's and then Laura Lynne's direction, "Get on up out of my kitchen! The two of you know better than to hang out in my space when there is work to be done. Go on now! Git!"

Grinning from ear to ear, Sawyer gives his best military salute. "Yes, ma'am!"

He and Laura Lynne scoot out of the kitchen and head to The Residence staircase. "You need me to go with you tonight to the book club? And what about Diane? And Mandy?"

Laura Lynne walks up the stairs with Sawyer. It occurs to Sawyer he hasn't done this since that fateful summer night in 1985. "No, there's no need. Gray will take me and plans to hang out in the bookstore away from all the women. But why don't you plan to pick up Diane and Mandy after it's all over? Probably be the least awkward way to handle it." She turns to go into her bedroom to get ready for the evening. "Just come to Wheelbarrow Books around nine. You can hang with Gray if we aren't done by then."

Sawyer nods in agreement.

"Oh, and let me work with Pearl this weekend on her list. Maybe I can take care of some of it and take something off your plate." Laura Lynne continues as she smiles at Sawyer, "And, listen, one last thing. In case we don't get a chance to talk alone again, I have a buyer for

River Oaks. I think I'm going to take it. It's a fair offer. Mabel and Ben are in agreement. Honestly, I think they are relieved."

"Are you sure about this?"

"I am. And so are the kids. I have some thoughts about what to do with the money too. I want to talk to you about purchasing Twin Oaks. Grace called after the drug drama and told me the property was ready to go into foreclosure. I say we buy it and call it Twin River Oaks, sort of a subsidiary of Tea Olive." She shakes her head. "I don't know. Something like that."

"If you're certain, I'm not going to turn it down. I would love to have the land. It used to be Cooper land at one time," Sawyer replies.

"So Uncle Gabe told me when I ran the idea past him this afternoon."

"He was pleased? I know he has wanted to expand operations for some time."

Laura Lynne laughs, "Pleased? I think he already called Ace and told him to start looking into it." Laura Lynne turns serious. "But I want to run it past Scarlet first. Have you seen her since you got back?"

"No. I have talked to her a few times." He looks around the hallway and then signals Laura Lynne to follow him into his rooms.

"What is it? What do you know?"

"I am not really sure." He relays the information John shared with him about their big sister.

"She's a maid?" Laura Lynne sits on the side of the bed, stunned.

"That's what he tells me. I decided not to say anything about it. What are your thoughts?"

"Something is weird. I can't imagine Scarlet cleaning hotel rooms for money. It just doesn't compute with the sophisticated, classy woman who I saw last time I was here." She looks at him. "You said she has been there for about six months?" He nods. "Well, that explains why she is so hard to get in touch with. And why she hasn't been around. But what about Buck? And the boys? Where are they in all this?"

"I don't know about Buck. I reached out to Grady and Charlie, neither have heard or seen from him in a year or so. Though Charlie did say he has business ventures that keep him in Biloxi quite a bit." He clears his throat. "Umm, Grady told me that over the years Robert has been in and out of rehab."

Laura Lynne stares at him with a dumbfounded expression, "Drug rehab?"

Sawyer nods. "And maybe alcohol. He wasn't positive. Last he heard, he was in the Midwest somewhere."

"What about Cooper?" Cooper is Buck and Scarlet's youngest son. He went to Auburn on an engineering scholarship. He's a brainiac.

Sawyer shrugs. "I have no idea."

Laura Lynne sits in silence, staring off into the distance. "I just don't know what to say." She looks at her brother. "I had this idea, ya know? That while I was gone, Scarlet was leading the life that was meant for me. She was a wife and mother living at Twin Oaks in the big house—all the things I should have been doing. It's hard to fathom she's a maid with an addict for a son, a missing husband, and living in a farmhouse outside of town."

"I know."

"Is that clock on the wall accurate?" Laura Lynne points to the antique, baroque wall clock behind the desk.

"Yep, looks like you have about 15 minutes to get ready."

"I can do it. Plenty of time." She gets up and heads for the door. "Any other revelations I should know about?"

"Not right this minute. But hang around for a while. I imagine something new will creep up."

"I may need to rethink my visits." Laura Lynne turns her head to the door as she hears clamoring coming up the stairs. She smiles. "That husband of mine is a bull in a China shop! I'm always surprised he doesn't break more things than he does."

"I like him."

She smiles like the cat who ate the cream, "Me too."

"Laura Lynne! Where are you? We got ten minutes to get this show on the road!" Gray yells as he barrels up the stairs.

"In here with Sawyer! Be right out!" She glances at Sawyer. "Thank you for not hiding stuff from me. As hard as it is to hear, I need to hear it."

"I know. I just wish it wasn't me telling you."

"No. I'm glad it's you. I told you before, and I mean it. You're my hero."

"I am nobody's hero," Sawyer mutters to himself as he watches his little sister slip through the door and meet her husband on the landing.

Three hours later, Sawyer finds himself in the parking lot across the street from Wheelbarrow Books. He would have parked in the bookstore parking lot, had there been a spot. Or even the café, but the parking lots were full, so he settled on the sheriff's department. Plenty of spaces available there. He texts Gray and gets a quick response. "Meet u at back door. Good vittles."

Getting out of the Yukon, Sawyer sees Gray at the front door of the bookstore, propping the door open with his leg while holding a small plate of food and a soda. He smiles as he reaches the door. "You timed it perfectly. I just got the signal from my wife that we can pillage the food. Diane went all out on the charcuterie boards. Come on."

Having never been to a book club meeting in his life, Sawyer was surprised by the number of women engrossed in the book's discussion. "Wow, is it always like this?"

Gray nods. "Not quite this rambunctious, generally. But these women came prepared. Laura Lynne is being put through her paces."

Sawyer looks concerned, "Anybody out of line?"

"Nah. Diane's got it all under control. Not that Laura Lynne can't handle herself." He nods toward the room. "Look for yourself. She's having a blast."

Sawyer glances into the café and sees Laura Lynne sitting ensconced in a wing-backed chair, her reading glasses perched on her head, laughing and articulating with her hands as she answers the volley of questions being launched at her. He catches Diane's eye, and he receives a wink. She looks excited.

"Come on. Food's this way," says Gray.

"How much longer will this last?" asks Sawyer.

"I have no idea." He glances at his watch. "But I wouldn't guess more than another 20 minutes or so." He gestures to the food. "Grab a plate. Laura Lynne gave me a brief rundown of your talk about Scarlet. I have some questions."

Sawyer gets a plate and starts filling it. "I'm not sure I have any answers." He starts loading the charcuterie on his small plate. "Why do these things always have such small plates? Can't get anything on it."

"Hmmph. Here, let's do this." Gray loads the nearly empty charcuterie board with fruits and cheeses. Then, he adds some nuts. He picks up the board. "Get a drink. We can sit in the bookstore while we wait."

The two men settle in next door to wait for their women. Sawyer has little to add to Gray's understanding of the Scarlet situation; however, he has questions of his own. "Listen, Gray. Are you okay with Laura Lynne selling River Oaks?"

Gray takes a swallow of his Dr. Pepper Zero, "Absolutely. The property is Laura Lynne's. It was never ours. We have our place in New Mexico. Besides, she's not ready to admit it yet, but I think she wants to come back here. At least part-time. Can't say I blame her. I love it here myself."

"You would be okay with that? Living part-time in Mississippi?"

Gray smirks. "You just don't get it, do you, Sawyer? My home is wherever my bride and her pretty little butt are. Makes no difference to me if it's here or Timbuktu. That woman is my home." He picks up a piece of gouda. "Now, for Laura Lynne, it's different. She needs a physical place to create a home for herself and for me. I think it's mostly security. Females need that more than men do."

Sawyer stares at him with new eyes. "You're smarter than I gave you credit for."

Gray laughs. "Don't worry about it. Happens all the time."

"So, what else can you tell me about women? Uncle Gabe informed me recently that I could use all the help I could get."

Gray laughs and slaps him on the back, nearly knocking him out of his chair. "Hell, man. I got plenty."

Laura Lynne and Diane find the men laughing uproariously when the women are finally dismissed from the book club. "And what is it we missed that has y'all laughing so hard?" asks Laura Lynne.

Gray wipes his mouth and gets to his feet, grabbing his wife and planting a big kiss on her lips. "We were just discussing the complexities of women." He leans in for another kiss. "No finer topic." He looks over at Sawyer, "Thanks for the conversation. I'm gonna help Laura Lynne see everyone out."

Laura Lynne wraps her arm around Gray's waist and pats his stomach as they walk away, "Y'all have a good time?" Gray asks.

"The best," replies Laura Lynne.

"I love their relationship," says Diane as she watches Gray and Laura Lynne.

"Yeah, I think she chose a good one," Sawyer replies. He comes up in front of her and grabs her hands. "How was book club?"

She turns her face up to his, and he obliges with a kiss. She parts her lips and invites him in. He takes full advantage, deepening the kiss and drawing her closer. She lets out a low hum when they break apart. "Mmm, that was nice." She takes a step back. "But we need to save it for later." She looks around. "Mandy is around here somewhere."

Sawyer catches her chin with his hand and gently kisses her lips. "I missed you."

She sighs deeply and walks back into his arms. "Me too."

He hugs her closely and then kisses the top of her head. "Come on. Let me help you clean up." He releases her and then bends over to get the charcuterie board. "You sure you're good with coming to Tea Olive tonight?"

"I am." She looks at him closely. "Are you?"

He stands up with the board in hand, indicating with his head to get her to move forward. "I am. It took me a minute to get that way, but yeah. I'm good."

"Mandy is thrilled. She can't wait. Laura Lynne told her she was staying in Princess Mary's room."

"Is she? Seems fitting," Sawyer replies.

"Did Princess Mary really stay there?"

"That's the family folklore. If Mandy is interested, I'm sure Uncle Gabe can give her more details. His mother was a child when Princess Mary visited, or so she told us."

"Hey, ladybug! Thanks for helping tonight." Diane walks over to where Mandy is helping clean up the coffee station.

"Are you kidding? I wouldn't have missed it. I thought, at one point, Miss Natalie was going to punch Miss Candy in the throat. It was very exciting," Mandy replies enthusiastically.

Gray stops rearranging the chairs and looks at Mandy. "This wouldn't be Nasty Natalie would it?"

"The one and only. Though, she wasn't being nasty, at least not to Miss Laura Lynne. It was Candy who set her off this time," answers Mandy.

"Candy Westerman? As in Bubba Westerman's daughter?" asks Gray.

"Yep. She got smart with your wife. Which, I have to say, is quite a surprise as Miss Candy is usually as sweet as her name," Mandy replies.

"Well, aren't you the little magpie tonight, Mandy? Don't you know what happens in book club stays in book club?" Laura Lynne walks over and puts her finger on Mandy's lips. "Shh."

Mandy looks around at the adults, realizing she has been chattering and working while everyone stopped to listen to her. "Whoops. I said too much, didn't I?"

"Not at all. What exactly did she say to my wife?" prods Gray.

"Oh, nothing really. Momma?" asks Mandy, looking at her mother.

"Oh, no. Don't look at me! You're the one who started it; may as well finish it," Diane replies.

Mandy clears her throat, "Uh, just that Miss Laura Lynne was a lightweight lush who couldn't hold her liquor like any decent Southern lady can."

Laura Lynne rolls her eyes. "Thanks, Mandy. Remind me to give you a lesson on tact when we are at Tea Olive this weekend."

Sawyer smiles at Laura Lynne. "And you didn't punch her in the throat?"

"Well, I was about to, but Natalie just swooped in and went for the jugular. Mentioned she had no room to throw stones considering where her daddy was currently residing."

"Ouch!" Gray looks at Laura Lynne. "You're right. She did go for the jugular."

Diane finishes the story, "It was dead silent. Everyone was looking to me and Laura Lynne for comment. I couldn't think of a thing to say. Thank God Laura Lynne was more coherent than I was." Diane starts laughing. "She said, 'Well, thank you, Natalie. You took the words right out of my mouth.'"

"You did not!" Gray slaps his leg and starts laughing. Sawyer and Mandy join in.

"I did! And it was true! I swear, had you asked me a month ago if Nasty Natalie and I would think the same, I would have called you a liar and ignored you the rest of my life!" Laura Lynne starts to giggle. "Bless Candy's heart. She didn't know what hit her."

Diane looks around the space. "Come on. We've cleaned it up well enough. The Magnolia crew can get the rest in the morning. I'm beat."

"Sounds good to me." Sawyer walks up to Diane and Mandy. "You have your things?"

"They're in Gray and Laura Lynne's car already. I just need to lock up, and we can get going." She wraps her arm around Mandy, "Come on, sweetheart. You ready?"

"Yep, let's go," says Mandy.

Sawyer and the girls turn out lights and lock doors on their way to the Yukon across the street. Sawyer holds Diane's hand as Mandy walks in front of them, chattering the entire way.

"Wow! Cool truck," Mandy says as she climbs into the back seat.

"Thanks. I like it much better than my mom's pink Cadillac."

"Your mom has a pink Cadillac? That's great," says Mandy.

"I'm glad someone thinks so." He shuts her door and opens Diane's passenger door. "Climb aboard." She complies and he shuts the door, walking in front of the car before climbing into the driver's side. It occurs to him as they begin the short drive to Tea Olive he has never been in this particular situation. He has never ridden with a mother and her child, especially one who he currently has a kind of relationship with.

Sawyer looks in the rearview mirror and catches Mandy's eye. "You excited to spend the weekend with Laura Lynne? I know she's thrilled to have some time with you, not to mention working the store."

"Yeah. Laura Lynne is cool." She looks at him with a steady gaze. "How about you? Are you excited to be spending the weekend with my mom?"

"Amanda Raven Hopkins! Don't you dare be rude," Diane exclaims.

Sawyer smiles as he pats Diane's hand. "It's a fair question, Mandy. And the answer is 'yes.' Yes, I am very excited to spend some time with your mom and get to know her. Are you okay with all this?"

She nods. "Absolutely." She taps her mom's shoulder gently. "Mom, I wasn't trying to be rude."

Diane rubs her daughter's hand. "Sorry, sweetie. I guess I'm more nervous than I thought. Just got real all of the sudden."

As Diane apologizes to her daughter, Sawyer turns toward the front gates. Tea Olive is alight in all its splendor. The garden's gas lanterns are all glowing with dancing light. The fairy lights on the oak trees add a magical quality to the scene. The streetlights strategically placed along the route to the house, again lit with gas, make it feel as if the threesome had gone back in time when horse and buggy were the main means of transport.

"It sure did. Get real, I mean." Mandy had her nose pressed to the window. Sawyer smiles as he rolls down the window for her. He does the same for Diane, who is silent as she allows her hand to rest on her heart. She squeezes Sawyer's hand.

"Wow. I have driven by here a couple of times at night. I have never seen this before," Diane whispers.

"Uncle Gabe probably wanted to be sure you felt welcome. Isn't it gorgeous? I always loved it when we had parties at the house because all the outdoor lights were lit for the guests. My friends and I would play in the gardens for hours."

Sawyer pulls up to the front porch and Gabe is waiting. He opens the car door for Mandy and Diane. "Welcome to Tea Olive."

Diane walks over and gives him a hug, Mandy close behind. "Wow! I love it here!"

Diane murmurs in Gabe's ear, "Thank you. It's beautiful. You made us both feel like princesses."

Gabe gives her a gentle squeeze. "I wanted you to know how much we want to have the two of you in our home. Besides, what's the use of having it if we don't use it?"

Gabe disengages and walks around to the driver's side. "Hop out, son. I'll go park this heap of metal." He rubs his hands together. "Been wanting to take her for a spin."

Sawyer opens the door and gets out, watching as his uncle makes his way into the car. "Be careful, now. She's a lot of car."

Gabe sniffs. "Hmmph, I drive tractors every day. You think I can't handle a truck?" He puts the car in gear and speeds off, barreling down the drive and out toward the fields. He honks twice as he disappears.

"Well, ladies. Welcome to my home. Come on, let's get inside." Sawyer invites them in.

Laura Lynne and Gray come down the stairs when the threesome enters The Residence. "Hi, y'all," says Laura Lynne, "Wasn't that sweet of Uncle Gabe to turn on the lights? I haven't seen it lit since I was a teenager. Made me cry."

She hurries down the rest of the stairs and gives Diane and Mandy a hug. "Thank y'all for tonight. I just got a text from Ashley, and our sales from the evening may break my record! Presales for the new Bluebird Book have her very pleased. Me too!" She looks over her shoulder at Gray, "Come on, sweet man. Let's celebrate with some hot chocolate and a walk through the garden. I'm too wired to settle." She continues to chatter, sounding more and more like a magpie herself. "Y'all's stuff has been delivered to your rooms. Feel free to join us if you like."

Mandy turns to her mom, "Can I, Mom? I know it's a school night, but the gardens..."

"Of course." She looks at Laura Lynne, "You don't mind?"

"Of course not! I invited her, didn't I? And I don't say what I don't mean. Come on to the kitchen when you get settled Mandy. You might want to bring your sketch book."

Mandy runs up the stairs, all teenage energy and excitement. Laura Lynne looks at Sawyer and smiles. "Feels good to hear that noise. I hope she slides down the banister on her way down."

"Please don't give her that idea." Diane laughs.

Sawyer grabs Diane's hand. "Come on. I think a stroll through the gardens sounds great. Let me show you your quarters." He and Diane start up the stairs, Gray watching with a knowing look.

"Take your time. We got Mandy." He winks at Sawyer as he follows Laura Lynne into the kitchen.

Diane lays her head on Sawyer's shoulder and then wraps her arm around his waist as they head up the stairs. He kisses the top of her head. "You, okay? Tea Olive can be a little overwhelming."

She looks at him with a smile. "You think?" She snuggles back into his shoulder. "It's magnificent. I just feel really blessed." As they reach the landing, Mandy emerges from the long hallway. She has her sketch book in hand. "Did you find your room?"

She nods excitedly. "Mom, it's gorgeous. And my clothes are already put away! It's like I live here or something." She starts down the stairs, "Are y'all coming to the garden?"

"Absolutely. I just need to change my shoes."

"'Kay." Mandy flies down the stairs toward the kitchen. Sawyer and Diane look at each other with a smile and laugh. They hear Laura Lynne and Gray greet Mandy in the kitchen as the door swings back and forth.

"Come on. She seems fine. Let me show you to your room." He walks down the hallway Mandy had just vacated. "The room is for lady's maids, so it is not as elaborate as the Princess Mary room. But it's connected to Mandy's room."

Sawyer opens the door and ushers Diane inside. Before she can fully appreciate the beauty of the room, Sawyer has her pressed up against the wall. "I have been dying to do this since I saw you tonight in that outfit and heels." He leans close to her mouth. "Do you mind?"

She gives him a sexy smile, "Not at all."

Sawyer takes his time, slowly lowering his mouth to hers, gauging her reaction before taking her lips. He caresses her lips with his tongue before sliding into her mouth. She is equally as leisurely, meeting his tongue with gentle strokes of her own, causing his knees to buckle when she runs her tongue along the roof of his mouth. He pulls his lips away and rests his head next to hers, his forehead on the wall. Their breathing is heavy. He closes his eyes and takes a deep breath. "Diane, before this goes too far, there are some things you need to know about me." He clears his throat. "Things that might change your mind about me." She gently pulls his head up by his chin so she can look in his eyes.

"And I want to hear all of them." She gently kisses his mouth. "But I don't think anything can change my mind."

He holds her tight. "I hope not." He gently releases her. "Come on, change your shoes. Let's go enjoy the garden tonight. Plenty of time this weekend for serious conversation."

Diane and Sawyer find the rest of the gang out in the gardens. Mandy and Gabe sit on the bench, Mandy sketching busily. She inundates Gabe with questions, and he answers each one, sipping his mug of hot chocolate. Sawyer looks over Mandy's shoulder. He is surprised by how talented Mandy is with a pencil. Her sketch of the scene captures the images but also the feel of the night.

He rubs his hand gently on her head. "Any more hot chocolate?"

Without looking up, Mandy indicates the table laden with mugs of hot chocolate. Diane and Sawyer walk over to the table. There is also all the equipment and ingredients needed for smores. "What is all this?"

Laura Lynne joins them, handing Diane her mug. "I found it in the cupboard, exactly where Queenie used to keep them. I thought it was fitting for tonight. Uncle Gabe lit the firepit for us."

Sawyer laughs, sounding like a kid. "I can't wait."

28

Chapter Twenty-Eight

June 1986

Graduation Day

Tripp leans over his bed at The Residence, packing the last of his belongings. He looks around his old room, covered in all the trophies, ribbons, and awards he had received over the years. He looks at the deer mount over his bed, an eight point and remembers the day fondly. He was 13 and with his dad, Mr. Cunningham, and Grady at the Cunningham's hunting property. He remembers his heart pounding, his palms a bit sweaty, his breathing increasing. His father leaning over and whispering in his ear, "Close your eyes, son. Take a deep breath. Now, squeeze the trigger. Aim to kill, we don't want to wound him."

The shot, the kill. The immediate whooping and hollering from his dad and Grady. Mr. Cunningham assessing the kill and then signaling them all to come over. His father, with his hand on his shoulder, squeezing. "Good job, son. Good job."

Tripp shakes off the nostalgia. He can't help but think today should be that kind of a day. Instead, he and his family will put on a show at his graduation and then Gabe will drive him to the airport. No party or celebration. He refused his mother's multiple requests, much to her distress. And, he knew he had hurt her. His success was as much hers as it was his. But he just couldn't bring himself to cave in to her wishes.

265

"Son, can I come in?"

Tripp straightens from folding his clothes, "Sure, Dad."

Sawyer clears his throat, "You got everything you need? Money?"

"Yes, sir." Tripp says stiffly.

"Gabe tells me you have a place to stay in Charleston. With a friend of his from his Clemson days?"

"Yes, sir. I'll be staying in their FROG."

"Their frog? What's a frog?" Sawyer asks with a frown.

"I'm told it's a finished room over the garage. Like an apartment."

"Oh, okay. I was worried it was some weird treehouse thing." He walks over to Tripp's trophy wall, "What's your plan for the summer?"

"I was able to get a job at the Parks and Rec center. Mostly doing summer camps in athletics for the kids." Tripp shrugs, "Should be fun and low stress. I just want a summer of fun before I have to go through knob year."

"Isn't that going to interfere with your football schedule?"

Tripp takes a deep breath then dives in, "No, sir. I decided not to play. I plan to focus on my studies and being a cadet."

Sawyer turns to his son, "And you didn't think to tell me or your mother of your plans."

Tripp shrugs, "It has no bearing on my scholarship, so I really didn't think it mattered. I'm sorry I did not inform you earlier."

"What is your end game here, Tripp? To ostracize your mother and I for our decisions. Just keep us out of your life."

Figuring he had nothing left to lose, Tripp decided on truth. "Yes, sir."

"And your legacy? Taking over Tea Olive. Do you plan to walk away from that as well?"

"I honestly have no idea."

Sawyer nods his head thoughtfully, "I see. Well, that changes things then, doesn't it? I will give you a word of advice, even though you have not asked for it." Sawyer walks toward the bedroom door, "Be careful about making decisions based on only partial knowledge. You do not have the full picture of why your mother and I made the choices we did. And you are not a parent, so you don't have a clue of what it means to protect your family. Not that you ever did." Before his father shuts the door, he gives one last parting word, "I hope you find what you are looking for, son. But I think we both know you won't. Your home, your legacy, your life is here."

"Not if I can help it," Tripp mutters under his breath after his father leaves the room.

Checking the time, Tripp has about 30 minutes before he needs to get over to Moseley. He takes his duffle bag and back pack downstairs and loads them into his uncle's truck. Returning to his room, he gets his graduation hat and gown in navy blue and takes one last look around. He shuts the door behind him.

"Mr. Tripp, you comin'?" Queenie asks over the intercom.

Tripp leans over the stairwell banister and shouts, "I'm comin' Queenie." As he starts to descend the stairs, Avery comes out of his room dressed in his customary Moseley uniform of khaki's and blue blazer. Then, grinning, Tripp reverses course, going back up the stairs.

"Race you down the banister," Tripp says.

Avery's eyes light up, "Really? Cool. Hang on."

Avery goes across the landing to the other staircase and hikes his leg over the banister. Tripp does the same.

"On your mark, get set, GO!" Tripp shouts, lifting his gown with one hand as he pushes himself backward with his other hand. He looks at his brother, who is doing the same. The two flying down the banister, barely stopping before hopping off at the end.

Avery walks across the foyer toward Tripp, adjusting his pants and kicking his left leg, "Man, that was a lot more fun when we were kids. I think maybe I chafed something."

"Serves you right, you hooligans. What in the world were you thinking? Acting like a bunch of buffoons. You're lucky it's just me who saw you. Now get in here, I got something for you, Mr. Tripp."

Queenie shoos the boys into the kitchen, using her ever present dishtowel.

"Go on, now. Open it up."

Tripp walks to the kitchen island where there is a small box wrapped in a light blue ribbon, Citadel blue. He carefully unwraps the box and nestled in the tissue paper is a note. He pulls it out and reads it out loud, "So you never lose direction and can always find your way home."

He looks inside the box and lifts out a brass compass, small enough to fit in his pocket.

Tripp turns around and Queenie is standing by the stove, in her customary place, but instead of her hands busy at the counter, they are cupped lightly together at her waist. "Lincoln and I wanted you to have something for your big day. We sure are proud of you."

Tripp walks around the counter toward Queenie and she opens her arms pulling him in close. Little as she is, she barely reaches his chin. He drops his head and puts his cheek on top of her head. "Thank you, Queenie. I'm sure goin' to miss your cookin'."

"I'm goin' to miss feedin' you. It's been a full time job."

Tripp lifts his head and turns it toward Avery, "Avery here will make up the slack. Won't you, Av?" Tripp releases his one arm from around Queenie and opens it to Avery, "Come on, bring it in. Group hug."

Tripp indulges himself for one more moment, taking it all in one last time.

"Let me go, you buffoons! You're gonna to be late for your own graduation. Now, go on! Scat! I've got work to do."

Laughing, Tripp releases her and Avery. He retrieves his gown and the gift and walks out of Tea Olive's mud room, letting the screen door slam shut. Avery is on his heels.

"Want to ride with me? I have to get their early, but you can come if you want."

"No, I can't. I have to go with Momma and Daddy. United front and all that shit. Gabe is riding along with us."

"Oh, yeah. That makes sense. He's taking me to the airport. Lot goin' on, I need to go."

They get to Gabe's truck and Tripp turns to his brother. "Not sure when we might see each other again. I'll call you when I have a phone number you can reach me at. I expect you to call if you need me."

"I know." Avery's eyes tear up.

"Oh, man. Don't cry, Avery. I'm hanging on by a thread."

"Then don't go. Not yet."

Tripp walks to his brother and pulls him in for a tight hug. He has hugged Avery more in the last two days then he has in the last two years. "Its gonna be okay. I love you little bro. Wave to me from the stands."

He squeezes him tight, releases him and jumps into his uncle's truck. Tripp starts the vehicle and backs out, seeing from the corner of his eye Avery wiping his face with his hands. He toots the horn twice and heads toward the front gates. His heart breaking and soaring all at the same time.

29

Chapter Twenty Nine

Present Day

Sawyer's alarm goes off at 4:30 AM. He is shocked that he slept so hard that he needed an alarm to wake up. This hasn't happened in years. He lays there, remembering the evening in the garden. He has to agree with Mandy; it was magical. He had not had that much fun with family since, well, since that summer in 1985. Maybe, just maybe, his soul was beginning to find peace.

He gets out of bed and takes a quick shower. He shaves and puts on his traveling clothes. Before Pearl left yesterday, she had made sure his clothes were pressed and his bags packed. It's a convenience he could get used to again, something he took for granted as a kid but would never again. By 5:00 AM, he heads into the hallway to fetch Diane.

She quietly shuts her door. He waits for her on the landing. "Good morning," he whispers quietly.

"Good morning," she responds.

He takes her suitcase and follows her down the stairs. The light from the kitchen is burning. He leaves the luggage at the front door and takes Diane's hand, saying, "Come on. Maybe there is some coffee."

"Wouldn't that be fabulous?"

The two walk into the kitchen to the smell of freshly brewed coffee and toasted bread. Gabe is at the island, sipping at his mug and eating a piece of toast. Laura Lynne sips a mug of tea. Both smile as the two enter.

"Wow, I didn't expect y'all up this early," says Sawyer.

"We are up this early every day. It's you who sleeps in." Laura Lynne pulls out two mugs from the cupboard. "Y'all got time for a cup before you go?"

"No, on a tight schedule this morning. But if we could take it to go?" Sawyer asks.

Laura Lynne hands them each a mug of coffee.

"Smells like Magnolia's house blend," comments Diane.

"You have an excellent nose, Diane. Here, take these with you. I packed a thermos and some egg and cheese biscuits for the road. You still have quite a drive before you reach the airport." Laura Lynne hands Sawyer a packed lunch box and thermos.

"You made biscuits for us?" Diane asks.

Laura Lynne laughs. "Heavens, no! Those are Victoria's. All I did was add the egg and cheese." Laura Lynne waves a piece of paper at them. "She left instructions."

Gabe gets up from his stool. "Y'all need to get a move on. Car is out front."

Sawyer raises an eyebrow at his uncle. "You're getting mighty comfortable driving my car around."

"Uncle rights." Gabe follows the couple out of the kitchen and to the front door with Laura Lynne trailing behind. Gabe picks up Diane's suitcase, and Sawyer picks up his. Laura Lynne loops her arm through Diane's as the two women follow.

"I promise to take good care of Mandy. And I will call if I need anything. I promise," says Laura Lynne.

Diane turns watery eyes to Laura Lynne, sniffing. "It's so silly! I don't know why I'm teary! I know you will take good care of her. And she could not be more thrilled to be here." She glances toward the upstairs windows. "You may not get her out of her room today."

"Don't worry. I have some experience with teenagers." Laura Lynne gives her a big hug and walks over to Sawyer, who is patiently waiting by the car door. "Stay safe, big brother. And keep us posted on your reunion."

Sawyer gives Laura Lynne a side-armed hug. "Will do. You do the same."

Sawyer walks around to the driver's side after shutting Diane's door. Laura Lynne joins her uncle at the back of the vehicle. She wraps her arms around Gabe's waist, and the two wait patiently as Sawyer starts the car and heads down the drive. He rolls down his window and sticks out his arm in a wave. Gabe and Laura Lynne wave them down the drive.

"What kind of reunion?" asks Diane. She hands him his coffee as she sips her own.

"Thanks." Sawyer takes a sip as he turns out of Tea Olive's gates. The gates slowly close behind them. "I'm meeting with the old headmaster of Moseley—a guy by the name of Elijah Kolensky. I'm hoping he can shed some light on why my daddy gave him half a million dollars in 1986."

Diane bobbles her coffee. "A half a million dollars? Good Lord."

"My sentiments exactly. I spoke with my mother, and she said the amount she and my father agreed on was closer to $50,000."

"Am I allowed to know why money was exchanging hands in the first place?"

Sawyer places his coffee in the cup holder and reaches over to squeeze her knee. "If this is going to work, I don't want secrets between us." She nods as he continues, "I graduated from Moseley Hall in 1986. My senior year had basically been shit. Laura Lynne had been sent to Georgia, Scarlet was at Ole Miss, and all my buddies had stopped talking to me. I'm not sure what happened, but I know that Robert Huger threatened my dad with a lawsuit. After that, things dried up socially for our family. Mom even lost her position as president of the DAR."

"Wait. Robert Huger. As in Scarlet's father-in-law?"

"The same." Sawyer picks up his mug of coffee as he reaches the highway. He leans back and settles into his seat. "I had one friend that year—a guy named Clay Newhouse. He was a transfer from Natchez, and his father owned a company called Modern Farming." He glances at Diane, who is listening intently. "It was my responsibility to make him feel welcome at the school. Dad and some of his friends had wooed his dad to Venice. They wanted first dibs on his equipment."

Sawyer continues, "Anyway, Clay and I ended up being the best of buddies. He was my only friend that year, and he stood by me through all the bullying and rumors. We played football together. He was my wide receiver."

"And you were the quarterback, of course."

Sawyer grins, "Of course. We won state that year. We would not have gotten that far if Clay had not been on the team. He was that good. Anything I threw, he caught. He was an amazing player." Sawyer puts on his blinker, preparing to exit. "By the spring, things had begun to settle. We were still on the outs socially, but Mr. Huger dropped the lawsuit. Or at least he and Daddy came to some sort of agreement. I'm not sure." He glances at Diane, who continues to sip her coffee and listen. "This is where you get to see a side of my family you may not like. I know I don't."

She nods, "Okay, lay it on me."

"The night of the Moseley awards ceremony, it was as if I was the town golden boy again. I won multiple awards, my friends all wanted to hang out, and Momma and Daddy were back in the fold again as well. But Clay, he didn't get one award. Not academically or for his athleticism. And he should have. In fact, a couple of the ones I got should have been his."

"What happened?"

"From what my mother tells me, she and Daddy paid Headmaster Kolensky to ostracize Clay and his family." He glances at Diane. "Somehow, they found out he was gay."

"So? Oh, wait, in 1986 in Southern Mississippi, that's a death sentence."

"Exactly. I found out from Clay later that night that Kolensky had approached his father and told him if they did not leave quietly, Clay would not be allowed to graduate. To make matters worse, he threatened them with an article in the Gazette outing their son. And the guys from my school knew. All my old friends were talking about 'that fag Clay and his Jew momma.' Though I don't think Mrs. Newhouse was actually Jewish."

"I'm so sorry for your friend."

"It broke my heart. I called him that night, but he wouldn't speak to me. I told his mother to have him meet me at Pickett's, so we could talk. He showed up, and we ended up at the cabin on Tea Olive. He was furious and crying. He couldn't figure out how anybody knew unless I had told them."

"Did you?" asks Diane.

"No, and I'm still not certain how my father found out." He looks at her.

"From the looks of you I would say it bothered you. Quite a bit."

"You have no idea. That night messed me up for a lot of years." He clears his throat. "And that was the last time I saw Clay. And from that night forward, I refused to stay at The Residence with my parents. I opted to stay at the cabin."

"Really? Why?"

"My parents, I lost respect for them. First, it was Laura Lynne; then, Clay. Just seemed like they had no compunction about tossing aside anyone who might endanger the reputation of the Cooper/ Beauregard name. It could just as easily be me."

She reaches for his coffee mug and puts it in the holder. She takes his hand and puts it to her cheek. "I'm sorry for you. You must have been terribly lonely."

He rubs her cheek with his finger, "Yes, I was." Somehow, she got it: the worst of the emotions that night, worse even than the faith he had lost in his family, was the utter loneliness he felt. Abandoned. Shattered. "There were only a few weeks left of school. Once I graduated, I went to South Carolina and worked until school started." He takes his hand back. "I just wanted time to think. I didn't come back home until Christmas, and even then, I only stayed for a couple of days."

He glances at Diane before finishing, "So that is the end of my sordid tale. Think you can dig out an egg biscuit for me? I'm starved."

Realizing now is not the time to ask questions about his family, Diane easily changes the subject, handing him an egg biscuit. "So, what happened to Clay? Do you know?"

Swallowing the bite of biscuit, Sawyer shakes his head. "I haven't personally heard from him, but from what I could gather from the company's website, he is the current CEO of Modern Farming. He lives in Oregon." He washes down the biscuit with coffee and then hands Diane the empty mug. "Can you please give me a refill?"

"Sure." She opens the thermos, refilling both their mugs. "Well, at least he ended up on his feet."

"I sure hope so." He glances around. "Listen, I need a bathroom break. You good if we stop at a rest area or do you prefer a gas station?"

"No preference. But a break would be nice."

Sawyer exits at the rest area and parks the car. It's still dark outside. He walks Diane to the ladies' room before going to the men's room. He relieves himself and then when at the sink, splashes his face with cold water. He looks at himself in the mirror. He doesn't look any different, but he feels different. Lighter somehow. He exits the restroom, and Diane is waiting. She looks at her phone.

"Everything okay?"

She looks up and smiles. "All is well. Laura Lynne just texted me. Mandy is up and in the shower."

"Great." He places his hand on the small of Diane's back. "Come on, we have another hour before we get to the airport."

The two walk quickly to the car and climb in. Diane goes straight to the lunch box and pulls out the remaining egg and cheese biscuits. She tops off their coffee.

Sawyer drives out of the rest area, putting on his blinker as he exits. "I'm done talking about me. How about we talk about you for a while?" Diane nods as she takes a bite. "Where did you grow up?"

Diane swallows and grins. "Hold on a second. I'm having a food orgasm in my mouth." She looks at Sawyer. "How is it possible to make an egg and cheese biscuit taste so good? That Victoria can sure cook. I had no idea."

He glances at the biscuit. "I think it's the cheese. Smoked gouda. And Victoria's special touch."

"God, it's good." She opens her eyes and smiles. "So, you want to know about me? Well, there's not nearly as much to tell. I guess the best way to explain is to ask if you have ever watched the television show *Dharma and Greg*." From his blank expression, she surmises he is clueless. "Okay, well. Dharma's parents are old hippies who lived on a commune: hug trees, believe in spirituality, use plant medicine, and eschew the government."

"Yeah? And, what, these are your parents?"

She laughs, "To a 'T.' My brother and I were born in a commune. My parents never married, though they acted married. They both died in a car accident when I was 19." She looks at Sawyer. "They were the best people. I miss them every day. Dad worked with his hands, mostly carpentry. My mother made medicinals and read palms." She sighs. "We were homeschooled before it became a thing. My brother and I had a great time growing up."

"I'm sorry about your parents. Your brother?"

"He's a musician in San Fransico. At least, that was the last time I heard from him. He has a girlfriend. He takes after my parents the most. He took care of me when our parents died. Until I met Mandy's father." She sips on her coffee. "Another musician and an artist. My brother introduced us."

"Tell me about Mandy's father? You married?"

She laughs. "Yes, I'm a bit more traditional than my parents and brother. But I was pregnant with Mandy, and we had no insurance. I was working at a bookstore, and he was getting gigs where he could. It wasn't enough. One day, he came home and told me he had joined the Navy. It would provide us with healthcare, housing, benefits. He never asked me. I guess he knew I wouldn't let him. Anyway, I had some complications with my pregnancy. Mandy came super early and was in the NICU for 42 days. If he hadn't done what he did, I'm not sure we would have made it. The care we received saved our lives."

She clears her throat, "His plan was to serve his term and then get out. It didn't work out that way. Mandy was two when he died. We were stationed in Biloxi. I decided then and there I was going to make a more stable home for Mandy then I had. I owed her, and I owed Thomas. I packed up what little we had acquired, took our savings, and started driving. I ended up in Venice, Mississippi. Looked like a nice enough town, and it didn't have a bookstore. Mandy and I went into the real estate office, and that was when our fortunes turned for the better. I met Grace. She is simply an angel disguised as a woman."

"Yeah. I can't disagree. Grace is good people."

"Is she ever! Before nightfall, I had a job working at Magnolia Café and was renting a sweet little duplex on Birch Street. The Gaillards let me bring Mandy with me for shifts until I was able to get her into a little school at the Baptist church. Grace introduced me to your father, who wanted to give me a business loan to start a bookstore. The rest is history."

"What's your brother's name?"

Diane slides her eyes over to Sawyer and starts to giggle, "You won't believe it."

"What? Is it something hippie? Like Snow or maybe Tree?"

She bursts out laughing. "Close. You are so close. His name is Ashbury. As in Ashbury, the center of the Hippie movement." She continues to chuckle. "I'll tell you a secret if you promise to keep it to yourself."

"Ashbury? That's really not so bad." He looks at her dancing eyes. "Yeah, I'll keep your secret."

"My real name is Daisy. I changed it after my parents died."

He looks at her seriously. "Daisy? I like it. It fits your personality. Sunny and bright."

Diane rolls her eyes. "Oh God, you sound like my brother. He was devastated when I did it. He still calls me Daisy."

"Your secret is safe with me." He exits the highway. "We're here." He pulls up to the stoplight and reaches for her hand. "I love you told me about your people."

"Same. Though I think you have more to share."

"Stop reading my mind, woman." He takes away his hand as the light turns green. "Yes, there is more to share. But not now. Now we find parking and catch a flight to Atlanta."

"I can't wait."

30

Chapter Thirty

Three hours later, the couple lands at the Hartsfield International Airport. To Sawyer's surprise, there is a gentleman holding a sign with his name on it as they exit the terminal. With some trepidation, Sawyer walks over and introduces himself.

"Come with me, sir. Twin Rivers has arranged for your baggage claim and transportation. I'll escort you to your car."

Diane looks at Sawyer with wide eyes. "Wow. Just wow."

Sawyer smiles. "Come on. This has Laura Lynne all over it. Can't wait to see what she has arranged for us at the house. I bet it'll be pretty nice."

"Oh, it will, sir." The concierge steps to the side to allow his guests to proceed him down the escalator. "I believe you have a chef for this evening and a picnic on the grounds for tomorrow."

"Really? How would you know?" asks Sawyer.

"I work for Twin Rivers. Ashley keeps me up-to-date on itineraries and the like. It's been a great retirement gig. I was sorry to learn of the potential sale," says the concierge.

"Itineraries? I'm a little confused," says Sawyer.

"Oh, wait a minute. I might have one of the brochures with me." The concierge fumbles through his pockets. Locating what he is looking for, the old man hands him a glossy trifold. "Here you go. This explains everything."

"Thanks," Sawyer says, still confused.

281

"Of course. Here we are, sir, just through these doors. Your car is the black Mercedes. Your luggage is already in your trunk. There is also a light lunch located in the floorboard of the passenger's seat." He opens the passenger door. "Ma'am."

Diane blinks a few times before sliding into the front seat. Sawyer tips their escort a $20 and walks around to the driver's side. He gets behind the wheel and looks at Diane.

"That was immensely easier than I imagined." He hands her the brochure. "Here, take a look at this and tell me what my sister has been up to at Twin Rivers."

Diane accepts the brochure. She leans over and extracts the lunch basket. It is decorated with the Twin Rivers horse logo. Diane reads the label, "Enjoy your romantic weekend getaway at Twin Rivers. We are delighted you have chosen us as your weekend destination." She starts rummaging through the basket. "Charcuterie, cheese, pickles, two mason jars of sweet tea, and crackers. Very classy."

Sawyer finishes plugging in the address of Elijah Kolensky's nursing home. The phone says it will take them one hour and twenty minutes. Sawyer begins to pull out of the parking garage, "What does the brochure say?"

"Hmmm, okay." Diane switches from looking through the lunch basket to the brochure. She is quiet for a moment, reading. "Wow, again. It looks like Twin Rivers is more of a bed and breakfast. There are four different rooms you can stay for the night or the weekend. It is only available Thursday through Sunday." She flips the brochure over. "There are different types of packages you can order. There is the Horse Enthusiast, the Outdoor Enthusiast, the Romantic Getaway, and the Privacy Package."

"I wonder if we will be there with other people?" Diane asks.

Sawyer shakes his head in the negative, "No. She told me we would have the place to ourselves."

"Well, I say we just enjoy ourselves." Diane leans over and puts her head on Sawyer's shoulder. "I really like your family."

"That's good, love. Because most of the time they are a pain in the butt."

Diane laughs and sits up straight. "Want some snacks?"

"No, I'm good. But you go ahead. I want to get this meeting with Kolensky over first." He rubs her leg, gently. "Then, I want to focus on nothing but you."

"Sounds like a plan." Diane fishes out her phone from her purse. "I just want to check with Laura Lynne first. Make sure all is well at the store and with Mandy." She takes the phone off airplane mode, and it lights up like a Christmas tree. Diane laughs as she scrolls through the texts.

"Everything good?"

"Better than good!" She shows Sawyer her phone. There are half a dozen pictures of Mandy at Tea Olive. "Hysterical. Mandy sent me pictures of her entire morning. She is happy."

"Good. She's a great kid." He glances at Diane who is rapidly texting. "Who are you texting?"

"Laura Lynne. I am thanking her for the weekend."

"When you get done can you make a call to Peachtree Downs Skilled Nursing Facility? Let them know we will arrive at..." he glances at the phone, "12:45 and would like to see Elijah Kolensky."

"Sure. Got it." He listens as she makes arrangements. She hangs up and glances at him. "No problem. He will be finishing up lunch. You're to meet him in the dining room."

"No, *we* are going to meet him. I don't want secrets between us, *Daisy*."

She laughs. "Don't you start." She turns serious. "Okay. To be honest, I can hardly wait to see what he knows. It's a bit like a puzzle, isn't it?"

"With more missing pieces than pieces that fit together, I'm afraid."

She pats his leg. "Don't worry. I am good at puzzles."

Promptly at 12:45, Diane and Sawyer arrive at the nursing home. They are escorted in to the dining hall. Elijah is sitting in his wheelchair gazing listlessly at his empty place setting. The nurse walks over to her ward and speaks gently.

"Your guests are here, Mr. Elijah. Why don't we take you out to the gardens? It's a pretty day for company."

He acknowledges with a wave of his hand, keeping his head bent. Diane and Sawyer follow discreetly behind as the entourage goes out the back doors to a stunning greenhouse. The entire property is very high-end. It put the Venice Pineview Nursing Home to shame. And Sawyer knows exactly how much the care there runs. He can only imagine how much this place costs.

The nurse positions the wheelchair across from an iron bench and locks the wheels. "Y'all call me if you need anything. Otherwise, I'll be back in an hour."

"Thank you," Diane says as she sits across from Kolensky. She pats the seat next to her for Sawyer to join her. He nearly groans as he sits his large frame into the uncomfortable and small bench.

Sawyer leans forward, his forearms on his thighs. "Headmaster Kolensky, I am not sure you remember me, but I am Sawyer Beauregard. You used to call me Tripp."

Kolensky lifts his head, his eyes laser sharp. "I remember you just fine, young man. It's my body that is failing. Not my mind. No matter what these people think." He turns his focus on Diane. "Now, you I don't remember."

Diane smiles warmly. "No. You wouldn't. My name is Diane. I own Wheelbarrow Books in Venice. You were gone by the time I got to Venice. My daughter Mandy goes to Moseley Hall, though."

He looks back at Sawyer. "She your girlfriend? I like her."

Sawyer smiles. "She is. I like her too."

"Now that we have everyone straightened out, what brings you to my current prison?" Elijah lifts his hand as he speaks. Sawyer notes the fine tremors.

Sawyer begins, "Well, just recently, I became the trustee of Tea Olive. I ran across some discrepancies from 1986. The accounts just don't add up. I did some digging. Your name came up. I am hoping you can shed some light on why my father gave you a half million dollars."

Kolensky nods his head and then gazes down at his lap. He is silent for a few minutes. Diane starts to speak, but Sawyer shakes his head. His silence works. Elijah looks up and answers, "Guess now is as good a time as any to get this burden off my shoulders. Doc says I don't have long left on this planet. May as well die with a clear conscience."

"I know it has something to do with Clay Newhouse," says Sawyer.

"It did, but that was just part of the scheme your father, Robert, and I cooked up," says Elijah.

"Robert? You mean Robert Huger?" asks Sawyer.

"Hmmph, don't know much, do you? Yeah, your daddy and Buck's daddy. I had a great side gig going. I had to do something since being a headmaster wasn't going to put my girls through school." He looks at Sawyer. "Still don't get it do you?" He settles back in his wheelchair. "How much do you know about Robert Huger's business ventures in Biloxi?"

"Only that he had them. But Robert Huger was a genius at the stock market, at least according to Buck. And my father." He looks at Diane. "Mr. Huger was never much of a farmer. Before Robert Huger took over from his father, the farm produced as much cotton as Tea Olive and Cotton Mill. But Robert preferred the stock market. And he was good at it." He looks back at Kolensky. "At least I thought he was."

"Oh no, he was very good at it. He made a lot of money for me and your father. He also had some other investments in Biloxi. More lucrative but also more unseemly." He glances at Diane and says quietly, "Stripper joints." Sawyer stares at him blankly. "Boy, do I have to spell it out for you? Robert owned nudey houses. I went to see one of them once. The place was packed. He had 50 women hanging on poles, dancing around in string things. Left nothing to the imagination. Not only that, you could purchase any of them for a price."

None of this fits Sawyer's perception of Robert Huger. He was as clean-cut and classy as his father. The idea of him owning a strip joint just did not compute.

"Prostitution?" asks Sawyer.

Kolensky slaps his leg. "Now you're getting it! He also dabbled in porn. Made a few skin flicks. Good money."

"So, what, you cleaned the money? For a fee?" asks Diane.

"Smart woman you got there, Sawyer. I did. At first, it was just me and Robert. He would bring me the cash, and I would launder it through the school. I took 10%. In those days, we didn't have a separate accountant, so it was easy enough. The money then went to an offshore account."

"How much are we talking, here?" asks Sawyer.

"It was mostly small amounts, as I couldn't do much more than that without suspicion. But then, your daddy got involved after that mess with your sister. In his defense, he had no idea what Robert and I were into until it was too late for him. He should have kept his mouth shut."

"Wait, which sister?" asks Diane.

Kolensky all but rolls his eyes. "Laura Lynne." He looks back at Sawyer. "That summer, your daddy goes off half-cocked at Robert, accusing Buck of taking advantage of her, giving her VD. Robert, being Robert, believes him. Hell, Buck had been visiting his daddy's prostitutes for years. Beats that poor boy within an inch of his life. Then, he hauls him off to Dr. Goldbug to run tests. Buck kept telling him he hadn't had sex with Laura Lynne. Then, Robert finds out Buck has been telling the truth the entire time. Robert, though, he is smart and plays the long game. He meets with your daddy, Buck, and Dr. Goldbug, who shares the results. Buck is in the clear. Sawyer apologizes. He's all tore up about it. Robert, he's all conciliatory, tells him we all make mistakes. They shake hands and leave."

Elijah takes a deep breath. "But it's not over for Robert. In fact, it's just beginning. He and Suzanne start freezing out your family from social functions. Suzanne feeds the gossip mill with tidbits, just enough to get everyone's tongues wagging. Plenty of people want to see the Coopers and Beauregards come off their pedestal. Your momma made plenty of enemies over the years, and they took advantage. And then, Robert starts calling in favors. Your daddy basically has to give away his cotton crop that year. Couldn't find anyone to harvest it, much less buy it. Robert asked me to set up a meeting with him, in my office. I did. Left the two men in my office alone, and when your father left, he was white as a sheet. Robert, on the other hand, was grinning like a Cheshire cat."

Sawyer can feel his arm pits sweating. Kolensky is having entirely too much fun telling him this story. He waits, breathing through his nose slowly and steadily. It takes everything in his power not to punch the old man in his throat and be done with it.

"And being the canny, smart guy you are, you taped the conversation, didn't you?" Diane leans forward, smiling as if Kolensky is a gladiator instead of a slime ball.

He chuckles. "I do like you." He smiles. "I did. Very enlightening." He refuses to go any further, making Sawyer ask. He loves being in control. This is the most fun he has had in ages.

Swallowing his bile, Sawyer asks a question, "And what happened in that conversation?"

"Robert showed his true colors. Told your daddy what he had been up to, how he planned to destroy the family, and how he would do it. First, he would tell everyone about Laura Lynne, and then, he would out Clay and insinuate you two were lovers. Finally, he would destroy Sawyer financially. Of course, all this would go away if your father started working for him. He really left him with no choice."

"So, it *was* blackmail," says Sawyer.

Kolensky claps his hands together, "Now you're getting it! Yes. Blackmail. Robert did a lot of it and did it for a lot of years. Anybody who came through his club that could potentially benefit him was secretly recorded. Anybody from a street vendor to a legislator, if Robert thought he might be helpful in the future, he would threaten to expose him. He had quite the racket."

"So, my father fed him half a million dollars through you. For this, Robert would keep quiet and life would go back to how it was before the summer of 1985." Kolensky nods in agreement. "I only saw the one payout, though. No way would Robert Huger not keep pumping his new cash cow for money."

"You're catching on quickly now, my boy. You're right. Two things happened, though, that put a stop to Robert's plans: Black Monday and Buck marrying into the family."

The door to the garden opens and suddenly, the alert and devious Eiljah Kolensky drops his head and stares blankly at his hands, startling Diane and Sawyer. The nurse appears from behind one of the bushes, quietly approaching Kolensky. "Mr. Elijah, you must be all worn out." She looks at his guests. "I'm sorry, but the hour is up and he needs to return to his room."

Diane stands up, pulling Sawyer to his feet. "Thank you...Brandi. We had a lovely visit." She walks over to Brandi. "If you don't mind, let's give them a bit of privacy to say good-bye." She leans in for a whisper, "They probably won't see each other again."

Brandi nods in agreement, "Of course. Would you like some tea for the road? Our cook makes the best peach tea in Atlanta." The two women wander off toward the door.

"You can drop the act. She's gone now," says Sawyer.

Elijah looks up, grinning.

"Got 'em all fooled."

Sawyer leans down and puts both his hands on the wheelchair arms, he gets close enough to Kolensky's face to smell the musty pong of his old man skin. He is done with the games. "Enough games. Things have changed since you were in Venice. My father is dead, and

Laura Lynne is vindicated. You have no power over our family. What else do you know?"

Elijah stares cruelly into his eyes, "Hurts knowing about your daddy, doesn't it? I sure hope so. Son of a bitch made sure I resigned. Then, I couldn't get a job anywhere else. I found out later he and Robert agreed to get rid of me. Robert tried to blackmail me, but then I told them about the tape. We ended in a stalemate."

Sawyer tips Kolensky's wheelchair back, startling his old headmaster. "You make my skin crawl. I'm glad you're dying. It prevents me from having to kill you myself."

Kolensky grins. "Son, your wrath is focused on the wrong person. It wasn't me who put your daddy in the crosshairs."

Sawyer tilts the wheelchair a little further before slamming him down, causing Kolensky to cry out in fear. "Good riddance, old man."

Kolensky cackles as Sawyer makes his way to the door, calling out, "Better watch your back, young Sawyer. And stay away from me and my family. I still have the tape."

Sawyer ignores the old man as he opens the door into the dining room where he immediately sees Diane and Brandi talking and laughing. "There's my guy! We were just coming to check on you." Diane looks closely at Sawyer, "You okay, honey?"

Sawyer forces a smile. "I am." He wraps his arm around Diane. "Mr. Kolensky is ready to come in, Brandi. Thank you for allowing us to see him."

"Of course. He has been looking forward to your visit since Sabrina told him you had reached out."

"I'm sure." Sawyer squeezes Diane. "You ready, sweetheart?"

She nods as the two walk arm-in-arm across the dining hall and out the front door. She looks up at Sawyer, his jaw rigid and his eyes steely. "Ummm, Sawyer? Is Mr. Kolensky still alive in the garden? Just wondering how quickly we need to leave."

Sawyer finally smiles, looking into Diane's eyes. "Yes, he is still alive. Though it was touch and go whether or not I was going to punch him in the throat."

"He's a despicable old man. He was gloating. Who gloats over someone else's misfortune?"

Sawyer kisses the top of Diane's head as he opens the car door. "Hop in. We can talk on the road. I want to loop in Laura Lynne and Uncle Gabe. As terrible as he is, at least now we know what happened to the half million dollars."

31

Chapter Thirty-One

Sawyer slides into the driver's seat and plugs in the address for River Oaks. "Can you text Laura Lynne and see when she is available for a call?"

"Already on it." Her phone pings. "She said give her a few minutes to get Uncle Gabe. She'll call us back." Diane starts messing with the car's Bluetooth system, hooking her phone up to the car speakers. When the phone rings a few minutes later, Sawyer almost wrecks from the volume of the ring. "Sorry!" Diane turns down the volume as she answers the call.

"Laura Lynne, hey. Everything going good on the farm?" Sawyer asks.

"Yes, all is quiet. I have Uncle Gabe. We're in the barn, away from the staff. What did you learn?" Laura Lynne replies.

Sawyer relays the information that he and Diane gleaned from Headmaster Kolensky. "When I was leaving, he did warn me to watch my back. And that he still had the tape in safekeeping."

Laura Lynne and Gabe are quiet on the other end. "Y'all still there?" asks Sawyer.

Laura Lynne clears her throat. "Yes, we're still here. Go ahead Uncle Gabe."

"Black Monday was in 1987, right? What year did Scarlet and Buck get married?" asks Gabe.

"1989," Laura Lynne replies.

"When Scarlet married, your father gave her her portion of the trust. It makes sense now," Gabe says.

"Why do you say that? Do you think it was more blackmail money?" asks Sawyer.

"That or it was to keep the Hugers afloat. Robert was heavily invested in the stock market. Black Monday would have been disastrous for him," replies Gabe.

"I am shocked Headmaster Kolensky ended up being such a sleaze bag. I remember him as kind of a quirky Ivy League guy. He always wore bowties and blue blazers," Laura Lynne says, "Not to mention Robert Huger owning a strip club. I can't wrap my head around it. Do you think they still own it?"

"I have no idea. And I forgot to ask him the name of the club. I'm sure it can't be too hard to figure out," says Sawyer.

"I wish your daddy would have confided in me. I hate that he didn't feel like he could," comments Gabe.

"Daddy played his cards close to the vest. Now, I see why he did it; he had a house of cards. One wrong move and the entire thing would collapse. I am surprised it didn't," says Laura Lynne.

Laura Lynne turns matter-of-fact. "Okay, now we know. What do we do with it? I vote we address it head on. But first, we have to talk to Scarlet and Avery. They deserve to know what's going on."

"I agree. And I want to talk to Buck face-to-face. I think he probably knows a lot more about this than the rest of us. In the meantime, let's sit on the information. We can't do much about it right now anyway," replies Sawyer.

"Okay, y'all enjoy the rest of your weekend. Thanks for keeping us up-to-date," says Gabe.

Diane and Sawyer sign off. Diane is quiet as she picks up the lunch basket and pulls out the mason jars of tea. She opens one and hands it to Sawyer. He takes it, lost in his own thoughts. Diane's phone pings, and a text message from Laura Lynne pops up on the car monitor.

"Uncle Gabe and I are fine. I'll call Avery and Scarlet. We will deal with it when you get home. Enjoy River Oaks."

"She's right, you know. There is nothing we can do about it right now," says Diane.

Sawyer nods. "I know." He looks at Diane and smiles. "Can you hand me some of that meat and cheese? I'm getting hungry."

As the couple drive down I75 toward River Oaks, Diane's phone pings. She looks at the text messages and says, "Oh, Lord." She shows the picture to Sawyer. He smiles and laughs.

"Don't worry, Diane. He did it with all of us. She can't hurt that old truck. Plus, the farm is as safe a place as any for Mandy to learn how to drive."

Diane studies the picture of Mandy and Gabe sitting in the front seat of the farm truck, her daughter behind the wheel. She is grinning from ear to ear. And much to Diane's surprise, so is Gabe. Her phone pings again. This time, Laura Lynne sends a video of the farm truck cruising down the dirt road toward the fields. Her text reads, "So far so good."

"If you're that worried, tell Laura Lynne. She will tell my uncle the lessons need to stop."

Diane shakes her head. "No. It's not really that. I am just not used to having someone else help me with Mandy. It's just been me and her for so long. Don't get me wrong, there has always been a bevy of people willing to babysit and carpool. But not the big stuff. I'm just processing how that feels."

"And how does it feel?"

"Today, it feels good. Besides, she is having a wonderful time. She has been dying to learn how to drive, and I have been reluctant to let her. Hard when your baby starts growing up on you. Once she gets a car, that means freedom. It certainly did for me. But I am glad she is getting this opportunity." She looks up from the phone in time to see the gated entrance for Twin Rivers. "Wait. Are we already here? It looks like a scene from *Black Beauty*."

Sawyer pulls up to the electrical box to enter the gate code. He checks his phone for the digits before entering the sequence. He waits as the electrical box turns green and the gates begin to open. "We're in."

Sawyer drives down the long and winding road to the main house. It is lit up in a welcoming glow. There is an old man standing on the front porch, waiting for their arrival. He meets the car at the bottom of the front porch steps. "Welcome back to Twin Rivers, Sawyer. I hope the ride in was not too bad."

"Mr. Ben! I didn't expect to see you. How are you and Dr. Mabel?"

"We're just fine. Laura Lynne told us you were coming. I wanted to make sure you had everything you need for the weekend." Ben shakes Sawyer's hand and then nods as Diane approaches. "Ma'am."

Sawyer pulls Diane to his side. "Diane, please meet one of Laura Lynne's favorite people in the world, Mr. Ben. Mr. Ben, this is Diane."

"Pleasure, ma'am," Ben says in greeting.

"It's really nice to meet you." Diane looks around. "You have a gorgeous place here."

Ben leans back on his heels, hooking his thumbs in his overalls. The gesture reminds Sawyer of Gabe. "We do. The missus and me, we live on up the road a bit. Take care of the farm animal orphans." He starts walking backwards a bit. "I will leave you two lovebirds to enjoy your visit." He gives a little wave. "Be sure to stop by and see us before you leave. We won't be far."

"Thanks, Ben. We will definitely swing by," assures Sawyer.

The couple watch as Ben ambles away. "Old Ben there was here when Laura Lynne came to live with Aunt Eileen. He and his orphan animals helped her through the rough times. His wife, Dr. Mabel was Laura Lynne's therapist. It's how the two met." He gives her a squeeze. "Come on. Let's get inside and look around. Plenty of time to unload the car."

Sawyer opens the door to the main entrance. The house is a typical farmhouse, just much, much bigger. There is a large basket on the entrance table with a note from Laura Lynne. Diane reads it aloud. "Sawyer and Diane, the house is yours for the weekend. Ashley has arranged for a personal chef to come for the evening to prepare your meal for tonight. The rest of your itinerary is enclosed. Make yourself at home. Love, Laura Lynne."

"Cool. What's in the basket?" asks Sawyer.

"Fresh fruit, eggs, bread, and jams. From a place called Royal Farms. Apparently, there is raw milk and butter in the fridge."

"A nice touch. Royal Farms is a neighboring farm. Want to look around?"

Diane shakes her head and walks up to Sawyer. She puts her arms around his neck and gives him a sweet kiss. "What I really want to do is take a shower. With you."

Sawyer wraps his arms around her body and kisses her back. "I like your plan." He bends down and slides his right arm under her legs, lifting her against his chest. He carries her up the stairs and into the first bedroom he can find. Shutting the door with his foot, he carefully lays her on the bed. He gazes into her eyes, brushing the whisps of hair that are falling in her eyes away from her face.

"This means something to me, Diane."

"I know. It means something to me too. I am just not sure what, yet. But I can honestly tell you I have never been swept off my feet and carried up a flight of stairs before in my life." She puts her hand over her heart. "I now know why Scarlet fell for Rhett."

Sawyer grins rakishly, looking every bit the scoundrel from *Gone with the Wind.* "That is apropos since Momma insisted on naming two of her children after one of the characters in the movie."

Diane looks at him with a laugh, "I always wondered if that was her inspiration."

Sawyer laughs, "Yep. Mom is Melanie, Scarlet is well Scarlet, Avery's middle name is Rhett." Sawyer pulls Diane off the bed. "Come on. Let's clean up."

The two lovers undress and enter the walk-in shower hand in hand. Diane runs her free hand along the fresh scar on his arm. "What's this?"

He looks at it, "My most recent war wound. Doc says I'm healed."

She kisses it gently. "That's good."

An hour later, entangled in the sheets, Diane props herself on Sawyer's chest. "You do good work."

Sawyer laughs, rubbing his hand down her smooth back. "It's been a while for me."

Diane snickers, "Not nearly as long as me!"

"You're good then? I didn't hurt you, did I?"

Diane gently slaps at him, getting ready to tease him. But then she notices he looks worried. She changes her tone, gently kissing him on the lips. "No, you didn't hurt me. I loved every minute of it." She sits back, wrapping the sheet around herself. "Sawyer, you could never hurt me."

He sits up and caresses her cheek. "No, I could never intentionally hurt you."

Diane drops her sheet and moves into Sawyer's embrace. The next hour passes as the previous hour, with sighs, murmurs, and sweet caresses.

"Come on, lazy bones. I heard the chef come in thirty minutes ago. I imagine we need to eat something," Diane says.

Sawyer grins and stretches. "I've worked up an appetite." He swings his legs to the side of the bed, fishing around the floor for his underwear and jeans. He buttons his shirt while Diane gets dressed. "I'll go get our luggage. You good?"

She smiles from the other side of the bed. "I'm good. Meet you on the back porch? There is a back porch isn't there?"

Sawyer laughs, "Yes, there is a back porch."

Ten minutes later, Sawyer finds Diane on the back porch, a golden retriever sitting next to her. "Look, Sawyer! The back porch comes with a dog."

He laughs as he walks over to the auburn-haired retriever. "Hi there girl, you gotta name?"

From the doorway, Diane and Sawyer hear a female voice, "Her name is Mayella. I'm told she is the great-granddaughter of Scout." She smiles as she walks over to the couple petting Mayella. "Your aunt liked Harper Lee." She gently drops her chin in acknowledgement, keeping her hands tucked in her apron pockets. "You must be Sawyer and Diane. I'm Stella, your chef for the evening. Are you interested in a cocktail?"

Sawyer looks at Diane before answering, "I think we'll stick to softer beverages tonight."

"Very good. We have all range of sodas and of course, sweet tea."

"Sweet tea," the couple says in unison.

Laughing, Stella smiles. "I'll bring you some, along with an appetizer of fried green tomatoes. Tonight's dinner will be Brunswick stew, barbeque, cornbread, and collards. I hope that suits."

"Sounds wonderful. Thank you," says Diane. She looks at Sawyer as Stella departs. "I had a chance to look around before I came to the back porch with Mayella. The place is fabulous. I am surprised your sister wants to sell."

"I was too, at first. I talked to Gray about it before we left. He said Laura Lynne is ready to claim her birthright. But she wants to make it her own, not leave it to what it has always been. Plus, it was always Aunt Eileen's dream to expand Tea Olive and live there. She just died before she could make it happen." Sawyer sits next to Diane, twirling a piece of her hair. "You would have liked my Aunt Eileen. When I first met you, she was who you reminded me of."

"From everything I have heard about her, I think I would have liked her too."

Stella comes out bearing a tray with appetizers and mason jars filled to the rim with iced tea. She puts the tray on the small side table, shooing Mayella off the porch. "Y'all enjoy."

The rest of the evening and that weekend are spent much the same way Friday was. Sawyer and Diane take advantage of their time alone to learn about each other. Much to Sawyer's surprise, his usual cadre of night terrors do not present themselves. Diane's favorite pastime is riding the four-wheelers throughout the property. She and Sawyer spend endless hours driving through creeks, across the hills, and over the fields. Sawyer loves watching her whip around corners, her hair blowing loose from her ever-present topknot, a huge smile on her face.

Sunday morning, before leaving to return to Mississippi, Sawyer and Diane join Ben and Mabel for breakfast. Mabel and Diane hit it off immediately. Mabel is fascinated by Diane's knowledge of plant medicine, a recent hobby of the doctor. So, after their meal, Mabel takes Diane to her garden to show her the herbs she has planted. The men go to the barn.

"Ben, I have to ask you about selling the place. Laura Lynne tells me you and Mabel are on board, but after spending a weekend here, I have my doubts. You have a mighty fine set up here." Sawyer leans over to stroke the nose of Maybelle as she wiggles her way around his legs.

"I appreciate you asking, but Laura Lynne is right. Mabel and I are ready to fully retire. We have a place waiting for us, but we didn't want to leave until Laura Lynne was ready to sell." He looks at Sawyer. "I owed Eileen that. With Laura Lynne settled and happy, I feel like my debt is paid."

"Your debt?" Sawyer asks.

"Your aunt never told you about me? Hell, I was the worst of the worst when she found me sitting out by her gate. I was drunk and beat up, been dropped on the side of the road by somebody." He shakes his head. "What she saw in me I will never understand. Took one look at my sorry hide and said, "Well, aren't you just a mess? Come on, get in. I like your aura.""

He chuckles. "I was still half drunk, not sure what she was even sayin' and no idea what my aura was. But I climbed in the back of her truck, and she dumped me off at the barn. I woke up with a goat staring at me. Eileen was there with coffee and a shotgun. She told me she was looking for someone to care for her animals. Offered me a job. I told her I was a convicted felon, a drunk, and no-good cowboy. She told me her spirit guides told her different. I've been here ever since." He hangs his head. "I sure did love that woman. Finest human being a soul could ask for. She turned my life around."

Ben blows his nose. "Anyway. I owed her. Seemed like she left this earth too soon. Had some unfinished business. I finished it for her."

Sawyer takes Ben's stooped shoulder in his firm grip, "You did a fine job. She wouldn't be happy if you called it a debt, though. She loved you, too. So does Laura Lynne, which is why I want to make sure you and Mabel are cared for. What can you tell me about the buyers?"

"You met one of them. Miss Stella and her husband Toby are offering a fair deal. And I like that they want to keep things going just like they are, at least for now." He looks around the barn. "They have three boys, all married, a couple of grandchildren. Be nice to see the place filled with family."

Sawyer nods. "Okay, then I will work with Laura Lynne to move things along." He holds out his hand to Ben. "Thank you, Mr. Ben, for looking after my family when I couldn't. I am the one who has the debt."

"No, son. Family looks after family."

Sawyer and Diane go back to the main house to pack their bags to leave for the airport. "I'm going to miss this place." Diane glances at Sawyer. "I will always remember it as the weekend I fell in love with you."

Sawyer stills, stopping his packing. He looks at Diane, who won't meet his eyes. Sawyer asks, "You love me?" He walks over to her and pulls her back against his chest, rubbing his chin on her head. "That's good, because I love you, too."

Diane turns in his arms. "You don't have to say it back just because I said it first. Loving shouldn't be a 'have to,' it should only be a 'want to.'"

He takes her chin in his hand. "Shhh. I want to love you. I don't feel obligated." He kisses her on her pert nose. She wraps her arms around him and burrows against him. "This is nice."

She sighs. "I feel a 'but' coming."

Sawyer laughs, "*But* we have to get going or we are going to miss our flight. Mississippi is calling." He pulls away and swats her bottom. "Come on, let's go."

She returns the swat to his very impressive rear-end. Then gives a salute. "Yes, sir, Colonel, sir!"

He rolls his eyes as he zips up his luggage and hauls it off the bed. Diane does the same before double-checking to make sure they have everything. "Okay, looks like we're ready."

Sawyer kisses Diane and takes the suitcase from her, nodding for Diane to lead the way. He looks at Diane as she walks down the stairs, enjoying the view but eager to return to Tea Olive. He has loved his time here, but to his complete surprise, he misses Tea Olive. He misses the family there: Gabe, Pearl, John, Victoria, Lamar, and young Liam. "I want you and Mandy to be a part of my life, Diane. This is not an ending; it is just a beginning."

She glances over her shoulder at him, a twinkle in her eye. "Damn straight. You can't get rid of us now. And, honestly, I am not sure Mandy will leave to come home with me. She keeps texting me all she is doing and how much fun she is having."

The two exit the house, securing the door. They walk to the car and put the luggage in the trunk. "I'm glad they are having so much fun together. I hope Mandy and I can get to know each other better. I don't know much about teenage girls."

Diane laughs as she climbs into the passenger seat, "Don't worry! Mandy will break you in." Sawyer kisses her as he shuts the door and walks to the driver's side. He takes a moment to look around the farm one last time. He knows in his heart that he will never be back. He takes a deep breath and lets it out. Time to go meet his future—a future that is waiting for him at Tea Olive.

32

Chapter Thirty-Two

Spring 2018

And, now, his father was dead.

He stands next to his mother on the left and Avery on the right. Scarlet, Buck, and their two boys are to the right of Avery. Tripp is embarrassed to admit he had not recognized them when he was brought to the family room prior to the funeral proceedings. There had been little time to talk, but he hoped to at least do more than say hello while he was in town.

Laura Lynne had chosen not to attend.

"Sawyer, go on." his mother nudges him with her arm.

Sawyer shakes himself from his musings and walks to the head of the casket. He leans over and picks up a handful of dirt. The casket is lowered, and Tripp waits before throwing in his dirt clod. His siblings follow suit. His mother completes the ritual.

Tripp and Avery escort Melanie away from the crowd and into the waiting Mercedes. Lincoln is at the wheel. Everyone climbs in, and the funeral procession goes to Tea Olive, where Queenie and Pearl have laid out an appropriate spread for the funeral company.

"I think that went well. Glad you were able to get here, Tripp," says Avery.

"Me too." He looks at his baby brother. "Glad to see you, man. Sorry it's under these circumstances."

"I know, right?" Avery looks at Melanie. "How are you holding up, Momma?"

She doesn't answer the question; just turns her gaze on her oldest son. "Are you here to stay? Assume your legacy as is your birthright?"

"It's not that simple, Mom. I have a responsibility and a life in the military." He pats her leg. "Can we talk about this later? We're here."

"This is not done. You are expected to fulfill the role, Sawyer. No excuses. You have a responsibility to your family. One you have chosen not to fulfill. It's time you quit thinking about yourself and started thinking about the family."

And, with that, Melanie Louise Cooper Beauregard—the grand dame of Venice society—exits the Mercedes. And, now, she is a widow, a widow of considerable means, especially if Tripp chooses not to accept the role of conservator of the trust. He assumes the responsibility would fall to his mother. In his eyes, it seems appropriate since she is the oldest living Cooper.

The next several hours are spent talking to his father's long-time friends, business owners, country club members, and hunting buddies. Tripp is surprised at the esteem in which his father is held. The man everyone portrays is not the man that Tripp knew. This version of his father is, well, philanthropic and community-driven. Tripp only knew him as a shrewd businessman and philanderer. He has a hard time reconciling the two versions in his mind.

At five sharp, the bell rings, signaling the end of the event. As people disperse, the Beauregard family heads to the study to hear the reading of the will. Gerald Lally is already there, sitting in a chair next to the desk.

"Tripp, could you please get Gabe? I think he needs to be here for this as well," Gerald requests.

"He has no business in Sawyer's will. I will tell him what he needs to know. This is Beauregard business," Melanie states rather tartly.

"Melanie, I hate to correct you on such an occasion, but this is Cooper business, and it affects your brother. He needs to be here," Gerald insists.

"Mother, don't make a fuss. Let's just get this over with," Scarlet says as she sits next to her mother on the couch.

Tripp walks to the intercom and asks Queenie to send his uncle in. Gabe arrives a few moments later, looking slightly confused.

"Gerald, what's this all about?" asks Gabe.

"I think it best if I just read the will, and all questions will be answered. Avery, could you shut the door, please?" Gerald asks.

Avery closes the door, and Gerald clears his throat. He begins to read.

He was right. It all became clear. Crystal clear.

His father had made Gabe executor of the trust. Tripp was not sure if he was relieved or upset. His mother, on the other hand, was visibly upset.

"Gerald! This is nonsense. Sawyer is to be named. Everyone knows it gets passed on to the oldest male in the next generation when the current executor either dies or gets too old and passes it on! That is Sawyer!"

"No, Momma. This makes total sense." Sawyer stands up and walks over to his uncle, who has been staring at Gerald in stunned silence. He holds out his hand for a handshake. Gabe looks at his hand blankly and then, as if on instinct, takes it with his own. "It should have been yours when Poppy Cooper died. Daddy was just righting a wrong."

Tripp looks around the room, gives a slight bow, and walks out the back door. He heads to the river. He had been given a reprieve, nothing more. But it is a reprieve nonetheless, and he is grateful.

"Hey, you're Uncle Tripp, right?" asks a young man approaching Tripp.

Tripp turns toward the voice. "I am. You must be Cooper."

"I am. It's nice to finally meet you. You're a legend around these parts, especially Moseley Hall."

"That was a long time ago. So, you went to Moseley too. Miss Witherspoon still there?"

Cooper laughs. "Yep, well, she was when I was there. That's been a while now. I'm working in Raleigh these days."

"I think I heard something about that. An engineer, right?"

"Right. And, you, the military has been your life." Cooper looks out over the water. "Can I ask why?"

"Uh, sure." Tripp puts his hands in his pockets. "I guess it was the routine. I like schedules. Plus, it was cool. Carrying a gun, shooting the bad guys...I don't know. I never really thought about it. Why do you ask?"

"Just could never figure it out. I mean, if I was set to inherit Tea Olive, I would never leave. I loved growing up in these fields with Uncle Gabe and Pappy."

"Then, why'd you leave? I'm sure they would have loved for you to stay here and work with them."

Cooper looks down before gazing back at the river. "Well, it just wasn't in the cards. Better for me to be away from here." He takes a breath. "Unfortunately, both sides of the family reside here. Makes things..."

"Hey, you two! Time to get back. Both your mommas are waiting on you," Queenie hollers as she walks up the trail.

"On the way, Queenie," says Tripp. Tripp puts his arm around Cooper's shoulders. "So, does Bobby feel the same way?"

Cooper starts walking back toward the house, Tripp beside him. "Yes, but let's just say he's more Huger than Beauregard."

"Would you two get the lead out? Miss Melanie is wearing herself out over this will. You need to quit hiding and go help out your brother and sister. You hide plenty already."

Chastised, Tripp and Cooper increase their pace and return to the chaos of the post-will reading. And, once again, Queenie was right. He had not seen his mother this upset since Laura Lynne came home from the doctor's office in the summer of 1985.

33

Chapter Thirty-Three

Present Day

Laura Lynne and Mandy wait expectantly on the front porch when Diane and Sawyer arrive from River Oaks. Mandy races down the steps when the Yukon pulls up the drive and envelopes her mom in a hug. "Hey, Mom! How was the trip?"

"Wonderful. And I don't have to ask how your weekend was. Laura Lynne has been keeping me updated. How did the driving lessons go?"

Mandy and her mom walk slowly up the stairs, with Mandy talking the entire time. Sawyer watches them when Laura Lynne sidles up beside him. "Have a good time, big brother?"

He glances at his little sister before letting his gaze return to Diane. "Sure did." He steps back and slams the car door, walking to the trunk to retrieve their bags. "How were things around here?"

"A whirlwind. I forgot how hard it is to work all day and then take care of a family at night. I have no idea how I did that for 25 years. I'm exhausted." Laura Lynne picks up a suitcase out of the trunk. "What do you think of River Oaks?"

He slams the trunk closed, and the two wander up the front steps. "You have done a remarkable job with it. I had no idea you had put so much work into it. It's a first-class establishment."

"Thanks. It was mostly Ashley's idea. I let her run with it."

"I'd like to go over the numbers with you. I met Stella and talked to Ben. If you're sure you want to sell it, then I think they are the right buyers. Ben and Mabel agree."

Laura Lynne shrugs her shoulders. "I already said 'goodbye' in my heart. It is absolutely time." She looks at him. "I'll call Ashley and get the ball rolling. I do want to talk to you for a minute about Twin Oaks, though. Grace came by the bookstore Saturday. She has it on good authority the property is going up for auction. I'm hoping we can put in an offer before that happens."

"Have you spoken to Scarlet?"

"I tried calling her after you called and told me about Mr. Kolensky. She has not returned my calls. I thought about going to the B and B where she works but thought that was weird. I did talk to Avery, though."

"What was his take?"

"He didn't remember Mr. Kolensky much. He was gone when Avery started high school. He didn't have much of an opinion. I think he was like the rest of us, surprised. It's hard to wrap your head around the fact our father was being blackmailed by Scarlet's father-in-law, who dabbled in prostitution and porn."

Sawyer grimaces. "When you put it that way, it does sound pretty bad." Sawyer looks around the front porch. "Where is Uncle Gabe? and Gray?"

Laura Lynne grins. "Waiting for you at the dock."

"The dock?" Sawyer leaves his suitcase in the entryway. "No way. Did Gray get *Miss Melanie* sea-worthy?"

"Go see for yourself. They're waiting on you for her maiden voyage," Laura Lynne replies.

"You don't want to come with us?"

"Of course, I do, but I am told it's men first. Some backwoods male bonding ritual. You get thirty minutes before you come back and get the women. Go on, quit staring at me like that! I'll take care of the luggage."

Sawyer doesn't hesitate a second longer. He hadn't been on *Miss Melanie* since he was in high school. His father taught him how to skipper on that boat, though he was rarely allowed to take it out solo. The *Miss Melanie* was his father's boat. He and his siblings were relegated to the johnboat.

As he approaches the dock, Sawyer sees *Miss Melanie* gleaming in the water. She is a classic, navy blue to accent the oak decking. Her name is painted in white at the helm. Gray and John are grinning like schoolboys as they wait for him on the dock.

"Gray! You are a wizard! How on earth did you get her ready so quickly?" asks Sawyer.

"My wife told you I am a sales guy, right? Come on, we're waiting for you to captain her. We can talk on board," replies Gray.

Sawyer climbs on first, helping his uncle before Gray climbs up. Gray hands him the key. "She's all yours."

Sawyer starts her up, and she purrs like a kitten. He grins as Gabe unties her from the dock, and Sawyer backs the boat off the dock. Gabe makes his way over to Sawyer. "How does she feel, son?"

"Just like she did when I last drove her." He maneuvers down the river. "Would you like a turn?"

"You enjoy it for a bit. But, yes, I want a chance." He looks at Gray, "And I know this one is chomping at the bit for his turn."

Sawyer looks at Gray. "How did you manage this in three days?"

"Mr. Gabe helped me. Once I knew who to talk to, the rest was easy. I actually found the mechanic who worked on her last. Guy by the name of Pete. He and his dad owned Taylor and Sons Boat Service before he sold it a few years back. When I asked Pete if he was willing to take on the challenge to get her up and running, he jumped at it." Gray looks chagrined. "Truth be told I think retirement has bored him to death. He came over Friday around lunch. He finished not long before you arrived. I asked him to stay, invited him to join us on the water, but he declined. He did tell me it was the most fun he had had in a long time."

"Well, come on, Gray. Take her for a spin." Sawyer hands the steering wheel off to his brother-in-law. "I would have never thought you could get this done so quickly."

Gray grins. "It cost you a pretty penny."

Gabe gazes off into the distance. "It was well worth it." He looks at his two nephews, one by birth, the other by marriage. "I can't tell you how happy it makes me to watch you young men bring this place to life. Tea Olive's been dormant for far too long."

Sawyer stands beside his uncle. "Only you would call 55 young, Uncle Gabe."

Gabe snorts. "Boy, from where I'm standing, it is." He silently grabs Sawyer's hand and gives it a squeeze. Sawyer squeezes back in understanding. The baton has been passed.

"Come on, Mr. Gabe. It's your turn." Gray slowly turns the boat back toward Tea Olive. "We need to go pick up the women. Might be we can catch the sunset." Gray hands the boat over to Gabe and stands with his hands on his hips. "Your daddy chose well."

Sawyer turns toward Gray and holds out his hand, saying, "So did my sister. Welcome to the family, Gray."

Gray shakes his hand with a firm grip, "Glad to be here. Really glad to be here."

Gabe expertly maneuvers *Miss Melanie* to the dock where Diane, Mandy, and Laura Lynne are waiting with a cooler. "Good evening, ladies. Welcome aboard."

Laura Lynne hands Sawyer the cooler while Gray helps her, and then Diane gets on board. Mandy has already hopped on and is currently standing in front of Gabe, her hands on the wheel. Diane grimaces as she sees her daughter prepared to steer. Before she can intervene, Laura Lynne nudges her and then whispers in her ear, "She's fine. Leave her be. Uncle Gabe loves having another protégé."

"Has she been this way all weekend?" Diane asks.

Laura Lynne shrugs. "Pretty much. He is a patient instructor, and she is a quick learner."

With a sigh, Diane acquiesces. "If she starts to be a nuisance, tell me. I don't want her to become a bother."

Gray and Sawyer walk over to their women. "What are y'all jabbering about?"

Diane looks at her daughter, "Just how quickly our children grow up, I guess." Gabe and Mandy begin slowly trolling away from the dock. Diane smiles as she watches Gabe instructing Mandy how to use the controls and adjust the speed. Mandy is listening intently and nodding. Her expression is serious. "She loves Mr. Gabe. I can't thank you enough for all y'all did this weekend for Mandy."

"Our pleasure. And I mean that." Laura Lynne chuckles as she sinks back into her husband's arms. "I don't know what we would have done without her at the store yesterday. She was a whiz behind the cash register. We had a lot of fun."

"Mom! Do you see the sunset? Isn't it gorgeous?" Before Diane can answer, Mandy continues, "I'm thirsty. Can I have one of those Diet Cokes, Miss Laura Lynne?"

Diane and Laura Lynne look at each other and start laughing. "Do you want to answer her, or do you want me to?" asks Laura Lynne.

"I got this one. You've had her all weekend." Diane pulls away from Sawyer and opens the cooler, hunting through the ice for a Diet Coke. She walks over to her daughter, smiling.

Laura Lynne nudges her husband. When he leans down, she whispers in his ear, "Look at Sawyer. He's got it bad."

Gray glances at Sawyer and notices his eyes never leave Diane, watching her every move. He has a gentle smile on his face and looks relaxed for the first time since he met him a few days ago. "Leave him be. He deserves to be loved by a good woman."

She nuzzles his ear. "You're right. He does."

Everyone has a turn at the wheel, and the boat performs beautifully. It's close to 9 PM when Sawyer brings *Miss Melanie* back to the Cooper dock. Gray ties her off and helps get everyone off. "Mr. Gabe, can you take the ladies back to the house? I'll help Sawyer batten down the hatches," asks Gray.

"My pleasure." Gabe slaps Gray on the back. "Good work, Gray. It was great to be out on the water again. It's been way too long." Gabe takes the empty cooler from Laura Lynne. "Come on, ladies. Let's head back. The morning will be here before you know it."

As the group disappears down the trail, Sawyer jumps off the boat onto the dock and walks over to Gray. "Okay, what's up? Considering all I need to do with the boat is turn the key off in the ignition, I figure you want to talk."

"Yeah, I didn't want to talk in front of the women. No need to frighten them." Gray pulls out a walkie-talkie from his jacket pocket. "Mind if I call John? I asked him to join us so we could talk together."

"Sure."

Gray radio's John, who was obviously waiting for him to call. "Can you meet us in the barn?"

"Sure, be there in five."

Gray and Sawyer start walking toward the barn. "So, my brother, you planning to marry Diane?"

Sawyer laughs, "No beating around the bush with you, is there?"

"I'll take that as a yes." Gray slaps him on the back. "Welcome to the club, buddy."

"Whoa, I haven't decided anything yet. We're just getting to know each other. The weekend was great and all, but marriage? Becoming a stepfather? That is a mighty big leap."

"I am going to give you my two cents worth of advice and then leave you alone. You would be a fool to let a woman like Diane get away." He points to a light flashing in the big azalea tree behind the barn. "Look, there's John."

Sawyer and Gray arrive at the barn door, followed closely by John. "Thanks for meeting us, John. I have something I want to show y'all. I found it in *Miss Melanie* when I was cleaning her out. Looks like someone's been hiding in there."

Gray goes to the corner where the boat had been residing up until this weekend. He pulls out a crate and trash bag. "There is a sleeping bag, lantern, books, food, water bottles, even a toothbrush and toothpaste."

John shines his light over the contents. "Any alcohol or drugs?"

"Not that I saw. At first, I thought maybe it was one of Freddie's gang, but that didn't make sense. Up until a few weeks ago, they were all living in the bunkhouse." Gray pulls out a wrapper. "The expiration date on this bag of crackers was three months ago. Whoever it is, he or she has been here for a while."

Sawyer is not pleased. "Shit, who would want to hide in the boat? And, why?"

John looks at Sawyer, "I think you need to call Grady and let him know."

Sawyer sighs. "You're probably right." He looks askance. "Maybe a vagrant?"

John shakes his head. "We haven't had an issue."

Sawyer looks at Gray. "When do you and Laura Lynne leave?"

"Our flights are tomorrow, but we can change them," Gray replies.

"No, no. It's fine." Sawyer looks around the barn, thinking of all the potential hiding places in the 8,000-square-foot structure. "John, after I get Diane and Mandy dropped off, I'll stop by and talk to Grady. Then you and I need to go over all the structures on the farm with a fine-toothed comb. There is a hell of a lot of places a person could hide."

"Sure, Colonel," John says.

Gray looks at Sawyer, "I can't hide this from Laura Lynne. I plan to tell her. I just wanted to show y'all first."

Sawyer nods, "I know. She has a right to know, but damn, sometimes I wish it was the 1950s again, and we could just keep the 'little women' in the dark."

Gray looks pointedly at Sawyer. "You need to tell Diane too."

"I know. I will." Sawyer starts pacing and asks John, "You see or hear anything from Scarlet since we last spoke?"

"No, but then I haven't been looking too closely. Why? Something I should know?" asks John.

"Laura Lynne tried to call her this weekend and hasn't heard from her," says Sawyer.

Gray watches the two men talk over him, and finally, he interjects, "Something I should know here? Why would John know where Scarlet is?"

John looks at Sawyer, and Sawyer nods in agreement. John answers, "I've been keeping an eye on her. From a distance. I got an itchy feeling in my gut when I met her the day Roger was killed. I don't ignore gut feelings, so with Sawyer's permission, I've been looking after her."

Gray is quiet for a moment. "She won't like it when she finds out, but from everything Laura Lynne has told me, I think you have a right to be concerned. I know Laura Lynne thinks something is off."

"I can do a little reconnaissance over the next couple of days now that you're back home."

Gray looks at Sawyer. "I'm gonna tell Laura Lynne about this too. Just thought I should warn you."

"Is there anything my sister doesn't know after I talk to you?" Sawyer asks.

Gray shrugs his shoulders. "No. We deal in truth." Gray gets up from his perch, "But don't worry, I got your back. If she was my sister, I would do the same." Gray walks toward the door. "Come on, Sawyer, let's not keep our women waiting any longer." He looks at John. "You're welcome to join us."

"Thanks, but looks like I have other plans," says John.

Gray replies, "Understood. Sawyer?"

"I'm coming." He walks out the door with John. "Thanks, man."

John quietly walks to the back of the barn and out into the night. Gray watches him go. "I like knowing John is here with you and Mr. Gabe."

"Me, too. There are too many unanswered questions around here. I think I need to go visit my mother again. Maybe she can shed some light on Scarlet."

The back door opens, and Laura Lynne walks out onto the porch, followed by Diane. "Y'all ready to tell us what's going on?" asks Laura Lynne.

Gray smiles and hits Sawyer on the back. "I told you so." He raises his voice to answer, "We were just on our way to do that very thing."

Sawyer glances behind Diane. "Where's Mandy?"

"Inside playing chess with Mr. Gabe," says Diane.

Sawyer nods and replies, "Come for a walk with me?"

"Absolutely, let me just let her know." Diane disappears for a few minutes and then comes back out, walking past Gray and Laura Lynne sitting on the settee. Sawyer takes her hand as she walks beside him. "What's going on?"

Sawyer tells her about the potential "camper" in the boat. He also tells her his concerns about Scarlet. She listens quietly. When he is finished, she simply says, "Thank you for telling me."

Sawyer stops under one of the tea olive trees on the property. The bush is in bloom, and the air smells sweet with its fragrance. He pulls Diane around to face him. She is stunning in the moonlight, her hair piled on top of her head, her dark eyes full of mystery, her nose ring sparkling. He gazes into her eyes. "Listen, there is a lot going on here at the farm and with my family. Finding time to be together over the next few weeks might be difficult." He kisses her forehead. "I don't want you to think I'm ignoring you."

Diane scoffs. "Do I look like someone who is worried about being ignored? Please give me some credit."

He holds on tight to her hands as she starts to pull away. "No, don't. I'm sorry. That didn't come out right."

"It sure didn't." She takes a step closer to him. "Sawyer, I am as new at this as you are, but I am not some damsel in distress character from some Elizabethan novel. I've been taking care of myself and Mandy for a long time. None of that ends simply because we are now lovers."

"I know. I know. I'm sorry. Let's start over. I don't want our weekend to end on a sour note."

Not one to hold a grudge, Diane steps into his arms. "It won't. Just don't ever think of me as a needy female again. We're in this relationship as equals. Fair enough?"

"Fair enough."

Diane and Sawyer listen as the house bell rings three times. Sawyer smiles, it is the signal for the kids to come home. He looks at Diane, "I guess it's time for us to go back. Three rings means the kids are to come in." He grins. "I think that means us."

Diane and Sawyer walk back down the path they came from to the back of the house. Gabe is standing at the bell. "Come on, you two. It's late and Mandy won't go to bed until her mother can tuck her in." He looks at Diane. "You've done a great job with her. Y'all are welcome anytime."

"Thank you." Diane smiles at Sawyer and squeezes his hand. "I'll see you in the morning. Good night."

Diane walks into the house, and Gabe comments, "Looks like the weekend went well."

Sawyer nods. "It did." He looks at his uncle. "I love her."

Gabe breaks out into a grin, "Well, that's just fine. Diane is a fine woman. And an excellent mother. You gonna marry her? Be a stepfather?"

Sawyer chuckles. "Lord, you and Gray. He asked me the same thing. The truth is I don't know. I never considered getting married. Figured I would die on the battlefield." He sighs. "Not to mention there is quite a bit going on right now."

"There is; that's true enough," says Gabe.

"Did Gray tell you what he found in the boat?"

"He did. It has me a bit baffled. I can't imagine why anyone would want to stay in there, plenty of better hiding places on the farm."

The next twenty minutes are spent discussing the possible implications of the potential squatter and about adding an additional watchman to the boat during the night hours and possibly installing a security system, something that had never been done.

Finally, Sawyer cannot hide his fatigue any longer. "I'm beat. I'm calling it a night."

"I'm right behind you. I'm not used to the energy of a teenage girl. It's like having a new puppy. Even Liam doesn't have her energy. She plumb wore me out."

"But you loved it."

Gabe smiles widely. "I did. Every minute of it."

34

Chapter Thirty-Four

The next morning, the house is a loud din. Sawyer smiles as he stands at the base of the stairs listening to Diane as she pushes Mandy out of her room. Laura Lynne and Gray come down the stairs hauling their suitcases. Victoria and Pearl are busy in the kitchen fixing breakfast for everyone before they leave.

"Haven't seen it this busy in a long time. Kind of nice." Gabe says as he sips his coffee. He hands Sawyer a cup. "Here. You're gonna need the caffeine."

"Thanks." Gabe didn't know how right he was. Sawyer smiles to himself as he thinks of Diane sneaking into his room and waking him up. They didn't get much sleep last night.

Laura Lynne snags Sawyer on her way to the kitchen. "We need to talk before Gray and I leave. Spare 15 minutes?"

Sawyer listens to the woman currently in his thoughts threaten her daughter to get moving, and he grins. "Sounds like I have at least that much time."

Laura Lynne smiles. "Teenagers. I vividly remember school mornings. Nice to have the house full, though, isn't it?"

Gabe clucks his tongue. "I said the very same thing. Mind if I join you in the kitchen?"

"No, come on. I need some tea." She looks to her husband, currently fishing his keys out of his pocket. "You want some coffee, sweet love?"

"Absolutely. I'm going to pull the car around first, though. I'll meet you in there."

Laura Lynne leads the way, her brother and uncle following. The kitchen is busy with Victoria at the stove and Pearl performing the role of sous chef. "Come on, we can sit at the island," Laura Lynne says. She bumps Pearl on her way to the coffee and tea. "Sorry! Just need the caffeine. I'll get outta the way."

Pearl looks at the invasion of her kitchen. "Victoria, I think you're right. We need a coffee station *outside* of the kitchen if we're going to keep having all this company." Pearl gives her guests the hairy eyeball.

"Fine, fine. We'll go to the study." Sawyer and Gabe exit as quickly as they entered. Laura Lynne retrieves the coffee and tea and follows. Of course, she had to rib Pearl a little more before she left. That's what besties do.

"Okay, Laura Lynne, what did you need to talk to me about? I know Gray told you about the boat and Scarlet. I swear I don't know anything more than what he told you," Sawyer says.

Laura Lynne waves her hand. "No, no, it's not that. While you were gone, I got an interesting phone call. Well, I shouldn't say I did, but I answered the phone. It was gentleman by the name of General William Williamson. He had some interesting information to share with me." She looks at him inquisitively. "Why didn't you tell me you plan to retire?"

"Bill called here? What did he want?" asks Sawyer.

"I think he wanted to convince you to stay in, but he was under the gun to turn in your paperwork. He said if you had changed your mind to let him know by today. Otherwise, the paperwork is going through." She sighs in frustration. "Well? Are you retiring?"

"Yes. Tea Olive is my home now. I am back to stay."

Laura Lynne puts her mug of tea down and gives him a big hug. She whispers in his ear, "I'm so glad." She steps back with tears in her eyes. She glances over her shoulder at Diane and Mandy who had appeared in the doorway. "I think this calls for a celebration." She looks at her uncle. "Think we can book the country club for next month?"

"Shouldn't be a problem. Just give me a date," says Gabe.

"Laura Lynne, no. I don't want a big shindig," Sawyer argues.

"I think she's right. Our family hasn't had anything to celebrate in a good long time. Retiring after, what, thirty years in the military seems fitting," Gabe says, backing up his niece.

"Thirty-three years," Sawyer corrects his uncle.

"Thirty-three years! An even better reason." Laura Lynne looks at Diane and sees Gray as he comes in the entrance, coffee mug in hand. "Don't y'all agree?"

Gray looks at his wife and smiles. "I have no idea what I am agreeing to, but whatever you want, darlin'." He looks at Sawyer. "What's got her all fired up this morning? I was only gone five minutes."

Sawyer explains, "She wants to throw me a retirement party at the country club. I don't want one."

"I have to agree with my wife," says Gray.

"Me, too," says Diane with a smile.

"Me, three!" Mandy chimes in, making her mom laugh.

Laura Lynne turns to face Sawyer. "Looks like you are outvoted. Ashley and I will handle everything. I'll let you know the date. All you have to do is show up in your dress blues or whatever you call them."

Gray walks over to his wife and kisses her on the nose before winking at his brother-in-law. "You may as well just agree. It makes life much easier."

Sawyer nods. "Fine. Whatever. Just don't invite the whole town. Let's keep the thing simple."

Laura Lynne smirks, unwilling to commit. She hugs her brother again. "Keep me posted." She lowers her voice, "And watch out for everyone, okay?"

"I will," Sawyer confirms.

Laura Lynne pats him on the back before releasing him and turning to her uncle to give him his hug. "Thanks for having us. It was lovely. And now I have an excellent reason to be back next month."

Gabe holds on to his niece and gives her a squeeze. "You never need an excuse."

She smiles as she walks over to Mandy and gives her a big hug. Mandy burrows into her arms. "I had the best time with you. We must do it again." She reaches out to Diane to make it a three-way hug. "Thank you for entrusting me with your daughter."

She looks over her shoulder. Gray is shaking hands with Sawyer. She calls to her husband, "Come on, Gray. We need to go before I start crying. I still have to say goodbye to Victoria and Pearl."

"Right behind you, love." He passes Diane and Mandy, roughing up Mandy's hair and pretending to air box with her, "See you later, Mandy."

She laughs, "You bet, Mr. Gray."

Gray laughs as he leaves the room. Sawyer looks at Diane. "Y'all ready for some breakfast? Victoria and Pearl are cooking up a storm."

Diane glances at her watch. "If we are quick about it. Somebody didn't want to get out of bed this morning."

"It was soooo early," Mandy whines. "Besides, we're just doing dumb testing today." She looks at Sawyer and Gabe, rolling her eyes. "So boring."

"Come on, we can eat at the kitchen island," says Sawyer.

The four of them enter the kitchen as Gray and Laura Lynne leave. Pearl takes one look at them and sighs. "Fine. Sit at the counter. Victoria can feed you here." She looks at Mandy. "Next time you want to sleep in around here, remember it impacts more than you." She leans closer, her wooden spoon in hand, and gently taps her head. "Got it?"

Mandy hangs her head sheepishly. "Yes, ma'am."

Victoria puts out plates full of eggs and bacon, fresh toast smeared with butter, and fresh cut cantaloupe. "Eat it while it's hot."

Thirty minutes later, Sawyer pulls up in front of Moseley Hall to drop off Mandy. Mandy hops out of the Yukon with a quick, "See ya," before joining a group of students. She looks back over her shoulder and gives a little wave.

"That's her signal to leave. You're embarrassing her," Diane says.

"What? I am? Aren't I supposed to watch her go *into* the school before I leave?"

Diane laughs. "When she was six, yes. Not in high school." She looks at him. "She's fine."

"Whatever you say." He pulls forward. "To your house or the bookstore?"

Diane glances at her watch. "I want to go to the store. I haven't been away from it this long, and I'm not sure what I am going to walk into today. I'm sure your sister and Mary did a good job, but…"

"But not as good as you would do?"

"Well, something like that." She looks at the luggage in the back of the car. "I can just put this in the storage room and grab a ride home from the Gaillards. Harvey will want to hear all about Mandy's weekend anyway."

"All right, but if Harvey can't take you and Mandy, I expect you to call me. I'll come and get you, but no walking home." He looks at her. "Promise me."

She holds up three fingers, "Scout's promise." She leans back. "You know you're a bit overprotective."

"Probably. But with so much going on, I don't know who to trust. I have had three people tell me to watch my back. That means watching out for those I love." He pulls into the Wheelbarrow Books parking lot and puts the car in park. "Can you live with that?"

"I can live with that." She opens the car door. "Because I love you too."

Sawyer meets her behind the Yukon, pulling her close and giving her a big kiss in front of the whole damned town. They pull apart when they hear the clapping. To both their mortification, the Magnolia Café crowd had a clear view and apparently appreciated the show. He pulls Diane close and kisses the top of her head, "Well, no keeping it a secret. I hope you don't mind."

She rolls her eyes. "I couldn't care less. Other people's opinions have never held sway over me. Do you mind?"

He sighs. "No, but my mother will. Public displays of affection are very un-Beauregard-like and, therefore, unacceptable. I need to stop by and see her anyway. I want to talk to her about Kolensky."

"Smart. I imagine she knows more than she's letting on. She is definitely coy."

"If by 'coy' you mean a cagey old broad, then I agree." He pulls the luggage out of the trunk. "I think I've got it all if you want to unlock the doors."

Sawyer meets her at the door, where she stands in stunned silence. Sawyer looks over her shoulder to see what has her speechless. He smiles; Laura Lynne has definitely left her mark on the place. In every corner, there are fresh flowers. A huge display sits on the counter. Sawyer leaves the bags at the door, pushing Diane through. He plucks the card out of the hydrangea and tea olive display and opens it. He reads, "Diane, thank you for entrusting me with your two most precious gifts: Mandy and Wheelbarrow Books. I hope Mary and I didn't leave anything too wrecked. I love you like a sister, Laura Lynne. P.S. The receipt of sales for Saturday is in the envelope. Mandy tells me we did good."

Diane walks slowly around her store, sniffing flowers and fingering their petals. Sawyer opens the envelope and look inside, pulling out the receipt. "Found the receipt. Looks like the total is $5,743.55."

Diane's fingers come to her mouth in awe. "What? In one day?" She rushes over to him. "Let me see."

He hands her the receipt. She looks and begins hopping up and down.

"You're pleased?" Sawyer asks.

"Pleased?" Diane opens her arms and does a little twirl. "Thrilled. I don't do that many sales in two weeks. I wonder how she did it?"

Sawyer goes to the wall and points his finger at the flyer. "I think I have your answer. Looks like your daughter had a hand in it. She should consider graphic art and marketing as a career."

Diane walks over to the wall and gazes at the flyer. She knows her daughter's artistry anywhere. "Wow, looks like they played on the 'whole guest author as a bookseller for a day' as a promo. Even lists some of her favorite authors."

"Smart."

There's a knock at the door. Sawyer goes over and unlocks it to find Grady leaning against the door jamb. "Welcome back," he says. He leans back so Diane cannot see him and mouths, "Gazette." Sawyer nods in understanding. Grady leans in the store and says, "Hi, Diane."

She comes to the door. "Hi, Grady." She shows him the flyer. "How did Saturday go?"

He laughs. "It was a zoo. I ended up directing traffic and coordinating parking. Even Grace came in to help man the cash register and the crowds." He pointed to the flyer. "Mandy posted that thing all over social media. People were coming from all around. It was crazy." He starts walking backward. "Gotta run. See ya later, Sawyer."

Sawyer nods as he shuts the door. "He wants to meet me at the Gazette, so I need to run. You good here?"

She turns a smiling face up at him. "More than good. I am great!" She laughs. "And I was worried they messed up my shop."

He squeezes her hand. "Glad you're happy. I can't promise when we will see each other again, but I promise to call."

She squeezes back. "I love you, Sawyer Avery Beauregard. You stay safe."

He smiles and walks out the door, waiting until she locks it behind him. He stops at the Magnolia Café and gets a regular coffee before walking down Main Street to the Gazette offices. Mary is just opening the front door. "Hello, young Sawyer. How was your weekend?"

"Lovely, just like you." He smiles at her blush. "That rose color is my favorite on you."

"Thank you." She fumbles open the door. "He's in the back."

Sawyer holds the door open for Mary and then walks behind the counter to the back office. Grady is perched on the edge of the desk with his hat off. He looks up from his phone when Sawyer enters. "Hey, buddy. Thanks for meeting me. How was the weekend?"

"Let's just say enlightening." He leans against the door frame. "But first, tell me what you know. I'll fill you in after."

Grady nods agreement. "I found Buck."

Sawyer perks up. "Really, where? Is Scarlet with him?"

"I don't know about that, but Buck is in Biloxi, Mississippi. From what I gather, he's been there on and off for years. As of late, he's been staying in a dump off the strip. From what the landlord tells me, he's been living there for the past six months." Grady looks at Sawyer with sad eyes. "I saw him. He looks like shit. I barely recognized him."

"He didn't see me, so I followed him for a few hours. He went to this joint on the strip called the 'Lucky Lady.' It's a strip club." He clears his throat. "He was well-known there and an obvious procurer of the services, if you know what I mean." Grady looks closely at him. "You don't seem all that surprised. I was shocked."

"Well, prepared to be shocked again, then," Sawyer explains in detail his conversation with Headmaster Kolensky. Grady sits in stunned silence.

"I don't know what is more stunning, the fact that the nerdy Robert Huger owned a strip joint or our old Headmaster was a money launderer? Crazy."

Sawyer looks at Grady. "I'm telling you this as a friend. I need some time to figure out what the hell is going on. And with what you told me, I'm more concerned than ever about Scarlet. She's not returning phone calls." He hesitates and then decides if he can't trust Grady, he can't trust anyone. "She's working in Wisteria as a cleaning lady at the bed and breakfast there."

"What? Your sister, Scarlet?"

"The very same. John has been keeping an eye on her. I quit worrying about her once I found out what she was doing every day, but after our discussion I'm thinking perhaps that was the wrong move." Something occurs to Sawyer. "Wait, you said Buck has been living in Biloxi the last six months."

"Yeah, why?"

"John told me he saw a guy go in and out of Scarlet's house one night while he was keeping an eye on things. I assumed it was Buck, but now I'm not so sure. But if not Buck, then who?"

"I can go by and see her, do a bit of a wellness visit. See if I can suss things out a bit."

Sawyer shakes his head, "No. I'll have John amp up his efforts. But you could do one thing for me. Maybe Grace would be the better one to ask, but can you find out who owns the Lucky Lady? And maybe talk to your dad, find out what he knows. He and Mr. Huger ran in the same circles."

"God, I hope not. It would kill Mom."

Sawyer grins. "Grady, one thing I am more certain of than life itself is your daddy would never cheat on your momma. Ever." His grin disappears. "Unlike my old man."

Grady's radio crackles. Sawyer recognizes Beth Bodeen's voice. Grady listens and then looks at Sawyer. "I need to get back, buddy. How about we meet again tonight, say 9 PM, at the ridge?"

"Before you go, Gray found evidence we've had a squatter on the property."

"Where?" Squatters are not unheard of along the river estates.

"Well, that's the curious thing. It looks like someone's been living inside *Miss Melanie*. And what is even more odd is *Miss Melanie* has been in the barn for like 25 years. There are plenty better spaces to hide inside that barn. The thing is a monstrosity."

"Christ, Sawyer. You got some weird shit going on."

"Not to mention Dead Doe. Any word on him?"

"Nothing more so far. Crickets from the DA's office. Today, I am taking some guys with me to do a walk-through of the Laurel place. Hoping Bubba is right and Freddie and the gang are hanging out there." Grady's radio crackles. Beth Ann is obviously perturbed. "Listen, Beth Ann is going to skin me alive if I don't handle this call. I'll see you tonight."

Sawyer nods as he watches Grady make his way out the back door. He follows at a more sedate pace, walking out the front office. Mary sits at the front desk, perched on her stool reading a novel. "Heard you had a good turnout on Saturday."

Mary looks over her glasses, "Most fun I have had since Laura Lynne was coming here every day. That sister of yours sure can stir up the excitement." She takes her glasses off and puts the earpiece to her lips. "And you, lockin' lips in the parking lot with the owner this morning. Hmmm, must have been a good weekend."

Sawyer grins. "The best." He walks around the counter. "Thanks for the space."

"Any time. By the way, congratulations on your retirement. I'm looking forward to the party." He stops and looks over his shoulder, rolling his eyes and shaking his head. Saying nothing, he walks out the front door, the bell tingling. All the while Mary is laughing. Will he ever get used to the rapidity of the Venice grapevine?

35

Chapter Thirty-Five

Sawyer checks his watch and decides to visit his mother at Pineview. Maybe she can shed some light on the Kolensky situation. Sawyer pulls into the assisted living parking lot and kicks himself for not picking up some flowers. Oh, well.

He walks into Pineview and to his mother's room where she is sitting regally in her chair, piecing together a puzzle. To her credit, she doesn't blink an eye at his appearance.

"Did you forget how to knock, Sawyer?" She goes back to her puzzle. "I know you forgot how to behave in public; seems like your manners need some work."

"I'm sure you're right, Momma. I went to see Elijah Kolensky this weekend." He walks to the puzzle table, moving it out of the way so he can stand in front of her. "No more cat and mouse." He leans down and whispers, "I know about the blackmail."

She looks pointedly behind him at the open door. "I have no idea what you are talking about."

Getting the hint, Sawyer walks over to the door and shuts it firmly. He then walks over to her radio and turns it on, placing it in front of the intercom. "Okay, Momma. Nobody's listening now. Tell me what you know, and don't leave out any details." He sits in the chair opposite her.

For the first time, he sees his mother flinch. Her hands are in her lap, worrying her handkerchief. She talks quietly, "It all started that summer Laura Lynne went to Eileen's. This was all before I found out what happened to her that summer. Your father and I, well more your father, was certain Buck Huger was to blame. I learned later why he assumed it was him." She looks at him.

"I know about the strip club."

"Yes, well, I didn't. And your father didn't tell me until much later. He made quite the fuss, going over to Robert and Suzanne's with his shotgun. I couldn't talk sense into him. Robert was able to calm him down. From what Suzanne told me later, Robert had to get in front of Buck for fear your daddy was going to kill him. And, then, well, your father was wrong. And it was too late. Robert knew all about Laura Lynne's secret. And he kept it. But things started happening: business dropped off, we couldn't hire field hands, I was excused from the DAR as president, and we were being iced out."

She looks at him for a moment and then drops her gaze. "You were there. You remember." Sawyer nods his head slightly. "Then, well, Robert told us about your *friend* Clay. That is when the blackmail started. Though Robert referred to it as an *investment*."

Melanie continues, "At first, it was relatively small sums of money. We would make 'donations' to the school, and Elijah would launder the money, taking a percentage. But then, Robert put the screws to us, and we had to use the last of the Beauregard money. Right at half a million dollars. It was all we had that was not in the trust. And, still, he wanted more." His mother looks to the right and gazes out the window for a moment. She then faces Sawyer directly, staring into his eyes. "We had no choice, you see."

"What did you do, Momma?" Sawyer leans forward off his chair and grabs her hand. "Tell me."

She rubs his hand with her thumb. "Suzanne came to see me one day. She said she had a deal for me. And she swore if I accepted, then the blackmail would cease. I listened. If I could arrange for Buck to marry into the family, then the blackmail would cease. At first, I thought she meant Laura Lynne, but in Suzanne's eyes, she was damaged goods. No, the prize was Scarlet. I knew then that had been the plan all along. They wanted Buck to marry a Beauregard."

"So, you sold Scarlet?" Sawyer can feel the bile rising in his throat.

"It wasn't that way! I agreed not to stop any romantic overtures from Buck. And, well, I didn't."

"You did a hell of a lot more than that, didn't you, Momma? Don't lie to me. I mean it, or I swear I will tell Scarlet myself."

"Don't you cuss at me, young man! I am still your mother." She sighs. "But fine. You might say I *encouraged* the union. And to help things along, your father sponsored Buck in his fraternity at Ole Miss." She squares her shoulders. "And it worked out, didn't it? She and Buck are still married and have two sons to carry on the Huger name. Suzanne got what she wanted, and your father and I were able to stop the blackmail and save the farm."

Sawyer hangs his head in shame. "And as part of the deal, Scarlet's part of the trust was liquidated and given to the Hugers, right? They needed it to save Twin Oaks after Black Monday in 1987."

"They threatened us one last time. Your father was going to call the whole thing off: the marriage, the payments, everything. We had decided we would just deal with the fallout. But somehow, Robert suspected it. He would have destroyed us all."

Sawyer is silent, watching his mother. "Is that all?"

"There should be a legal document somewhere outlining the terms of our agreement. Gerald Lally drew it up. I know he has a copy."

Sawyer looks at his mother. "Again, you sold your daughter?"

"No more than I was sold to your father. It was an arranged marriage, perfectly acceptable."

"I imagine you have had to tell yourself that over the years, Mom. But don't try and sell that bill of goods to me." He cocks his head to one side and gives his mother a look of dawning understanding. And he feels the bile rise in the back of his throat. "We were all just pawns, Laura Lynne, Scarlet, me...even Avery. Chess pieces on the board of Tea Olive's legacy. You used us not as children but as a means to achieve your own goals. Everything was justified as long as it was to 'protect the legacy.'" He walks backward toward the door. "It's no wonder we're all so fucked up."

Melanie stares blindly after him as he walks out the door.

To his surprise, when he gets into the car after leaving his mother's room, the one person he wants to talk to is Diane. He decides to take a chance and run by the bookstore. He glances at his watch; the morning is all but over. As he drives down Main Street, he notices both the café and bookstore are in a flurry of activity. There would be no way to see Diane now. So, at the one stoplight in town, he texts her.

The response is almost immediate. Diane replies, "What's wrong? U never text."

He thinks for a minute. What is wrong? He misses her. He grew accustomed to her being around to talk to, consult with, and share his day. He pulls over on the outskirts of town. He texts her back, "Miss u. Talked to momma. Bad." He figures that about covers it.

"Call tonight. Or coffee in AM."

"Coffee. 8 AM. Luv u." He looked at his texts, not sure his abbreviations make sense.

She sends back a thumbs up emoji and a heart. "Luv u 2." He smiles.

He pulls back into the road and back home to Tea Olive. There is a strange pickup truck in the back of the house. Sawyer quickly parks in the barn and heads to the mud room. He opens the door, removes his shoes, and enters the kitchen. Sitting at the island, being fed by Victoria, is an ancient-looking man wearing paint-smattered overalls. He smiles a toothless grin at Sawyer as he enters, moving quickly off his stool. Sawyer is shocked by his agility.

"Sir," the man addresses Sawyer.

Sawyer nods his head. "Now, Mr. Gates, no need to be so formal with Sawyer," Victoria says as she looks at Sawyer with a twinkle in her eye. "Sawyer, this is Bill Gates. Mr. Gates, Sawyer Beauregard." Sawyer shakes his hand. "Momma hired him to paint the rooms upstairs and fix that hole in the wall."

"Nice to see you again, Mr. Gates," Sawyer says.

"Oh, you can call me Bill. And it's okay; you can go ahead and laugh at my name. I've heard it all. Truth be told, Mr. Richest Man Alive was named after me. I'm a good twenty years older than he is," says Gates.

Sawyer smiles, enjoying this Bill Gates immensely. "Glad to see you here. I sure don't care for a rose-colored room."

"I remember painting that room for Miss Melanie. I thought it was fussy then, but she insisted. I like the blue color better. It should be done by the end of the day tomorrow. But you'll want to wait until next week to move back in. Takes a bit of time for the walls to set up nice in an old house like this," advises Gates.

"I'll remember that. Victoria, you have any more of those chicken and waffle sliders left? I've missed your cooking this weekend," Sawyer asks.

"Sure, pull up a stool. I'll serve 'em to you hot off the griddle," says Victoria.

He passes the next thirty minutes being entertained by Bill Gates and fed by Victoria. He enjoys himself immensely.

"I'm just not comfortable calling you Sawyer. You got something else I could call you?" asks Gates.

Sawyer thinks about it and responds, "Well, the farmhands call me Colonel. Would that suit you better?"

"It would. I'd appreciate it if you just called me by my last name. Think you can do that?" asks Gates.

"I can, Gates. Join me for lunch again tomorrow. I can't wait to hear more of your stories," invites Sawyer.

Gates looks at Victoria. "As long as this lovely lady plans on doing the cooking. That was a fine meal, ma'am." She smiles at him as he gets off the stool. "Well, I need to get back at it. The walls won't paint themselves." He walks out the swinging kitchen door.

Sawyer looks at Victoria. "He is some character."

"He is. Momma throws him work whenever she has it. He sold his company a few years back, but then his wife took ill. Rumor has it the bulk of his money went to cover her medical expenses. She died about a year ago."

"Think he might be interested in picking up some other projects? There's plenty of work to be done around here. I know Pearl has a list a mile long she would like to tackle."

"That's right nice of you, Colonel," Victoria says, sounding just like Bill Gates. Sawyer starts laughing.

"Ask your momma, and let's figure out a schedule that works for him. See if we can get him on as an employee."

"Okay, I will." Victoria studies Sawyer with a keen eye. "Everything okay with you? When you walked in, you looked a bit peaked."

"I'm fine. Just heard some news that didn't sit well with me." He nods toward his empty plate. "The meal helped a lot."

"Good food has a funny way of doing that." She smiles. "Shrimp and grits for supper. That should cheer you up."

"Homemade grits? Like your granny used to make us?"

"The very same. I don't know any other way to make them."

"I can't wait. Any idea where my uncle is today?"

"No, can't say I do know. He left not too long after you. Said he had some errands to run and would be back for supper," she replies.

"Hmmm, okay."

"Oh, by the way, you had a call while you were out. I left a message on your desk. It was Miss Grace. She said no reason to call her back. She just wanted to remind you this Thursday morning the board meets at the club. She wanted to be sure you were in attendance. I told her I would let you know."

"Thanks, Victoria." Sawyer sighs as he walks through the kitchen door toward his study. He texts Grady, "Ridge tonight? 9 PM." He notes the thumbs up signal and then with a sigh, begins to work on the stacks of paperwork from the vault.

36

Chapter Thirty-Six

Sawyer sees Grady sitting in one of the Adirondack chairs as he approaches the Ridge. He could smell the fire burning about a half mile down the hill. He watches as Grady pokes at the fire, then leans back in the chair, his hands in his pockets. He looks up when he sees Sawyer approaching.

"I love how you can stare at a fire, and it just makes your mind settle, don't you? After my conversation with Dad and Grace, I needed that to happen." Grady smiles and pats the chair next to him. "Pull up a seat. You aren't going to believe what I learned today."

"It can't be nearly as heartbreaking as what my momma told me," Sawyer says as he takes a seat.

"I want to hear all about it, but first let me tell you after quite a bit of digging and calling in some favors, we now know who owns the Lucky Lady. And it isn't Buck. At least, not directly." He waits a beat. "It is none other than Green Acres, LLC. The same company that owned Virginia Phillips house."

"Daddy's maybe mistress?"

"Yes, but it gets even more weird. Green Acres, LLC, is owned by the Overpass Development Partners. The very same company that bought Twin Oaks." He lowers his voice. "It's all the same people, Sawyer. It has to be a front of some kind. It only makes sense."

Sawyer gives a low whistle.

Grady continues, "When the feds came down to investigate Laura Lynne's case, they mentioned to Jerry and me that they had been looking at Venice for a myriad of crimes. Those crimes included drugs, money laundering, prostitution, sex trafficking, and gambling." He looks back at Sawyer. "At the time, I was focused on the crimes against Laura Lynne. I just didn't pay much attention, but when I put this together, that conversation came back to me. Made me start to wonder and...think."

Sawyer is quiet for a long time, pondering the ramifications of what Grady just laid out. If what he said is true, then this was much bigger than Sawyer had originally thought. He finally speaks, carefully and softly, "Grady, who else other than us knows what you just told me?"

"You think they could be in danger? I think you could be right." Grady thinks for a second. "Grace and my daddy know bits and pieces, but they don't have the full picture. So, I would say it's just us."

"You trust Jerry, right? Laura Lynne seems to like him. She thinks he is on the up and up."

"I have to agree. So far he has been straight as an arrow. If you are asking me whether we should let him know what we know, the answer is a resounding yes. I don't like it one bit. Too many unknowns."

"I agree. How do you recommend we handle it? I don't trust the sheriff's department. Bubba still has too many connections."

Grady is quiet as he considers his options. "Can you make it to town in the morning? Without drawing too much attention to yourself?"

"Sure. I'm meeting Diane at 8 for coffee at Magnolia Café."

"That's perfect. Have your coffee, then say around 9 make your way to the Gazette. I will have Jerry with me. We can give him a rundown then."

Sawyer starts to get up. "Hey, don't you want to tell me what your momma had to say today?"

"It can wait." Sawyer holds out his hand. "It was more of a personal nature than anything. Nothing to do with what we are talking about right now."

Grady shakes his hand. "Be careful, Sawyer. Somehow, your family is right in the middle of all this."

"I will be. Thanks for having my back, buddy."

The two men part company. Sawyer's mind is working through different scenarios when he spots John's cabin. He decides to stop. He has no doubt John has been tracking his movements since he walked this way to the ridge. "Hello the house!" Sawyer hollers as he approaches the front door.

"Hello, Colonel." John comes around the right corner of the house, loosely carrying his rifle. Sawyer has to admire his preparedness.

"You have a few minutes we can talk? I found out a few things today, hoping I can pick your brain."

"Why don't you come in? I have a fire going and some decaf coffee hot. Figured you might stop by."

"Thanks, I appreciate it," Sawyer replies.

John opens the front door and places the rifle next to the door. He walks behind the kitchen island and fills up two mugs with the hot brew. Sawyer takes a seat in one of the cowhide chairs. He appreciates John's sense of style and comfort. "I like the chairs. I think they are new since I was here last."

"Yeah. I have been working on them for a while."

"You *made* them?" Sawyer asks in amazement.

John smiles. "It's not all that difficult." He sits down in the other chair. "Now, what brings you to my cabin?"

Sawyer takes the mug of coffee John offers him and leans back, "Remember the other day you were telling me that you saw a guy in and out of Scarlet's house one night?"

"Yeah, sure. You thought it was probably her husband."

"Well, I found out today that her husband has been living in Biloxi for the past six months. So, there is a large chance it's not him. Are you sure it was a man?"

"Not 100%, but based on his stature and build, I immediately thought the person was male. She has grown boys, doesn't she? Could it be one of them?"

"Maybe. Though from what I gather, they live out of state. Her oldest, Bobby, has been in and out of drug rehab over the years. Grady thinks he is somewhere in the Midwest. Her other boy, Cooper, is working as an engineer in North Carolina, according to Uncle Gabe." Sawyer sips his coffee. "Maybe we are looking at this wrong. Could be she has a lover? Might make more sense."

"Maybe. Though it would have been a mighty quick rendezvous. He was in and out in 15 minutes," John replies as he takes a sip of his coffee, "You really think your sister would take a lover? She seems pretty conventional to me."

"Two weeks ago, the possibility would have never crossed my mind. But then I never would have considered Scarlet being a maid, either." He looks at John, contemplating his next move. John has been a source of support for Sawyer. He has had his back since he got here and has become a trusted friend. "Listen, I wouldn't even bring this up except I have to trust someone." Sawyer leans forward and props his forearms on his knees, cupping his mug of coffee. "I just finished talking to Grady. I don't want to go into too many details, simply because right now it is a lot of supposition. What I do know for certain is Scarlet's father-in-law was involved in a strip joint in Biloxi where he engaged in pornography and prostitution. He blackmailed my parents for years."

John nods. "Okay. And does Scarlet know?"

"I have no idea. But here's the thing, Buck is in Biloxi hanging out at a strip club called Lucky Lady."

"Really? His pop's place?"

"Good question. And I don't have the answer. It is owned by a LLC, but we think maybe it's a front company. At least Grady is leaning that way." Sawyer stares into the fire. "I can't shake the feeling my sister is in danger. There are just too many things that keep coming back to Robert Huger."

"What's your take on Scarlet's husband? Buck, right?"

Sawyer hangs his head thinking of all the wonderful years he and Buck had playing together. He vividly remembers building forts, swimming in the creeks, climbing trees, and generally doing what boys would do. Charlie was with them most of the time. They were the Three Musketeers.

"Growing up, we were inseparable. He and Charlie were my best friends. Things didn't start to change until we were in high school. And it was just subtle things, like copying homework, picking on one of the nerdy kids, or being a player with the girls. It bothered me, but whatever, you know?" He looks up at John who is leaning back in the chair, his left ankle propped up on his right knee, listening. "But then he was doing things on the football field that just didn't sit right with me. You know, late tackles, getting into fights, he was just an ass on the field. We had stopped hanging out by then. He made a play for Laura Lynne, and I put the kibosh on that."

Sawyer finishes his story, "When I found out Scarlet and Buck were getting married, well I was shocked. But my parents were very pleased. It was a good match for all intents and purposes. And from the outside looking in all these years, I would have said they were right. Scarlet was bred to take over as the matriarch of the family, the same way I was raised to inherit the responsibilities of the trust. She played her role well. I haven't seen Buck in years. I guess the last time we spoke was at Daddy's funeral. That was five years ago."

"So, I guess you're wondering if Buck has taken up where his daddy left off? And you're worried Scarlet is somehow involved?"

"Yeah, I guess that about sums it up." Sawyer gets to his feet. "I need to talk to her, but she's avoiding my sister and me. I could have my mother summon her; she wouldn't refuse her. But honestly, I don't think that's a smart move." He looks out the window, and John remains seated. "I don't know what's going on, and I don't want to do anything that might put Scarlet in more danger than I think she's already in."

John replies, "I'll keep an eye on her. You can't be two places at once. And, you're right. At this point, I don't think you should upset the apple cart. Best to wait and see how this plays out."

"I'm happy to pay you for your services. Just let me know what I owe you."

For the first time since meeting John, Sawyer sees the trained killer in him. He is mad and trying to contain his anger. John stands up slowly, as if careful not to move too fast for fear of hurting someone. "Colonel, I'm going to let that slide tonight because I know you're worried about your sister. But don't ever offend me again by offering to pay me for my help. I told you once I owed Mr. Gabe."

Sawyer meets his gaze squarely. "Okay, I won't."

John nods and visibly shakes his entire body as if getting rid of his anger. "You want a ride back to The Residence?"

Sawyer realizes he is being dismissed. He has overstayed his welcome. "No. Thank you, though. And thanks for the coffee." Sawyer walks to the door and lets himself out. John remains where he stood. Sawyer shakes his head. John seems to have a trigger when it comes to Scarlet. Sawyer finds that bit of information interesting.

37

Chapter Thirty-Seven

Sawyer wakes early the next morning. His sleep fitful and unfortunately, his nightmare came back last night. Maybe because Diane wasn't sleeping with him. He sighs. He is determined to get in his morning run, which he has been neglecting. He is a man of routine, and he needs to get back to some sense of order in his life. He throws on his running clothes and goes down the stairs. He doesn't run into anyone as he makes his way out the mudroom door, grabbing his tennis shoes on the way out.

He makes his way around the estate, encouraged to see the cotton fields beginning to green up. He waves acknowledgement to the field hands working security. He briefly stops at the broken wall between Tea Olive and Twin Oaks to speak to Lance, who is currently guarding the area. He is happy to note there has been no suspicious activity. He takes his time, covering the entire area. He even cuts through to Twin Oaks and runs some of the paths he played on growing up.

He finishes his run at the dock, enjoying the sunrise. He turns to walk toward the house and nearly plows his uncle down. "Whoa there, son! I thought I might find you out here. Brought you some water." He lifts his mug. "I'm going to stick with coffee."

"Thanks." Sawyer breathes heavily, gulping in air. He's not happy he is so out of shape. He clocks his time, and he has run nearly ten miles. He paces and drinks his water. "I have to do this more often. I'm getting out of shape."

"When I first took over for your father, I found it hard to make time for myself. It takes some time to find your balance. Lot of people and projects pulling you in different directions."

Sawyer looks at his uncle, "I missed you yesterday. Didn't hear you come in until late." Gabe ignores the comments. "I guess you aren't going to tell me where you were?" Gabe remains silent. "Fine, whatever. Just don't go off again where I can't reach you, too much going on."

"What's going on that's got you so concerned?" Gabe asks.

"Besides Dead Doe? And the drug runners? Isn't that enough?" Sawyer snaps his fingers snarkily. "Oh wait, maybe it's finding out Scarlet's father-in-law blackmailed our family? Or maybe it's that Scarlet was given to Buck as a peace offering? I don't know, Uncle Gabe. Take your pick."

Gabe waits patiently for Sawyer's temper to cool off. "You done, now, or do you need to go run again? Cuz, son, you talk to me that way again, and I'm liable to take you over my knee." He starts to walk away. "When you are ready to talk reasonable, you let me know."

Sawyer sighs heavily before jogging up next to his uncle. "Sorry. It wasn't fair of me to take my frustrations out on you. Can we start over?"

Gabe eyes him warily. "You gonna be civilized?" Sawyer nods as his uncle starts walking again. "I take it from your ranting that you spoke to Melanie yesterday?" Sawyer nods again. "All right, start from the beginning."

Sawyer tells Gabe everything about his visit with his mother and John. He decides against involving him in Grady's current speculations until after his meeting with Grady and Jerry this morning. "And Momma defended her actions, Uncle Gabe. I feel awful for Scarlet. I don't know whether to tell her or not. So, right now I am just doing nothing."

"It sounds bad to you, doesn't it? The idea of an arranged marriage between two families, but it is the way things were done. Melanie's marriage was arranged, first to Silas and then to Sawyer. I know for a fact money exchanged hands. I imagine Melanie condoned her behavior by comparing it to her own life. Doesn't make it right, but in this instance, I can see my sister's side of things." He ponders for a moment longer. "So, the Beauregard money is long gone, then?"

"Appears to be. Why do you ask?"

"I found out yesterday your grandparents' old place in town is going up for sale. The mansion on Tulmedge Street."

"Really? You thinking about a purchase?" asks Sawyer.

"I was against selling it in the first place, but given what you just told me, I think I now understand why your parent's needed to liquidate their assets." Gabe takes a sip of coffee. "Grace told me when I was in town yesterday. Before I left to attend to some personal business."

"And that is fine. I don't need to know what you are doing. I'm not asking, though I am curious. But you can't leave and not have a way I can contact you, at least for now."

"Fair enough. I will be more careful about keeping you informed of my whereabouts. I didn't mean to make you worry."

Sawyer looks at his uncle with surprise. He was right, he was worried. It was an uncomfortable feeling for him, one he had avoided since losing his men. Caring enough about the people in his life to worry about them. Maybe caring is not the right word, he loves his family. Maybe it's more being involved in day-to-day relationships that have caused him to worry. No wonder he stayed in the military so long. Shooting people is much simpler than being in a relationship with them.

"Just don't do it again. It's a new feeling for me, and I don't like it." Sawyer checks his watch. "Listen, I'm meeting Diane for coffee this morning and then seeing Grady and Jerry. I want to tell you all about it, but it will have to be later. You gonna be around today?"

"I am. And Liam is joining us today. It's apparently a teacher's workday at his school, so he has some additional free time. Maybe he can join me for breakfast since you are running off. I plan to teach him how to run the tractor. I think he's old enough."

"Sounds fun. Y'all be careful."

"Always. Tell Diane I said hello and to bring Mandy by again soon. I like having her around." Gabe heads toward the barn when Sawyer goes into the mud room. He glances at his watch. He has about thirty minutes before he needs to leave. Time enough to spare a quick chat with Pearl. He finds her in her office, fiddling at the computer.

"Good morning, Pearl. I was hoping I could catch you. I wanted to ask you about Bill Gates." Sawyer leans on the doorjamb. "Got a minute?"

"Sure, give me just a sec." She clacks at her keyboard for a moment and then turns her full attention to him. "Okay, thanks. I wanted to finish that invoice before I forgot about it again. Victoria told me you wanted to hire Gates on full-time. As long as you can afford it, there is plenty of work for him to do." She points at her computer. "I already have a list started. That alone will keep him busy for the next six months."

"Okay, well, he's yours. And so is Victoria," And remembering what his uncle said about righting the wrongs of the past as best as he could, he continued, "I am elevating your position to Head of House or whatever title you want. We can figure that out later, but all household staff are going to be reporting to you." Pearl's mouth drops open. "And hire a housekeeper or two. We need to be ready for guests and that shouldn't fall solely on your shoulders."

Sawyer smiles. For the first time in his life, he has left Pearl speechless. He continues, "Unless you object, of course."

"Uh, no, no." She shakes her head as if regaining her senses. "You don't think I'm gonna do all this extra work for free, do you? Supervising people's hard work."

"Ahh, there she is!" Sawyer laughs. "I thought maybe you forgot how to talk there for a minute." He starts to turn from the door. "Yes, you will get paid more. And listen, the same rules apply to whomever you hire for the house. They need to be well-vetted. I can help you out with that part."

"Of course." Pearl stands from her desk as Sawyer starts down the hallway. "Sawyer!" He turns around with a questioning look. "Thanks for the opportunity. I've been waiting a long time for this day."

"You earned it. Thanks, Pearl. I'll be home later this afternoon." She watches him with a small smile on her face, then rubs her hands together excited for the first time in a long time to get to work.

After a quick shower, Sawyer walks to the master suite and looks at the progress Gates has made. He is happy to note the rose-colored walls are slowly disappearing. He smiles as he makes his way down the stairs and out the back porch, his long stride eating up the distance to the barn. He notes Liam's bike propped up against the door as he backs out his Yukon and goes to town.

Sawyer meets Diane in the back corner of the Magnolia Café, a small private nook near the door to her shop. She has his coffee and a pastry waiting. Diane stands up when he comes in the front entrance, waving him over. He walks directly to her and takes her in his arms. The two kiss intimately.

"Mmmm, I have missed you and your kisses," Diane says as she steps back to sit on the cushy chair, "I got you a muffin."

"Thanks." He takes a bite, then shrugs off his light jacket. "I missed you, too." He takes her hand and kisses her fingers lightly. She smiles, gazing into his eyes.

"I wanted to talk to you yesterday. I want you to know I swung by your shop first, but there were too many people. I want points for that."

"I didn't know we were keeping score." She sips her tea. "But I will adjust the scorecard accordingly." She tilts her head. "I'm sorry I wasn't available. Do you want to talk about it now?"

"I do." He looks around. The back room is nearly empty. "I went to see my mother yesterday." Diane spends the next 15 minutes quietly listening as Sawyer recounts the conversation he had with his mother.

By the end, Diane has forgotten her tea and has her hands clasped together, absorbing the facts of the story. Sawyer looks at Diane for her opinion. "So, what is your first instinct? Do I hunt Scarlet down and make her come to The Residence and stay there where I can watch her, or do I let it go for now?"

Diane mulls it over as she watches Sawyer devour the rest of his muffin, sitting back to sip on his coffee. She is still silent when Sawyer prompts her, "Thoughts? I can see you have them."

Diane replies, "I do. And I don't think you are going to like them, but you did ask." She looks over at him, her lower lip curling up to the side in a half smile. "Scarlet strikes me as an intelligent woman. My guess is she knows more than you think she does about the entire situation. And, like it or not, may even be a participant."

Sawyer's ire rises, and Diane holds up her hand. "I know, I know, she's your sister. It doesn't mean she's perfect. You have no idea what has happened in her home or her marriage for the last 35 years. I imagine she has had to turn a blind eye to a lot of things, or she couldn't have survived." Diane continues, "I don't fault her one bit. I probably would have done the same. She would want to protect herself and her children."

"So, you think she knows? I hadn't thought about it from that angle."

"No, you wouldn't. I love that about you; you are a fierce protector of those you love. But it also blinds you to their potential faults and failings." She stirs her tea. "I think you are best to let this go for a while. Scarlet is a survivor, and she's figured it out on her own so far. Plus, if she is in danger, we have no idea by whom. Play your hand, and it may place her at more risk."

"Yeah, that's what I figured out for myself last night." He glances at his watch, it's almost time to meet Grady at the Gazette. "Listen, I have to run to another meeting. When can I see you again? Uncle Gabe misses Mandy."

Diane giggles. "The feeling is mutual. All I have heard since I got back is how wonderful Mr. Gabe is. How about we come to Tea Olive this weekend? The shop is closed on Sunday."

"It will have to be after church. I haven't been yet, and I need to go." He has an idea. "Join me. I'll come get y'all for services. You can be my shield from all the well-meaning people of this town."

"Church? We can go, but you need to know I am not a fan of organized religion."

"That's okay, me neither. But family obligation and all that. And it pleases Uncle Gabe to see me there. I know it would thrill him to have you join us."

"All right. I'm game." She waves him out the door. "Go on, don't be late. Text me the details." He kisses her on the forehead and scoots out the back door. His long strides get him to the Gazette right at the appointed time. Mary is sitting at the front desk. Today's outfit is chartreuse. She is waiting for him.

"Sawyer, lock that door behind you, please. I'm joining you, and I don't want any unexpected visitors," says Mary.

"Sure." He looks down at the gray-haired, wiry woman who today reminds him of a tree frog. "You know what we're doing?"

"No, Gray asked me for access to the conference room. He had a box of stuff with him. He asked me to print off some pictures and logos and bring them back when you got here. Just following instructions."

Sawyer and Mary enter the room to see Jerry sitting perched on the edge of the conference table and Grady at the front, near the corkboard mounted on the wall. Old storylines are thumbtacked to the board. It was obviously used during the golden days of investigative reporting.

"Oh, good Mary. Thank you for printing off the photos." Grady motions toward Jerry. "Everybody, take a seat, please."

"You want me to stay?" Mary asks.

"I do. I need your help Mary, and I know you are good at research. There could be some risk involved, though, so if you're not interested, I understand." Mary simply pulls out a chair and takes a seat.

Grady begins, "Okay, here is what we know so far. I thought it might be helpful if I diagrammed it out. Maybe if we look at it from a new angle, we will see something we missed before." Grady walks over to the corkboard and puts up three-by-five cards with the names Green Acres, Lucky Lady, Twin Oaks, MRM, Tea Olive, Overpass Development Partners, and Robert Huger. He then takes the logos and pictures Mary printed off and puts the appropriate picture next to the corresponding heading. He steps back.

Sawyer sits with his arms folded, staring at the board. All he sees is a jumble of odds and ends. "Now, what?" he asks.

Jerry gets up and starts rearranging the pieces of paper. "Now, we look for the connections." He looks over his shoulder, "Mary, do you have any yarn or string?"

"I have a ball of twine. Would that work?" she responds.

Jerry nods absently as he removes thumbtacks. "Do you have any scissors?" Grady hands him a pair. He takes the logos and cuts them down to size, attaching them to the pictures or leaving them to stand alone. Finally, he has them where he wants them. Mary hands him the twine. Using the thumbtacks, Jerry strings up the twine from one section to the next. "Get me a few blank three-by-fives and the markers. I have an idea."

He adds 1985, Dead Doe, Bubba Westerman, Dr. Butler, Dr. Goldbug, and Virginia Phillips. He attaches them to the board. Once he is done, he takes a step back.

Sawyer and Grady stare at the board. Jerry had placed Tea Olive at the center, and all the connections, as depicted by the twine, lead back to Tea Olive.

"I keep coming back to this." Jerry looks at Sawyer. "With everything we have talked about, what is the one common denominator? Tea Olive Plantation. Every road leads right back there. Why? Is it the property or the people? Or both?" He turns back to the board. "The only deviance from Tea Olive is Twin Oaks."

Mary chimes in, "Well, if I remember my history right, Twin Oaks used to be owned by the Coopers. It was a part of the original estate. The property was given as a gift to one of the daughters when she married."

"Really?" Jerry looks to Sawyer for confirmation.

"She's right. Nathaniel Cooper had numerous sons but only one daughter. He doted on her, and when she married, he wanted to keep her close. So, in essence, the Hugers are very distant cousins of the Coopers."

Jerry puts the Twin Oaks card side by side with the Tea Olive card, and the wheel is complete.

Grady asks, "So, what does all this mean? I still don't see the connection. I agree all of it seems to revolve around Tea Olive, but why?"

"I think that *is* the question. Once we can figure out why, we can figure out the who," says Jerry, "Do you have any ideas who would want to destroy your family?"

Sawyer quietly stares at the board. Jerry is right. All roads lead to Tea Olive, and Tea Olive is the Cooper family. "Who would want to destroy my family? And who could be smart enough to do it?"

"Not only smart but willing to play the long game. If all of what the sheriff here is saying is accurate, then this has been going on for at least four decades." Mary takes her glasses and puts the earpiece to her mouth, what Sawyer refers to as her thinking pose. "Or maybe not one person, maybe a familial grudge. You know, something that passes from generation to generation. A Hatfield and McCoy type of hate."

"Well, there is only one family that comes to mind who has that kind of anger toward our family that I am aware of, but to this level, I just don't see it," says Sawyer.

"You thinkin' of the Monroes?" asks Grady. "It's the first one that came to my mind."

"But how do they connect to the Hugers?" asks Sawyer. "I think we all agree Robert Huger was involved. Maybe he and Silas were working together? It's a lot of speculation." Sawyer looks at Mary. "And no offense to Mary, but it could just as likely be one person or not even a family, but a company. Somebody who wants the land."

Jerry nods. "Now, that could make sense. The land your property sits on is valuable, especially if you were able to buy up the plantations along the river and make them into commercial properties or even neighborhoods. The real estate alone has to be worth several million."

Grady gives a harsh laugh. "You're not even close. Daddy was offered a pretty penny for Cotton Mill when Twin Oaks was sold. I'm sure Mr. Gabe was approached around the same time." Grady grins. "Daddy pulled out the shotgun and told the man that if he or any of his other carpetbagger friends came by wanting to buy his property, they would be met with buckshot in their nether regions." Grady waves his hand toward Sawyer. "I'm sure Mr. Gabe's response was along the same lines. We don't sell the land, ever. That's why the entire sell of Twin Oaks was met with such ferocity and bewilderment."

"Okay, so a land grab is a possibility. If they could get Tea Olive to topple, would the others fall?" Jerry asks.

Sawyer answers, "It would be much harder for them to stay afloat. The plantation owners have unwritten rules regarding the river and its use. Without the river, the plantations die. Uncontrolled development would make that much harder to ensure."

Grady gets up from his perch on the table. "I want to talk to my dad about this. Maybe he can shed some light on the whole thing." He looks at Sawyer. "But I won't if you don't want me to."

Jerry chimes in, "I'm gonna ask you to wait on that for now. Both of you. I want to pass this by the feds. The two guys who helped us with Laura Lynne, they can be trusted. This has an organized crime bent to it, and they're involved with the drug piece already."

"If y'all don't mind, I would like to do some digging myself. I'm pretty good with research, and no one would suspect me. I do historical research for my boyfriend and Laura Lynne all the time," says Mary, "And there is something that is ringing a bell. I just can't put my finger on it. I have heard the term 'Lucky Lady' before somewhere. I don't know."

"So other than Mary doing research, we do nothing? Just wait for the next shoe to drop?" Sawyer asks.

"I hate this part, but Jerry's right, Sawyer. We wait until we have a clear path to move forward or something else breaks. In the meantime, it's business as usual," Grady agrees. Grady takes out his phone. "I want to get a picture of this before we break it down. And, then, Mary, do you mind shredding it?"

"Is it wise to take a picture? Laura Lynne would never do it. She kept paper copies of everything and then took them to the vault at Tea Olive. She told me it was under triple lock." Mary holds a piece of paper she was working on to Grady. "Here, I sketched the diagram."

He looks at the paper and shows it to Jerry. Jerry smiles and looks at Mary. "Do you want a job? We could use someone with your talents on the police force."

She smiles. "I already have one, and I need to get back to it. Y'all see yourselves out when you're done."

"Who is her boyfriend?" Jerry asks.

"Matt Waring, he used to be a reporter here. Now, he writes books on Venice," answers Grady.

"Lucky man," says Jerry.

Grady takes all the papers down off the corkboard and slides them into a manila folder. He hands them to Sawyer. "Go straight home and lock it up. I have a weird feeling about all this."

"Will do." Sawyer takes the papers from Grady.

Jerry clears his throat. "Listen, Sawyer, this is not to be shared, but I want you to know we brought in Freddie, Froggie, and Greg."

Sawyer stops in midstride and turns toward the two men. "You have them in custody?"

Grady nods. "We found them in one of the deer stands on the Laurel property." Grady smiles. "I think they were actually glad to be taken in. Looked like they had been living on bologna and cheese sandwiches and whiskey and not much else."

Jerry continues, "We're keeping this on the down-low. We don't want to tip anyone off. We have eyes on the deer stand and some undercover cops as decoys."

"A sting operation?" Sawyer asks.

Jerry cracks his first smile. "You watch too much TV. No, not a sting operation. We're simply trying to lure in the big fish. Freddie and his boys are lackeys."

Grady continues, "But not stupid. They aren't talking much, either. They did have a thing or two to say about you, though, Sawyer. None of them are too fond of you."

Sawyer smiles. "Well, this is good news. I can't believe Bubba's tip actually panned out." He holds out his hand to Jerry, saying, "I appreciate you keeping me informed. It won't go past me, but there is a great deal of relief knowing at least some of them have been apprehended."

Jerry shakes his hand. "You gave us the tip; figured you deserved the trust."

As the three men walk out the door, Grady slaps Sawyer on the back. "By the way, congratulations on your retirement. I'm looking forward to the party. I got the invitation just this morning, and Prissa and I have already RSVP'd. Always fun to go to a black-tie event at the club."

"Got mine, too. Thank you for the invitation. The wife and I will be there," Jerry says.

Sawyer sighs, knowing before he opens his mouth that Laura Lynne has been busy behind the scenes. "Dare I ask what y'all are talking about?"

"You mean you don't know about your own party?" Jerry asks.

"Laura Lynne told me she was planning to throw one at the club, but I haven't even seen a date, yet. When is the thing?"

Grady laughs. "You gotta love our sisters! I will send you the save the date, though I bet if you checked your phone, you would see it yourself."

"I just checked it yesterday, and there was nothing from Laura Lynne on it, I swear!" says Sawyer.

"A lot can happen in 24 hours. The party is two weeks from Thursday." Grady grins cheekily. "I hope you can make it."

Sawyer rolls his eyes as he takes his leave—like he had any choice.

38

────────────────────

Chapter Thirty-Eight

It is amazing how quickly two weeks can go by when you are running a farm. The last fourteen days were spent in a whirlwind of activity. Pearl took Sawyer's advice and hired two new housemaids, though that's not what Sawyer is supposed to call them. He is supposed to call them Domestic Cleaning Specialists. Seriously. Regardless, they have been cleaning all the closed rooms in the house, deep cleaning bathrooms, and washing windows. Gates has been painting every wall, freshening up the unused spaces. Victoria has been in her element, cooking for all the farmhands and now the new staff. She requested some help in the kitchen, and Pearl agreed. Laura Lynne and Ashley have been making arrangements for the party, firing questions to Sawyer at all hours of the day and night, until finally, he metaphorically threw up his hands and told them to do whatever they thought was best.

And everyone is going to begin arriving today. Laura Lynne and Gray would be there, as well as her children and their spouses. Avery would be coming, though he would be solo. Scarlet had even RSVP'd for two. It would be the first time since 1985 that all four of the siblings would be together at one time.

And it had Sawyer's anxiety at an all-time high. How he could execute complex military missions with less stress than going to his own retirement is still an area of bewilderment to him. Sawyer shakes his head as he rounds the corner to the dock at the end of his morning

355

run. To his surprise, standing on the dock are John, Gabe, and Malcolm.

"There you are, Sawyer. Pearl kicked us out of the house for the day. We're not allowed back in until this afternoon, so I decided we could all use a day out on the boat. Malcolm has the fishing poles, John carried the cooler of food from Victoria's kitchen, and I have the keys."

Sawyer hesitates and then says, "What the hell?" before he follows the men up on the boat. Since Freddie and his gang are behind bars, Sawyer has felt a small bit of peace. He refuses to be complacent, even though there have been no problems in weeks. "Just one question: who is watching the farm?"

John answers, "I left Lance in charge. But I would feel better if we didn't stray too far." He looks at Malcolm. "Any good fishing spots close by?"

"Absolutely." Malcolm looks at Gabe, who is manning the wheel. "Take us to the rope swing, Mr. Gabe."

"Excellent choice." Gabe waits for John to untie the boat from the dock before motoring out to the middle of the river and downstream.

Sawyer leans close to John, whispering, "Any updates?"

John gives a negative shake of his head. "Nothing, Colonel. Just going to the Whistle Stop B and B each morning and coming back home each night. No stops in between."

"Any nighttime visitors?" asks Sawyer.

"Negative. It's been quiet."

"She RSVP'd to the party, and added a plus one. I hope that means Buck will be there. I want to lay my eyes on him," Sawyer says before leaning forward to pull out the cooler. "I'm starving, anybody else want a snack?"

Sawyer received a chorus of yeses before he opens the cooler to find it fully packed with a plethora of culinary delights. Each of them is labeled. He even finds serving utensils. "I swear, Malcolm, that niece of yours needs to start her own catering service. Look at this: deviled eggs, sweet tea-drenched tenderloin, smack your lips pimento cheese." He looks up. "We may never go back."

Sawyer sees the rope swing hanging from the tree. It is frayed now, and the tire is no longer attached. Gabe trolls the boat around, and Malcolm throws the anchor out. Gabe shuts down the motor and reaches for a fishing pole. "You boys eat while I drown a worm. I can't remember the last time I went fishing. Should be a fine day for it."

The rest of the morning and into the afternoon, the men fish, eat, and relax. Sawyer and Malcolm even take a swim, though the water is still a bit chilly. The cool water revives Sawyer's skin, and the tangy smell makes him nostalgic. So many days growing up were spent just like this. The only difference was that back in those days, his dad manned the wheel, and his companions were Buck and Charlie. Sawyer enjoys the time with his new friends, realizing the importance of taking time off and playing with the people you work with. In the military, it was pick-up games of football. It built teamwork.

As Sawyer pulls into the dock, his uncle finally relinquishes the wheel, and waiting to greet them are Gray, Beau, and Chris. Beau and Chris, Laura Lynne's son and son-in-law, tie *Miss Melanie* off as the men unload from the boat. Handshakes and introductions are made, and then Sawyer hands Gray the keys and asks, "You want to take her for a spin?"

Gray grins before snatching them out of his hand, "I do. Come on, boys. Let's do a run." He climbs on board, watching as the men he is grateful to call his sons untie as Gray starts her up. He calls down the dock, "Let the women know we will be back in an hour. Promise."

Sawyer waves as the crew and boat depart, trolling upriver instead of down. He looks toward his uncle, "Guess everyone is arriving. Let the festivities begin."

The men are greeted by a gaggle of women. The cutest, by far, is the overly pregnant Savannah. She is glowing and rubbing her extended abdomen while she talks excitedly about the trip. Savannah introduces Claire, Beau's wife, to everyone before wrinkling her nose. "Don't let us keep you."

Sawyer laughs. "Smell like dead fish, don't we?" He and Gabe walk to the back door, the cooler between them. John and Malcolm say their goodbyes, taking off to their vehicles. The men carry the cooler into the mudroom and call for Victoria. She peeks her head in, and the men open the cooler to show her their catch of the day. She is delighted.

"Y'all did good. Just leave them right there. I will ice them until I can get to them with my knife," Victoria says.

"You want me to help fillet them? I don't mind." Sawyer offers.

The look Victoria gave him told him she was not happy with the suggestion. "Sawyer, do I offer to help you shoot a gun? You stick to what you do best and I will do the same." She wrinkles her nose, "Go on now, both of you. You stink. Momma will have a fit if she thinks you made the house smell like anything other than lemons. She has been in a frenzy all day." She looks at Sawyer and gives him a broad wink, "Besides there is something special for you in the bedroom."

Sawyer looks at her questioningly, and she just shoos him out of the way. Sawyer and Gabe head up the stairs. Both have moved back to their original quarters. Sawyer is much more comfortable in his new grayish-blue room with his grandfather's furniture. He actually enjoys relaxing in there in front of the fire, or occasionally reading a book Diane has given him.

He hasn't seen too much of her lately, though the two talk on the phone almost nightly. Other than taking her to church on Sunday, he has not been to town, and she has not been back to the farm. However, she is his date for the party tomorrow night. As if he conjured her up from a dream, Diane is standing in front of the closet of his room with her hands on her hips when he opens the door.

She smiles as he comes over to her and gives her a big kiss. "What are you doing here? Victoria told me I had somethin' special up here. I didn't think it would be you."

She wraps her arms around his shoulders, swaying into him. He is pleased the fish smell is not keeping her out of his arms. "It was a surprise. I closed the store for tomorrow. And since Mandy is on a field trip with her class, Laura Lynne invited me to stay here." She kisses him soundly. "I hope you don't mind."

"No, I don't mind," he murmurs as he nuzzles her ear. "What had you so mystified when I came in the room?"

She takes a step back. "My clothes. They are hanging in your closet. And I didn't put them there."

Sawyer smiles at her look of bewilderment. "It's a Tea Olive thing. Pearl usually unpacks everyone's things and puts them away. She and Queenie have always done it. She will pack for you too. I've told her not to do it, but she likes to get everything organized." Diane's cheeks turn pink. "What, why are you embarrassed?"

Her shoulders start to shake, and Sawyer realizes she is silently laughing. "What's so funny?"

"Oh God, Sawyer." She snorts. "I brought something special to wear tomorrow night." He looks at her blankly. "For *after* the party." She wipes her eyes. "I can only imagine what went through her mind when she saw my lingerie."

Sawyer wraps his arms around her from behind. "What's going to go through my mind?"

"Would you cut it out? Listen, this is all your fault. You have to tell me stuff like this. She didn't unpack my stuff last time I was here. How was I supposed to know?

Sawyer plants a kiss on top of her head before letting her go. "Don't blame me. I had no idea you were going to be here. Blame Laura Lynne. She's the one you cooked this up with." He walks into the bathroom and turns on the shower. He strips and climbs in, Diane trailing behind him. "You joining me?"

"Yep, once the water heats up." She takes off her outfit. "So she didn't empty it last time because we were leaving the next day, right?"

He puts his finger to his nose, telling her without words she had "hit it on the nose." She gets in behind him, running her hands over his back. "Oh, well. Too late now. I'm not sure how I am going to face her, though."

Sawyer steps aside, letting the water flow over Diane. "Don't worry about it. I can only imagine what she has seen over the years. She is the soul of discretion." Then he takes her mouth in his, and she promptly forgets all about the sexy underwear hiding somewhere in one of Sawyer's drawers.

Refreshed and very clean, the couple emerges from the bedroom to join the family downstairs. As they hit the landing of the staircase, Sawyer hears Laura Lynne open the door and let out a little gasp and squeal. She turns around and shouts up the staircase, "Sawyer, get down here! You have a guest."

Sawyer smiles at Diane and says, "Let the festivities begin."

39

Chapter Thirty-Nine

He goes down the staircase. The two walk up behind Laura Lynne who has gone out on the front porch with Pearl close on her heels. Sawyer spots two men, good-looking and well-dressed standing on the porch. Laura Lynne is smiling and talking. The two men are captivated.

Then, Laura Lynne turns her smile at Sawyer. "Sawyer, I have a few surprises for the weekend. One of them just showed up." She walks over to Sawyer and takes his arm, steering him in front of the men. Sawyer turns dumbstruck. He stares at one of the men in recognition. He thinks, "No, it can't be."

"Sawyer, I think you remember Clayton Newhouse." Laura Lynne takes a step back and gently shoves her brother forward. "Clayton, my brother, who has completely lost his manners. You knew him as Tripp back in the day, but we call him Sawyer now that Daddy passed."

Clayton's eyes are bright with tears, but his smile is wide. He holds out his hand and Sawyer grasps it before coming in for a hug. The two men laugh and slap each other on the back. Finally, Sawyer speaks, "Clay, I had no idea. What in the world.."

Clayton smiles at Sawyer and nods his head over at Laura Lynne, "That baby sister of yours is hard to turn down. I got your email a few weeks ago and to be honest, just needed to think on it. Then, I receive a call from this lovely lady inviting me to your retirement party." He glances over his shoulder at the man standing a foot or so away. "My husband and I agreed it was high time for him to see my home state." He steps back from Sawyer and walks next to the well-heeled man watching the exchange. "Sawyer, meet my husband, Gordon Turner."

Sawyer holds out his hand and Gordon grasps it, no weak handshake from him. "It's nice to meet you, Gordon. I don't have to tell you what an amazing man your husband is. He was my best friend senior year." He steps back with one foot and pulls Diane into the mix. "I'd like you to meet my girlfriend, Diane Hopkins."

Gordon grabs both her hands and smiles. He looks over at Clayton, and they grin at each other. Gordan says, "Yes, we heard all about the romance between the town son and the bookstore owner. She is as lovely as Mrs. Gaillard told us."

Diane rolls her eyes. "Oh, Lord. Let me guess, coffee at Magnolia Café."

Clayton chuckles. "Well, Gordon and I decided it would be best to get the grapevine buzzing, so before we came here, we stopped for coffee. Didn't realize the grapevine is nearly overloaded with activity. The town is electric with Beauregard news."

Laura Lynne steps in. "Why don't y'all come in? Meet the rest of the family, well, at least some of them. Everyone is out on the back porch." She looks at Pearl. "What room are the gentlemen staying in?"

Clay shakes his head. "No, no. We have reservations at the hotel."

Laura Lynne gives him her best haughty Southern Lady look. "Well, just cancel it. You and Gordon are guests of Tea Olive and our family. Pearl?"

"I have them in The Beauregard Suite."

"Pearl? Pearl Jackson?" Clay walks over to Pearl and smiles as he swoops her up in a big hug and lands a kiss on her cheek, "Girl, you haven't changed a bit." Clay turns toward Gordon with Pearl tucked under his arm, "Gordon, this is the Pearl I told you all about."

Gordon walks over and, with a gentle smile, takes her hand and brings it to his lips. "Thank you for all you did for my husband. He talks highly of you."

Pearl smiles, her eyes bright. She is not used to being fawned over, so she does what she always does. "Now, it's nice to meet you, but there is work to be done. Clay, give me the keys to the car." She holds out her hand, and he stares at it. "Come on. I don't have time for this foolishness. You're staying here in the Beauregard room, just like Laura Lynne told you. No sense arguing. See?" She points to Laura Lynne, who is sending a quick text. "She already texted Ashley to cancel your reservations."

Laura Lynne looks up and smiles. "I certainly have. I'm not going to hide it. You are our guests. Sawyer?"

Sawyer has Diane tucked up under his arm, watching with interest the exchange between Pearl and Clay. Realizing his agreement is needed, he answers, "Absolutely. The house has plenty of room, and we would love for you to stay." He looks at Clay. "I would love for y'all to stay."

Gordon steps in over the slightly awkward moment, "Then, we accept with gratitude. I was not looking forward to staying at the motel. This cute little town could use a nice bed and breakfast."

Clay gives Pearl one last hug before she takes the ever-present dishtowel off her shoulder and swats Clay with it. "Git on with your own self now! Food a-plenty on the back porch."

Everyone laughs and talks at once as the group moves through the house. Gordon, an architect and landscape artist, is delighted by The Residence and talks animatedly about the design and structure as they make their way to the back porch. Laura Lynne comes up beside Sawyer and squeezes his arm. She whispers, "You aren't mad, are you?"

"No, not at all. But how did you know?"

"Uncle Gabe. He told me to invite him." She smiles at Sawyer. "I'm so glad I did."

"Me, too. Are there any more surprises I should know about?" Sawyer asks.

"Maybe one or two, but we're going to let them be surprises." She gently pats his arm. "Trust me."

The back porch is alive with activity. Gabe is keeping everyone entertained with stories of the plantation and the Cooper family ancestors. Everyone stops talking when Sawyer and Laura Lynne appear with the additional guests. Introductions are made all around, and John mans the bar and begins doling out cocktails. Victoria and the new servers hired for the weekend are passing out hors d'oeuvres. The conversation is lively and before too long, Avery arrives.

Sawyer and Laura Lynne descend on their baby brother, enveloping him in a hug. The moment is bittersweet; the three have not been together since the summer of 1985, but Scarlet is missing from the party. Laura Lynne wipes her eyes with her husband's arm around her, supporting her as she experiences the long bottled-up emotions. Gray reaches around her and holds out his hand. "You must be Avery. Glad you made it. I'm Gray."

Avery smiles and shakes his hand. "Heard a lot about you." His eyes widen. "And who is this? You are a Beauregard through and through."

Beau reaches out his hand. "So I've been told. I'm Beau, and this is my wife, Claire. Nice to meet you, Uncle Avery."

The introductions continue and the conversation and drinks flow. Pearl announces dinner is served and the group proceeds into the formal dining room. The table has all its extensions in and seats 24 guests. The tablescape is elaborate, and he learned Savannah had her hand in its preparations. Gabe goes to his seat at the head of the table. Sawyer goes to the other end. All guests have assigned seating. The men help the women to their chairs, and Gabe gives the blessing. As the food is served, there are toasts and stories, everyone obviously enjoying the comraderie.

As the main course is served, brisket with collards, pecan-encrusted sweet potatoes, and cornbread, Clay looks at Pearl and asks, "Who is the genius in the kitchen? I feel like I am back in Queenie's kitchen."

Pearl smiles and says, "Well, you're close. My daughter, Victoria. She took all of Momma's recipes and added her own spin to them."

"Your daughter? Well, be sure and let her know how fabulous the meal has been. Absolutely divine." Pearl nods her head in acknowledgment.

The rest of the evening meal is consumed, and Laura Lynne's children are anxious to go out on the boat. "I'm fine with y'all going, but you have to have somebody with you who understands the river. It's dangerous," says Laura Lynne.

Sawyer chimes in, "Your mother's right. The river is not a toy, nor is *Miss Melanie*. Give me a minute…"

In a hushed voice, Avery asks, "You got daddy's boat running?" He has a stunned look on his face.

Sawyer says, "Well, Gray did. You want to go give her a run? You spent more time on her than the rest of us did combined."

Avery looks to Laura Lynne with a huge grin. "You mind if I captain your children around? Didn't have a drop to drink. Wouldn't mind getting on her again."

Laura Lynne smiles and nods. "Of course! You have my absolute trust."

"Come on, kids. Let's see what she can do," Avery says, getting up from the table.

"Got room for one more? I wouldn't mind joining you." Gordon asks.

"The more the merrier," says Savannah.

Gordon walks over to Savannah as the group heads to the dock, he whispers to her, "They do know you are full grown adults, right?"

Savannah laughs. "It's a Southern thing. No matter how old you get, your parents have to give approval. If my grandmother Melanie was here, it would be the same for my momma. It's a respect thing."

"Weird," Gordon says.

Sawyer, Laura Lynne, Gray, Clay, Diane, and Gabe are the only ones left on the back porch. "Come on Gray, we need to help Pearl," says Laura Lynne, "Not that she needs help, but I want to thank her and Victoria. They have done a ton of work to make this happen."

"Then let's go. Maybe I can snatch another one of those peach pie things."

Sawyer nudges Diane. "Laura Lynne, Diane is going to join you. I'd like to speak to Clay and Uncle Gabe for a moment."

Diane gives him a quick kiss and starts chatting with Laura Lynne and Gray as they make their way back to the kitchen.

Sawyer asks, "How about we walk a bit? Maybe the front gardens?"

"Great choice. Malcolm helped me with the lights. I'd like to check on them now that it is getting dark," says Gabe.

The three men walk around the side of the house, along the pathway toward the front gardens. Sawyer looks at Clay. "That spring of our senior year. It's been eating at Uncle Gabe and me. Can you tell us what happened?"

"Truthfully, it was the worst night of my life. Pearl probably saved it. I met her on the way back from the cabin early that next morning. Thought maybe I would just walk into the river and never walk out." He smiles softly. "She convinced me otherwise." He clears his throat. "And I am really glad she did. I went to MIT, and that is where I met Gordon. We've been together ever since. We moved to California and then Oregon; got married as soon as it was legal. I have had a great life."

Sawyer takes a deep breath. "I'm really glad to hear it. I was worried I had somehow ruined it. Me or my daddy."

"Naw, what happened at the school? That was all Buck's daddy."

Sawyer stops walking. "Wait. Robert Huger?"

"Hell, yeah. Mean son of a bitch." He looks at Gabe. "Sorry, sir, but it's the best way to describe him. I found out later he was blackmailing my father. When my mother found out, she put a stop to it and well, the result was what happened at the awards' assembly."

"How did he know?" Sawyer asks.

"Ever heard of a strip joint called the Lucky Lady? A place in Biloxi?" Clay asks.

"Only recently. It's Buck's current hangout."

Clay snorts. "So, he still frequents his pop's place." He slows his pace, reminiscing, "I was a naïve fool." He looks at Gabe. "I was feeling boxed in here. I just needed to be myself for a while, you know? Anyway, I went to Biloxi with my dad, and while he was at his meetings, I trolled the strip. I found a gay bar and went in. I had a lovely time. It felt good to be with my own tribe, ya know?"

He walks over to one of the rose bushes and fingers the petals. "Thought nothing more of it. Eventually, after the falling out in Venice, my dad told me he was being blackmailed by Robert, who had video footage of me in Biloxi. At the bar."

"How does the Lucky Lady play into it?" Sawyer asks.

"My dad did some digging and discovered Robert was at least involved, if not an owner of multiple establishments in Biloxi. The Lucky Lady is the crown jewel. The video surveillance equipment was all housed there. He had quite the scheme. Wouldn't be surprised if Buck was carrying on the family business." He continues, "Once mom and I knew what was happening, I was firm we were not going to be blackmailed. Let the chips fall where they may." He grins as he looks at Sawyer. "But my dad got the last laugh."

Gabe has his hands in his overall pockets, leaning back on his heels. He asks, "What did he do?"

"My father had an automatic shut-off in the computer program designed for the farm equipment. It was created for people who didn't pay their bills or if the equipment was stolen. My father could remotely turn off the capabilities, rendering the equipment useless." He smiles larger. "On our way out of town, Dad shut down all of Twin Oaks equipment."

"Wait! I remember this! Caused quite a stir. Figured there must have been some computer virus or something" Gabe looks at Clay, "Pretty smart."

"It's not like it caused any major disruptions, but my father was determined that SOB was not going to benefit from him. I like to believe Robert Huger saw it as a parting shot from the Newhouse family. Anyway, that's what happened." Clay looks at Sawyer. "I accused you and your father that night of outing me. I'm sorry."

"No need for that, to be honest I'm not certain my dad didn't have a part in how this all played out. But I appreciate it." Sawyer says. "I've been worried we messed up your life."

Clay replies, "You didn't. Or, if you did, it needed to happen. I look back at my time in Venice with gratitude. It forced me to face who I was and deal with it. When I went to MIT, I didn't hide. I didn't flaunt it, mind you, but I didn't fake anything either. Venice gave me freedom."

Gabe pulls out his handkerchief and blows his nose, "I'm going to walk down to the gate, just need to be alone for a bit. Okay?"

Sawyer nods. "Of course. Take all the time you need."

He begins to walk away, and Clay calls to his back, "Mr. Gabe, the gardens are beautiful. I love the lights." Gabe waves over his shoulder. Clay looks at Sawyer with concern, "Is he going to be all right?"

Sawyer stares after him. "I think so. The idea our family had somehow hurt you messed him up. He has a gentle soul. He takes things to heart." Sawyer decides it's time to change the subject, "It's really good to see you, man. I still can't believe you're here." Sawyer starts to walk toward the house, "Come on. Let's go meet *Miss Melanie.* Avery should be bringing her back soon."

"You know," Clay says, "I've thought about you often over the years. Followed your career, *Colonel.* Wondered how you were. I was pretty messed up when I left the cabin that night. Thought maybe the same had happened to you."

Sawyer is silent for a moment as he walks next to his old friend. "It did. Messed me up quite a bit. I didn't know who I was or what I was. Took me years to work it out for myself. That night, at least for me, was just love. Love for my best friend. A friend I lost abruptly. I just felt bewildered, ya know?"

Clay looks over at him and then off to the setting sun. "For me too."

"But you're happy now? You have a good life with Gordon?"

Clay smiles widely. "I am very happy. It all worked out the way it needed to for me. Gordon is my rock. We made a good life together. Hell, we even have a couple of kids. Grown now, but I have a family. All the stuff I didn't think possible as a gay man in 1980s Mississippi."

"You have kids? That's great! I know it made your parents happy."

"It did. Mom was over the moon." His face drops. "I lost them both a few years back. Dad had been sick for a bit. Mom stayed by his side as she always did until the very end. Two weeks later, she passed. I swear, Sawyer, it was from a broken heart. They had 63 years together."

"I loved your parents." Sawyer laughs and points. "Look, *Miss Melanie* is coming in." He slaps Clay on the shoulder, "Are we good, pal?"

"We're good. I missed you, buddy."

"Me, too. Let's not wait 40 years to see each other again, okay?" Sawyer says.

"Deal. Come on, I can see Gordon on the back looking a bit green. He is not one for boating."

"Why did he go then?"

"He knew we needed to talk. There are no secrets between Gordon and me. He knows our story. Shoot, he is the one that pushed me to come. In his words, 'It's time to put that Venice shit behind you.'" He smiles as he starts to jog. "He was right. As always."

Sawyer spots Diane and Laura Lynne on the dock, and he looks at Clay. "I'm pretty sure she's the one."

Clay glances where Sawyer is looking. "Then grab her with both hands, man. Nothing better than doing life with somebody else."

The two men slow their jog down as the boat idles up next to the dock. Laura Lynne helps to tie her off. Sawyer walks behind Diane and gives her a hug. She snuggles against his back. She turns her head and kisses his cheek. "Hey, you. All good?"

Sawyer nuzzles Diane's neck. "Better than good. Remind me later to thank Laura Lynne."

The rest of the evening is spent playing board games on the porch. Gabe dominates chess, though Clay makes him work for it. Gordon and Diane become fast friends in the kitchen, putting together snacks and drinks. The surprise winner at the Scrabble tournament is Savannah, beating out her mom for the coveted spot. By midnight, everyone is exhausted and ready to turn in. As Sawyer is locking up the house, he hears John's bird call. He walks out the back porch and heads to the azalea bushes. John appears.

"Hey, John. Everything okay?"

"Yeah, just didn't want to interrupt y'all's family time with business. I have Lance and the boys pulling double duty tonight and tomorrow. Just being extra cautious. Wouldn't want anything to ruin the celebration."

"I appreciate it, John. Any word on Scarlet?"

"She drove by the front gate a few times. I thought she might stop, but she ended up going back to her house. I followed her to make sure she got home safe."

"Hmmm. Laura Lynne and Avery texted her and told her we were all here and to stop by. She was the only one missing tonight." He drops his chin and shakes his head, scuffing the ground with his boot. "I wish she would have stopped." He looks up, "Oh, well. Maybe I can pin her down tomorrow. You comin'?"

"Plannin' too. Laura Lynne got my dress blues cleaned and sent back today." John shakes his head. "That woman is a marvel."

"She is. Thanks, John. See ya in the morning."

As Sawyer returns to the porch and walks into the house, he shuts the door. Clay clears his throat. Sawyer kicks himself for being startled.

Clay apologizes, "Sorry, man, didn't mean to startle you. Heard the bird call. Everything good?"

Looking at Clay, Sawyer decides to confide in his old friend. Clay had always proven to be trustworthy. Besides, he could use the reinforcements. "Interested in a cup of coffee and a really long story?"

"Let me just run upstairs and let Gordon know."

Sawyer walks over to the wall of the study and points to the intercom, "Which room are y'all in tonight? The Beauregard rooms?" Clay nods. Sawyer inserts some numbers, and Gordon's voice comes over the speaker. Laughing and shaking his head, Clay informs Gordon of the plans, and Sawyer goes to the kitchen to fix coffee. Clay follows.

"I forgot about the intercoms. I remember the first time I saw them. I think that is when it dawned on me that I didn't have any clue about people like you." He waves his hands around, encompassing the house. "Daddy did well. Hell, he was rich. Probably had more money than most of the plantation owners, but what we didn't have was this: culture, history, an intercom system."

"Yeah, it's hard to explain to anyone who doesn't grow up like I did. And why we protect it. They don't understand." He hands Clay a mug of coffee. "So, you heard about the body found here a couple of months ago?" Clay nods as he sips his drink. "Well, from what we can tell, it all dates back to that summer you got here. The summer Laura Lynne went to live with my aunt." Sawyer rehashes the events of the past eight weeks. Clay listens intently. When he is finished, Clay gets up from his perch on the stool and begins to pace the kitchen. Sawyer smiles. He remembers this from when they were kids. Clay prefers to be on the move when he is working out a problem.

He comes to a stop. "So, what is the one thing?"

"The one thing?" Sawyer asks.

"Yeah, what would motivate someone to carry on a vendetta for forty years? Not money, no I think the money is a side benefit. It has to be revenge. Who would hate you and your family so much they would spend their life working to destroy you? Who has that kind of hate for you?"

Sawyer leans across the kitchen island, putting his weight on his forearms. He rubs his eyes. "I haven't really thought 'hate,' but maybe it is. My family has not been without its share of bad deeds, but something like this…to go after my sisters, that is an entirely different level of malevolence." He rubs his eyes. "And, I have no idea."

"Follow the money. I still think you follow the money. And, if you want, Gordon and I can take a trip to Biloxi and visit The Lucky Lady. I still have a bone to pick with Buck Huger. Dickwad."

For the first time in two hours, Sawyer laughs. "Haven't heard that since you called him a dickwad during spring baseball practice. Coach made you run laps."

"Yeah, well, it didn't make him any less of a dickwad." Clay looks at the clock; it is 2 AM. "Come on, let's go to bed. Gordon is an early riser. He's probably gonna want to go for a run in the morning."

Sawyer turns off the kitchen lights, and the two men walk out the kitchen doors to the staircase. "Why don't y'all join me? I like to run the farm. It's about six miles. We can show Gordon the Ridge. Oh, and you won't believe what John did to the cabin. The man is a regular artist with a piece of wood."

They reach the landing, and Clay comes in for a hug. The two men hold on tight. "Thanks, man," says Clay. They part. "See ya in the morning."

Sawyer watches as Clay walks down the hall toward his room. He is exhausted. He quietly opens the bedroom door. Diane is snuggled in the bed, the light on and a book laying on her chest. She is sound asleep. Sawyer walks over and gently moves the book and removes the glasses from her hand. He pulls up the comforter and turns down the lamp. He kisses her head. She snuggles in to her pillow. He smiles and walks into the bathroom for his third shower of the day.

40

Chapter Forty

It's the day of Sawyer's retirement celebration, and the house wakes up early. The girls go to the country club to help with decorations and meal preparations, while the men stay at the farm. Avery, Chris, and Beau plan to take the four-wheelers out while Sawyer, Clay, and Gordon go for a run. Before they leave, Sawyer calls Avery into the front sitting room. He has the safe open.

"Hey, Sawyer, what's up?" asks Avery.

Sawyer walks out of the safe with a hunting rifle and shotgun. "You still remember how to use one of these?"

Avery walks over and takes the shotgun. He plays with it a minute. "Don't make me whoop your ass at the target range, asking me a question like that." He grins, "Why?"

"With everything happening on the farm these days, it makes sense to be prepared." He holds up his chest holster. "I even run with a gun." He hands him some shells for the shotgun. "Store it in the four-by-four; just keep it close by."

Avery takes the shotgun. "It's the same one I used as a kid." He looks at Sawyer. "I knew things were bad. Don't think I realized it was to this level."

Sawyer looks at him seriously and, for the first time, sees him as a man and not as his baby brother. "We have a lot to talk about." He lowers his voice, "But someone is after our family. We can't be too careful. Watch your back and trust no one except our kin, John and Malcolm. Otherwise, no one is above suspicion."

"Okay, I trust your judgment. But I want to know what's going on."

Sawyer nods as he shuts the vault, securing the multiple latches. "I will, promise. I haven't been keeping anything from you, or Laura Lynne for that matter, on purpose." Sawyer smiles as he hears Beau and Chris calling for Avery, "It's been a bit busy. How about tomorrow after church? That work?"

Avery loads the shotgun and puts on the safety; his adept maneuvers bely his earlier comments. Sawyer looks at him with a question in his eye. "Told you I still had it."

Avery looks at Sawyer and asks, "What about the girls? Are they good at the club? I can go there instead of riding around the farm."

"Gray went with Laura Lynne. Also, Grady and Charlie are there. Their wives are helping with the preparations."

Avery nods, then grins when he hears his name for the third time. "I have to say, Laura Lynne has done a fine job with her kids. That Beau is something else, and Savannah is Laura Lynne's mini-me. Like their spouses, too. Glad to spend some time with them." He lifts up his rifle. "And I will protect them with my life." He walks to the doorway and hollers, "I'm in the front room!"

Within moments, Chris and Beau are standing in the doorway. "This house is so big we couldn't find you." Chris says, "What's with the guns?"

"Just playing it safe. Come on. There is daylight burnin'." Avery looks at Sawyer. "We will be back by lunch. If you need us beforehand, ring the bell."

Sawyer holds up a finger and unstraps his walkie-talkie. "Take my radio. I'll grab another one before we head out. Keep it to the family channel."

"Got it." Avery runs herd on the boys as he hustles them out through the kitchen. "Always go out the mud room, never know what kind of good food you can snatch from the kitchen on the way out. Plus, Pearl won't tan your hide for traipsing mud through the house."

Sawyer smiles as he listens to the door swing open in the kitchen. Good sounds and smells emanate from the room. It feels great to have the house full again. He walks out to the main entrance and opens the front door, walking out on the front porch. His uncle is already out in the garden with his cutting shears.

"Awful early to be cutting flowers, isn't it?" Sawyer teases.

Gabe gently places the hydrangea he just cut into the water-filled bucket. "Laura Lynne needs them for tonight's shindig. Convinced her to wait until this morning to cut them." He goes to the next bloom. "Pearl is going to put together the arrangements." He looks over his shoulder. "You were up kind of late, everything okay?"

Sawyer comes up behind Gabe and places his hands on his shoulders. "Everything is fine. You okay?"

Gabe's shoulders sag. "Been worried about that boy since we talked. He's had a good life, right?"

"A really good life. He and Gordon made their own family. Raised two kids who are grown now."

"A family?" Gabe goes back to his blooms, shaking off Sawyer's hands. He says to himself, "Now, wouldn't that be something." He raises his voice, "Go on, now. I got work to do if I'm going to go to that party of yours tonight. Go on. I'm fine."

Sawyer smiles and returns to the front door. He opens it, ready to holler up the stairs to Gordon and Clay. Then, he sees them coming down the stairs. "I thought you said Gordon was an early riser? Doesn't he know farm work starts at 4:30 AM?" He laughs at the stink eye Gordon gives him. "Come on; let's go. We can snag a biscuit from Victoria on the way out."

The rest of the day passes in a blur. The women arrive back around lunchtime, full of excitement and energy. Around the same time, the guys come in from the fields. Victoria has a huge buffet on the back porch of charcuterie boards, sandwich meats, pickle platters, and gallons of sweet tea. After grabbing a bite, the girls hurry upstairs to start getting ready. The men play chess, watch TV, and doze until it was time for them to start getting ready. Gabe looks at Sawyer with a grin as the men go up the stairs, listening to the feminine voices as they laugh and gossip, the smell of hairspray and beauty products in the air.

"Reminds me of happier times here at The Residence. My mother would have the house full of guests and host the best parties. Listening to the ladies, they were always a fascination." Gabe shakes his head. "It will take me twenty minutes to get ready. What do they do for four hours?"

Beau chuckles, overhearing the conversation. "Whatever it is, I sure do appreciate it."

Chris, Avery, Gray, and Sawyer say in unison, "Me too!"

The men laugh as they head to their perspective rooms. Finally, at 6 PM, everyone is in the front room, ready to go. The women are dressed in floor-length gowns of lace in pale pastel colors, their throats and ears bedecked in jewelry from the family vault. Sawyer notices Diane is wearing his mother's emerald pendant against her throat, off-setting her simple lavender gown. "You look beautiful."

"And you look so handsome in your military attire. I always appreciated a man in uniform." Diane turns serious. "You ready for tonight? I warn you, Laura Lynne has pulled out all the stops."

"I guess we are about to find out," Sawyer replies.

The cars pull up. Laura Lynne has arranged drivers for the cars this evening. She looks at Sawyer. "You and Diane are in the Yukon. You will pull in last. Everybody else, just find a seat." The men escort the women off the porch and into the waiting cars. Sawyer waits as Diane climbs into the backseat of the Yukon. He gets in behind her. "Well, I can honestly say I haven't ridden back here yet."

The entourage arrives at the club fifteen minutes later. As they pull up, Sawyer sees the club entrance has luminaries leading in, the music is softly playing in the background, and it appears that most of the town has turned out for the occasion.

Diane waits for their driver to open the door before sliding out of the seat, followed by Sawyer. Sawyer is caught off-guard by the flashing lights and the microphones, surprised there is press here. He holds out his elbow for Diane to take, watching as the reporter is escorted away from him.

As he and Diane enter the ballroom, the music stops, and the conductor walks over to the microphone. "Ladies and gentlemen, it is my pleasure to announce the arrival of the guest of honor for this evening, Colonel Sawyer Avery Beauregard III."

The guests erupt in applause as Sawyer and Diane make their way through the crowd. Gray and Laura Lynne walk over and immediately give them drinks and begin escorting them around the room, to speak with all the guests. Sawyer is amazed to see Gates in his overalls with a suit jacket talking to Mary, who is dressed in the palest pink. "Is that Gates? Who all did you invite to this Laura Lynne?"

She looks over at him, "Everyone who is important to you." She stares over his shoulder, then grabs Gray's arm. She points her head in the direction of the door. "Sawyer, Scarlet just arrived. She has Cooper with her, I think." She releases Gray and takes his arm, "Come on. Where is Avery?"

"Right behind you, baby girl. Right behind you," Avery says as he walks up behind Laura Lynne. Scarlet sees them coming and loses her reserve. She hurries across the room and into their arms. The four siblings hold tight before stepping back and all talking at once. They create quite the scene: the four Beauregard siblings. Each is beautiful to look at, but seen all at once, they are staggering. The photographer is taking shot after shot. Beau walks over to Cooper, holding out his hand, "Hey, cousin. Nice to finally meet you."

Scarlet and Laura Lynne seem to remember their manners at the same time. Scarlet turns toward Cooper, waving him into the circle. Laura Lynne waves over her family, and Diane follows. Introductions are made, and then a family photo is taken. Sawyer assesses Scarlet; she is too thin, but she is stunning for a woman of her age. She has on a gold dress and their mother's pearls, every inch the lady. Her hair is coiffed, and her makeup is perfect. He walks over to her as she takes a drink from the procured tray. "Hey there, stranger. Missed you."

She says nothing and simply smiles. He continues, "I have a surprise for you." Her face drops, fear crowding her eyes. "Scarlet? It's a good surprise." He takes her arm and feels the tremors. "A blast from the past. You remember Clayton Newhouse from Moseley? You taught him how to dance?"

She immediately relaxes, the tension in her arms dissipating, "I sure do. How are you, Clay?" Scarlet reaches over for a brief hug and air kiss from Clay who is impressive in his tuxedo. Gordon is no less striking in his formal attire. Sawyer looks over at Laura Lynne and Avery. The two walk over.

Laura Lynne says, "Listen, Momma will be here shortly. Uncle Gabe drew the short stick tonight and is bringing her from Pineview. Y'all good with a family photo?" After receiving consent, she looks at the clock. "Fifteen minutes until dinner. We have the founder's table to ourselves tonight."

The three other siblings stare at her. Scarlet stutters, "What? How…?"

Laura Lynne just waves it off. "I got it all worked out. I just didn't want y'all surprised when we got up there." She looks at Sawyer. "There is someone here to see you, so once Momma gets here, and the picture is done, I promised him a few minutes." Then she smiles warmly and leans in. "I'm so glad we are here together. I love you. Okay, Beauregards, let's show them how it's done."

41

Chapter Forty-One

Melanie and Gabe arrive, and the two walk proudly across the ballroom floor to where the Beauregards are all standing. Glimpses of Melanie as a young woman are evident as she walks with a straight spine wearing a dark grey silk dress lined with lace. Avery walks over to Gabe and bows slightly, taking over as his mother's escort. Laura Lynne smiles at her mother. "Momma, you look beautiful. We are going to get pictures first, and then Avery will escort you to help welcome everyone."

Melanie, to her credit, simply nods her agreement. Pictures are taken, and Laura Lynne takes Sawyer by the arm. "Diane, I need him for just a few minutes. Promise to bring him right back." Laura Lynne takes Sawyer by the arm. "Come on, we're going to the billiards room." The walk is slow as Sawyer and Laura Lynne are waylaid repeatedly by well-wishers. Finally, they get to the door, and John is waiting. He looks staggeringly handsome in his dress blues. He salutes Sawyer. Sawyer does the same. And that should have been his clue.

John opens the door, and there, standing near the fire is General Bill Williamson and another young soldier that Sawyer does not immediately recognize. Sawyer jumps to attention, saluting his commander. Bill returns the salute and then smiles. Bill extends his hand. "Thanks for meeting me here. I brought someone with me I want you to meet."

Sawyer looks over at the young soldier, who is around 30 years old. He is already a first lieutenant. He salutes, "Sir."

Sawyer stares at him, and he sees his nameplate, "Valz." "Are you related to Brady Valz? Dodger?" asks Sawyer.

"Yes, sir. He was my father. My name is also Brady." Sawyer is stunned into silence. "I asked if I could come and meet you. I got your email, sir. But, what I want to tell you I wanted to do it in person." He clears his throat. "My father, he wrote to my mother nearly every day. His letters were filled with stories about his commander, "Tom." I asked my mother, and she told me I could read one of the last ones we received before he was killed in action." He fishes it out of his pocket. "I'd like to read it to you."

Sawyer is silent.

"Go on, son. Read it," General Williamson says.

Brady nods and reads, "My dearest heart, I hope this letter finds you and Junior well. I'm also doing well. The missions are getting more and more complex, but each day is one day closer to me coming home to you both. Tom trains us hard, and he has put me in for a promotion. He says I'm a natural-born leader; the other soldiers look up to me. Can you imagine that, Audrey? A street hustler from the hood who was called no-good from the day he was born, a natural-born leader.

He's a good man, Tom. Carries some dark garbage, though. I hear he's some gentrified type and lives on a plantation or something. I don't know and don't care. He's a man's man. Taught me a thing or two about life, about being a gentleman, about loyalty and dignity. All stuff I plan to teach Junior one day.

Audrey, if I don't make it back, you tell Junior how his daddy was somebody, a natural born leader. Don't ever think he is from a no-good. If a man like Tom thinks I'm somebody, then I am. I hope one day I can repay the favor.

Love, Dodger"

Brady folds up the letter and puts it back in his pocket. Sawyer's eyes are wet.

Brady continues, "Sir, I wanted you to know my daddy knew what he had to do to get me and Momma out of the slums. And he did it. I don't mean any disrespect, but you blaming yourself for his death takes away what my old man did for my mom and me. You understand?"

Sawyer holds out his hand, "I do. And I will do my best. Losing men like your father takes a toll, but I will absolutely remember what you said."

Brady shakes his hand. His grip is strong.

"First lieutenant, huh? I'm very impressed. How's your mother?" asks Sawyer.

"Good, sir. She lives with my wife and me, and our two..." he grins sheepishly, "almost three children."

"Congratulations." Sawyer glances at Laura Lynne as she comes over to his right. "Time to go?"

"I'm afraid so." She looks at Brady. "We would love it if you would stay for the party."

"No ma'am, thank you. I need to get back." He looks at Sawyer and asks, "So, my old man, was he as good a guy as my mother claims? I mean really."

Sawyer smiles and then turns serious. "He was. The finest man in my battalion. He would have been very proud to know how well you have done." Brady nods and then salutes Sawyer and the General before leaving with John.

Sawyer looks at Bill. "You didn't have to do that, ya know."

"Yes, son. I did," says Bill.

"Hate to break up the macho military thing, but dinner cannot get started until we sit down. General, I have you sitting with my very best friend. I assure you the dinner will not be boring." Sawyer listens with one ear as he recounts his conversation with Brady. Diane walks over and gives him a light peck on the cheek.

"Happy?" she asks.

"Extremely." He takes her arm. His step is light and his manner cheerful. "Come on, let's eat and dance. I'm ready to relax. And celebrate."

The rest of the evening is filled with congratulations, dances, toasts, and a meal that could have only been prepared under Victoria's watchful eye. The steaks cut like butter, and the garlic mashed potatoes melt in Sawyer's mouth. Sawyer laughs with everyone else as Bill regals the crowd with stories of "Tom" and his military adventures. The night is a tremendous success.

Sawyer watches as the last of the party-goers leave the premises. His family gathers together, with only a few people missing from the group. Cooper comes over to Sawyer. He looks like his father, but his eyes are kinder, more gentle, like Scarlet. He says, "Hey, Uncle Sawyer, do you mind if I bunk over at The Residence tonight? Avery is taking the boat out early for fishing and invited me to join. Momma said it was okay."

"Love to have you. Why don't you see if your momma wants to join us? Her room is ready and waiting," Sawyer says.

"Uncle Avery already asked her, and she said no. I wish she would. I don't like her staying out at the house by herself. She won't listen, though," complains Cooper.

"Your dad's not there?" asks Sawyer.

Cooper snorts. "He hasn't been there in years. Stays in Biloxi for the most part. I've tried to get her to sell and move up near me. I have a nice place. Hell, she could live with me. But she loves it here. Says she doesn't want to leave. And, well, there is always Bobby to think about."

"What does that..." Sawyer begins.

"Coop! Come on to the billiards room. You too, Sawyer, cigars and bourbon for the men. Laura Lynne tells me it's for a job well done." Gray rounds the men up.

"What about us women? We did a good job, too," Claire says.

"You absolutely did, which is why there is champagne and canapes in the bridge room. Though we are playing Scrabble, not bridge," Laura Lynne replies.

Scarlet walks toward the coat check to collect her wrap. "Scarlet, please join us?"

"I would love to, but I need to get home. I will see everyone at church in the morning," Scarlet replies.

Laura Lynne walks over to her and puts her hands on her arms. "Scarlet, please. We would love to have you. We haven't seen each other in ages. You can get to know Savannah. I know she would like to know her aunt."

Scarlet shakes her head. "No. Another time, perhaps?" She looks around the club and then back at Laura Lynne. "It was a spectacular night. Like when we were kids growing up. I had more fun than I have had in, well, ages."

She walks out as Laura Lynne looks helplessly at Sawyer. Sawyer follows her out. "Let me at least walk you to the car, Scarlet."

"Oh, there is no need. Cooper already brought it around." Scarlet says, brushing her brother off.

Sawyer comes up beside her and offers his arm. "I'm walking you out, Scarlet. Like it or lump it."

She looks at him and then takes his arm. "You always were a pest."

They walk out of the building arm in arm, neither saying anything, just enjoying each other's company. Sawyer walks her to the driver's side and opens the car door. "I love you, Scarlet. I know you are hiding stuff from us, and I am not asking you to tell me what. But, no matter what, Tea Olive is your home too. You come home whenever you want to. We're all waiting for you."

Scarlet's eyes begin to tear as she hastily climbs into the front of her Cadillac. She firmly shuts the door behind her. She looks through the window at her brother as he gazes back at her, strength and compassion all rolled into one look. She puts her key fob in the ignition and starts the car, speeding off down the club drive. Sawyer watches as she drives away.

"John? I know you're there. Follow her, would you? Let me know she made it safe?" Sawyer asks.

"Sure, Colonel," replies John.

"Any word from Tea Olive? Everything good there?"

"Just talked to Lance. Everything is quiet. Malcolm took Pearl and Victoria home a couple hours ago. He said all was quiet when he was there too. You got a funny feeling, Colonel?"

Sawyer looks up at John on the stairs. "I do. I can't seem to shake it. Thanks for looking after Scarlet."

The two part company, and Sawyer returns to the billiards room. Gabe is telling tales, and Avery is adding his own spin to living at Tea Olive. Everyone has a cigar and is sipping bourbon. Sawyer gazes at his nephews, happy to share this experience with them.

A tired but happy crew returns to The Residence. Everyone says their goodnights and heads up to bed. It is 2 AM. Clay looks at Sawyer before turning in. "Would you like Gordon and me to do a ground check or lock up? You've had a big night."

"I appreciate it. But honestly, I like doing it myself. Y'all go on to bed." He turns toward the door with Diane on his arm. "Thanks for coming, Clay. Both of you. It was a really fabulous night."

Clay smiles. "It really was. We enjoyed ourselves so much we are thinking about buying something down here. Maybe set up shop again. Who knows?"

"Really? Venice would be better for it if you did." He looks at Diane. "Shower or coffee? Your choice."

"How about I make coffee and meet you in our room after you lock up?" Diane suggests.

"Perfect. Give me ten minutes," says Sawyer.

Sawyer methodically checks the doors and windows. He verifies that the gate is closed and the surveillance camera is on. He makes his way upstairs, and when he opens the door, he sees exactly why Diane was so worried about what Pearl had seen when she unpacked Diane's suitcase. Sawyer shuts the door with his foot. "I think the coffee can wait."

42

Chapter Forty-Two

Sawyer cannot help but think, as he is lying with Diane curled in his arms, that the rest of the house is probably enjoying the same bliss he and Diane just shared. At least, he hopes so. He smells her hair and rubs Diane's back. Then, he gets an itchy feeling in the pit of his stomach moments before he hears a horn blasting, the screech of brakes, and, within a matter of moments, the bell clanging.

Sawyer jumps from the bed, rolling Diane off of him as he pulls on his shorts and throws on a t-shirt. He grabs his gun. He looks at Diane as she puts on her sweatpants. "Watch yourself," he says as he rushes out of the room.

He is out in the hallway and headed down the stairs with Avery close behind him with his shotgun at the ready. Laura Lynne and Gray follow. Laura Lynne texts as she hurries down the stairs.

"Avery, open the vault and get the guns. The bell is still ringing; this is not good!" Sawyer shouts.

Laura Lynne is close on Sawyer's heels.

"Laura Lynne, don't you go out that door! You wait for me!" Gray shouts as he pulls Laura Lynne back.

Clay and Gordon suddenly appear. "What the hell is going on?" asks Clay.

"I have no idea." Sawyer looks out the window before opening the door. "John? What is it?"

John stops ringing the bell. He is in the bed of his truck, holding his gun with one hand still on the pull for the bell. It is the most frazzled Sawyer has ever seen him. He braces for the worst news. "He tried to kill her, Colonel. I didn't know. He was in the house when she got there, and I didn't sense something was off."

"Scarlet? Where is she?" Sawyer asks, panicked.

John lifts her limp body to his chest. Even in the dark, Sawyer can tell she has been badly beaten. Sawyer hears a gasp from the door. He knows it's Laura Lynne. "Christ. Bring her in." Without looking at them, he orders Clay and Gordon to help. Avery and Gray are staring into the dark, ready to shoot.

"John, what happened?" presses Sawyer.

As if John flipped a switch as soon as he handed Scarlet over to Clay, he goes into full military mode. "I followed Scarlet home as requested. She went in the house, no issue. I waited thirty minutes, and when the lights went out, I headed out. Something felt off. I returned to the house some twenty minutes later, and the lights were back on. I could hear screaming and the muffled sounds of beating. I barged into the house and found Scarlet on the floor, being repeatedly hit by a man in his thirties. I shot him as he fled from the scene. Hit him too. She made me swear I wouldn't take her to the hospital. Then she passed out."

John looks up as he hears a whistle. He whistles back. "Give me a minute. I need to talk to Lance. I don't think there is any threat to Tea Olive. Look after your sister. I got the men."

Sawyer nods as John trots off. He looks at Beau as he walks into the house. Sawyer asks, "Where is she?"

"Momma put her on the dining room table for now. Uncle Gabe and Cooper are in there with her. They called somebody named Truelove. He's on the way," says Beau.

Sawyer puts down his gun and walks into the dining room. His beautiful sister, who only hours ago was stunning in all her finery, had a face that looked like it had been through a meat grinder. "How bad is it?"

Laura Lynne answers as succinctly as possible, "Broken nose and several lacerations to her face and head. Maybe broken ribs? I am worried about internal bleeding." She looks at Scarlet as she stares unseeingly into her eyes. "I don't think this is the first time this has happened."

"It isn't," Cooper states.

Everyone in the room stares at him. Laura Lynne asks, "Was it your father?"

"This would be my big brother Bobby's handiwork." He pulls up his sleeve, showing a long scar, "This is what he did to me the last time I interrupted his use of our mother as a punching bag."

Scarlet becomes increasingly agitated. She tries to sit up. Laura Lynne and Gabe simply push her back down.

Cooper looks at his mother. "Mom, I am not going to protect him any longer. You have to tell them."

Laura Lynne looks at her sister with compassion in her eyes. "Scarlet, nobody knows better than me how much we Mommas want to protect our children. But you need to tell me the truth; was it Bobby?"

She closes her eyes and nods her head slightly in confirmation.

Laura Lynne's eyes begin to tear up. "Why, Scarlet? Why would he beat you like this?"

In a raspy, broken voice, Scarlet whispers, "Drugs."

Cooper sighs heavily. "He was hopped up again? Figures."

Scarlet stares at Laura Lynne and mouths, "No." Then shifts her eyes toward her son. Laura Lynne understands the request. "Cooper, could you leave us for a few minutes? I want to check out your mom, and I need some privacy. You too, gentleman." She looks at Sawyer. "Can you send Diane in, please?"

The men exit, and Diane enters, carrying a steaming hot bucket of water and washcloths. "Thought you might need these," she says, dabbing the blood off Scarlet's forehead.

"Thanks. Okay Scarlet, the men are gone. What don't you want Cooper to know?"

With painstaking gasps, Scarlet whispers, "Bob-by. M-R-M. Heeeere." She wheezes out the last. "Ttttried to s-s-s-stop hhhhim."

Laura Lynne glances at Diane and then back at Scarlet. "Wait. Are you saying Bobby is behind the drug running at Tea Olive? Freddie and the gang? The guys that killed Roger?"

"Yy-y-yes. Shshshot. Jjjjohn," Scarlet whispers.

Laura Lynne looks confused. "John is fine. He didn't get shot."

Diane interrupts, "I think she means John shot Bobby. Is that right, Scarlet?"

She nods and then as if she can do no more, loses consciousness. Laura Lynne calls out, "Sawyer! Avery! Can you please come here?" Cooper sticks his head in. "Cooper, can you please check the gate for Dr. Truelove?"

He hesitates. Sawyer steps in. "Son, do what your aunt asks. Take Beau or Chris with you." He waits until Cooper leaves down the hall before joining Diane and Laura Lynne. Avery steps in behind him. "Is she okay?"

"She passed out again. I'm sure it's from the pain, but her pulse and blood pressure are steady. She's breathing easily." Laura Lynne looks from one brother to the next. "Before she passed out, she told us that Bobby is Mississippi Rebel Mafia. He was the one running the drugs through Tea Olive and Twin Oaks. She tried to stop him. She said John shot him."

"Shit. Just shit." Sawyer starts to pace back and forth. "But it makes sense. Grady and I agreed it had to be someone local, someone who knew how the rivers worked and the farms functioned. We thought it was a farmhand."

"Bobby would know. He ran the fields when he was little. Worked the farm with Uncle Gabe and Daddy, just like we did. He was such a cute kid," says Avery.

"And from what I heard, he knows drugs too," Diane chimes in. "It's no secret he has been in and out of rehab over the years."

The four are silent. Finally, Laura Lynne asks, "Now what?"

From the table in a barely audible whisper, Scarlet answers the question, in the strongest voice she has mustered since her arrival, "Find him. Arrest him. It ends today."

"Aunt Laura Lynne, Dr. Truelove is here. And Uncle Sawyer, so is Mr. Grady," Cooper says as he gently taps on the door before walking in.

Sawyer looks at his nephew and then at his older sister. "Scarlet, I'm going to tell Grady what you told me. And I am telling Cooper too. No more secrets."

She stares at him with fear before closing her eyes and giving a slight nod.

"Come on, Coop. Let's go talk to Grady," Sawyer says.

Dr. Truelove enters as Sawyer begins to walk out. The doctor clucks his tongue and leans over her, in a gentle voice he says, "Well, I'm glad to see he didn't kill you this time. I thought maybe he had." He looks at Sawyer and Laura Lynne, "She told you it was Bobby?"

They nod and he goes back to his exam. Sawyer leaves the room, walking with Cooper to the study, "He knows?"

He nods. "He's been treating Mom and me for the last few years. It was Bobby, wasn't it? Not who beat her; I know it was him, but who killed Roger? And running the drugs?"

"I'm afraid so, son. And apparently, John shot him. I'm sorry."

"I'm not. I hope he killed him."

Sawyer does not have time to respond to Cooper's statement because Grady and Jerry are waiting to speak with him. Sawyer invites them in, "Come on in. We can talk in the study." He looks at Beau. "You know how to make coffee? We could all use some."

"My sister is making it now. Chris tried to keep her upstairs and tucked in bed, but she was having none of it." He pushes himself off his perch on the back of the couch. "I'll go see what I can do to help."

Sawyer nods and says, "Jerry, this is my nephew, Cooper Huger. I'm not sure if you have met." The two men shake hands. "Here's the thing: my sister Scarlet is in the other room beat to a pulp. And John shot her abuser." He looks at Grady. "She tells us it was her son, Bobby Huger."

Jerry looks at Sawyer. "Does she want to press charges?"

Grady holds up his hand. "Wait, sheriff. What are you not telling us, Sawyer?"

Sawyer walks over to his desk and leans his hip against it, crossing his arms. He looks at Cooper before answering, "From what Scarlet tells us, she has reason to believe he is the mastermind behind the whole drug smuggling deal at Tea Olive. And, probably the one who shot Roger." He looks at Jerry. "We can probably surmise he is the leader of the Mississippi Rebel Mafia."

Grady looks to Cooper. "You think he is behind all this?"

Cooper doesn't hesitate. "Absolutely. I know he is my brother and all, but he is pure evil. And smart with it, like genius smart. Daddy used to say he was the reincarnation of his grandfather, that he and Momma had named him right."

"Okay, say he was hit by John. Where would he go to hide or to get cleaned up?" Grady asks.

"Twin Oaks. He knows the place like the back of his hand. Plenty of places to hide too. He would wait there until our father came to get him." Cooper holds out his hands. "And not because he wants to help out his son. He is as scared of him as the rest of us."

Beau comes in with a tray of coffee just as Jerry says, "Who here knows how to handle a gun?"

Sawyer thinks a moment. "Me, Avery, Gray, Clay, John."

"I can too," Beau responds.

Sawyer shakes his head. "No can do. Your mother would skin me alive."

Beau begins to posture.

"Whoa there, son, before you get all bent out of shape," Jerry explains, "We need your gun too. But I need you here, along with your uncle. From what I hear Sawyer and Cooper saying, Bobby knows his way around. If he gets cornered, he may just as likely come here." Jerry looks at Sawyer. "It's what I would do."

Jerry continues, "Okay, I don't want to spook him with sirens. Get your men. I officially deputize them. Is everyone armed?" Sawyer just looks at him with a steady gaze. "Right, stupid question. Let's meet out back." Jerry and Grady each grab a mug of coffee on their way out the back door. "Grady, call your dad and give him a heads up. His property is the next closest one."

"On it," says Grady, pulling out his phone.

Gabe comes in from the dining room, his eyes sad. "Is it true? Bobby caused all this? Beat his mother like a dog?" He looks at Cooper. "Cooper?"

"It's him," Cooper says.

Sawyer looks at Gabe. "I need y'all to watch the house. Do whatever you have to do to protect the women."

Diane rolls her eyes. "How about we protect ourselves? I know how to shoot, Laura Lynne too. And given the kind of mother she is, I imagine Savannah can hold her own."

Sawyer sighs. She is totally right. "Sorry, you're right. Hard to dispel my upbringing, little lady." He gives a cheeky grin before turning serious. "Y'all work it out. Just stay safe." He looks at Cooper. "Come on. Grab a coffee."

The men meet outside and prepare a quick plan. They partner and load up in the back of John's truck. He drives down the driveway, and two teams get out of the bed, making their way along the fence line over the stone wall. John takes a right at the gate, turning off his lights and slowly making his way along the front of Twin Oaks. He drops a team at the front before parking his truck and moving quietly along the left hand side of the property. Sawyer and Cooper get to the main residence first. The yellow crime tape is still up and flapping in the wind.

The two men enter the front door, which is wide open. Sawyer points to the blood along the front porch and entryway. Cooper follows close behind Sawyer, protecting his back. All of a sudden, Sawyer stops in his tracks, causing Cooper to bump into him.

"What are you doing?" Cooper whispers.

"You don't have to whisper; pretty sure your brother can't hear you," Sawyers says at a normal volume.

Cooper turns around and sees his brother, dead, lying on the floor in front of the fireplace. He had been shot in the head. "Whoa. Shit."

"Come on, walk back the way we came in."

Sawyer and Cooper return to the front door and out on the front porch. Sawyer gives a long, loud whistle and waits while everyone comes into view. "We found him. Gunshot to the head." He looks at Grady and Jerry. "He's all yours. I'm taking my family home."

43

Chapter Forty-Three

"How is she?" Sawyer asks Dr. Truelove when he emerges from Scarlet's bedroom. Scarlet had been moved there the night before.

"She's going to be fine. At least physically," Dr. Truelove replies.

"Christ. How long has she been abused?"

"It's hard to tell. She has some pretty old scars. The X-ray we took showed multiple healed fractures. Some appear at least 20 years old." He looks at Sawyer. "But the physical part is not even the worst of it. Scarlet has been severely abused emotionally. I have no idea how she has kept it together all these years."

"Does she know about Bobby?"

"Yes, Laura Lynne told her."

"How did she take it, doc?" Sawyer asks.

He shrugs. "She didn't say anything. She just nodded her head. Then, she closed her eyes and went to sleep. She has been asleep ever since." He checks his watch. "Listen, I have to go. Laura Lynne is going to stay with her today. I will come back in the morning to check on her. Call me if you have any questions."

Sawyer watches as the doctor descends the staircase before pushing the door to Scarlet's room open. He glances at the bed and sees Scarlet sound asleep. He signals for Laura Lynne to join him in the hallway. "Hey, you okay?" Laura Lynne shakes her head in the negative and walks straight into Sawyer's chest, wrapping her arms around his waist. Sawyer pulls her in for a hug. He feels her shoulders shake as she cries. Finally, after several moments, she stops crying and wipes her nose and eyes on his t-shirt.

"That poor thing. What she has been through, Sawyer. How did we miss it all these years?" Laura Lynne lifts her head when she hears the voice of her daughter coming from one of the upstairs bedrooms. "I thought for sure everyone would be asleep," she says, looking up at Sawyer. He shrugs his shoulders and releases Laura Lynne. The two siblings walk over to Savannah's bedroom to see what is happening.

"I don't know, Chris. Uncle Gabe always wears a bowtie. I think when in Rome..." Savannah waddles over to Chris with a blue bowtie in her hand.

"What is all this?" Sawyer asks.

Savannah smiles. "Chris would prefer not to wear a tie to church. What do you think?"

"Tie is not necessary. Acceptable but not required." Sawyer walks into the room and takes the tie from Savannah. "But if you want to score points with Uncle Gabe, then go with the tie."

Chris sighs. "The tie it is, then."

Sawyer smiles as he wraps it around Chris's neck and expertly ties the bow.

"Y'all know you don't have to go to church today. Nobody expects you to attend after last night," says Sawyer. "Nobody is in the mood, plus we are all exhausted."

Beau and Claire stand at the door where Laura Lynne is propped against the doorframe. The couple is dressed, and Beau is sporting his bowtie. "Uncle Sawyer, you said it yourself. Cooper-Beauregards don't miss church."

"You also said we don't hide from gossip and scandal," Savannah chimes in, "We walk right into it with our head high and our spine straight."

"I think that was Uncle Gabe who said that part," Laura Lynne says.

"Either way, we're going to church. Uncle Gabe is already dressed, and we decided we weren't going to let him go by himself. We need to stand together on this. Regardless of what proves to be true about our cousin, he was still a Cooper-Beauregard," Savannah concludes.

Sawyer looks at Laura Lynne. She has tears in her eyes. "Well, I guess I better get dressed. Do we have fifteen minutes?"

"Closer to twenty, Uncle Sawyer, we can handle this ourselves," Beau says. The four young adults all nod in unison.

"I know you can, but y'all are right. Cooper-Beauregards don't miss church." He heads to the door and looks at Laura Lynne. "You got some great kids, baby girl."

Laura Lynne sniffs. "I know." Then she stands up straight. "Let me see if I can find someone to watch Scarlet for an hour. I want Gray and me there with y'all. The more of us there, the better the show of solidarity."

"I'll ask John. I know he has some medic experience. I'm sure he wouldn't mind," says Sawyer.

Laura Lynne nods her appreciation. "He won't have to do much. Dr. Truelove gave her some pretty strong pain medicine, though she didn't want to take it. She should sleep for a few more hours." Laura Lynne hangs over the banister and shouts, "Gray! Are you down there? Gray!"

A moment passes, and Sawyer hears the kitchen door swing open. "Right here, love. Everything okay?" Gray calls out.

"Everything is great. We're going to church. We leave in twenty minutes," Laura Lynne informs he husband.

Sawyer just shrugs his shoulders and leans over the banister like his sister, the two hanging by their hands like they did as kids. "Is Diane down there? Can you tell her our plan?"

Avery comes to the platform in his sweatpants and joins the fun. He hangs over the banister and begins calling for breakfast. The three siblings laugh like loons as they re-enact a favorite childhood pastime.

Gray goes back into the kitchen, and Sawyer and Laura Lynne continue to shout down the staircase. Gray comes out of the kitchen followed in hot pursuit by Pearl. "What are y'all doing up there screaming down the house? I know your momma taught you better than that! Now quit hanging over that banister like a chimpanzee. You're liable to break your neck falling over onto those blockheads of yours!" She stands in the entranceway, hands on hips with her dishtowel over her shoulder. "Go on, now. Git dressed!" She points her finger at Avery. "Don't you dare slide down that banister! At your age, you're liable to get a hernia!"

By then, the entire second floor is out on the platform, watching the scene unfold. Laura Lynne and Sawyer look at each other, grinning. Avery unhooks his leg from the banister.

Clay comes over to them. "I swear if I didn't know better, I would think that was Queenie setting you straight. Brings back memories." He looks over the banister. "I think I would comply."

Laura Lynne and Sawyer stand up, and Clay gives the two a hug, "Thank you for a really wonderful weekend. I'm so sorry it ended the way it did, but it was definitely memorable." He looks over his shoulder. "Gordon and I have an early plane to catch, but we will be back." He looks at Avery and shakes his hand.

Sawyer shakes Gordon's hand. "Here, let me see you out."

Beau comes over. "Claire and I will see them to the car, Uncle Sawyer. You get ready for church."

Sawyer looks at his doppelganger and acquiesces. "Very good. Y'all have a safe flight."

Fifteen minutes later, all of the family is at the front door. As the group determines who is riding with whom and in what car, Cooper comes down the stairs looking dapper in his khaki pants, buttondown, bowtie, and navy blue coat. Sawyer looks at him with concern. "You sure, son?"

"I am. Momma would want me to go, but even if she didn't, I want to be there."

"Then let's go," says Sawyer.

Cooper walks next to Laura Lynne on the way out the door. "Aunt Laura Lynne, is Mom okay with John? You trust him?"

"I do. He's a good man. But if you'd rather, I can stay with her," offers Laura Lynne.

"No, she wouldn't want that. I just wanted to make sure," says Cooper.

Laura Lynne pats his arm. "I'm sorry, Cooper. For all of it."

"It's over now; that's all that matters," Cooper says.

Sawyer overhears the last of Cooper's words and as he looks over the brood of family he has somehow managed to surround himself with over the last month, he feels his soul at peace. He feels a deep love for Diane and their budding relationship, a renewed and strengthening bond with his two siblings, a glowing respect for his uncle, an appreciation for the team of men and women who keep Tea Olive running, and excitement over his nieces and nephews who he can mentor and nurture. For Sawyer, it is all over: the running, the nightmares, the loneliness.

But in his heart, he knows the same is not true for his sister. Scarlet's journey has just begun.

Contact the Author

Thank you for supporting a new author!

If you are interested in receiving a monthly author newsletter, please go to

https://whisperwoodholdingsllc.com

and register for The Red Bird.

Or visit

https://linktr.ee/whisperwoodholdings

for more information on the author.